THE GIFTED HEART

Marks of Inheritance: The Orkeia Cycle
Book 1

Tiffany Davis

To Mom

I did it.

You can stop bugging me now.

PLAYLISTS

SOUNDS OF ORKEIA
00:00
04:10

CHARACTER PLAYLIST
KENNA
00:00
04:10

CONTENTS

Chapter One

WHERE THE DEAD REST

Bodies of Orkeian knights scattered the rocky beach all around me. My eyes darted across the carnage in horror before landing on the stone shelter built into the cliffs. No visible movement came from inside my clan's home. I sprinted forward and stumbled through the open door, tripping over something on the ground.

My bag fell to my side as I collapsed. I cried out, realizing that the thing I'd tripped over was a knight's arm. Beneath me, the ground was stained red with blood, but it didn't stain my dress and hands. It was already dry. My stomach twisted in knots as I looked up.

They were all dead.

A sob escaped my throat. *No, no, no...*

Through my tears, I stared at the faces of my clan members. Logan, Greta, Elizabeth—

Not Elizabeth...

Her gray hair was stained red from the massacre, and her eyes stared blankly into the stars through the fallen ceiling. I crawled over the bodies separating us and took her lifeless form in my shaking arms.

A seal barked on the beach, the only sound to break the silence other than my choked sobs. Elizabeth was the Mother of our clan. More than that, she had raised me for the past seventeen years, ever since I was left on the beach as a baby—the same beach that was now littered with the bodies of our enemies.

I buried my face in her cold, stiff shoulder. She'd been dead at least a day. *A whole day.*

And I hadn't been here.

I don't know how long I stayed in that position. It felt like hours. But eventually, I took a deep breath and looked up once more.

Everything was gone. Our cauldrons, candles, talismans, even our cooking pots. The knights had destroyed all that they could, not content with murdering my family. What was once a home was now a burial chamber—four thick, crumbling stone walls surrounding this massacre. The rest of the world wouldn't even notice their deaths. All we'd had was each other.

Now, I was alone.

I lowered Elizabeth gently to the ground, my sobs still coming in spurts. I had nothing left.

Except for my candles...

Numbly, I reached for my bag and emptied the contents onto the dirt floor. The salt crystals shattered and I gasped, but my concern was short-lived. The supplies I'd gathered for Greta and the other green witches no longer mattered. Brushing the shards aside, I took my fourteen summoning candles from the pile, setting them up in a circle on the ground.

Elizabeth helped me make my candles when she first started teaching me how to use my powers. I hadn't planned on bringing them when I left for the gathering trip—they just took up extra space—but Elizabeth had insisted. It was like she had known what was going to happen, and that if they had been left here, they would have been destroyed with everything else. And it was my only comfort to know that since they weren't, I would be able to see her again.

I still had a lot to learn as a white witch, so it took a moment of closing my eyes and muttering what I remembered from Elizabeth's lessons to be sure I placed them correctly. She had usually been the one to place them for me. Once I felt sure they were in the right places, I stood in the center and traced a pentagram against my chest, chanting the Sacred Words of

Passage. The candles lit magically, illuminating the massacre around me. I raised my eyes upward.

"Do you desire to visit the Saved or the Lost?" came a whisper in my mind.

"The Saved," I breathed.

A swift breeze extinguished the candles. My spirit left my body with a familiar, light sensation, traveling upwards until I could see the golden gates of the Land of the Saved. Translucent beings crowded in the light around the gates, waiting for them to open for the day. I slowly made my way across the clouded ground, scanning the crowd for familiar faces.

Eventually, I heard a familiar musical laugh echoing through the air. My lips quivered when I saw Elizabeth's spirit near the gates. I also recognized Greta and her husband, Logan, who had been our Father green witch and sent me out gathering. Logan noticed my approach and nodded in my direction, causing Elizabeth to spin around. Her lips split into a smile, and she ran gracefully to my side, the crowd of spirits parting politely for her. Her characteristic laugh lines were gone, and her gray hair was now a brilliant blonde.

"Kenna," she said, beaming.

I instantly wanted to embrace her and clenched my fists together to hold back the impulse. Even though I was in spirit form, I could not physically interact with any of the spirits who had passed on. It made seeing her again bittersweet.

"I am so glad we picked you as our gatherer this week!" She clasped her hands as she so often did.

I struggled to find my voice. "Did you know?" I whispered.

"Know what, My Heart?"

The tender nickname caused the knot in my throat to double in size. "Did you know they were coming? You—you didn't want me to go, and then you just changed your mind out of the blue, did you—?"

"No," she said gently, her eyes softening with understanding. "But I'm glad I changed my mind when I did. Otherwise you would be here with us. Now, you can find a new home."

"How could I find a new home?" I croaked. "With you gone, and the knights everywhere…"

She frowned. "You can't think that way. This is only the beginning for you. You will find a new family, I'm sure of it. Maybe even a clan with members closer to your age."

I shook my head. Being the only child in our clan had never bothered me. Elizabeth always lamented that I was alone, but I had never felt alone until this moment.

As if reading my thoughts, she gave a small, encouraging smile. "It will be good for you," she insisted. "You'll discover parts of yourself you didn't even know were there. Be comforted that all of us are here and accounted for."

I gazed towards the golden gates before me, seeing more familiar faces waiting to enter along with Logan and Greta. They were all smiling and content. As I watched, Logan ran towards the gates to greet a spirit on the other side, and with a shock I recognized Alan—his brother who had been the first of our clan killed when all of this started five years ago. They were overjoyed to see each other again, and eager for the gates to finally open.

As grief-stricken as I was, the sight did bring a small amount of comfort. The king of Orkeia and his knights believed that all of the Gifted were destined for the Land of the Lost, that anyone who could use magic would do so for evil. But these people—my family—had always used their powers for good. And now, Logan and Alan—and so many others—would be reunited.

My fists slowly opened. "I'm glad to know that, but how did they find you? Did they take you by surprise? Could I have helped?"

Elizabeth shook her head. "There's nothing you could have done against an entire army, Kenna."

I turned my face away. I knew I hadn't gained enough experience to be a true asset to any clan, but there must have been *something* I could have done.

"Not because you aren't capable of fighting," Elizabeth continued in her motherly voice, "but because it was the Giftgiver's will that we meet Him."

"But why would the Giftgiver allow the king to do this?" I said, keeping my voice low as I threw a glance at the bright gates in front of me. "Why wouldn't He stop him? Doesn't the king need to be stopped?"

Elizabeth sighed. "He is wiser than we are, and He knows the minds and hearts of His children," she said, repeating the mantra I'd so often heard.

"But certainly the king—"

"That's enough," she said kindly.

Just then, the gates opened behind her, revealing the city beyond. The golden buildings almost looked like they were floating on clouds but somehow had blooming gardens growing in front of them. Numberless angels made their way through the iridescent streets, some of them approaching the gates to greet the new arrivals with bright, welcoming smiles. The Giftgiver's House towered above it all with splendid golden arches that sparkled and shone in the sunlight almost as if they were studded with diamonds.

It was breathtaking.

Logan and Greta rushed inside, and the brothers embraced. They held each other so tightly I was sure they'd never let go.

Elizabeth's smile brightened with excitement as the crowd began to move forward, and she turned to join them. I could only watch longingly, knowing that if I followed her, I would forfeit my own life. Once a spirit passes through the gates, it can no longer return to Earth.

"Do you really have to go?" I whispered.

I already knew the answer, but that didn't stop me from asking.

"There is work for me to do here," she said matter-of-factly. Her smile was wider than I'd ever seen it. "And people that I miss. It's time for me to move on to the next stage of life."

I bit my lip. "I want to go with you."

Elizabeth's face hardened. "No. There is work that *you* still have to do in mortality, or you would have been taken with us. Don't throw away the life you have yet to live."

I sighed and looked down. I'd learned a long time ago to trust Elizabeth's words. She reached out as if to touch my brown hair before she too sighed. As hopeful and wise as she was, I knew this was hard for her as well.

"I hope you'll visit...but don't waste your life waiting outside these gates longing for the dead," she said gently. "Your place is with the living, My Heart. The Giftgiver has great things in store for you, I am sure of it."

I nodded, the lump in my throat too hard for me to speak through. My legs felt like stone, but somehow I willed myself to step back. Elizabeth joined Alan, Logan, Greta, and the rest of my family. I wanted to speak to them each in turn, but I knew the longer I stayed here the more tempted I would be to enter the gates. They waved, smiles all around. I tried to smile back but couldn't force my face to make the necessary changes. Instead, I stared after them, watching their spirits brighten with a celestial glow.

I forced myself to close my eyes. The first time I attempted communication beyond the mortal world, I was unable to return for hours. When I asked Elizabeth why I had so much trouble, she explained that if I thought of nothing but returning, the transition would be much more difficult. I needed to relax and think about what I would do next after I returned.

This time, my spirit returned to my body quickly. My mind was made up. Finding a clan to live with temporarily was the wisest thing to do, but all I could think about was the man who caused my family's murder.

Someone had to stop the king. And somehow, I was going to be the one to do it.

***

I walked into the night and away from what was left of my home. My father brought me to the beach when I was less than a year old and asked Elizabeth to take care of me. I used to wonder if my parents simply hadn't loved me or if they'd tried to give me a better life among the Gifted. But now, their reasons didn't matter. I was leaving behind the bodies of the only family I had ever known

I wanted to march straight to the castle and get revenge, but facing the king would have to wait. I didn't have the slightest idea where to begin in my quest or even how to get to the capital city, and if I attempted to barge into the castle, there was no chance I would survive long enough to speak a single word. Elizabeth was right—I needed to find a new clan, at least temporarily.

But that was easier said than done. I traveled across the hilly, cliff-lined island for days without meeting a soul. I shouldn't have been too surprised—clans stayed hidden and kept their groups small to avoid detection. All I could do was keep walking and hope luck was on my side.

The cold season was approaching, making the nights particularly difficult with the lack of trees or natural shelter, and my bread and small supply of fruit was almost gone. When I saw a herd of wild goats after four days, I felt some hope, thinking I might be able to catch one. But they were much too quick for me.

On the sixth day, I spotted a village, but I wasn't comfortable trying to get food there. What if I gave myself away? After all, I didn't know anything about their culture or customs. Would they see through my ruse and report me to the knights?

Most Gifted wouldn't even be able to consider going into the village as an option due to their marks. Every witch or sorcerer has one, usually on their shoulder or neck. Every mark is unique: a green witch might have one that looks like some sort of flower or other plant, while a white witch's could be a human silhouette, a wisp of smoke, or a spiral. Sorcerers vary the most—although they can learn all types of magic, each sorcerer has a defining power that is their strongest ability or skill. This is usually manifested in their mark, such as a flame for fire magic.

Gifted societies used to be able to explain these away as peculiar birthmarks, but the knights discovered the linking thread four years ago when the king officially declared war against magic. It became almost impossible for us to blend in.

I, however, am an enigma. My mark is the shape of a heart, which is where Elizabeth got my nickname. No one in our clan had heard of a white witch having that mark before, and at first they weren't even sure what my powers were. It was only when I saw my first spirit that Greta theorized the heart represented a human soul.

Stranger still, my mark isn't on my neck or shoulder—it's on my thigh. Theoretically, I could go to the village for food as long as I didn't use my magic in public. The knights couldn't prove I was Gifted without seeing my mark, and there was no reason they would ever see it. But if I drew too much attention, I was sure that wouldn't matter.

Knowing Elizabeth had once lived in Ungifted society, I decided to seek her advice. I made the transition into the Other Worlds and traveled upward to the Land of the Saved, but she was still within the city when I arrived. Sighing, I walked up to the gates and asked a man on the other side if he could look for her, but I knew the chances were slim. Spirits only exit occasionally to greet those joining them or meet with white witches, and I hadn't told Elizabeth when to expect me. After waiting for a little less than an hour, I returned to my body, discouraged.

When I opened my eyes, I was no longer alone.

A boy about my age sat a few feet away, staring—intrigued—at my face. I let out a startled gasp, putting up my hands in a pitiful attempt at defense. He quickly jumped up, a little startled himself, and stumbled backward as he brushed off the dirt on his pants.

"I'm sorry, Sister," he stammered. "You seem lost, I thought maybe I could help you..."

My breathing started to calm. Though I knew I should still be cautious, against my better judgment, I stared as intently at him as he had at me. His clothes were simple, but he had a strong body underneath. His hair was golden as a sunset, almost as if it was stealing all light from around him. My eyes met his and I subtly caught my breath. They were a striking sky blue, the type of blue one never sees but only imagines.

He took a step forward into my summoning circle, and I felt the spell around me break. Coming back to my senses, I scrambled to pack up my supplies. My heart raced with adrenaline and I was keenly aware of his gaze on my back.

"My name is Gideon Grison," he said. "My father is the Father of our clan. He saw you while on lookout yesterday and sent me to ask if you needed shelter."

Pausing, I looked back at him. He ran his hand through his sunset hair and shifted the weight on his feet. I was unsure how to respond. If this was an act to lure me to the knights, it was an exceptionally good one. But something told me that he was being sincere.

I tentatively reached out my hand. "My name's Kenna."

His shoulders relaxed and he shook my hand. His grip was firm, yet not forceful. He glanced at the candles on the ground. "You're a white witch?"

"Yes. You?"

"A sorcerer," he replied, then asked gently, "Is anyone else with you?"

I shook my head, looking down at the grass.

"I'm sorry for your loss," he said reverently. Without asking, he knelt and began rolling up my sleeping mat. "Is there anything left to retrieve from your camp?"

"Unfortunately, no," I responded, kneeling next to him. We fell into silence as he forced my mat into my bag and I gathered the candles on my left. Once he finished, he helped me pick up the rest of them. I reached for the last one just as he did, quickly drawing my hand back as his brushed mine.

"Sorry," he muttered, withdrawing his hand.

I found myself momentarily staring at him again. I had never been around a boy my age before, and I felt a strange rush of heat to my neck and cheeks. Feeling suddenly awkward, I tore my gaze away and tied off my bag of candles. But when I reached for my pack, Gideon had already stood and hoisted it over his back.

My cheeks burned even hotter. "You don't have to do that."

"I don't want you to carry this all the way to camp."

"I've carried it myself for the past week and I've been fine," I insisted.

"I just want to help," he shrugged. "But I understand if you don't trust a stranger with your things."

"It's not that, it's just—"

I couldn't think of how to finish the sentence. After a moment, I sighed and relented. "Thank you," I said, motioning that he should lead the way. With a smile, he reached his free hand toward me, palm outstretched, to help me to my feet. I hesitated for a moment before taking it, my fingers tingling in the brief moment our skin touched once more.

"If we move fast we'll make it there before nightfall," he said.

Chapter Two

BENEATH THE HILL

My multiple layers weren't enough to keep my teeth from chattering as the night wind beat against my face. Ahead of me, Gideon didn't appear cold at all in his large overcoat. His coat reminded me that Elizabeth had been working on a new one for me when I left on my gathering trip. The knights probably had it now. I wondered if one of them would keep it for himself, give it to a loved one, or simply throw it away. The thought made my jaw clench.

We approached a rocky hill, and Gideon began climbing. My hands had been clutching my arms in a desperate attempt to stay warm, but I forced them to open and followed him, my frozen fingers struggling to keep a hold of the rocks. He reached the top before I was even halfway up and frowned when he saw my progress.

"Is everything all right?" he called down.

"Fine," I insisted, but my shaking voice betrayed me.

He knelt on the ground and extended his arm. "Take my hand, I'll help you up."

Elizabeth had always warned me that not being able to accept help was a sign of pride, but I wrinkled my nose and stubbornly continued to climb on my own. Only when I started to slip backwards did I finally relent and reach for Gideon's offered hand. He pulled me up with a strength I hadn't expected and caught me as I stumbled backwards once on my feet.

"You're freezing," he said, alarmed. "Is there a coat in your bag?"

"No," I said as he began lowering the bag from his shoulder. "But I'm fine, really. We must be getting close to your camp by now."

"It's not too far," he said. "We're just about halfway there."

"Halfway?" I breathed out.

He sent me an apologetic glance. "It won't be long, I promise."

Stopping briefly, he set my pack on the ground and took off his coat, revealing a sleeveless tunic underneath. On his shoulder, a circle was clearly defined. His mark.

A circle. Where had I heard of that mark before?

"You'd better put this on, before you catch a cold." He held his jacket out to me.

"What about you?"

The corner of his lips twitched. "I'll survive. Take it."

I took a deep breath before reluctantly doing so. The twitch of his lips turned into a smile, and he picked up my pack once again.

With his jacket around my shoulders, the cold wind wasn't nearly as unbearable. Thankfully, the majority of the walking we had left to do was on level ground, and I was able to keep my arms wrapped tightly around myself. I let Gideon walk a few paces ahead of me, all the while looking past him for any sign of a shelter.

"We're here," he finally said as the sun disappeared on the horizon.

I scanned the area, furrowing my eyebrows. All I could see was a small, grassy hill in the middle of a plain. There were no structures and no signs of any people.

"Gideon," I said slowly, "you can admit if we're lost."

He smiled at me, the kind of smile that tells you he knows something you don't. Instead of responding, he walked around to a small bush growing on the side of the hill. He pushed aside the top of the bush, revealing a slab of stone tucked behind it. As I watched, he knocked three times, waited a moment, then knocked again. I started in surprise as a door opened from the inside, and Gideon disappeared from view.

Tentatively, I peered into the opening. A set of about ten steep steps led underground. Gideon waited patiently at the bottom. Someone else stood behind him, but I couldn't make out any features. The chamber was lit behind them, but the steps themselves were mostly obscured by shadow.

I hesitated before squeezing myself through feet first, pushing the stone slab back into place once inside and carefully descending the steps. Gideon handed me my pack when I reached the bottom and motioned for me to follow. He and the other figure headed down a corridor, their silhouettes eerily illuminated by the unseen source of light. I took a deep breath and followed.

The light grew brighter with each step down the tight passageway. We emerged in a large room with a bright fire in the middle. I gazed upwards, and my mouth fell open in awe. We were inside the hill, in a completely hollow space with no timbers to hold the roof. My eyes lowered to find Gideon and two other men standing in front of me, and I quickly closed my mouth.

"Welcome, Sister," said the tallest one. He and Gideon had the same golden hair, though his was much longer, and the same kind blue eyes. "I am Julius Grison, father of this clan."

"I'm Kenna," I answered quietly.

"Pleased to meet you."

He smiled and my shoulders began to relax. When I glanced at the man to his right, however, my anxiety returned. He had hair so dark it was almost black and eyes to match. Though he smiled as well, I could tell he was wary of bringing a stranger into the clan, and while I didn't exactly blame him for that, I too felt wary of him.

Julius gestured to him. "This is Darius Bain, my counselor."

"Though the roles should be reversed," Darius said.

I tensed, my uneasiness growing. No one in my clan had ever questioned Elizabeth's leadership. But without any hesitation, Julius laughed and clapped Darius on the back.

"He's also my best friend," he added.

They both chuckled, and I forced my shoulders to relax. With the atmosphere eased, I let my eyes wander around the room in amazement. Four doors left this common area, and a small kitchen and well were located on either side of the room. Clothes hung on lines over the warm fire to dry. Apparently the rest of the clan members were already sleeping, because the four of us were the only ones here.

"There must be a lot of you," I observed. My clan hadn't had nearly this much space, the twenty of us sharing just a couple of rooms.

"Hardly," said Julius, his smile fading. "There used to be twenty-seven of us, but the others were killed the last time we fled from the knights. There are only twelve of us now."

It took a moment for me to respond. "Then why make such a large shelter? This must have taken months—"

"It only took a few hours, actually," Darius said casually.

This statement shocked me into silence, and Julius and Darius chuckled.

"More than a few hours," Gideon frowned. "We spent the night outside."

"Well, you can't expect me to work on it without stopping," Darius defended.

"Darius has power over the elements," Gideon explained. "He can manipulate earth into almost any shape he wants."

"I've had a lot of practice." Darius shrugged, but his smirk told me his humility was insincere.

"But what about the fire?" I said, looking at where it was burning. "How do you stop the smoke from filling up the room?"

"Darius's power also allows him to put a spell on the fire, eliminating the smoke," Julius said. "It's not trapped in here, but the knights won't see it, either."

My mind raced. The Grison clan had found a place to live completely hidden and undetected. My heart ached when I thought of Elizabeth. She and the rest of my clan might still be alive if we'd been fortunate enough to have a similar shelter.

"Mostly everyone's settled down for the night," Julius said, indicating the empty common room. "My daughter has a room to herself that I'm sure she would be happy to share."

"Oh, no," I said, grasping onto my pack's shoulder strap. "I don't want to intrude. I can set up my mat out here—"

"Nonsense," said Julius. "Unless you plan to leave us in the morning, you should get used to having a bed to sleep in."

While I'd hoped to find a clan to take me in, I hadn't expected such a warm welcome. I wasn't sure why—if the roles had been reversed, I was sure Elizabeth would have been just as welcoming to them. I still felt a bit flustered at their generosity, but I didn't protest further.

"Thank you," I said.

"In times like this, we all need to do what we can to take care of each other, don't we?" Julius said before motioning for me to follow.

Gideon waved me forward, and I followed the three men through the door to my right. We passed into another room, smaller than the common area, containing a large table and twelve chairs. Because the table took up most of the space, this room was lit by candlelight instead of a fire. There were three more doors extending from the eating area, one on each wall. Julius knocked on the door to the left, and a young girl, about thirteen, opened it, dressed in her nightgown. She too had golden blonde hair, and it fell just past her waist in a fountain of light curls.

"What is it, Papa?" she asked.

"Shae, I'd like you to meet Kenna," he said, stepping aside so she could see me. "Kenna, this is my daughter, Shae Grison. Shae, you wouldn't mind sharing your room, would you?"

Shae's eyes widened. She stared at me for a moment, obviously surprised at a stranger's sudden appearance in the clan, before her lips split into an enchanting smile. "I don't mind at all. How long will you be staying?"

All eyes were immediately on me, waiting for my answer. I thought I saw Gideon lean forward, listening intently, and I felt the heat from before travel up my neck once again.

"I'm not sure," I said. "I don't really have anywhere else to go..."

There was a moment of awkward, almost reverent silence before Shae smiled again. "Well, stay as long as you need," she said, pulling me into the room.

Julius and Gideon left in search of bedding while Darius began to shape the earth into a bed. With seemingly little effort, the ground began to rise and twist into the form he wanted. I watched in awe.

As he worked, Shae struck up an eager conversation, clearly excited to have a girl close to her own age to talk to. Apparently, all of the other women in the Grison clan were adults. She started telling me about what she was learning about potions as a green witch, and when she discovered that I was a white witch she immediately started asking me questions about the Lands of the Saved and the Lost. I'm sure she would have kept chatting the rest of the night if her father hadn't returned with the bedding and gently reminded her I'd been traveling all day.

When Darius finished the bed, Shae quickly quieted to let me rest. I laid down with a pillow for the first time since leaving my clan and was almost instantly asleep.

***

I awoke just a few hours later with a parched throat. Groggy, I took a small cup from my pack, pulled on a simple dress over my nightgown, and headed to the common area, careful not to disturb Shae.

A woman with fiery red hair sat next to the well drawing water, a bag of clothes at her feet. She was about ten years older than me and possibly the most beautiful woman I'd ever seen, but she was grimacing even before she became aware of my presence. The door to the eating area closed loudly behind me, and she sat up with a start, locking her bright green eyes with mine. Hers narrowed.

Silence. She didn't ask who I was or why I was there, just stared at me with her accusing eyes. I shifted my feet, partially afraid to approach the well. After what felt like an eternity, she released me from her gaze, an expression of disgust frozen on her face. As she stood, I recovered from my shock and stepped forward.

"My name's Kenna," I said in the friendliest way I could. "What's yours?"

She turned, just enough so she could again penetrate me with her biting eyes. "Helen," she said coldly, disappearing through her door before I could attempt any more conversation.

The polite smile I'd put on to greet her faded. Something in my stomach tightened, and I closed my eyes. Despite the warmth of the fire, I felt a chill in the air.

I can't stay here.

Letting out a slow breath, I laid down and willed my spirit to leave my body. Summoning candles were necessary for visiting the other worlds, making spirits visible to others, and other rituals I hadn't learned, but a white witch could roam the earth as a spirit without any assistance. I gazed down at my body for a moment before allowing my spirit to travel through the ground and out of the shelter into the night sky.

In spirit form, I was able to move much faster than I would have physically, which I needed if I was going to find where to go next. Orkeia was a kingdom of islands, and I didn't know for sure if the main city was on this one or another. If I was going to find a way to stop the king, that was the first thing I needed to figure out.

The stars were bright as I began to explore the coast. There were only a few villages on this island that I could find. I didn't really know what was a normal size for a village, but based on stories Elizabeth had told me, these seemed small. The largest was a few days of travel away, and I saw ships docked on the beach beside it.

I felt a rush of rage. For all I knew, these were the same men who had murdered my clan. Those ships would be filled with the things that they stole—Elizabeth's talisman, my coat, all of my clan's possessions that hadn't been destroyed.

Likely to bring back to the king...

That thought made me pause. I could spend more time in spirit form searching through the other islands for the castle, but even if I found it, figuring out how to get there was another matter. Making my way to this village and seeking passage to the capital city seemed like a good start.

Resolved, I quickly journeyed back across the island to return to my body. When I opened my eyes, I stood and turned to go back to Shae's room and get my things—walking straight into Gideon as I did.

"Sorry!" I gasped, stumbling back. "I didn't expect anyone else to be awake..."

"No, I'm sorry," he said quickly. "I just came out to get some water and saw you laying there. I wanted to make sure you were all right."

"I'm fine," I said, shifting my feet.

We fell into a brief awkward silence before he cleared his throat. "Listen, I can only imagine how hard this is...if there's anything I can do to help..."

His words trailed off. I found myself staring at him for a long moment. He ran a hand through his hair with a bit of nervous energy, his blue eyes darting from mine to the wall and back again.

I suddenly felt guilty. Leaving in the middle of the night wasn't the right thing to do. Even if Helen had been less than friendly, everyone else I'd met so far was welcoming. And as eager as I was to get moving, if I didn't take time to rest and resupply, I'd just find myself in the same situation I was before—hungry, cold, and exhausted as I wandered the hills alone.

"Thank you, Gideon," I said softly. "I appreciate it."

"Don't mention it," he said, then added, "You can call me Gid, if you'd like."

I nodded. "Thanks, Gid."

"You should get some more rest," he said, stepping out of my path.

I gave him a friendly smile before returning to Shae's room. A heavy sigh left my lips as I laid down, staring at the ceiling for a while before drifting back to sleep.

Chapter Three

WARY WELCOMES

Some of the members of the Grison clan were more receptive than others. The Paterson family welcomed me with open arms. Nathanael Paterson was the Father green witch. He and his wife, Brynna, had two sons who were a few years older than I was, and all four of them were green witches. My first morning there, the older son, Neal, brought me a delicious plate of fruit and cheese from their family breakfast. I didn't get much of a chance to thank him, however, before his brother coaxed him out of the shelter. After that, I didn't see them much over those first few days. The two of them were almost always outside. I thought it was reckless, but everyone else seemed confident that they were being careful.

The three white witches, including Helen, weren't as welcoming. They had joined the clan individually, and since they didn't have their own families, they all shared the same room. Even though they weren't as friendly, I offered to give Shae back her own space and share with them as well, but she refused. She enjoyed having someone to talk to. Honestly, I didn't mind. Elizabeth had been right—it was nice to be around someone closer to my own age.

Shae was the youngest member of the clan, about three years younger than me. Her mother, Lyra, was also a green witch, and due to her training, Shae's gift had developed exceptionally fast for her age. She had high ambitions for the future, despite the Slaughters. During my second night there, she exclaimed that she was going to invent a potion to make the drinker happy for the rest of his life.

"Well, that would be a bit unfair," I said thoughtfully.

She sat straight up in bed. "Why? They would never feel sad again!"

"Yes, but if they had never been sad, they could never really be happy, could they?"

Shae stared at me for a moment, then shook her head. "Kenna, you sound just like Sybil. Sometimes I think all you white witches are old hags from birth."

I couldn't help but laugh. Sybil Freeda was the Mother white witch of the clan and not particularly friendly. She was nothing like Elizabeth in that she had no patience for mistakes. When she heard me telling Shae about my initial struggles learning to travel to the Other Worlds, she scoffed, muttering to herself that if you couldn't do something right the first time, you weren't fit to do it at all. If she'd been the Mother of the clan I grew up in, I doubt I ever would have learned any magic at all.

Generally speaking, I did not like the white witches in the Grison clan. All three were constantly in bad moods and bickering. One of them, Ethel Brewer, brazenly told me in the middle of the common area that she should be the Mother white witch instead of Sybil. Of course, she left the room when she met Sybil's harsh glance.

"Why doesn't she challenge Sybil?" I whispered to Gideon as she left. "If she thinks she would be a better Mother white witch, why doesn't she do something about it?"

"It's not exactly her call. The talisman chose Sybil years ago."

I raised an eyebrow. Each Mother or Father witch, white or green, wears a talisman to signify their position. I'd of course seen them before—Elizabeth always wore hers—but there'd never been contentions about who should lead in my previous clan. I hadn't known that the talismans *chose* who wore them.

"So what happens if someone other than the Mother or Father tries to take a talisman?" I said hesitantly. I probably sounded incredibly naïve.

In answer, Gid called to his father, who was crossing the room.

Julius joined us by the fire. "What can I help you with?"

"Would you mind putting your talisman on the ground?"

Julius's eyes darted from Gideon to me, and he grinned knowingly. He reached behind his neck and unlatched the talisman's cord, pulling it from beneath his tunic. It was an opal, as they all were. The talismans were ancient—Elizabeth told me as much—but they were not all identical. Julius's was a square with a simple casing, while Elizabeth's had been a delicate, beautiful oval. He laid it on the ground, then stepped back.

"Try to lift it," Gideon instructed.

Eyeing him curiously, I reached forward, wrapped my hand around the cord, and pulled. To my surprise, it didn't budge. I stood to get more leverage and only succeeded in barely lifting the opal off the ground.

"So anyone other than the rightful Father or Mother won't be able to lift it," I observed, releasing the cord.

I looked up, surprised to find that Julius was frowning. When I looked back at Gideon, his eyes were wide.

"Did I do something wrong?" I asked.

"It's just that usually people can't lift it at all," Gideon said slowly. "But you were able to get it off the ground."

I opened my mouth to speak but didn't know what to say. Slowly, I sat back down. Julius bent over and retrieved his talisman, still watching me curiously.

"You must be a special witch, Kenna," he mused.

With that, he left. Gideon was still staring at me. I shifted uncomfortably.

"What's Helen's story?" I said, changing the subject. "My first morning here, I thought she was going to demand I leave."

"I'm surprised she didn't," he said, lowering his voice. "She doesn't trust outsiders."

I frowned. "But you saw me with my summoning candles. I'm obviously Gifted."

He shook his head. "It has nothing to do with whether you're Gifted or not."

"Then what *does* it have to do with?"

His eyes darted around the room before he leaned in close to me. "When she was little—six or seven, I think—she and her parents were traveling to a new clan. They met another traveler, a sorcerer, who didn't have a tent or anything with him. Since theirs was large, they let him take shelter with them for the night."

He dropped his voice even lower. "He killed both her parents while they were sleeping and took all their supplies. She didn't wake up until he was gone."

My eyes widened and I opened my mouth to speak, but stopped when a door behind me slammed. We both spun to see Helen standing outside her room. Our eyes met for a second and, again, hers narrowed dangerously. Darius, who'd been speaking with Julius in the corner, crossed to her and took her arm. He kissed her cheek before they headed down the hallway out of the shelter.

"Darius's parents found her," Gideon explained when I raised my eyebrows. "From what my dad said, he was immediately attached to her and promised to protect her. They're engaged."

"So Darius and your father have known each other for a while?"

Gideon laughed. "They're practically brothers! In fact, Darius's father was the Father of the clan before he died."

I furrowed my eyebrows. "Then why isn't Darius the Father? Doesn't it usually stay in the family?"

He shrugged. "The talisman chose my father. Darius understands."

I frowned, my mind wandering back to Darius's comment that his and Julius's roles 'should be reversed.' Julius had laughed it off, but it made me uneasy. Maybe the magic in the talisman knew something about him that the others weren't seeing...

Shae's voice interrupted my thoughts. "Kenna! Will you go to the beach with me? I need some shells for a potion."

"Sure," I said, standing.

"Can I come, Shae?" Gideon asked.

She rolled her eyes. "You just have to follow Kenna everywhere, don't you?"

My mouth opened slightly and Gideon's cheeks turned pink. "Don't be ridiculous. I just want to make sure the two of you stay safe."

Shae sighed exasperatedly. "If you *must*."

As she turned away, Gideon rolled his eyes. We both chuckled before heading after her.

Shae wasn't exactly wrong, though, at least not over those first few days. When I visited Elizabeth in the other worlds, Gideon watched me, claiming he would protect me if the knights attacked. When I practiced conjuring spirits, he asked me to teach him, excusing the extra time he spent with me for his studies. Honestly, I didn't mind—in fact, I think I enjoyed it. It was familiar and comforting, like falling back into my old routines with Elizabeth.

Of course, not *exactly* like that. For one thing, we were the same age. And I still felt that uncomfortable heat in my cheeks occasionally, which I hadn't ever experienced before. But the warm connection between us was similar. For some reason, it seemed like I'd known him much longer than a few mere days. Already, his friendship was the one thing keeping me from trying to get closer to the castle. Closer to justice for my family.

I sighed as the three of us walked to the beach. I *should* be moving on and making my way to the village I'd found my first night here. The security I felt in this underground shelter and friendships I was forming shouldn't matter. The king of Orkeia had my family killed. I would have been killed had I been there, and every time we left the shelter—like now—we were taking a risk.

Someone had to do *something*.

It didn't take long to gather the shells Shae needed, and she eagerly headed back to the shelter with them to get started on her potion, but froze after just a few steps.

"I forgot I told Nathanael I'd get some angelica for our stores," she groaned.

"Angelica?" Gideon asked.

"It's a plant with white flowers. It's really useful during the cold season for healing potions. It grows just west of here."

"Okay, so we head west," he said.

"But I already started boiling the water I need for my potion! I'll have to start all over!"

She groaned again and I glanced at Gideon before sending her a supportive smile. "We can get some for you. I know what it looks like."

Shae beamed and gave me a huge hug before running back towards the shelter. Gideon rolled his eyes.

"She always does this."

"Does what?"

"Conveniently 'forgets' what she's been asked to do and gets someone else to do it for her," he said.

I shook my head as we started to walk towards the hills. "I don't think she does it on purpose."

"You haven't been here long enough to know better."

I chuckled, changing the subject to describe angelica in a bit more detail as we walked. Plants were few and far between on this part of the island, and we fell into silence as we searched. It wasn't until we reached the third hill that I was able to show Gid what it actually looked like, but we would need much more than what was there to gather enough for the clan.

My heart ached as we moved to the next hill. The last time I'd been searching for supplies like this, I'd come home to a massacre. My lips quivered as the images flashed in my mind, and I quickly redirected my thoughts back to my plan. Somehow, I needed to get close to the king. Once I found passage, it would be easy to get into the city, but much harder to get into the castle. Maybe I could get a position as a maid? Then again, I didn't know any of their traditions. Hiding my mark was one thing, but blending in was another.

And then there was Gideon. How would he feel if I left? Even though we still didn't know each other that well, I felt comfortable with him in a way I hadn't really experienced before, and it was obvious that he enjoyed spending time with me. Surprisingly, I had to admit that I would be sad to leave him behind.

Maybe I'll ask him to come with me...

I sighed at the thought. He couldn't come. His mark was clearly visible on his shoulder. Only I would be able to enter the city unnoticed. Not that I knew where to go from there.

"What's your mark?" Gideon asked, making conversation.

Great timing, I thought, looking up from a bush. "A heart."

He turned and raised an eyebrow. "I've never heard of a white witch having a heart as a mark."

"Neither have I. Elizabeth wasn't sure what it meant for a long time, either."

He frowned. "Are you sure you're not a sorcerer?"

I bent to inspect the plants. "Don't be silly, Gideon."

"You don't actually know, do you?"

"Gid—"

"I mean, sorcerers can learn other magic, right? So what if it *is* something else?"

I sighed. I wasn't going to get out of this conversation.

"I don't know what to think," I admitted, looking up at him. "When I was younger, people thought it meant I had power over the human heart, but that never seemed right to me."

"Why's that?"

"Because I don't read people very well," I laughed. "I never know what they're thinking or feeling, and I'm horrible at manipulating them to get what I want. Believe me, I tried with Elizabeth my entire childhood. It never worked."

He raised an eyebrow. "So why do you think you're a witch and not a sorcerer?"

"When I saw my first spirit, one of the sisters in my clan—I think it was Cassandra—guessed that the heart represented a soul. Elizabeth started teaching me, and while it wasn't *easy* to learn, the skills seemed to come pretty naturally. So we just kind of...went with that answer. I mean, what else could it be?"

"Well," he said, scratching his head. "Where is it?"

The corner of my lips twitched in an awkward smile. "My leg."

"Can I see it?"

I blushed. "The upper half of my leg."

"Oh." His face turned even redder than I imagined mine was and he quickly stooped down to inspect some flowers in the grass.

"What's your gift, Gideon?" I said quickly. "You've never told me. I saw your mark the night you found me, but I can't think of what it means."

He forced a laugh, his cheeks still flushed. "Maybe you could tell me."

My lips curved into a smile. "You don't know either."

He shook his head. "Any theories?" he said, lifting up his right sleeve.

I inspected the perfect circle. "Is it supposed to represent a shield? Defensive powers?"

"My father and I already thought of that one."

"And?"

"And he had to try hard *not* to kill me."

I bit my lip. "Let's see, something round...seeds are round, fruits are round—"

Gideon let out a loud laugh. "You make it sound like I should be a green witch."

I placed my hands on my hips. "What's wrong with being a witch and not a sorcerer?"

"Nothing," he said quickly. "It's just that I can't even make the simplest healing potion without blowing something up or making whoever I'm trying to heal even sicker."

He returned his attention to the plants, his easy-going nature turning more melancholy. I frowned. I could certainly relate to being discouraged about not fully understanding your gift, but it seemed like he'd already given up.

"What else is round?" I mused aloud.

"It doesn't really matter, Kenna," he sighed. "You asked about it and I was curious what you thought. You don't have to—"

The clouds parted, letting the heat warm the back of my cold neck. "The sun!" I exclaimed. "The sun, stars, moon, and earth are all round!"

He stared at me. "What are you suggesting?"

"You've heard of Hanson, right?" I asked. "Elizabeth used to tell me stories about him. They said he had power over the planets."

"Yeah, and they called him World-builder," he said. "But that's just a legend, Kenna."

"All legends are based in truth, right? Elizabeth said his mark was a circle—"

He snorted. "You can't be serious."

I opened my mouth to respond but was interrupted by a thundering sound in the distance, growing louder every second. Gideon motioned to me to remain silent and crouch down. He climbed the hill to peek over the top and his face turned white. Even without seeing it myself, I knew what he saw.

Knights.

CHAPTER FOUR

ONE LEFT BEHIND

"Come on," Gideon whispered, backing up.

I scrambled to my feet and grabbed the bag of plants. The shelter wasn't far. As long as we didn't do anything to draw their attention, we should be able to make it back and warn the others without raising an alarm.

Just then, one of the Paterson brothers—the one with the ponytail—ran around the hill, tripping over his feet. We all froze at the blare of a battle horn.

"They saw me," he gasped out between heavy breaths. "Run!"

We took off as fast as our legs would carry us. They could see us and would follow us to the shelter, but there was nowhere else to go.

"How are we going to lose them?" I panted.

"Julius has power over space," ponytail-boy explained, falling to his knees and knocking forcefully on the stone door. "He'll get us out of here."

I didn't have time to react to this new information or even really process what it meant. As soon as the door opened, the three of us pushed our way through the entrance, almost knocking Darius over. Before the opening was covered, the knights blew their horn once again, filling the shelter with a terrifying echo.

"What's going on?" Julius shouted, rushing into the common area just as we reached it.

"Knights," Gideon said. Everyone froze.

"I'm sorry, Julius," ponytail-boy said quickly. "I should have been more careful—"

Julius forced a kind smile in his direction. "It's all right, Jonas. It was bound to happen eventually. How far away are they?"

"Close enough that they saw us run for the shelter," Gideon panted.

Julius nodded and turned to address the entire clan. "Grab only essentials and meet in the cellar."

"Do you really think they'll find us?" Darius asked incredulously. "The shelter's entrance is well hidden. For all they know, the kids just disappeared."

"I'd rather not take the risk," said Julius.

Darius grimaced but nodded. Without another word, everyone hurriedly dispersed.

"The cellar?" I asked Shae as we rushed into our room.

She nodded. "Darius built a chamber under the common area, and we store emergency supplies down there. It's our escape route."

I still didn't entirely understand, but now was not the time to ask questions. I threw my pack over my shoulder—I'd never actually emptied it—and helped Shae with her things.

Even with the two of us working together, we were the last ones out. Gideon was just entering the door at the far end of the common area when we joined the others, and I closed it behind us. Everyone else was on the first landing twelve steps down, climbing down the last steps to the bottom of the chamber. Gideon, Shae, and I hurried to catch up, reaching the landing as everyone else reached the floor.

"Is Sybil behind you three?" Lyra, Gideon's mother, called as we helped Shae down.

I turned, my stomach dropping. No one had been behind me when I closed the door, and no one was following us now.

"I'll find her," I volunteered, running back up the stairs before anyone could stop me. I hadn't been there for my last clan when they were attacked, and I wasn't about to leave anyone behind this time—not even Sybil.

I couldn't hear the march of the army through the hill, but I knew there was no time to lose. My heart pounding, I entered Sybil, Helen, and Ethel's room. It was empty. Quickly, I turned to check the rest of the shelter and ran into Gideon in the doorway.

"What are you doing?" I yelled.

"If you think I'm going to leave you up here alone, you're crazy, Kenna."

I groaned. There was no arguing with him.

"Fine. You check the eating area and the three rooms over there, and I'll check the others."

He nodded, and we separated. She wasn't in the Patersons' rooms, and I could tell from Gideon's expression when he re-entered the common area that he hadn't found her either. We ran back to the cellar. Judging by the pounding of the footsteps above us, the knights were dangerously close.

Soon we were on the first landing, looking down at everyone waiting impatiently.

"She's not down there?" I called, knowing the answer before Lyra spoke.

"No. You didn't find her?"

"It's like she disappeared," Gideon answered, but I was no longer listening. To my right, a sliver of light caught my eye, and I turned towards it. A small crawl space led upwards towards the surface. Someone was huddled at its exit.

I ducked into the tunnel, not giving any mind to the dirt soiling my clothes. Behind me, I heard Gideon call my name, but I ignored him and approached the slumped figure.

"Sybil!" I called, struggling toward her. She didn't turn, staring blankly through a small opening ahead of her. Through it I could see the knights. They weren't far off, but they were no longer advancing. The men closest to us appeared to be fighting off invisible creatures, and my eyes widened in understanding.

"She's holding them off," I called back to Gideon, not surprised that he'd crawled in after me. "She's summoning spirits. I'll find her spirit and get her down there—you go tell the others."

Only when Gideon had reluctantly squirmed out of the crawl space did I close my eyes, willing my spirit to leave its physical home. I flew through the ground above to see about twenty spirits battling the front lines of the knights, their spiritual swords leaving nothing but bruises on the enemy's skin. Sybil's spirit floated just ahead of me, focused on controlling the small army.

The knights yelled in confusion, those further back unsure why the line wasn't advancing. A man on a horse rode forward, an angry scowl on his scared face, and Sybil sent one of her spirits to spook the animal. The horse whinnied and bucked, and the man barely managed to stay mounted. It was enough for him to apparently realize what was happening, and he growled.

"Onward, Men! These paltry spirits are nothing but a distraction!"

I frowned. He was right. Twenty spirits were definitely not going to be enough to fight them off. There's only so much a spirit can do, even when it's summoned for battle purposes. It's not like fighting another human being—it's almost like fighting against birds pecking at your skin. The knights would soon be at the shelter, and even with how well-hidden the entrance was, it wouldn't take them long to get in once they found it.

I hurried to Sybil's side. "Sybil, we're leaving. If we go back now, there's enough time for us to join the others."

Her eyes narrowed. "Why don't you do that, then?"

"I came back to get you."

Sybil shook her head. "As soon as I let these spirits free, the knights will be upon us. There would hardly be enough time for both of us to escape. You are young and have a life ahead of you—I have lived mine."

I groaned in frustration. There would be no point in forcing her body back down the tunnel while her spirit remained here—she would have to search for wherever we went, and it was very possible she might not ever find the new shelter. If she couldn't find us, she would end up a lost spirit and her body would die anyway.

"Let me help you, at least," I insisted.

"I've summoned all the spirits nearby."

I furrowed my brow. "That can't be possible. Dozens of people died when the knights attacked my clan, and that's just on the other side of the island."

She let out an incredulous scoff. "And have any of these spirits passed into rest?"

"Yes, but—"

She shook her head at me condescendingly. "You can't summon spirits who have already passed on, Kenna."

"Have you ever tried?"

She broke concentration for a moment to glare at me. "Are you suggesting you know more about summoning spirits than I do?"

"Of course not," I said, exasperated. "But if there's even the possibility—"

Sybil scoffed, but her dismissal only made me more determined. Leaving her to the battle, I quickly flew to my previous home. The bodies had begun to decompose, and some had clearly been mutilated by animals. My stomach turned and the desire for revenge filled my heart anew, but right now I had to stay focused on my goal.

I thought back to the few times I had summoned spirits before under Elizabeth's instruction. While I had never summoned more than one or two at a time, theoretically, I should be able to summon those of any bodies in the area. Even if I couldn't summon my clan members who had moved on as Sybil claimed, there were bound to be at least some of the knights in the Land of the Lost or still wandering the earth that I could call to our aid.

"Arise, those who have died in this place," I said, my eyes skyward and my hands extended toward the ground.

A surge of power coursed through me as spirits began ascending from the Land of the Lost to come to my side. To my relief—and some satisfaction that I would be able to prove Sybil wrong—I also saw spirits descend from the Land of the Saved. I recognized the members of my clan, including Elizabeth, but when they were summoned this way, they were no longer individual beings. All summoned spirits exist solely to carry out orders. There was a knot in my throat at seeing Elizabeth's form floating in front of me, but I dismissed it as quickly as I could, focusing on the task at hand.

"Follow me," I commanded, "and delay the knights."

All their ghostly heads nodded in unison, and we hastily returned. The knights had gained ground since I left, and Sybil had lost most of her spirits. Her eyes widened at our approach. As her last spirit disappeared, I set loose the ones following me. They pushed forward, creating a wall of force between us and the advancing army. Horses bucked in fear and the knights stumbled backward from the sudden barrier, waving their swords and shields wildly against the invisible attacks.

I watched the scene carefully, sending more spirits to those sections of the army that were advancing, but my energy quickly began to falter. It was getting harder and harder not to return to my body, and my hold on the spirits was weakening—to control that many at once was draining my powers. As I directed them in the attack, a few of them disappeared, returning to their places of rest. *Focus, Kenna!*

Sybil's spirit rose up to mine, eyes still wide. "These spirits passed on?"

"Some of them, yes."

"And you still summoned them?"

"Yes," I said, struggling to keep my focus.

She shook her head before taking control of the spirits into her own hands. The attack was stronger now, proving her skill as a white witch. I wasn't yet that skilled in controlling spirits.

"I'll keep holding them off. Return to your body, Kenna," she instructed, "and take my talisman. You are the Mother white witch now."

I stared at her. "Me? But I—"

"Do not argue. You are worthy. Now go!"

Reluctantly, I allowed my spirit to sink through the ground and rejoin my body. As soon as I opened my eyes, I retrieved the talisman from Sybil's neck and placed it around my own. It was practically weightless.

As I started squirming out of the hole, the sounds of the battle drew closer. When I reached the landing, to my relief, everyone was still there.

"Where's Sybil?" Lyra called.

"She's not coming," I answered.

There was no time for anyone to argue. Julius had already drawn a circle in the ground for his spell, and everyone but Gideon stood inside it. He waited at the bottom of the steps, watching anxiously as I half climbed, half fell down the steep flight. As I reached level ground, Julius started chanting and Gideon pulled me into the circle, keeping his arm protectively around my waist.

When Julius finished his spell, the world around me disappeared into darkness. Forces pulled on me from all directions, as if they were trying to rip me into pieces. I felt a rush of panic and nausea as the world seemed to spin out of control. It only lasted a few moments, however, and we soon stood on a quiet beach. The struggles of the knights could no longer be heard.

Okay, this is what they meant by power over space...

Tentatively, I stepped outside the circle and surveyed the area. At the moment, it didn't look like a home, but it was perhaps the best location Julius could have chosen for us.

The beach was even more secluded than where I'd lived with my previous clan—it looked like we were the first people to set foot on it and there were cliffs surrounding every side. Seals barked on the rocks and seabirds flew all around. The scene was eerily similar to where my clan had died, and my thoughts turned to Elizabeth. I closed my eyes, listening to the waves beat against the rocks, grateful I'd been there this time. I said a silent prayer that Sybil wouldn't suffer and would be able to join Elizabeth and so many others in rest soon.

Above the noises of nature, I heard footsteps behind me and turned to face a very disgruntled Ethel. By now everyone had noticed the opal around my neck, and she held out her hand expectantly, glaring at me.

"I would like my talisman, please."

I wanted to snap at her that there were more important things to think about, like the fact that Sybil had just sacrificed herself for us. But even though I didn't know Ethel well, I knew enough just from the last few days that comments like that wouldn't go over well.

The whole group was watching me. I fingered the clasp, but then hesitated. It didn't make sense for me to have the talisman at all—I was the least experienced of the white witches in the clan, and I hadn't even planned on staying with the clan long-term. But I felt a pulsing of power from the talisman, almost as if it was warming my skin, and knew it was a confirmation of what Sybil had said.

Whether or not I wanted it, I had been chosen as the Mother white witch.

"Sybil told me to keep it," I said as evenly as I could.

Ethel's eyes grew cold with fury. "You must have misunderstood. Give it to me!"

Her sharp tone made me wince. "You're welcome to try to lift it," I said, not seeing another way to settle this. I unlatched the talisman and set it on the ground.

The whole clan watched silently as Ethel eagerly bent to claim it. With her hand securely around the cord, she began to straighten, only to be stopped by the unexpected weight, unable to move it even the slightest amount.

"What kind of trick is this?" she demanded. "Do you have a spirit helping you?"

"I can only control spirits when I'm outside of my body. You know that."

She let out a sound that resembled a growl before trying again, but after multiple failed attempts, her face reddening more and more each time, she finally stomped away. The beach seemed almost more deserted than before.

Helen sighed. "Well, I guess it's only fair that all three of us try, isn't it?"

After exchanging a glance with Ethel, she calmly stepped forward and attempted to pick up the talisman at my feet. When she too was unable to lift it, she stared at me, shocked. I bent down to her level, met her sharp eyes, wrapped my fingers around the talisman, and stood. Slowly, I wrapped the cord back around my neck and hooked it, acting more confident than I actually felt. Helen stood as well.

"I suppose you were telling the truth, then," she said, her eyes narrowing as she turned to join Ethel. The two of them walked away, and I let out a breath I hadn't realized I was holding. Darius's eyes narrowed and he stared at me for another moment before turning to join the two women. Others were quick to look away and begin exploring the area. I wrapped my hand around the opal, my heart racing.

Chapter Five

PLANS AND PROMISES

Since we were on a beach now and not in the middle of the hills, Darius built the new shelter above ground, far enough away from the ocean and close enough to the cliffs that it wouldn't be seen by passing ships. I requested to have my own room, a decision Shae was very unhappy about.

"Do you not like me anymore?"

"Of course I like you, Shae."

"Then why don't you want to share a room again?"

"It's just—"

"Is my talking annoying you?"

"No!" I sighed. "I just need time to myself occasionally. And now that I'm the Mother white witch, I'm going to have to speak privately with Ethel and Helen from time to time, and your father might have me working on projects for him. Do you understand?"

Shae pouted. "Promise we'll still spend time together?"

"Promise."

When she left to help her mother find some food, I sat on the beach and buried my head in my hands.

How am I going to leave now?

It wasn't just the attachments I was forming with Gideon and Shae—how could I leave now that I had responsibilities in the clan? Could I really just abandon them and give it all up? I wasn't even sure what my responsibilities *were* as Mother white witch, aside from being part of

Julius's council and helping Helen and Ethel if they needed it. But they were both so much more experienced than I was.

I fingered the talisman around my neck. Sybil had entrusted this to me. And yet, when I closed my eyes, all I could see was her mangled body, lying with those I had already lost. Wouldn't it be better to try to put a stop to all of this than just stay with the clan?

But even if I did decide to abandon my new responsibilities, for all I knew, we were now on a completely different island than before. The village where I'd been planning to start my journey could be far, far away, and I'd need a new plan for how to get to the main city for when the time came.

The sound of someone running up to me from behind interrupted my thoughts. I looked over my shoulder and saw ponytail-boy—Julius had called him Jonas—jumping down a hill to land on the beach, his eyes darting this way and that. When he saw me, he put a finger to his lips before taking off to the right and diving behind a boulder just large enough to hide him.

I scarcely had time to raise my eyebrows before another person appeared at the top of the hill and jumped down. It was the other Paterson boy, his brother—not that I should really call them 'boys' since they were both a couple years older than I was. He had green eyes and black hair that fell to just below his shoulders. It was pretty clear he was looking for his brother, but when he saw me, he stopped and smiled.

"Hey, did you see Jonas run by here?" he asked.

"Um ..."

I glanced at the footprints he left in the sand, and his brother followed my gaze. He smirked, but rather than immediately running to go after Jonas, he brought his attention back to me and sat down.

"I don't think we've been properly introduced—I'm Neal," he said, extending a hand.

There was something about his smile that made me smile, too, even in the midst of my confusing thoughts. "Kenna," I responded as I took his hand.

"So, Kenna - how does it feel?" he asked, gesturing to the talisman.

I sighed, looking down at the ground and absentmindedly drawing in the sand. "I'm not really sure ..." I said awkwardly.

"Well, I for one think you're brave to accept it," he said, leaning back a little and looking up at the clouds. "My dad's the Father green witch, and he's made it pretty clear that that's probably going to pass on to me, but honestly, I don't want to be tied down like that."

"Tied down?"

"Yeah—stuck here, having to help lead the clan, not being able to run out and have fun anymore," he said with an exaggerated yawn.

I raised an eyebrow. "You don't plan on staying with the clan?"

"Oh, I didn't say that," he said, sitting back up and turning to look at me more directly with those dark green eyes. "I'd just rather spend my time *living* while we're young, you know? After all, who knows how much longer any of us have?"

A lump formed in my throat at that and I looked away. He seemed to sense that his comment had been a bit crass given recent events, and he cleared his throat.

"Sorry, I'm not really expressing myself well—do you want to go for a swim?"

I stared at him. "What?"

He smirked and jumped to his feet, extending a hand to help me up. "Come on, life's short, we're young, let's go for a swim."

"The water will be freezing," I protested.

"You get used to it pretty quick."

"Our clothes will get soaked."

"So?"

He asked the question in such an innocent, casual way that I actually laughed.

"Aren't you at all worried about getting sick?" I asked.

"Nah," he said, shrugging. "Mum's soup pretty much cures anything."

"I thought you were looking for your brother."

He smirked a little more. "Yeah, but you're much prettier than him."

My cheeks warmed. As I stared at him in indecision, Jonas moved out from behind the boulder and started to sneak up from behind. Before I could decide whether or not to warn Neal, Jonas tackled him to the ground, and both of them rolled around in the sand shouting at each other. Their scuffling finished with Jonas on top. Neal threw a handful of sand at him and Jonas simply messed up his brother's dark hair in response, which was apparently all it took for Neal to admit defeat.

"Enough!" he said with some annoyance. As the two of them straightened, Neal furiously tried to fix his hair. I held back a laugh.

"Thanks for keeping him distracted," Jonas said to me with a wink.

Neal's jaw dropped in a look of betrayal. "You were in on this?"

"What? No! I was just sitting here!" I said quickly.

"Well, you can make it up to me by having dinner with us," Neal said, his offended expression replaced by another smile. Up until that point, I'd only ever dined with the Grison family. The Patersons had their own eating area in the previous shelter and the other white witches had kept to themselves.

"Um...sure," I said.

"Great!" Neal said enthusiastically. Jonas elbowed him in the side, which resulted in another brief wrestling match. Shaking my head, I stood and left them to it, moving in the direction the rest of the clan had gone.

With shock I saw that Darius had almost completely finished the shelter. From first glance, it looked like just a cave set into the side of the cliff. From the outside, it reminded me of my former home, and all of the levity I'd felt talking to Neal and Jonas vanished. I swallowed the knot in my throat as I entered, looking around the new space.

Darius lowered his arms when he saw me, his exhaustion only just apparent, and forced a hesitant smile. No doubt he thought Helen should be the next Mother white witch. I felt an awkward heaviness in the air between us, but we both seemed to be pretending it wasn't there.

"Your room's the second one on the left," he said, nodding toward it. "It's already finished."

He walked toward one of the other rooms before I could say thank you. I let out a breath as the air lightened and approached the door to enter my new room.

The fire was already lit, but it wasn't too warm. The bed still needed bedding, and the dresser had yet to be filled, but it was a nice, cozy room. I could be comfortable in here.

For the moment.

I stood in the center of the room for a few minutes before setting down my pack and opening it. My mind still swimming with my earlier thoughts on the beach, I pulled out my summoning candles and set up the circle.

Just before I stepped inside, I heard a knock on my door and turned. Part of me wanted to just ignore it, but instead I said quietly, "Come in."

Gideon opened the door, glancing at the candles briefly before meeting my gaze with a small smile. "Hey...I just wanted to check on you," he said. "Are you okay?"

My lips quivered as I tried to smile back. "I'm fine," I said. He raised an eyebrow and I sighed as I sat on the edge of the bed. "At least, I'm doing as well as can be expected."

He slowly moved to sit down next to me, glancing again at the candles before looking ahead at the wall. For a long moment we sat in silence, but it was a comfortable silence. I could feel his quiet support and concern.

"I know you weren't planning on staying with us," he eventually said.

Surprised, I looked up at him. He was still looking at the wall.

"How do you know that?" I asked.

He shrugged. "You never unpacked. And I just felt like...like there was somewhere else you thought you needed to be. You get this distant look in your eyes."

I bit my lip and looked down at my lap.

"You can tell me, you know," he said after another moment of silence, tearing his eyes from the wall to look at me.

I hesitated, rubbing my hands on my skirt. My plan would likely sound crazy to him, and I wasn't even sure if it was worth repeating at this point, not when everything had been upended by the knights' attack.

"I just feel like someone needs to do something," I finally said, meeting his gaze. "I mean, what is it going to accomplish, just constantly running and hiding? The last shelter—it should have been easy to stay hidden, but the knights found it anyway. The Slaughters are never going to stop if someone doesn't confront the king."

He frowned. "And you think you're the one to do that?"

I pressed my lips together. "I just know *someone* has to. And there must be a reason the Giftgiver spared me when my clan was murdered."

"Have you considered that maybe you were meant to find us?" he asked, and I was surprised to see color come to his cheeks. "I mean, you're the Mother white witch now, not just because of what Sybil said. The talisman *chose* you. And...well, selfishly, I haven't really felt like I could talk to anyone else the way I can talk to you, especially about not knowing what my gift is. I just...I think there's a reason we're the ones who found you..."

His voice trailed off and he looked away once more. I watched his expression, frowning slightly as I pondered what he said.

"You could be right," I admitted quietly.

Gid sighed, looking back at me with a soft smile. "Well, whatever the reason, and whatever happens, you're going to do great," he said. Reaching out, he took my hand and gave it a supportive squeeze. I returned his smile with a shaky one of my own.

"Thanks," I muttered.

He glanced at the candles again and nodded to them as he released my hand and stood. "I'll leave you to it...see you at dinner?"

"Actually, Neal Paterson invited me to have dinner with his family tonight."

This seemed to make Gid pause, but he gave me another smile, this one a little more forced for some reason. "I'll see you in the morning, then. Make sure you get some rest."

"I will. Thanks, Gid."

As he left the room, I let out another heavy breath. Maybe he was right. Maybe I *was* supposed to stay here. Maybe I was supposed to help strengthen this clan, and together we could come up with some sort of solution.

But for the moment, I turned my thoughts to other matters. Pushing myself up from the bed, I moved into the center of the circle and closed my eyes, whispering the Sacred Words of Passage. They'd become more and more familiar to me as I'd spent time visiting Elizabeth, and soon enough I was standing before the Golden Gates once more.

It wasn't a surprise to see Sybil near the gates. Her youth in spirit form had changed her. She looked much happier, even given the fact that she had just been murdered. She was speaking with others waiting at the gates, her smile bringing a brightness and beauty to her expression and visage. When I recalled the bitter old woman I had known, it was hard to believe that her beauty had once been so overwhelming.

Slowly, I approached. Sensing my mortal spirit, other spirits stepped aside to allow me to pass. As I drew closer, Sybil turned her head and her eyes met mine. Her smile brightened even more and she moved towards me.

"I must admit, I didn't expect to see you here so soon," she said. "But I'm glad. Is everyone all right?"

I nodded. "Yes, thanks to you."

She shook her head. "I never could have held them off effectively without your help."

There was a knot in my throat. Even though we hadn't gotten along in my few days in the clan, it was still emotional to know that she had sacrificed herself for us. And here she was, thanking me for the small part I played. It felt unfair.

"Sybil..." I started awkwardly after another moment. "Are you...are you sure I'm supposed to be the new Mother? I know the talisman has its own magic, but I'm only seventeen. I don't even know everything I'm supposed to do..."

"Kenna, what you did down there—summoning spirits that had already passed—that was incredible," she interrupted. "In all my years, I've never heard of anyone doing such a thing. I had no doubt the talisman would choose you once I was gone."

I shifted where I stood and looked down at the clouds beneath my feet. Sensing that I was still unsure, Sybil added, "As far as what you're supposed to do, Julius will help you. So will the talisman. Your main role is to support the other white witches and the clan in general. Make sure they are taken care of and have the spell components they need. Help Julius make decisions for the safety and betterment of the clan. Oh, and keep a record of our history—I passed mine on to Helen when everyone was packing, assuming she would be the one to take on the mantle."

"Keep a record?" I asked. I had seen Elizabeth write frequently while I was growing up, that much was true, but I always assumed it was notes for herself. I hadn't realized there was a history written of our people—a history that was now lost and destroyed thanks to the knights.

Sybil nodded. "It's tradition. Like Kindra and the Mothers of old."

Kindra. "The wife of Hanson?" I said in recognition. My eyes widened a bit as I thought more about it and added, "Hanson, the one that had power over the planets generations ago?"

"That's right."

"So it's more than just a story?" I asked hopefully.

"Oh, it's definitely more than just a story. My former clan used to have copies of some of Kindra's writings. They were left behind when we fled from the Orkeian knights, unfortunately, but they were very real. She set the precedent for us to keep records of our people and pass them down to the next leaders. That will be one of your responsibilities now."

Slowly, I nodded. The responsibility already felt overwhelming, but Sybil's calm demeanor soothed me. I felt like I finally understood why the talisman chose her to be the Mother white witch while she was alive. I wondered if her cold nature had been the result of hardships she faced in life, and now that she was relieved of them she was free to show the care and compassion she had really felt for those around her—the care and compassion that had led her to give up her life to keep them safe.

"Thank you," I said. "If you meet another white witch, a woman named Elizabeth, will you please let her know I'd like to speak with her again soon?"

I took a moment to describe her, and Sybil assured me she would relay the message if she could. As I returned to my body in the summoning circle, the weight of the amount of magic I'd expended in the past few hours suddenly hit me. With a groan, I closed my eyes and moved to the stone bed, not even caring about how hard it was as I finally did what Gideon suggested and laid down to rest.

CHAPTER SIX

BETWEEN SALT AND SAFETY

When I awoke, I didn't bother taking down my summoning circle. Instead, I began to unpack. It felt strange, and I still wasn't sure how committed I was to staying, but at least for now, I owed it to Sybil and the others to help the clan get settled in their new home.

It wasn't long before I heard a sharp knock on my door and turned to see Neal enter uninvited. "Nice place," he said. "I'm jealous. I still have to share with Jo."

"How dreadful," I said in mock horror.

One side of his mouth curved upwards. "Ready for dinner? My mother's an excellent cook."

Setting down the clothing I'd pulled from my pack, I followed him from the room. "I feel like all green witches are good cooks," I said.

He laughed and shook his head. "Not me. I'd probably manage to poison you with salt."

I chuckled. "Your whole family's green witches, right?"

"Yeah. It's been that way for generations. My dad's the Father green witch."

I nodded. Shae complained constantly that he didn't let her try half the potions she wanted to. He said she was 'too young.'

"Is that why you and Jonas were never really in the shelter?" I asked.

Neal paused as we entered the common area and looked at me, confused. "What do you mean?"

"Well, I just—I was surprised by how little I saw you around before," I said, stopping beside him. "So was it because you were doing things for your father, or...?"

"Oh." He shrugged and leaned against the wall. "I mean, sometimes, sure. But most of the time Jo and I were just exploring."

I raised an eyebrow. "Exploring?"

"Yeah. I've never been good at staying cooped up," Neal said wryly. "I used to sneak off to villages when I was a kid. Obviously I don't do that anymore, it's too dangerous, but being stuck underground wasn't exactly for me. It's a shame, though."

"What? That you can't sneak off to the villages anymore?"

"Sure, but that's not what I meant," he said, shooting me a grin. "It's a shame I waited this long to get to know you."

I bit the inside of my lip, feeling heat rush through my neck and cheeks once more. Thankfully, Jonas came and found us, saving me from having to respond. Together we entered the Patersons' living quarters. The dining area was in the first room, and Jonas and Neal's mother, Brynna, sat at the edge of a fire in the corner, stirring something in a cauldron. Her long black hair, even darker than Neal's, was pulled into a bun on top of her head.

"Welcome, Kenna!" she said cheerfully. "Please, have a seat."

"Thank you for having me," I said as I sat. Neal took the seat next to me. Jonas punched him in the arm as he sat, but Neal didn't respond. Apparently they didn't roughhouse as much in front of their mother.

Their father came out from one of the bedrooms. He also had black hair and Neal's same green eyes. When he saw me, his eyes crinkled with a smile. "Hello, Kenna."

"Hello, Nathanael. Thank you for inviting me to eat with you."

"It's about time we did. My wife is the most talented cook alive—she barely even uses her gift," he said warmly, kissing Brynna on the cheek. She giggled. Neal's leg bumped mine and I looked up to see him roll his eyes exaggeratedly. I suppressed a laugh.

"What is it tonight?" Jonas piped up.

"Vegetable soup," she said, filling the bowls. "I would have made something better if I knew you were going to invite Kenna to join us."

"That sounds wonderful," I insisted. "And it smells divine."

"Speaking of 'divine,'" Nathanael said, taking the seat at the head of the table next to me. "I've always wondered: what is the Land of the Saved like?"

I blinked, thrown off by the abruptness of the question. Brynna sighed and shook her head slightly, a bit of an amused smile on her face. Neal and Jonas exchanged a glance as well, and I gathered that they were used to Nathanael interjecting in conversations like this.

I chewed on my lip as I considered how to respond. "Well—"

"Is that not a question I'm supposed to ask?" he said.

"It's not that," I said. "It's just that we can't actually enter the city. We can only go up to the gates."

Nathanael nodded. "That's logical. My apologies for my ignorance. Sybil wasn't exactly open to talking to others about her powers, and I've had a lot of questions, seeing so much death in the past few years."

"Well, there will be plenty of time for questions later," Brynna interrupted, setting the bowls on the table. "For now, let's eat."

Neal and Jonas picked up their spoons eagerly, gulping down the soup. I'd barely started before they were asking for seconds. It was a delicious meal, and I was surprised at the amount of flavor she was able to bring out of the vegetables. I could see spices set out in containers on a shelf nearby and wondered how she knew to combine them so expertly.

Despite Brynna's caution to her husband, Nathanael was clearly eager to learn about the magic white witches held. I did my best to describe to him and the others what the Land of the Saved looked like from the gates, and I mentioned that I'd seen Sybil and how much she had changed being in her eternal spirit form.

"Are you sure you were talking to the same Sybil?" Neal asked with a laugh, bumping my leg again under the table.

His mother shot him a warning look. "Don't speak ill of the dead, Neal."

"I wasn't," he said, putting up his hands innocently. "She was just always snapping at us when we were growing up."

"Well maybe she wouldn't have if you weren't always making a ruckus and interrupting her spells."

"Sybil certainly appreciated order," Nathanael said, bringing a calming influence to the conversation. "She always found it difficult to be around rambunctious children. But I knew her for a long time, and she had a kind heart."

"Elizabeth—the Mother white witch from my previous clan—said our spirits don't change when we die," I said. "We stay the same people with the same personalities. But the Land of the Saved...it exudes peace. I'm sure being free from the stress of taking care of a clan and worrying about a war has changed her in some ways."

Nathanael nodded. "I'm sure. And what of the Land of the Lost? What is the fate of the spirits there?"

I shifted in my seat, frowning. "I've only been there once, with Elizabeth when she was teaching me how to travel between the worlds," I admitted. "There's a really dark forest. Elizabeth told me not to enter because the spirits there will try to make you get lost so you can't return to your body. I don't really know much else, just that Elizabeth said that anyone who goes there ends up miserable forever."

"My mother taught me that the Lost One tortures the spirits sent to him," Brynna said. "I'm not sure how you torture a spirit, but I'm sure it's an awful place to visit."

I nodded, shivering at the memory. The only time I'd felt more despair and sadness was when I had come upon the scene of my clan's destruction. I stirred my soup for a moment, staring into it as I began to get lost in my thoughts.

Neal cleared his throat. "So, Kenna, do you want to go exploring tomorrow? Get a lay of the land?"

I looked up at him and saw Brynna's eyes narrow as she did as well. "Don't drag Kenna into your trouble," she said before I could respond.

"The two of you need to be more careful so nothing like this happens again."

Jonas put up his hands defensively. "Hey, I was out gathering, not just messing around."

"Yes, but you'd become careless. That's why you were spotted," Brynna said with a gentle tone. "I'm not blaming you, Dear, but if it weren't for Sybil holding them off, we may not have had time to escape. We don't want to risk exposing ourselves again."

"Someone has to do some scouting," Neal insisted, setting down his spoon. "We need to know where we are and if there are any settlements nearby, after all."

"I agree with them, Brynna," Nathanael said, taking his wife's hand. "We also need to know what resources are nearby, and I feel more comfortable sending the boys out searching than Lyra or Shae."

Brynna sighed, taking a long look at each of them before nodding in defeat. Neal's smile brightened and he turned to me again.

"So, what do you say? Want to come along?"

My chest tightened, but Neal and Nathanael were right. If nothing else, we needed to know what was out there so we were prepared. What's more, I would need to know if there was a village or city nearby if I did decide to leave and find a way to the castle.

"Sure," I said.

"Then it's a date," Neal said with a wink.

I felt my cheeks suddenly burn and noticed Jonas elbow him in the ribs, but I was saved from any lingering awkwardness by Nathanael asking another question.

***

Brynna was kind enough to give me one of her old coats for our outing the next day. I buried my hands in the pockets, grateful for the extra warmth, as I waited for Neal and Jonas outside the shelter. I stared at the waves rolling over the rocky beach, once again eerily reminded of the home where I grew up. I used to sit on the doorstep of our shelter and stare out at the waves like this while Elizabeth braided my hair or we both sewed.

Breathing deeply, I imagined she was here with me. A sinking feeling settled in my chest, centered beneath the talisman I now wore, and I reached up to grasp it.

"See? There it is again."

I jumped, looking up to see Gideon, his golden hair bright under the morning sun. There was a pained smile on his face as he sat down and rested his arms on his knees.

"There's what again?" I asked.

"That distant look I was talking about," he said, nudging my shoulder with his. "Do you want to talk about it?"

I sighed, turning away from him to stare out at the sea once more. "This is a lot like the cove where I grew up," I muttered quietly.

"I'm sorry," he said after a moment. "That can't be easy."

He set his hand on my knee, drawing my gaze away from the waves. I stared at his fingers, not really sure why his touch made my throat feel tighter. After a short silence, I placed my hand on top of his and gave a gentle squeeze, realizing as I did that my eyes were watering.

"Thank you," I whispered.

He turned his palm upward to properly hold my hand and squeezed back. I felt his blue eyes on me and lifted my gaze to meet them. There was a soft, concerned frown on his face. His eyes darted across my features and he lifted his free hand to wipe away a tear. The touch brought some warmth to my cheeks.

"Kenna," he said, taking in a bit of a shaky breath, "I—"

"Ready to go?"

Gideon quickly drew back both of his hands and stood. Even though his touch was no longer there, I still felt the heat in my cheeks as I, too, stood and turned to face Neal. His characteristic grin spread across his face as he walked up to my side, but it seemed to be more forced than usual.

"Yes, I should be," I said, clearing my throat.

Gid's lips tightened into a frown. "Go where?" he asked, looking between the two of us.

"To scout the island. Figure out where we are, what resources are available, that sort of thing," Neal said nonchalantly, looking at Gideon only briefly before returning his attention to me. "Mum packed us some sandwiches for lunch."

"That was nice of her," I said, stuffing my hands in the coat pockets again. "Where's Jonas?"

"Jo decided not to come—something about getting settled in," he said with a shrug. "I think he really just wants to sleep."

"Hold on," Gid said, moving directly in front of Neal. "You're taking her out scouting *alone*?"

Neal's grin faded. He looked down at Gideon, who was about a head shorter than him, and crossed his arms. "Yes," he said flatly. "Is that a problem?"

"Of course it is!"

Neal scoffed. "Why? I don't seem to remember it being a problem when *you* were taking her out alone at our old camp."

"Yeah, well, I know how to be careful, unlike some people," Gid said under his breath.

Neal's green eyes flashed with anger. "It wasn't Jo's fault," he said. "And Kenna can decide for herself if she thinks it's safe."

"Um, I'm right here," I interjected, stepping between them.

Gid's mouth was partially open, ready to retort, but he swallowed whatever he was going to say when he saw my hard expression. "Sorry, Kenna," he breathed instead, shooting a sharp glance at Neal before stepping back. "I just don't think it's safe for the two of you to go out wandering alone, that's all."

"You're welcome to come with us," I suggested.

Neal shuffled where he stood and cleared his throat. "Yeah, sure," he said, though his voice sounded a bit hollow.

Gideon looked from me to Neal and back again. With each passing moment of silence, his expression softened. His narrow eyes relaxed and he unclenched his fists. But for whatever reason, the frown on his face deepened.

"No," he muttered finally, sounding resigned. "It...makes more sense for just two people to go, now that I think about it. Less people to be noticed, after all."

He tried to force a smile, but sadness remained in his eyes. I creased my eyebrows in concern, but before I could respond, I felt Neal's hand on my shoulder.

"Don't worry, Blondie, I'll make sure Kenna's safe," he said.

He caught my eye with a wink, looking as carefree as usual, and turned to go, steering me with him. Briefly, I looked back over my shoulder. My eyes met Gideon's. He let out a breath and waved, the corners of his lips twitching, before he turned and reentered the shelter. Something in my chest tightened.

I faced forward as Neal let his hand drop to his side. He walked with what I can only describe as a relaxed confidence. Any tension he'd shown when Gideon questioned our outing seemed to have melted away now that our journey had actually begun.

"For today, why don't we head north for a bit?" he suggested.

So that's what we did. We took a half day's trip north, walking along the foot of the seaside cliffs. They were magnificent, if a bit imposing. Neal wanted to climb them, an idea which made me nervous. But when he finally convinced me to go along with it, the feeling of hanging out above the water was exhilarating.

When we reached the top, Neal took out the sandwiches his mother had brought, and we sat down to eat. There was something peaceful about listening to the waves crash against the rocks below us. He sighed dramatically when he finished his lunch and laid down on the grass, resting his hands under his head as he looked up at the gray sky.

"It's nice to get away for a bit, isn't it?" he mused.

"It is," I admitted with my own, quieter sigh. "But...we should probably head back."

"What, are you tired of the view already?"

He nudged me with his foot and wiggled his eyebrows when I looked at him. I rolled my eyes.

"It's not that, it's just…Gideon was right about it being dangerous."

He rolled onto his side to look at me more directly. "I'm not worried about that. We haven't seen anyone all morning, so I don't think there are any settlements around."

"In *this* direction," I retorted.

"So we check another direction tomorrow," he said matter-of-factly. "We need to check them all eventually. Blondie really can come too, if he wants." He gave a slight smirk. "That'd be a shame, though."

I raised an eyebrow at him. "A shame?"

"Mhm," he said, sitting completely up and bringing his face level with mine. "I like having you to myself for a few hours."

My breath caught in my throat when I realized how close he was, and I stood, brushing off my skirts with a rush of nervous energy.

"Let's find a way back down to the beach," I suggested.

***

We took several more scouting trips together. Jo joined us sometimes, but Gideon said he didn't want to intrude and, eventually, I stopped asking if he wanted to come. Neal made each one an adventure with more climbing, exploring hidden caves, and chasing the wildlife. His carefree, easy personality was infectious. When I was around him, it was easy to forget about the weight of the war, or that of my new responsibilities.

I quickly decided that I didn't like being Mother white witch. Ethel pestered me endlessly, requesting increasingly rare spell components and special privileges that I didn't know how to accommodate. She said she was trying to develop new protection spells, but it was no secret that her keeping me busy was really retaliation for the talisman incident. To my surprise, Helen exasperatedly told her to stop after about a week, but Ethel continued to grumble and snap at me every time she had the chance.

Helen, on the other hand, gave me Sybil's writings without me even asking for them. She, at least, seemed to respect the talisman's decision, even if she still wasn't exactly pleasant to be around.

I wasn't sure how thorough I was supposed to be in keeping the clan's records. I often found myself staring at a blank page. But occasionally, I'd feel inspired to write about certain interactions between the clan members. I imagined they were coming from the talisman since they weren't usually things that seemed important, like noticing Darius and Helen leave the room immediately when Julius entered. But as I wrote about it, it did seem odd. I thought Darius and Julius were supposed to be best friends, but it was almost like they were avoiding each other.

Before I knew it, a month had gone by. I'd been too busy to think about leaving again. The weight of responsibility was definitely taxing, and I relished every opportunity to take a break. When Neal wasn't dragging me off on another adventure, I spent time with Gid, talking about everything and nothing at the same time. Sometimes the conversations lasted for hours, sometimes only minutes. Usually, there were long periods of comfortable silence in which we just walked together or sat overlooking the ocean. There wasn't necessarily anything that needed to be said.

During one of these moments, while listening to the beating of the waves of the shore, I closed my eyes and leaned back on the grass. I tilted my head back, letting the sun warm my face.

The sensation made me pause. I glanced towards Gideon sitting on my left. He, too, was enjoying the sun with his eyes closed. I hesitated for a moment, just watching him, but eventually couldn't hold in the thought any longer.

"Have you thought any more about what I said, Gid?" I asked tentatively.

"Hm?"

"About your gift."

He opened his eyes to look at me and sighed. "I told you, Kenna, it's impossible."

"It's not impossible," I insisted. "Why couldn't you have power over the planets?"

"Because no one can," he retorted.

"What about Hanson?"

"That's just a legend, Kenna."

I frowned. "Sybil didn't seem to think so. Neither did Elizabeth."

"Well, I doubt they're right."

I looked down at the grass between my fingers and realized they'd tightened around it in a fist. "Do you doubt that, or do you doubt yourself?" I asked quietly.

He looked hurt for a moment before shaking his head. "It doesn't matter, anyway."

"You don't really mean that."

"Yes, I do," he said. "My life is just fine how it is. If that doesn't make me interesting enough to spend time with, go run off with Neal."

"Gid—"

"I'm going back inside," he said, standing. "See you later."

I was momentarily stunned as he walked away, but found my voice just before he disappeared from view.

"I'm not going to let you just give up on figuring this out," I called.

He didn't turn back, acting as if he hadn't heard me. I groaned and laid down in exasperation, pulling up a fistful of grass and tossing it into the air. I wasn't sure why—maybe it was direction from the talisman, maybe I just wanted to spend time with him—but I felt the *need* to help him understand his gift. Something told me that even if he'd given up on ever knowing what it was, there was a special power within him that had yet to be uncovered. And for whatever reason, I felt like it was my job to help him find it.

CHAPTER SEVEN

IN SEARCH OF A LEGEND

I stayed there until it was almost time for dinner. Neal had invited me to join him again, but I'd eaten most of my dinners with the Patersons over the last month, and Shae was starting to take it personally. She was setting the table when I entered and gave a squeal of delight, wrapping me in a tight hug before Lyra called her over to help serve the food.

Julius had managed to catch a few birds earlier that day, and Lyra prepared them with seasonings she borrowed from Brynna. Gideon smiled at me from across the table, but the smile didn't quite reach his eyes. He was still bothered by our conversation. But as he looked away, his smile fading, he didn't seem angry anymore. Now he just seemed sad.

Lyra's food was of course delicious—I maintained that all green witches must be natural cooks—but as Shae talked my ear off about everything she'd been learning in the last month, I kept glancing at Gideon. I could just see the circular mark poking out of his sleeve. After some hesitation, and when Shae finally stopped to take a breath, I cleared my throat.

"Julius, what do you think Gideon's gift is?"

Gideon groaned and put his head in his hands.

"I don't know," Julius admitted, eyes darting to his son.

"I still think he's a witch," Shae teased. Lyra gave Shae a reproachful look. Clearly she said this often to bother Gideon, even though she herself was a witch and knew there was nothing wrong with that.

"Well," I ventured, putting down my fork, "I have a theory."

"An impossible theory," Gideon mumbled, through his hands.

"How do you know it's impossible?"

"Because it's insane!" he suddenly snapped, standing. "The more you talk about your idea, the more I'm convinced the power couldn't possibly exist!"

I flinched and Lyra and Shae both stared. I opened my mouth to retort, but Julius raised a hand to call for silence. Reluctantly, Gideon sat, his eyes locked on mine in a silent debate.

"What's your theory, Kenna?" Julius said.

"Dad—"

"That's enough, Gideon."

I broke eye contact with Gid and looked to his father. "I thought it may be power over the planets."

Gideon's lips pressed tightly together. Shae coughed as she almost choked on a bite of her food.

"Like the legend of Hanson?" she asked, wide-eyed.

"Exactly like that," I said with a breath. "It makes sense. The Earth, moon, sun, and stars are all round, just like Gideon's mark. And I'm pretty sure I remember Elizabeth saying his mark was also a circle."

"He didn't exist, Kenna," Gideon muttered.

"Yes he did," Lyra said matter-of-factly. "His wife's writings prove that."

"Those are just stories," Gideon retorted.

"I don't think so," Julius said, "but it doesn't matter. The only way to *prove* whether or not you have this power is to try."

He eyed his son sternly. Gideon shifted in his seat. Shae and Lyra watched him as well, and he sank under the pressure. Our eyes met for a second, and in that second I could tell he loathed me for voicing the idea. But at the same time, I thought I saw a glint of hope in his eyes.

Almost as soon as it appeared, the hope vanished, and he let out a deep sigh. "Fine. But who would be my mentor?"

Even I was at a loss for words. Young sorcerers need mentors to prevent them from exhausting energy or causing damage, and usually, mentors were someone with a similar power. I hadn't thought about the fact that if I was right, Gideon wouldn't have anyone on Earth to teach him how to control his powers...

Suddenly, it dawned on me, and I almost dropped my fork.

"Hanson would."

All eyes turned to me. For the first time, Gideon looked curious, not just incredulous.

"What do you mean?" asked Lyra.

"I'm a white witch," I said breathlessly. "Someone who can visit the other worlds. I could find Hanson there and relay messages back and forth."

Gideon opened his mouth slowly, considering my proposal. "If he's even real, how would you find him?"

I bit my lip. Searching for someone you had never met in the Other Worlds is difficult, but possible. The fact that I knew some information about him—his gift, his name, and the name of his wife—would add to the chance of success.

"It won't be easy," I said, "but it's possible. I'm willing to try if you are."

The room fell silent, no one touching their food. For what felt like an eternity, Gid just stared at me. Conflicting expressions and emotions crossed his face as we all waited for his response. Finally, he gave a small, hesitant nod.

"All right," he said. "You can look for him if you want. But I doubt you'll find anything."

My lips split into a smile. "We'll see," I said.

Gideon shifted in his seat, averting his gaze, and excused himself from the table. Julius frowned a little as we watched him go before looking back at me.

"I think it would be wise to temper your expectations, Kenna," he said gently. "This is a pretty far-fetched idea. You're right that it's worth trying, but Gideon has been disappointed enough times before. I don't want to get his hopes up with premature excitement."

"I'm going to start the search regardless—if nothing else, Hanson would be an interesting person to meet," I said.

Standing, I thanked Lyra for the food, gave Shae a hug and promised to come over to try some of her potions the next day, and left. While I understood where Julius was coming from, I couldn't help but feel a twinge of annoyance. Had Gid's own family given up on figuring out his gift as well?

I returned to my room and hurried to arrange my summoning candles. I felt a surge of energy and excitement despite Julius's words. When the candles were placed, I stood in the center, chanting and tracing a pentagram against my chest.

"Do you desire to visit the Saved or the Lost?"

"The Saved," I said. Someone as renowned as Hanson was probably not Lost.

The familiar breeze blew through the room, and my spirit was pulled away once more to the Land of the Saved. As always, a large crowd waited for the gates to open. I approached in anticipation. It was hard to tell which spirits had passed on and which hadn't, so I went up to the gates to speak to the spirits on the other side.

Not sure how else to start, I began by asking if anyone happened to have met Hanson or his wife. Unfortunately, none of them had, and most of them seemed surprised I would even ask. To my relief, however, there were a handful of people who said they thought they'd heard others here in the Land of the Saved talk about meeting him. I eagerly asked them if they could search for me and bring word back to the gates.

Just when I had decided to end my search for the night, a familiar voice called my name, and I turned to see Elizabeth running toward the gates.

"Kenna!" she called. "Sybil told me about the attack."

My delight at seeing her was tempered by that statement. "Oh?"

She nodded, her expression difficult to read. "Of course, she didn't really need to. I was there, after all."

My breath caught in my throat. "You...remember it?"

"It was very strange," she said, her eyes scanning my face as if searching for something. "Once you've passed through the gates, you're not supposed to be able to return. But one minute I was here, and the next..."

"I'm sorry," I blurted out. "I didn't—I didn't really think about what it would be like for *you*, I just—"

She shook her head and gave a comforting smile. "You did the right thing, Kenna. And what you did—well, it was incredible. Certainly more than enough evidence that you are worthy to be the new Mother white witch."

I bit my lip and looked down at my hands. She reached out through the bars, sighing when she remembered that we couldn't touch. After a long moment, she spoke again in a low tone.

"I hope this has changed your mind," she said.

"About what?"

"Going to the city."

I frowned and reluctantly met her gaze. I hadn't exactly told her that was my plan, but I probably shouldn't have been surprised that she guessed it.

"Shouldn't the king get what he deserves?" I whispered.

"You don't know what he deserves—only the Giftgiver does."

If I hadn't been standing in front of the golden gates, I probably would have argued, but that didn't exactly seem appropriate.

Time to change the topic.

"Can you help me with something?" I asked.

Elizabeth sighed, but didn't press the issue. "Of course. What is it?"

"I'm looking for someone. Hanson, the sorcerer with power over the planets."

She raised her eyebrows. "Have you made any progress?"

"Well, this is my first time searching, but no," I grumbled. "No one I've talked to has ever seen him, and most of them aren't even sure he's a real person."

"Oh, he's real," Elizabeth said. "I'll ask around. Maybe I can find other white witches who know his wife, Kindra. In the meantime, keep asking at the gates—you never know who might be passing by. And, though I know it's a long shot, it wouldn't hurt to look in the Lost as well."

I nodded, but I didn't really agree with her. If Hanson was indeed a real person, and if the records that his wife wrote were true, he couldn't be

Lost. I would just have to bide my time and hope he came out to welcome spirits, or that Elizabeth found him inside.

As I returned to my body, I had to admit that Julius was probably wise to tell me not to get too excited. But that didn't mean I was about to give up.

***

Over the course of the next two weeks, I checked the Land of the Saved every night to see if any of the spirits I'd spoken to had any news. Despite Elizabeth's counsel, I didn't feel comfortable journeying to the Land of the Lost on my own.

Shae had heard of him before, but she didn't know as many of the legends that I did. While I helped her work on her potions as promised, I recounted to her some of my favorites from when I was young. She knew the stories about him filling the sky with stars and stopping a never ending storm, but she hadn't heard the legend of Hanson and the Sea Serpent.

"Elizabeth said that this serpent had been sinking fisherman's ships for generations, always on the full moon," I said as I chopped up some roots for her. "The moon's power over the tides gave the creature power as well. The town reached out to Hanson for help, and he traveled from the South, arriving just before the full moon. When the serpent appeared, Hanson reached his hands to the sky and blocked out the moon with his gift, taking away all of the serpent's power and strength in an instant. To make sure the creature couldn't return, he then raised an island where the serpent had appeared, stranding it on land and bringing an end to its days. Elizabeth said that island was the beginning of the kingdom of Orkeia."

"Wait—are you saying that a *sorcerer* founded Orkeia?" she asked with shock.

I shrugged. "That's what Elizabeth said. I don't think it was called Orkeia then, obviously. But she said he created these islands, or at least some of them."

Shae stared. "If a sorcerer created them, how did the Slaughters happen? What made the king think magic was evil?"

"It's been hundreds of years, Shae," I said with a wry smile as I passed her the ingredients. "If the stories are true, even the Gifted barely remember them, and most people—like your brother—don't believe they really happened. The Ungifted probably don't have a record of him at all, or if they do they just think of them as myths and legends."

"But if it *is* true," she said earnestly, "wouldn't that make a difference?"

I fell quiet at those words. While I was sure that the king and his people would dismiss any such claims by the Gifted as being outrageous, it was definitely something significant to consider. Maybe there *was* something in their history that could be used to show that the Gifted and Ungifted had lived in harmony in Hanson's time.

But I couldn't make that connection without having access to Ungifted records, something that seemed impossible. Even if I could make my way to the city and blend in with their society, wouldn't any historical records be carefully guarded? And even if I did find something that seemed to make a connection between our legends and the founding of Orkeia, would the king ever listen?

No. He was too determined to destroy us.

The conversation did cause me to start thinking again about what I could do to stop him. It seemed clear to me that he would need to be stopped by force. Gathering an army would never work—even with our powers, we were severely outnumbered by the knights. In fact, no one was really sure how many clans were still surviving on the islands given how difficult it was for us to communicate. So if someone was going to put a stop to the king's crusade, it needed to be done carefully through infiltration.

I thought about my mark once again. Why would the Giftgiver have placed it somewhere it could be easily hidden if not to give me the chance to get close to the king? Why would I have been spared when the rest of my clan was destroyed if He didn't have a destiny for me to fulfill? As daunting as the task seemed, the more I thought about it, the more convinced I became that I had to be the one to make the journey.

But every day, it was harder to imagine leaving the Grison clan. My heart felt heavy as I returned to my room that evening. I didn't want to leave Gideon, or Neal, or Shae, and I didn't want to abandon the duties Sybil had passed on to me. But if I stayed here, nothing would ever change.

Before I closed my door, I heard a voice behind me.

"Hey, Kenna," Gideon said a little awkwardly.

I bit my lip and turned to face him. "Hey, Gid," I replied.

We hadn't talked much in the past two weeks. I was sure he had been avoiding me, and with how awkward that dinner was, I couldn't really blame him. Neal kept me distracted when I wasn't doing things for Julius or Ethel and Helen, but I had to admit that I had felt lonely without my regular walks with Gideon.

He glanced through my door past me to where my summoning circle was set up. I hadn't taken it down in the past two weeks, figuring it was easier to just leave it until I decided to give up on the search. I couldn't quite read his expression as he looked at it.

"How are you?" he asked, tearing his eyes away from the circle to meet mine.

I shrugged. "Tired. I spent the morning looking for stones that could be used for spellcasting focuses on the beach. Ethel is being *very* particular about the one's she'll use. Then your sister sequestered me for the afternoon."

Gid rolled his eyes. "Tell Ethel she can get them herself. And as for Shae, she'll understand if you just say you need to rest."

"Oh, spending time with Shae didn't bother me," I said with a bit of a smile. "It was nice, actually. She just—well, you know how much she likes to talk."

He chuckled and nodded. I watched the way his smile slowly started to grow and felt a pang in my chest at the thought of eventually leaving. Once again, I considered inviting him to journey with me to the city, and I almost said something before he spoke.

"I just wanted to apologize," he said after another minute, shifting his feet where he stood. "I know you're just trying to help me, and I appreciate that you think highly enough of me to even entertain your theory. I just ... I wanted to let you know that I'm okay. I'm not miserable and I don't feel useless to the clan. And...I don't want to feel like I can't spend time with you without you bringing up my gift."

"I'm sorry if I ever made you feel that, Gid," I said with a frown.

"It's all right, it's just—I've made my peace with it, you know?" he said with a shrug. He smiled again, a hopeful smile, and added, "Can we just go back to normal? I don't want you spending every night looking for someone who might not even exist."

I glanced back at my summoning circle. With a heavy breath, I looked back towards him and nodded, forcing a smile. "If that's what you want."

"Thanks," he said, sounding relieved. "Maybe I can help you look for the stones or whatever else you need in the morning?"

"Sure. I'd like that."

He gave me another smile before saying goodnight and heading back to his room. I shut my door and leaned against it, closing my eyes as I did.

One more night. Then I'll put the candles away.

Pushing aside all my other conflicting thoughts and feelings from the day, I moved into the circle and performed the now very familiar ritual to pass into the Land of the Saved. It wasn't long before I spotted Elizabeth's golden hair. Sybil stood beside her and to my surprise, they were outside the gates. As I approached, they saw me and stopped their conversation, both of them turning to smile.

"Back again?" Elizabeth said.

"Yes," I said with a pained smile. "I'm assuming you haven't heard anything?"

They exchanged a glance, and I saw a familiar glint of excitement in Elizabeth's eyes. "Follow us," she said, turning to walk along the wall of the city.

My heart leapt and I hurried after them, hardly daring to hope. The crowd began to thin as we moved further from the main gate, and at length, it finally parted enough that I could see a large man standing off to the side, clearly waiting for someone. He had golden hair that fell below his shoulders and a kingly beard to match. There was a sense of majesty about him, and when he saw us approaching, he beamed and stepped forward.

"Kenna," said Sybil, "I'd like you to meet Hanson."

CHAPTER EIGHT

A MUDDY START

"Pleasure to meet you, Kenna," Hanson said in a deep voice, his blue eyes shining in a strangely familiar way. "I heard you've been looking for me."

"I have," I said, struggling for words. "I was—well, we were hoping—what I mean is, I have this friend—"

"Gideon," he said with a nod. "Sybil told me. I'm sorry I wasn't already waiting for you before, but I lost track of time. I thought we were still on the thirteenth."

I blinked. "What?"

"The thirteenth generation."

When I didn't respond, his look of confusion turned to understanding. "So you don't know," he muttered. "I assumed you would have Kindra's records."

"Only some of the stories survived," I said. "If the records were still out there, the knights probably destroyed them."

"Knights?" he asked, raising an eyebrow.

"The knights of Orkeia—the ones who hunted us," Sybil explained.

Elizabeth nodded. "They want to destroy any trace of magic. That includes our records."

He looked to the two of them, his smile fading into a frown. "I knew there were witch hunts happening," he said somberly, "but I didn't realize it was so far spread. So *none* of you have had access to Kindra's writings?"

"My clan had some when I was a girl, but they were lost a long time ago," Sybil said.

He sighed and pinched the bridge of his nose. "That's...unfortunate."

There was a heaviness to his tone, and when he looked at me again, I saw some urgency in his eyes. "Well, now that you're here I can tell you myself. Every fourteen generations, a sorcerer is born with power over the planets and universe. It is that sorcerer's calling from the Giftgiver to serve and protect mankind. The power is carried through the male blood line."

My eyes grew wide. "So you're—"

"Gideon's thirteenth great-grandfather, yes," he confirmed. "He inherited my gift, and in fourteen generations, his descendent will inherit it from him, just as I inherited it from Varan, the world-builder before me."

He lifted his sleeve to show me his mark as evidence. It was identical to Gideon's. I felt a rush of joy as my suspicions were confirmed, but I was still speechless. A chuckle came from the back of Hanson's throat.

"So who figured it out? You or Gideon?"

I struggled to find my voice. "Well, it was my idea. He's still not sure you exist."

"I felt the same way about Varan," he said with a smirk. "But Kindra just seemed to know he was real and that she could find him. It doesn't surprise me that you'd play the same role as she did. You'll be relaying messages to Gideon for me, yes?"

"That's—yes," I said, still in shock. "Assuming he agrees. I mean, I'm sure he will, it's just—he really didn't think I'd ever find you."

Even though I was in spirit form, I felt the same sensation I did when my heart was pounding with nerves. I had hoped I would be able to help Gid, but I hadn't imagined the scale of the task. If he didn't learn how to use his gift in this life, he wouldn't be able to teach the next world-builder, and somehow it was up to me to make sure he was prepared.

It looked like I wasn't leaving the Grison clan after all.

"How old is he?" Hanson said, interrupting my thoughts.

"Seventeen."

He let out a breath. "I wish we'd been able to get started sooner," he muttered. "Let me know the moment he's ready. I'll be waiting near the gates."

I was at a loss for words and simply nodded. When I looked into his eyes—*Gideon's* eyes—I knew he would keep his word. As long as I could convince Gid to follow through with this, Hanson was clearly eager to take on the role of a mentor.

"Thank you," I managed to stammer. "So much, I—I'll be back soon."

His expression softened, and he bid me farewell. Sybil and Elizabeth both gave me encouraging smiles and turned to make conversation with him as I stepped away. I kept looking back over my shoulder with disbelief at the three of them, my excitement growing more with each step.

I was right!

I broke into a run, reaching the front of the gates quickly so I could return to my body. Once back on Earth, I stumbled out my door and across the common area, walking straight to Gideon's room and knocking on the door. Gid opened it, looking very confused.

"Kenna, what are you—?"

"I found him."

***

To say Gideon was shocked would be an understatement. If I was being honest, it sounded crazy even to me. But when I described Hanson's mark, as well as his other physical similarities, Gideon had no choice but to suspend his disbelief. Slowly, he sat on the edge of his bed, staring at the wall in deep thought.

"He's real..." he said after a long silence.

"He's real," I echoed, sitting beside him and reaching for his hand. He let me take it and gave it a small squeeze, shaking his head and rubbing his face with his free hand.

"This is crazy, Kenna. Even if it's all true, I—I don't understand what all of this means."

"Neither do I, but there's only one way to find out."

He let out a deep breath, but to my relief, he nodded. "Let me talk to my parents in the morning. Then we can make a plan on how to..."

"How to start teaching you how to use your gift," I finished as his voice trailed off.

He tried to say something else, but couldn't seem to find the words and instead just nodded. I squeezed his hand once more then, feeling a sudden surge of emotion, pulled him into a tight hug. He was stiff for a moment before returning it. When he did, he was shaking.

"Try to get some rest," I said as I stood, knowing well enough that would be almost an impossibility for both of us. I beamed at him, and he returned my smile with some effort. I thought I saw his eyes watering, but I didn't say anything, deciding it was best to let him be alone to process things for a while. I had enough to process myself.

By the time I awoke in the morning, the news had already spread through the clan. Gideon hadn't intended on telling everyone about what we were about to try, but when Shae overheard him talking to his parents, that didn't matter. She immediately ran into the common area and blurted it out to everyone there.

Everyone wanted to hear the details about meeting Hanson, even Helen and Ethel. They seemed disappointed that I hadn't met Kindra as well, but to be honest, the thought of asking about his wife hadn't even occurred to me the night before. Gideon was clearly uncomfortable with all of the attention, but he was trying to hide it, staying close to me as questions started to be directed towards him as well.

Most of the clan seemed focused on what this meant for Gideon, but Neal kept bringing the conversation back to me and my role.

"It sounds exhausting, constantly going back and forth," he said. There was a frown on his face as he looked between me and Gideon. "Aren't you worried about over-exerting yourself?"

"I'm sure Kenna knows what her limits are," Gideon said with a surprising amount of defensiveness. "And I'd never ask her to do anything she didn't feel comfortable doing."

I crossed my arms. "You didn't *ask* me at all—I volunteered."

"I'm just looking out for her," Neal said, not seeming to hear me and keeping his eyes on Gideon as they narrowed. "I'm worried about her."

"What, and you think I'm not?" Gid retorted.

The atmosphere in the room tensed, and everyone else was quiet as the two of them stared at each other. Uncomfortable, I moved to stand between them.

"I'll be fine, and I know how to take care of myself," I insisted, looking between them. "I promise, if things get too much, I'll say something."

Neal took a few steps back to stand next to Jonas. Thankfully, he dropped the subject, but he kept looking at Gideon with narrowed eyes. My shoulders tensed with some annoyance and I could feel Gideon next to me breathing heavily as he tried to calm down under so much scrutiny from Neal and the others. After fielding a few more questions, I managed to convince everyone to let us go on a walk and start making plans. It took Lyra's help to get Shae to stay behind, but once she relented, I didn't waste any time grasping Gid's hand and leading him outside.

Once we were alone, he groaned, running his hand through his hair in frustration. "Shae and her big mouth."

"It wasn't going to stay a secret for long," I said gently.

"Sure, but I would have liked to feel a little more confident that this is even going to work before everyone started expecting great things of me," he said with a frown, looking up at the sky above us. Both of us stared at it for a moment, thinking about the implications of the legends we had been told.

"What if I can't do it, Kenna?" he whispered.

"You can," I said, reaching for his hand and squeezing it. "It's your gift, and Hanson's your ancestor."

He squeezed my hand back, but pulled it away almost immediately and ran it through his hair. "How can we really know that? He could be wrong."

"He seemed pretty confident. Besides, his mark..."

My voice trailed off as we both continued to stare up at the sky. I hadn't thought much about it before, but according to Elizabeth, there were other worlds out there with their own suns, moons, and stars. She even seemed to believe that there might be people and civilizations living on those other worlds. My mind began to spin as I thought about the possible extent of Gideon's power if that were true, and my head started to ache.

Then, another thought occurred to me. If Gideon could master this power, it was a greater power than any other sorcerer of our age. If he was able to do half of the things that Hanson had done in the legends, he could take on a whole army of knights on his own, not to mention the king. Something caught in my throat as I turned my head to look at him, the possibilities in my mind making my heart beat a bit quicker with hope and excitement.

Maybe *he* was the answer after all. Maybe—maybe my whole role was to make sure he got the training he needed.

But I kept my thoughts to myself. The last thing he needed right now was even more pressure.

He slowly tore his eyes from the sky as well and turned to meet my gaze. I realized we were still holding hands, but neither of us let go.

"Thank you," he said at length. "For believing in me...whatever happens."

My cheeks and neck felt warm as I smiled encouragingly. "Whatever happens, I promise I'll be there for you...just like you were here for me when I lost everything."

His eyes scanned my face as he returned my smile. The warmth I felt increased, and after another moment I pulled my hand back and cleared my throat, feeling suddenly awkward.

"So...when should we start?" I asked.

***

I visited Hanson that night. Gid wanted to wait until the next day before beginning his training. While Hanson seemed eager to start, he also seemed to understand Gid's need to process everything. He told me that when we were ready, we needed to be outside in an open space. He also said that it would be easier for Gideon to learn to access his powers under the light of the sun, so if it was too cloudy we may need to postpone. Luckily, when the morning came, the sky was relatively clear.

As we left the shelter, Lyra ran interference with Shae once more, her and Julius both insisting that Gideon and I needed some privacy to be effective. Though he tried to hide it, the growing bounce in Gideon's step told me he was getting excited.

We moved inland a ways, and I set down my bag, pulling out my candles. Gid tried to help me set them up, unpacking them quickly and putting them in a random order. Chuckling, I rearranged them to the correct positions. Had I tried to enter the other worlds with the candles the way he had them, my spirit probably would have been separated from my body forever.

When I was done, I told him to sit outside the circle and wait. As I watched him take his place in the grass, I couldn't help but be reminded of when we first met and I'd found him watching me. I felt that strange heat rush up my neck again, but I pushed it aside and closed my eyes.

I traced the pentagram over my chest and was soon in the other worlds once more. Hanson was waiting directly in front of the gates.

He beamed as I approached. "Is Gideon outside, ready for his first lesson?"

"As ready as he's going to be."

"Fantastic! Now, the first thing I need you to teach Gideon is that his gift includes power over the elements."

I raised an eyebrow. "There's a sorcerer in our clan with that power."

"Yes, Sybil already informed me, but what Gideon has is very different. The other sorcerer—Darius, was it?—uses his powers to manipulate existing elements, usually to build homes, cross water, or other such things. Gideon's powers, on the other hand, are used to create elements in places that they were not before."

My jaw dropped.

Hanson chuckled, a glint in his eye. "Incredible, isn't it? Your friend is a human being who can actually *create* rivers, mountains, valleys, trees, plants—anything you can imagine!"

I felt an ache in my brain. "Okay."

"I know it's overwhelming," he said gently. "It was for me, too. But we'll take it slow."

I resisted the urge to rub my forehead, since I wouldn't have been able to touch it anyway. "Please do."

"The first we're going to create is water. It's the easiest element to produce. Where are you right now? In the mountains, in a forest—?"

"In the hills near a beach. We live on the Northern islands, in Orkeia."

I thought I saw a twinkle in his eyes and almost asked him about the legend of the sea serpent, but he continued before I had the chance. "Then a small pond will do fine. We want to keep it inconspicuous, after all."

He explained that Gideon had to understand what water was made out of and how the smallest parts of it—he called them molecules—fit and worked together. Most importantly, Gideon needed to clearly see the pond in his mind as he created it. If he didn't have a clear vision of what he was trying to make, it wouldn't appear as he wanted it to.

After repeating the instructions back to Hanson, I returned to my body and related them to Gideon. He made me repeat myself at least three times, overwhelmed at the possibility of being able to *create* water from nothing at all. Hanson had warned that it would probably take several hours, so he advised me to take a nap as Gideon practiced.

It took me a while to fall asleep, and it felt like once I did, shouts jerked me awake almost instantly. In a panic, I jumped to my feet, my eyes darting across the hills. There were no knights in sight, but my alarm only increased as I scanned the area.

Gideon was nowhere to be seen.

"Gid! Where are you?"

Muffled sounds came from behind, and I spun around. He was still nowhere in sight. My heart beat faster and my eyes darted this way and that. Just as I was about to run back to the shelter for help, I heard the sound again, coming from below the ground.

Where Gideon had been standing was a huge puddle of mud. Bubbles popped slowly on the surface.

"GID!" I exclaimed, rushing to the edge of the mud. Falling to my knees, I reached into the pit, grasping to find anything but the murky earth. After what seemed like an eternity, something solid brushed my fingertips. A hand wrapped around my wrist. I'd found one of his arms! Frantically, I felt around in the mud for the other one. After what felt like an eternity, I was able to grasp him by both arms and pull with all my strength.

His head broke the surface and he coughed up earth, gasping for air. I breathed a sigh of relief. With some effort, I heaved him out of the pit. We both lay panting on the ground, Gideon still coughing occasionally as he wiped the mud off his face.

"What—did—you—do?" I said in scattered breaths.

"I forgot to move the earth," he coughed. "I mixed it with water."

I turned my head to look at him. "Why were you standing on top of it?"

"I wasn't! I meant to start small—it got big!"

I burst into laughter. After a couple seconds, he joined me, and we lay there on the ground, covered in mud, struggling for breath as we laughed harder than we ever had in our lives. All the tension and uncertainty that had been hanging over both of us was suddenly gone. Even if it hadn't exactly been a successful attempt, now there was no way of denying the fact that this really was his gift.

"Let's not tell your father about this," I said as my laughter died down. "And I am *never* taking a nap while you practice again!"

He laughed even louder. We both struggled to gain enough hold on ourselves to stand and walk to the ocean. I turned my back as he undressed to wash himself and wiped the mud off my arms and dress on the other side of the beach. When he was completely submerged, I gathered his things and washed them as well, laughing all the while. I left them on the rocks for him and returned to my candles, moving them closer to the beach so Gideon wouldn't have to work around the mud. By the time I'd set them up again, he was on his way back.

"Ready to try again?" I asked.

"I've got it this time," he said, sounding a bit too sure of himself for someone who had just been buried in a giant pit of mud.

This time I watched him carefully as he worked. First he closed his eyes to focus, creating a picture of the pond in his mind. This took him a while—I think after the last incident, he wanted to make sure the image was complete. I stayed quiet, not wanting to distract him.

Eventually, he opened his eyes and extended his right hand towards the ground. The earth began to move, slowly forming a ditch. When the ditch was about the size of our shelter's common room, Gideon dropped his right hand and extended his left, hardening the earth.

He grinned at me as he finished that step. "At least I won't fall in the mud again."

I smiled, but the laughter was gone. I waited in anticipation, anxious to see him create water out of nothing. I'd seen Darius manipulate the earth before, and though I was proud of Gideon for accomplishing it, I knew it wasn't the nature of his gift. He turned back around to face his work and I held my breath, afraid to blink.

Gideon's shoulders tightened as he focused. He held out his hands in front of them and they shook. Slowly, the ditch began to fill. I could see the excitement in his eyes as water appeared, out of nowhere, exactly as he saw it. When the water reached the top of the pond, he crumpled to the ground, exhausted.

I sat next to him in awed silence. A bird flew in from the cliff's edge and landed next to the water, surveying it for a moment before leaning over for a drink. Cautiously, moved forward and dipped my fingers into the pond, my heart pounding against my chest as the cool liquid ran through my fingers.

"Amazing," I breathed.

With some effort, Gideon lifted his head. "How long did that take me?"

"This just now or including when you buried yourself in mud?"

He grinned. "Just now."

"About thirty minutes."

His eyes shone, but he soon closed them as he lay down. "Wake me up when Hanson tells me what to do next."

I laughed. "I already know what he's going to say."

"What?"

"*Sleep,*" I teased, poking him.

He swatted my hand away, smiling the whole while. "Just go ask him, will you?"

As he let his breathing settle, I stepped into my circle and quickly made the transition from our world to the Land of the Saved. Hanson waited near the gates, talking to a woman on the other side. When he noticed me approaching, he raised his eyebrows and cut his conversation short, meeting me partway.

"Is everything all right?" he asked. "Did Gideon have a question?"

"Not about the pond," I said. "He wants to know what he should do next."

Hanson's eyes widened. "He already finished the pond?"

"Yes."

He whistled. "It took me six hours to create my first pond, and I got myself stuck in the mud a couple times."

"Well, I didn't say he *didn't* get stuck in the mud," I said with a smirk. "But it was only once."

Hanson laughed and his lips split into a grin. "And he did it perfectly the next time? The boy is a sorcery genius!"

I thought I saw his shoulders relax, the anxiety and eagerness I'd seen before melting away. He shook his head with another, almost relieved, laugh.

"Tell him to keep practicing with water until tomorrow afternoon," he said. "We'll continue then."

With a wave, he turned to resume his conversation with the female spirit. Swelling with pride, I followed the path back to my body. I opened my eyes as rain began to fall and stepped out of the circle. Gideon sat up and looked at me with anticipation.

"What did Hanson say?"

I shrugged my shoulders. "You could have been faster."

His face began to fall until he noticed the glint of a smile on my face. He stood and punched me lightly on the arm. "You've been spending too much time with Neal. What did he really say?"

I smiled. "It took him six hours to make his first pond."

His eyebrows shot up. "Really?"

"Really."

He laughed, pulling me into a tight hug. I returned it, feeling our shared wonder and excitement. The rain fell steadily on my cheeks and the back of my neck, but it didn't bother me.

"What do I learn next?" he said eagerly when we parted.

"Practice creating water formations and get some rest until tomorrow afternoon."

For a moment he looked disappointed, but soon enough he smiled again. "I'm going to fill the well with water!"

I laughed as he ran toward the shelter. Kneeling on the ground, I gathered my candles and placed them in my pack before following him. It wasn't until I was near the fire that I realized just how cold I was, and I sat, letting the warm flames thaw my body. Gideon stood over the well, concentrating. Soon, I heard water rising to the surface.

As Gideon relaxed, Neal came bounding through the front door, soaking wet and covered head to toe in mud. "There's a huge bog out there!"

He never did figure out why we were laughing so hard.

Chapter Nine

INTERRUPTED VOWS

O ver the course of the next few weeks, Gideon's lessons continued. Though each was just as impressive as the last, they started to blend together after the first week or so. We occasionally had to take a day off to rest, but neither of us ever got tired of the lessons. Every day was a new adventure, and we were sharing it together.

After water, he learned how to create earth in its different forms—dirt, sand, rocks, and other small formations. The second week he started to create grass and small plants. He specifically had Hanson teach him how to create the herbs the green witches used most often to make a small but very useful garden in the common area. It was a great time saver, and we no longer had to take turns gathering, but not everyone appreciated his thoughtfulness.

"It's obnoxious," Neal said one day as we watched Gideon work on developing a pine tree—a type of tree that, Hanson explained, was very common in the South and lived all year round, with green needles instead of leaves. There aren't many trees in Orkeia to begin with, so it was difficult for Gideon to envision the finished product, and it was taking him a while. Neal had brought us lunch from his mother since we were taking so long and decided to stick around.

I looked away from Gid for a moment. "Why? It saves a lot of time, and it's much safer."

Neal smirked and threw his arm around my shoulder. "Because I don't get to spend as much quality time with you."

I rolled my eyes. "We spend just as much time together as we used to."

"But now we spend it around *other* people," Neal said, imitating disgust. "I'd much rather we were alone."

I shivered, but didn't remove Neal's arm from its place on my shoulders. Gideon must have noticed, because when we left the shelter the next morning for his lesson, he confronted me.

"What's going on with you and Neal?"

I stared at him. "What are you talking about?"

"Come on, Kenna. I'm not blind. You like him, don't you?"

"I mean, he's a *friend*," I said defensively.

"You do realize he's five years older than you."

"Gid! What is this?"

"You spend a lot of time together."

"Not *that* kind of time," I said angrily, my cheeks burning. "Besides, why should you care?"

"I care about you, Kenna, and he's too old."

"Your father is seven years older than your mother," I retorted.

He scowled. "So you do have feelings for him."

My jaw dropped. "No, Gideon Grison, I don't, and if I did it certainly wouldn't be any of your business."

"The only reason he's even flirting with you is because you're the only girl we've had here under thirty for ten years."

I flinched, feeling the sting of his words, but wasn't about to let it show. Instead, I let a sly smile cross my lips.

"Are you jealous, Gid?"

He stared at me, dumbfounded. "Of course not!"

I moved closer to him and playfully ran my fingers through his hair. "I think you are."

He blushed, knocking my hand away. "You're my best friend, Kenna. I don't—that's not how I feel."

"Then why did you blush?" I smirked, enjoying taunting him.

He closed his eyes and breathed slowly. "I'm just concerned, all right?"

"Well, don't be," I snapped, serious once more. "And stop being such a jerk to Neal."

This became a regular morning conversation: he accused me of caring for Neal, I accused him of caring for me, and we both left unsatisfied and full of bottled anger. Somehow, we managed to forget we were repeating ourselves.

But despite what I told Gideon, my relationship with Neal was growing stronger. He joined me for the lessons, he stole me away to picnic on the beach, and he always looked for excuses to be alone, even from Jo. And honestly? I was enjoying it.

***

Gideon's lessons had been going on for almost a month. He was now creating larger formations, combining plants and trees with them. At first it was difficult for him to create both simultaneously, but he eventually got the hang of it. It only took him three hours to make a mountain out of nothing at all—Hanson's record was seven. Of course, he had to destroy it immediately afterwards. It would be obvious to anyone in the area that the formation was new because of how large it was, and however remote we seemed to be, we couldn't take any chances.

I was constantly amazed by his talent. When Darius heard that it involved the elements, he offered more than once to give me a break and teach Gideon himself, but I refused. I enjoyed meeting with Hanson and seeing Gideon's excitement. Darius seemed a bit offended at this, but didn't say as much.

At least, not verbally. The more days that went on, the more Darius and Helen isolated themselves. I was so engrossed in Gideon's lessons that I didn't notice at first, but when they started leaving the common area any time Julius entered, it soon became obvious. Something must have strained the relationship between the two men, and I was reminded of the uncomfortable feeling I had when Darius said he should have been the

Father of the clan. But even though I was part of the clan's counsel as the Mother white witch, it wasn't my place to pry, so I kept my thoughts to myself.

Until Julius approached me himself. Gideon had just started creating valleys within his mountains. As he concentrated on sinking the ground in front of him, his father sat next to me on the ground. I continued eating a wonderful stew Brynna sent over with Jo and some bread from Lyra, waiting for him to speak. He was silent for a long time before sighing.

"Do you know how long Darius and Helen have been engaged?"

"As long as I've been here. So, six or seven months?"

"Three years."

I hid my surprise and placed my bowl on the ground. "That's a long time."

"Do you know why they haven't been married yet?" he asked.

Knowing he would tell me, I remained silent.

He sighed again before continuing. "Because I haven't let them."

I nodded. A marriage ceremony had to be performed by one of the three Mothers or Fathers. As Father of the clan and Darius's best friend, Julius was obviously first choice. Had he refused, they would ask either Nathanael or myself, or have to find another clan to perform the ceremony.

"Nathanael refused too?" I asked.

He nodded solemnly.

"Because you told him to?"

Again, he nodded.

I frowned. "Why haven't they asked me?"

"They're about to. At first they were against being married by someone so young, but they're becoming more desperate."

I shifted uncomfortably. "And you want me to say no?"

He stared at the back of his son's head as a new waterfall formed miraculously in front of us. "I'm not entirely sure."

A heavy silence fell between us, interrupted only by the sound of the water from Gideon's new creation. Gideon looked back and flashed me a smile, though his expression shifted to one of surprise at seeing his father.

Julius gave a nod, indicating that his son should keep working. When Gideon did so, I let out a breath.

"Why don't you want them to get married?" I asked.

"Because of Helen," Julius said, his usual calm eyes blazing with bitterness.

"She's not easy to get along with," I admitted.

He shook his head. "You didn't know Darius before, Kenna. When Helen first came into his life, he started to change. He became a different person."

"I've heard that can happen when you love someone."

He sighed, hanging his head. "I know it doesn't make any sense, but he's never been this unhappy—the more time he's spent with her, the more bitter he's become. I can't sanctify a union that I think is ultimately a mistake."

We were silent once more. In front of us, Gideon leaned against a rock, clearly getting tired, but he didn't stop his work.

"What are you asking me, Julius?" I said quietly.

He sighed. "You're on my counsel. I'm coming to you for advice."

I took a deep breath. I hardly thought I was qualified to do that.

When I spoke, I did so slowly. "You want Darius to be happy, right?"

He nodded.

"I think he would be happiest if his best friend performed the ceremony," I said. "Not a seventeen-year-old that neither of them even really like. And honestly, I think three years is long enough. If he hasn't changed his mind by now, he's not going to."

Julius frowned. Glancing over, I saw that Gid had finished. He stood and stared over the edge of the new cliff. When he looked to see my reaction, I sent him a huge smile of affirmation before turning back to his father.

"Unless you order me not to, if they ask me, I'll say yes."

He remained silent until Gideon reached us, at which point he enthusiastically expressed his admiration of Gid's progress. Gid knew perfectly well his father's thoughts had been elsewhere, but he was used to that when

Julius was troubled. He smiled politely and thanked Julius before turning to me.

"Were you timing?" His eyes shone. We'd decided to keep track of how fast Gideon accomplished all of his tasks and compare them with Hanson's records.

"Twenty-five minutes," I said grinning. Gid beamed before pulling me to my feet.

"Want me to wait for you to report to Hanson?"

I laughed. "If you must."

After I visited Hanson to gloat for Gideon (Hanson's record for a valley was an hour and a half), the three of us walked quietly back to the clan. I asked Gid to give me an hour to rest before we went on our walk.

As I lay on my bed, closing my eyes to relax, I heard a soft tapping on my door. I sighed and propped myself up on my elbows.

"Come in."

Cautiously, Darius and Helen entered. Darius looked hesitant, but Helen was determined. I closed my eyes once again and sighed inwardly before sitting up, forcing my best smile.

"What is it?"

"Julius has probably spoken to you, Kenna," said Darius, taking Helen's hand. "I don't know if you're aware, but we've been waiting for three years now. Neither of us is getting any younger, and—"

"Julius told me everything," I interrupted.

"And he told you to refuse us, did he?" spat Helen.

"No. He didn't order me either way."

The room went very quiet. Darius's eyes filled with hope, and Helen's visage softened.

"So will you do it?" he asked. "Will you marry us?"

I felt a sick feeling in my stomach, but ignored it. "I will, but I want you to ask Julius again first."

Helen raised her eyebrows. "He already refused."

"Give him another chance," I said. "If he still says no, I'll perform the ceremony."

"Thank you," said Darius, his lips splitting into a huge grin. I thought I saw a hint of a smile on Helen's face as well.

I followed them out the door, anxious myself to know Julius's answer. When they left the Grisons' rooms, eyes shining, I couldn't help but smile.

***

The marriage was set for just two days later. The day before was extremely busy—Ethel altered the dress Helen made two years ago, I helped Lyra and Shae create flower arrangements, and the Patersons prepared a menu and gathered ingredients. Gideon assisted them by growing whatever they requested. He also decorated his pond and the surrounding area, growing beautiful flowers and sprinkling the surface of the water with lilies. Darius took some time from his personal preparation to create an altar in the middle of the pond with a pathway leading up to it where Julius would perform the ceremony.

The morning of, Ethel helped Helen get ready while Julius helped Darius. The rest of us decorated the pond and altar. When we were finished, the scene looked splendid. A fountain of water from the pond squirted up behind the altar, thanks to Gideon, and beautiful bouquets of flowers lined the pathway on both sides, full of roses, tulips, and carnations—all of them white.

We finished around noon and all hurried inside to change. I chose my nicest dress—a long, straight, midnight blue dress with long sleeves and golden accents. Elizabeth had made it as a gift for me when I turned sixteen. It was the only article of clothing I owned that I could wear without layering, because it was made out of wool, which was why I had even had it with me when I was on my gathering trip for my former clan.

The opal talisman looked like it was made to go with the dress, but I decided it would be best not to wear it at Helen's wedding and placed it in my pack. As an afterthought, I pulled my curly mess of hair into a bun on the top of my head, letting only a few strands dangle out.

There was a short knock on my door and I opened it to see Gideon, dressed in his best tunic, waiting for me. His eyes opened wide.

"You look beautiful, Kenna," he said.

I smiled. "You don't look too bad yourself," I said, admiring the way the blue trim of his tunic complimented his already bright eyes.

He blushed, as I knew he would, and we walked to the pond together. Julius and Darius were already there, and soon after we arrived, so did the rest of the clan. Neal grinned when he saw me, making my cheeks burn. Gideon shifted at my side.

Moments later, Ethel and Helen appeared on the other side of the hill, walking ceremoniously toward the altar. The smile on Darius's face was one of the purest I'd ever seen as he watched his fiancé walk toward him, her red hair done up extravagantly, looking for once like she wasn't about to kill someone. Julius smiled halfheartedly when the couple reached him, but his smile seemed to become more genuine and relaxed when he saw the look of elation on Darius's face.

"We gather today," he began, "to join this woman and this man together with an everlasting bond. We—"

The blare of the horn filled the air. I spun around, my heart dropping out my chest. An army of knights climbed over the hills, at least twice as many than the previous attack. They'd already seen us, and there was no way we could get rid of the altar even if they hadn't.

I was frozen in place, but Julius immediately sprang into action. "We have to leave," he shouted, running to land and drawing a large circle in the ground with his finger. "Everyone, inside."

"What about our things?" Shae asked, her voice cracking in fear and desperation.

As silly as it seemed, everyone had the same concern. Without summoning candles, cauldrons, and spell components and ingredients, we wouldn't be able to practice magic. We could leave them behind, but they were virtually impossible to replace with the knights destroying everything in their path.

A sinking feeling settled in my chest. I couldn't let this happen, not again, not to this family. Something had to be done, someone had to stall the knights—

This is my chance.

"There isn't time," Julius said desperately.

"There will be," I spoke up. "I'll hold them off. The rest of you go."

"No!" Neal and Gideon said in unison as everyone stared at me with concern.

I ignored them and looked between Ethel and Helen. "The talisman is in my pack with my candles. The records are on my bed."

Without another word, I ran, kicking off my sandals. Someone yelled after me, but I didn't turn to see the source of the voice. The only thing on my mind was getting close enough to the knights to attack them, but far enough away that I would be able to hold them off for a while before they reached my body. Just as I'd reached a hill I could partially hide behind, a firm hand took hold of my arm and spun me around.

"We're not leaving without you," Neal panted, trying to drag me back.

I wrenched my arm out of his grasp. "I have to fight them, Neal. I wasn't there for my last family when they needed me, and leaving Sybil behind—I can't let something like that happen again. I need to do this."

I turned my back on him to look over the top of the hill and judge the distance. He let out an aggravated sigh and swerved in front of me. I tried to run past him, but he took a hold of my waist and pulled me into a sudden passionate kiss.

Shocked, I stopped fighting and let him hold me. I was even more shocked when I realized I was kissing him back. His arms tightened around my waist and my heart beat faster as I breathed in his earthy scent.

After a long, intense beat, he released me, and we stared at each other, breathless. He was about to speak when the knights' horn sounded again.

"Let me do this," I finally choked out.

He placed a hand on my cheek, his green eyes pleading. "I don't want to lose you."

He leaned in once more to kiss me, but I couldn't waste any more time. Closing my eyes, I willed my spirit to leave my body, pausing for the briefest moment to watch myself fall limp in his arms.

I flew as fast as the wind to our last home, summoning the spirits of the fallen knights and Sybil before repeating the process at the site of my first clan's massacre. By the time I returned, the knights were almost upon Neal. He'd laid me on the ground and was hovering over my body defensively. Panicking, I instructed my spiritual soldiers to attack. As the knights struggled against their unseen foes, I called to the spirits of Logan and three of the other brothers from my original clan. They retreated from the fight.

"Take him back to his clan," I instructed, hearing my voice crack. "There is a sorcerer who is going to transport him away. Make sure he gets inside the circle."

They nodded, receiving directions to the shelter from my mind, before falling upon Neal and taking a hold of his arms and legs. Neal cried out, but the expression on his face soon changed from astonishment and fear to understanding.

"Kenna, stop!"

I tore my eyes from him, focusing all my energy on fighting the enemy and ignoring the sudden ache in my heart as his cries became more distant. I thought I heard Gideon in the distance as well, but tried to block out the sounds, praying that the rest of the clan would be able to get them to stay in the circle long enough to leave.

The knights pushed onward, and the space between their matchless numbers and my limp body grew dangerously slim. My little army managed to fell maybe half a dozen of them during their relentless march forward. But soon, the spirits began disappearing one by one as my energy decreased, until it was useless to continue fighting. I closed my eyes, reuniting my body and spirit, and kept them shut tightly.

There was nowhere to run.

"Here she is!" one of them yelled, anger in his gruff voice. "She was conjuring the spirits!"

Footsteps hurried toward me and though I had intended to keep them shut, my eyes opened instinctively. I was surrounded by men covered head to toe in heavy armor. One of them drew his sword and I flinched.

Just get it over with.

Rough hands pulled me to my feet, forcing me to face a very large, very angry looking man with small, squinty eyes. With a start, I realized it was the same man who had been leading the army I fought with Sybil. He had his sword drawn, ready to strike.

"For the kingdom!" the same gruff voice yelled. I tried to force my eyes closed, but none of the muscles in my body wanted to move. His black eyes burned with the fire of hatred, and a whimper escaped my lips as he drew the sword back purposely.

Then, from out of nowhere, another voice suddenly rang through the crowd of soldiers.

"STOP!"

Chapter Ten

WHISPERS IN THE DARK

The man who was about to kill me froze mid-strike, seeming just as shocked by the outburst as I was. An older knight, face covered in scars, pushed his way through the crowd. He ran to me and took me in his arms, surprising my captors so much that they released me.

"Kenna! Kenna, dear, are you all right?"

As he pulled back to look at me, I stared at him open mouthed. So did the rest of the knights.

"H-how do you know my name?" I whispered, still trembling.

He smiled with kind eyes. "Poor girl doesn't remember me. She's probably in shock," he said to the onlookers before meeting my gaze. "It's Isaiah, remember? When your parents died, I took you in, and—"

"Out of the way, Balton," the first man said through clenched teeth.

"She's not one of them, Captain Lewin," Balton said firmly, surprising everyone—especially me. It was all I could do to keep a straight face, biting my tongue to keep myself quiet.

"And how could you possibly know that?" the captain spat.

"She was kidnapped five years ago from my village," he said.

Lewin scowled. "We'll see about that."

He pushed Isaiah to the side and took a hold of my left sleeve, ripping it off. When he was positive my mark wasn't on that shoulder, he violently turned me and repeated the process. When again he saw only bare skin, he checked both sides once more, pushing away my hair invasively to look at my neck and jerking my head to the side. I hardly dared to breathe.

When he was certain there was nothing to find, he lifted his sword and placed it against my neck. "What kind of trick is this?" he growled.

"It's not a trick," I said, surprised that any noise came out of my throat. "I—"

"Are you a sorceress?" His tiny eyes were bulging. "I'll know if you're lying!"

"*No*," I stammered, feeling tears fall down my cheek.

"I told you," Isaiah said, his kind eyes suddenly hard as he looked at the captain. "She's been their captive. She must have heard us and run for it."

The captain didn't seem convinced, but he couldn't disprove Isaiah's words. After a tense few minutes of silence, he pushed me away and sheathed his sword, still scowling.

"Well, what are you all waiting for?" he yelled to the rest of the knights. "Find them!"

His men hurried to obey orders, and I breathed out shakily in relief. I was *alive*. Silently, I prayed that the others had already escaped.

Isaiah remained by my side. His expression was still hard, but I thought I saw a similar relief in his eyes to what I felt. I opened my mouth, my questions written on my face.

"Not here," he whispered before I could speak.

"Balton!" the captain growled from the shelter's entrance. "Bring the girl!"

Isaiah's lips thinned in response to the order. He put a gentle hand on my back and urged me forward. I hesitated, but I had already cheated death once—resisting now would be foolish.

As we walked, Isaiah whispered, "Whatever you do, and whatever you see, don't show that you care about your clan. If you give yourself away now, there was no point in saving you."

My heart twisted with fear as we entered the common area, but to my relief, no one from the clan was there, and the knights searching the rooms left them empty-handed. But I barely had a moment to register this before the captain walked up to us and seized my arm. The muscles in his face were still contorted in a permanent grimace.

"Where did they go?" he demanded.

My eyes darted to Isaiah briefly, and I felt a rush of panic. I was sure a seasoned soldier like this captain would be able to tell if I were lying. So the best thing to do was to tell the truth.

He shook me. "Where did they go?" he repeated with a growl.

"I don't know," I muttered.

"Why didn't they take you with them?"

I couldn't help shaking. "They tried, but I ran from them."

His eyes narrowed and he tightened his hold. "They didn't stop you?"

"They weren't expecting me to run," I said, trying to ignore the pain in my arm.

Next to me, Isaiah's hands were balled into fists. "Let her go, Captain. Can't you see—?"

"*Quiet*, Balton!" he said, teeth clenched. "I don't trust her any more than I trust you."

Isaiah reluctantly stepped back. The captain glared at me, filling my heart with dread.

"We'll take her back to be tried," he growled. "If she's a witch, she'll be found out. If not, she'll be safe in the city."

From his tone, it didn't sound like he wanted me to be safe. Before Isaiah could protest, Lewin called two other knights over and pushed me towards them.

"Tie her to my cart," he ordered. "And keep watch on her."

There was no point in struggling. I let myself be led back outside, my arms bare against the wind, and the right one throbbing from the captain's harsh grip. Lewin ordered Isaiah to stay and help search, and the door to the shelter closed between us.

Each step felt heavier than the last. I was sure I would just be imprisoned until Lewin found a reason to execute me. But if he couldn't—if I somehow was set free—I would be in the city. Maybe, just maybe, I could find a way into the castle. Maybe I could avenge my family after all—

Are you crazy? You couldn't even stand still in front of one of his captains!

I sighed inwardly. The voice in my head was right. If I trembled with fear in a captain's presence, I couldn't imagine what it would be like to stand in front of the king. Despite my earlier convictions, it was clear now that I would never be able to face him.

Not that it mattered. Lewin was going to kill me anyway.

The supply carts were guarded by four disgruntled men. As we approached, all four reached for their swords as if glad they finally had the chance to fight.

"We're taking her prisoner," the guard to my right said. "We can't prove she's a witch, so we're bringing her to be tried."

The soldiers grumbled, looking disappointed.

I was led to the largest cart at the front of the company. The rest of the knights appeared to carry what they owned on their backs, but not the captain. His cart held a large tent and more blankets than I could count in one glance. There was a grotesque amount of food inside and three bags of clothes. Along with these comforts, swords of various shapes and sizes filled the left side of the cart, with a few bows and arrows thrown in for good measure. If I hadn't heard him say it was 'his' cart, I probably would have assumed it was meant to be provisions for the whole army. In the corner, I could make out a box that held spoils from war, such as clothing and jewelry. Talismans were carelessly thrown in with the rest of the loot, their magic extinguished when their clans were destroyed.

My hands were bound together and tied to the front right side of the cart, far from the supply of weapons, only giving me about three feet to move. One of the guards stood to my right and the other stood behind me, ready to march out. We stood in silence, waiting for the marauders to finish ransacking what had been my home. When they finally returned empty-handed, I stared at my feet to hide a smile. Captain Lewin ordered his men to march out, his scowl even deeper than before.

We traveled nonstop for hours. As I stumbled along behind the cart, I realized just how much energy I'd exerted controlling the spirits in the fight. My legs shook and my eyelids drooped from exhaustion. When I threatened to collapse, the guard next to me roughly pulled me back to my feet and ordered me to keep walking. By the time we climbed over the last hill and reached our destination, I was sure I couldn't take another step.

Two large ships were anchored ahead of us in the bay, each bearing Orkeia's symbol, the sea hawk. I had only been out to sea a handful of times growing up and had never felt quite comfortable being tossed about by the waves. Once, the fishing boat I was in had even capsized, making me weary of going out on the water again unless I had to.

With a start, I realized that I would be bound as we journeyed. I knew that the knights were skilled naval fighters, so they knew better than my clan how to navigate the ocean's tides, and their ships were much more soundly made. But if a storm hit, the last thing these knights would do was untie me. Childhood fears of drowning suddenly awakened, and I was petrified.

We reached the first boat, and Lewin halted the march. His eyes more chilling than any of the elements, he retreated and cut the rope that bound me to his cart, but not the one binding my hands.

"Take her aboard, and tie her to the mast."

My panic morphed into pure terror. If the ship went down, being tied to the mast would mean certain death. But I was too exhausted to fight back. Numbly, I allowed myself to be shoved onto the ship. Isaiah was sent to the other ship, a decision I'm sure the captain made on purpose. He gave me an encouraging smile as he passed, but it was impossible for me to return the gaze.

Once everyone was on board, the rowers pushed off. Too soon, the land behind us was out of sight, and we were out on the open sea. I shut my eyes tightly and leaned my head against the mast, trying to push aside the discomfort of the ropes chafing my skin and the continuing panic I felt at the rocking of the waves.

I knew the knights must know where they were going, but that didn't stop me from fearing we were completely lost. Lewin was commanding as ever on the ship, shouting at his men to keep their rowing in rhythm and increase their speed even though their arms must have been growing stiff.

Somehow, I eventually fell asleep from pure exhaustion. Had I not been so fatigued, my fear would have kept me alert and awake, whether or not I wanted to be. When I awoke, my body felt more sore than I could ever remember. Slowly I opened my eyes and saw land ahead. Relief washed over me, but that relief quickly changed to awe.

Ahead of us rose a set of brilliant, majestic cliffs, the waves of the sea crashing relentlessly against their base. A breathtaking city, rivaling the cliffs' magnificence, sat atop the rocks. Toward the edge, but still inside the city gates, a watchtower reached toward the sky, the king's banner flying proudly upon it. Several smaller tiers that I could only imagine belonged to the castle stood behind it.

This was the city of Orkeia.

I'd always wondered what the kingdom's main city looked like, but never imagined anything quite so fantastic. Elizabeth had told me many stories of her time growing up here—the always bustling marketplace in the middle of the city, the traveling bards that sang on every street corner, the mansions of the rich and shacks of the poor, the military quarter that citizens avoided at all costs, and the awe-inspiring castle seated above it all. Though I detested the king with every fiber of my being, I couldn't help but feel submissive as we drew closer to the grand sight.

No beaches touched the city itself, so we sailed past it to a port for the knights' ships. Even with my hands tied to Lewin's cart once again, I was eternally grateful to be on solid ground. I saw Isaiah move in my direction as we disembarked, but he was ordered to help unload cargo before he could reach me.

Lewin left one of his advisors in charge and set off—with me and a few men in tow—up the steep, grassy slope. We passed a number of small houses and farms, the overflow of the city's vast population. In a little less than half an hour we reached the front gate, and the knights standing guard immediately opened it for the captain. Their eyes lingered on me, but as soon as they realized it they turned away. The people in the town stared as well, and I couldn't understand why at first.

Then it hit me—this was not a war of prisoners, but of mass murder. The knights had probably never returned with someone in their company before, let alone a woman. A few citizens even dared to approach and ask questions of the men, but Lewin ordered them to move on, even shoving one man roughly to the side and spitting at where he landed.

After walking a short way down the road, we veered to the right, and entered what looked like the military quarter. I immediately understood why Elizabeth said people kept their distance. Not only was it visually intimidating, but the smell was horrendous. There were a number of men dressed in full armor, practicing sword-fighting and stances. A few wielded quarterstaffs while others practiced with a bow and arrow. There was a building that I assumed was housing for trainees to sleep in, but it appeared most of the men slept in the large number of tents pitched in the field.

Attached to one of the watchtowers against the city wall was a large building, larger than any of the houses we'd passed on our way in. When we reached the front door, Lewin cut the rope binding me to his cart. I whimpered from the sting of increased pain as he roughly grabbed my arm in the same spot as before.

As the rest of his men unpacked his things, he forced me inside and to a small door at the far end of an open room. He violently pushed me through it and we descended a long, spiral staircase into endless darkness that rivaled the Land of the Lost, illuminated only by sparse torches along the wall. I stumbled more than once, and each time he shoved me to keep me moving.

When we reached the bottom, my captor took one of the torches off the wall and held it ahead, revealing the poor souls trapped in cages on either side of us. A few looked up as we passed, but the majority seemed to have lost all hope of escape or sanity. The sounds of whimpering prisoners and the acrid smell of the unkempt cells filled me with both nausea and dread.

If I thought I was frightened before, I was sadly mistaken.

When we reached the end of the hall, Lewin produced a ring of keys and opened an empty cell to my left. I let out an involuntary cry of surprise and pain as he pushed me through the gate and I fell flat on the floor, cutting my lip on a loose stone.

The lock turned behind me. I spun around just in time to catch a glimpse of his glare, barely visible in the dancing flames of the torch.

"You can expect to be tried within the week," he said. A horrible grin spread across one side of his face before he strolled out of view, taking what little light there was with him.

***

The days I spent in that dungeon were the most terrifying of my life. I was the only sane person in the darkness. Constant moaning of pain or sorrow came from the other cells. Hearing that horrid sound while being completely blind would be enough to drive anyone mad, even without experiencing the neglectful treatment of a prisoner.

Only twice—I assumed once each morning—a flicker of light appeared down the hall just before a stale scrap of bread was tossed through the bars. I had to scramble to get it before the light disappeared, otherwise it would've taken me forever to find it sitting on the dirt. No liquid was offered to us, only the puddles in the corners of every cell. I heard many of the other prisoners lapping up the filthy water like parched dogs, and though I initially wasn't desperate enough to join them, that inevitably changed as time passed.

Aside from when the knights brought the pitiful excuse for food, we were left in frigid darkness. We were so far underground and the walls and floor were so damp that any hope of warmth was completely lost. The majority of my time was spent shivering on the ground, trying to stay away from puddles I couldn't see, and crying silently to myself as inhuman noises came from every direction and invisible insects crawled over my body. I wished that Isaiah had let Lewin kill me. If he had, I would have been with Elizabeth in the land of the Saved.

Instead, I was here.

It felt like an eternity had passed when the sound of voices interrupted the monotony of life in the cells. My first thought was that I was hearing things, starting to go mad like the rest of the prisoners, but one of the voices sounded vaguely familiar. After straining my ears for a moment, my heart sank. It was Lewin.

"There is no mark on her skin," he was saying, "but I suspect she is one of them."

"Why did you imprison her without my consent?" The second man sounded much younger than the captain.

"I didn't want to trouble you, Kiernan. This is a matter I can deal with—"

"She claims to have been captured by them," the man called Kiernan said matter-of-factly. "If it's true, she is the first person to have escaped. It is my duty as her king to speak with her."

The king...

The footsteps slowed to a stop as the light became visible. My heart dropped, and my blood boiled with rage simultaneously. On the one hand I wanted to face him, see his face, the face that had caused so much death and destruction.

On the other hand, I was terrified.

"What is this place?" The king's icy tone was barely above a whisper. When there was no response, he repeated the question, this time in a more commanding tone. "Where am I, Captain?"

"Holding cells," Lewin replied. "For those guilty of crimes punishable by death."

"I never authorized this!"

"Your father did, Your Majesty."

"Listen to me carefully," the king said, his tone threatening. "My father is not king anymore—*I* am. We've been through some dark times, but I am doing all I can to keep the darkness outside our walls. I will not permit this treatment of my people."

"Yes, Your Majesty," said Lewin reluctantly. "I will begin the trials at once and find a new holding place. If you would follow me back upstairs—"

"No. I'm going to speak to this girl."

"Kiernan—"

"*Stand aside.*"

The light slowly moved in my direction. I held my breath. My eyes squinted from the shock of the firelight as the ruler of Orkeia reached my cell, his face illuminated by a dim torch.

I blinked. A young man stood before me—he couldn't have been much older than Neal. Even in the poor lighting, he was strikingly handsome. His dark blonde hair was pulled back neatly, only one or two strands free to dangle in front of his face.

He wasn't at all the man I had expected to see.

The only thing I seemed to have had accurate about his character was his harshness. His features were like stone.

Frowning, he moved closer to my bars. Lewin stood to the king's left, his scowl ever present. The king didn't seem to be paying any attention to his captain. He studied me intently where I knelt in the dirt. I tore my eyes away and stared at the ground.

"What is your name?" he asked.

"Kenna," I said, surprised I was able to make any sound.

"How old are you?"

"Seventeen."

"Were you being held against your will by witches?"

My lips quivered and I kept my gaze on the ground. I knew I should lie and say yes, but my throat tightened so much that when I tried, little more than a whimper came out.

Out of the corner of my eye, I saw the king's expression soften. "Unlock her cell, Captain."

"Your Majesty—"

"*Now.*"

Lewin begrudgingly removed a ring of keys from his belt and fit one into my door. When the lock clicked, he let it swing open, stepping behind his king. I remained on the ground, too shocked to move.

Slowly, the king stepped into the cell. Taking a dagger from his boot, he knelt and cut the rope around my wrists, letting it fall to the ground.

I stared at the rope where it fell before slowly lifting my eyes to his. All the harshness I'd seen in his expression was replaced by what seemed to be genuine concern. He stood and extended a hand to me, his eyes kind.

Bewildered, I allowed him to help me to my feet, but my legs immediately threatened to give way. He wrapped an arm around my waist, catching me before I could fall and supporting me with his strength. I felt like vomiting.

"I can't imagine what those witches must have put you through," he said somberly. "And the treatment you received from my knights appalls me."

Lewin didn't dare make a sound, remaining stiff where he was. I was speechless as well, staring into the eyes of the man who had ordered my people's extermination. He seemed to be waiting for a response of some kind, but all I could do was shiver.

He sighed. "Let's get you out of here."

Without a second thought, he removed his cloak and wrapped it around my bare shoulders, silencing Lewin's outburst with his mere stance. Once it was fastened, he replaced his arm around my waist to steady me as I walked. I flinched at his touch, used to Lewin's rough treatment and surprised by how gentle the king was in comparison. We made our way down the damp hall and up the never ending stairs, stopping frequently as I stumbled. It was frustrating not to be able to support myself, and the last person I wanted to be relying on was the king.

Lewin was ordered to stay behind and move the prisoners to a more humane location, and relief flooded through me as the king's carriage pulled away from my prison. Once the cursed building faded from view, I stared at the man across from me. How could this be the same man who had started the Slaughters? I'd expected someone older, rougher, with evil seeping from his very skin. This man didn't seem evil—just hardened.

"Your uncle told me about you, Kenna," he said as we left the military quarter behind.

"My uncle?" I asked, confused.

He nodded. "He said you didn't seem to remember him. I'm sure the past few days haven't helped."

My eyes widened. "Isaiah?"

A small smile crossed his face. "That's right. Sir Balton. He's the one who told me where you were. You owe him your life and your freedom."

Questions that had been flashing through my mind days before returned. Was he really my uncle? If so, how did he recognize me when I'd been with Elizabeth since I was a baby? And if he was again lying to protect me, who was he?

"You've known a hard life," the king continued. "Losing your parents at a young age, being kidnapped and tortured by those monsters—"

I flinched at his last word, but he pretended not to notice, likely misinterpreting my reaction.

"—and now being imprisoned by my own captain of the guard," he said with genuine anger in his voice. "I intend to make it up to you, Kenna."

A knot formed in my throat. "You don't owe me anything—" I managed to say before he held up his hand for silence.

"I want to give you the opportunity to start a new life. If you don't object, Sir Balton and I have arranged quarters for you in the castle. You will be taught to be a lady of the court and you will be under my protection."

Quarters in the castle...

"Do you offer all young ladies this treatment?" I asked, squirming.

I thought I saw him smile, but I couldn't be sure. "Only those who deserve it."

He waited patiently as I considered his offer. A few months ago, I would have been leaping with joy inside at having found a way into the castle walls. After experiencing Lewin's dungeon, my reaction was quite the opposite. Not only was I terrified, but I'd realized the truth: no matter what he had done or how much I hated him, I would never be able to kill a man.

The only thing keeping me from running as far away as I could was Isaiah. I needed to understand who he was and how he knew me.

He never said I couldn't leave if I accepted...

I forced my lips into a shaky smile. "I don't deserve your hospitality. Thank you for your kindness."

"Then it's settled," the king said, clapping his hands. The moment his palms made contact, the carriage door opened, and I looked out at my new home.

CHAPTER ELEVEN

WITHIN THE CASTLE WALLS

A large iron gate stood open between two majestic stone towers. Dual flights of stairs led to the grand entrance beyond a courtyard buzzing with gardeners. Above the ornate door hung a beautiful stained glass window depicting a diving sea hawk. The architecture was magnificent, and the kingdom's blue banners—also bearing the sea hawk—brought color and life to the stone walls. As I stared, servants passed in and out of the courtyard, dressed in the finest clothes I had ever seen.

"Are you coming?"

The king's voice brought me back to myself. He stood outside the carriage, his hand outstretched. Dazed, I took it, digging my fingers into his palm to retain balance. Once my feet were firmly on the ground, he wrapped an arm around my waist again, almost protectively, supporting me as we moved slowly along the beautifully paved path. He didn't attempt to rush me, allowing me to take my time to get to the steps and instructing the staring servants to return to their duties. I must have looked ridiculous, walking into the courtyard of the castle wearing a worn out, wet, torn dress under the king's cloak. I can't imagine what they would've thought if they knew what I really was.

As we climbed the left staircase, the large, heavy doors ground against the stone floor. Four knights stood at each door and bowed deeply to their king when we reached the landing. These men had more elaborate uniforms than those I'd seen in Lewin's company. More guards lined the stairway inside, as well as the railing of a grand balcony, armed to protect their king. I pulled my eyes down from the dangling chandelier to see six maids standing directly in front of us, their hair up in tight, perfect braids.

"Show this young woman to quarters in the East Tower," the king ordered. "Give her a bath, new clothes, and anything else she might require."

All six ladies curtsied and stepped forward. I reached for the latch on the cloak I was wearing, but he gently placed his strong hand over mine.

"Keep it, Kenna," he said kindly.

He smiled, and there was a warmth to his smile that filled me with a surprising amount of comfort. For a moment, I almost forgot how terrified I was supposed to be of him. I realized as we stood there that his hand was still on top of mine. His eyes were filled with concern and...something else that I couldn't quite place. I took in a deep breath, my chest feeling tight.

At length, he tore his eyes from mine and turned to ascend the stairs to the throne room. As his entrance was announced, I glimpsed a gathering of people standing inside. The room fell silent the second he walked through the door. He must have been presiding over a trial—what probably should have been *my* trial.

The doors closed behind him and the attendants he had assigned to me led me down the hall. I followed them numbly, my eyes darting this way and that. It was impossible to take in every detail of every painting and sculpture we passed, but I still tried.

The maids brought me to an enormous room on the second floor. My eyes widened in wonder at the silk tapestries, the ornate gold furnishings, the elaborate portraits on the walls, and the rich rugs beneath my bare feet. I had never felt anything so soft, and I was suddenly self-conscious of how dirty I must be making them. An enormous wardrobe stood on the opposite side of the room, bursting with more colors and styles of dress than I'd ever seen. There were candles lit around the room as well, and I noticed that in addition to light, they gave off a pleasant, flowery smell.

As awe-struck as I was, everything else disappeared when I saw the bed. It was all I could do to stay awake long enough for a bath. If I'd been alone, I wouldn't have thought twice about jumping into those sheets in my drenched, muddy clothing. It was hard to remind myself that I was in the home of someone who wanted me dead, and that I couldn't afford to let my guard down.

When my bath arrived, the maids turned to give me privacy. I undressed and lowered myself into the warm water, gasping. I'd never had a hot bath before. It was the most wonderful feeling, especially after two winter days in that dungeon.

"If you need anything, M'Lady," one of the maids said, her face pleasant, "just pull that rope there next to the bed."

"Thank you." I gave her an awkward smile. She smiled back, and curtsied before she and the rest of my attendants left the room.

When the door shut, I lifted my right leg just above the surface of the water and slowly traced the mark on my skin, watching the water roll down my leg. Years ago I'd accepted that I would probably never know what it meant or why it was placed where it was, but curiosity returned as I sat there, a witch in the king's castle. Maybe my suspicions about some sort of destiny had been right after all—maybe the Giftgiver had known I would find myself in the castle one way or another and it would need to stay hidden.

Whatever the answer, I closed my eyes reverently and poured out my soul to Him, thanking Him for sending Isaiah to my rescue, and for keeping my identity a secret from the knights and the king. No matter how many times I'd wished for death in that dungeon, I was glad to be alive.

I briefly dozed off, but woke up shivering in the cooled water. Feeling cleaner than I'd ever been, I climbed sopping wet out of the bath. A beautiful, green velvet robe lay on my bed, and I wrapped it around me, amazed at how soft it was against my skin. As I climbed into the bed, there was a light knock on my door. The same six maids entered to clean up the bath, but I hardly noticed them. I'd never been in a bed like this, only the stone ones the Grisons padded down for comfort. But this—*this* was the most amazing feeling I could imagine! The closest thing I I had felt to it was laying on a soft bed of grass, but it was hardly a worthy comparison.

Before any of the maids could ask if I wanted anything else, I was fast asleep.

***

I dreamt I was in the middle of a field, my spirit hovering above my limp body. As I watched, Neal rushed out from behind the hills and tenderly took my body in his arms. "Please come back, Kenna," he whispered desperately. Tears came to my eyes as I watched him run his fingers through my hair, but for some reason I couldn't return to my body.

Suddenly, he disappeared, and Gideon took his place. He laid my head in his lap as the knights approached from all directions, led by their king on horseback. Gid closed his eyes and stretched out his hands, creating a moat around us. The concentration in his face deepened and his hands shook as he increased the size of the obstacle, making it impossible for the knights to cross. King Kiernan dismounted and walked to the edge of the water, drawing his sword.

"Hand her over."

Gideon's blue eyes glared at him with a harshness completely alien to them. "Never," he said.

King Kiernan's grip on his sword tightened, but he didn't attempt to cross the moat. Instead, he lifted the sword into the air and pointed toward us.

"Shoot him."

I screamed silently as hundreds of arrows flew at Gideon. He cried out and collapsed to the ground, his blood staining the green grass red. My spirit snapped back into my body and I pulled him into my arms.

"MONSTER!" I screeched, tears staining my face as I turned toward the man who had killed my best friend.

His lips curved upward wickedly. "So you are one of them."

Chilling my bones with his laughter, he mounted his horse.

"What are you waiting for? Shoot her!"

I squeezed my eyes shut as a hundred bow strings were pulled back.

When I opened them, I sat upright in my bed, sweating and panting heavily. A nightgown was laid out at the foot of my bed. In the dim light of the moon, I changed and sat on the edge of the bed, still shaking.

I stared ahead in the darkness. Despite how long I had dreamt of infiltrating the castle, now, I wanted to run as far away as possible. At the same time, another part of me wanted to find the king's quarters now and kill him as he slept.

But no matter how many times I had wished for his death, I'd never be able to go through with it. And as hard as it was to admit, how that I'd actually met him, he was nothing like the horrible, ruthless monster I'd imagined. He was kind and seemed genuinely concerned for my well-being. While I knew that his demeanor would change if he knew the truth about my Gift, it was hard to imagine the man in my dream and the man who'd pulled me from the dungeon could be the same person.

And then there was Isaiah. I couldn't leave without speaking to him. I needed answers.

It was dark outside, but I'd slept as long as my body was going to let me. Right as I decided to stand up, a long, rattling breathing sound came from the side of my bed. The hairs stood up on the back of my neck and I clutched the blanket, turning my head towards the sound.

A shadow hovered there, the shadow of a man. The evil emanating from the figure seized my throat. In a rush of panic, I threw my blankets into what I thought was his face and lunged for the candle on the other side of the bed. My fingers fumbled with the match, my breath coming out in gasps. With the candle finally lit, I spun around.

There was no one there.

Shaking, I pulled the rope next to the bed, my eyes lingering fearfully on where the figure had been. It didn't feel like any spirit I'd sensed before, but I couldn't come up with another logical reason for its quick disappearance. Could it have been a malevolent spirit that somehow escaped from the Land of the Lost?

A soft knock jerked me out of my thoughts. The same maid who spoke to me the day before opened the door, a kind smile on her round face as she suppressed a yawn.

"You rang, M'Lady?"

My words came out in slow, staggered breaths. "Are there any other ways in and out of this room? Aside from that door?"

She eyed me curiously. "No. Might I ask why?"

I bit my lip. "I just had a bad dream. I'm sorry for disturbing your rest."

"'Twas no disturbance, M'Lady," she said with another smile. "Anything else I can do for you?"

I was about to say that I was fine when my stomach rumbled loudly, and painfully for that matter. The maid smiled again, not waiting for me to speak. "I'll fetch you something to eat," she said with a bit of a chuckle, hurrying out of the room.

The sun rose as I waited for her to return. My eyes continually darted to where I'd seen the shadow. She returned with a platter of fruit, and my stomach rumbled again. She hid an amused smile as I devoured everything in front of me. I bit into a juicy apple, closing my eyes to relish the sweet taste.

"I'm sorry I didn't bring more, M'Lady," the maid said, "but the king has requested your presence at his breakfast table, and I didn't want you to eat too much beforehand."

I almost dropped the apple. She no doubt attributed my reaction to the shock and awe of the king's hospitality and concern, but as hungry as I was, the thought of sitting civilly and having breakfast with this murderer made my stomach turn.

Just play along.

"Oh—of course," I breathed with a small nod.

As I ate, the maid opened the wardrobe, searching through the gowns. After a few minutes of silent debate with herself, she picked an emerald green one with gold accents, laid it on the bed, and pulled the cord to summon more maids.

The last grape was barely in my mouth when the door swung open and I was swarmed. The maids gave me some privacy as I pulled the dress on, enough that I was able to hide my mark, but no sooner had I put my arms through the sleeves than they were lacing up the back and fussing with my hair. I had to be presentable for their king. I did my best not to scream at them as they pulled my hair and pinched my cheeks, but I'm afraid I did let out a few involuntary sounds of protest. They pretended not to notice.

When the six pairs of hands finally stopped poking and prodding me, the maid who'd been helping me all morning turned me to face the mirror. I couldn't believe my eyes. The person staring back at me was a complete stranger, a lady in the king's royal court. Her brown curls were pulled up, expertly controlled in an elaborate style. My hair could never be controlled, and I did not have the figure the woman facing me did. With the dress hugging her body elegantly, she looked more like Helen than any version of myself. It was all I could do to take my eyes off the disturbing image and follow my attendants out of the room, back through the endless halls.

Time seemed to pass faster than normal, and soon I stood in front of a large set of doors. One of the maids knocked. I tried to appear pleasant and even managed a small smile to aid in my façade. The door opened and the king and his captains came into view.

"Ah, there you are!" King Kiernan said, standing. The other men at the table followed his example, though the surprise and confusion on their faces was evident. I recognized the two men who guarded me as we traveled and Lewin himself, his perpetual frown directed toward me from the moment I entered the hall. I averted my eyes and stared at the uncomfortable shoes on my feet, trying to hide my fear.

One of the maids passed me and pulled out a chair. I felt a slight relief from my panic when I saw Isaiah standing next to my seat. I joined him, wishing we were alone and not surrounded by these monsters. As soon as I sat, the men took their seats once more, the majority of them averting their gaze. The king and his captain of the guard, however, continued to stare at me. I stared at my plate in response.

"I trust you slept well?" the king inquired.

"I slept very well…Your Majesty."

I glanced up and our eyes met for a moment. His, which I had deemed emotionless just the day before, were shining.

"I am glad to hear it," he said. "Now, enough conversation—you must be starved."

He clapped his hands, and servants immediately entered from the opposite end of the room. They filled the table with freshly baked bread, hot soup, more fresh fruit, eggs, and some meat I didn't recognize. I almost forgot how uncomfortable I was at seeing the food, and I struggled to eat politely rather than shovel the food into my mouth as quickly as possible.

The meal passed in silence on my part. Occasionally I met Isaiah's gaze, and he sent me an encouraging smile. I searched for answers on his face, but I knew I wasn't going to get them until we could speak in private.

The conversation was uninteresting until halfway through the meal. The younger of my two guards mentioned preparing ships for departure, and the king set down his fork.

"When will they be ready, Captain Stole?"

"Within the next few hours, Your Majesty," Stole said. He appeared to be the youngest captain present, but he was still quite a bit older than the king. "We are ensuring we have all the necessary supplies and precautions in place for your voyage."

Kiernan glimpsed the surprise on my face and turned. "I will be leaving with my captains for a short while, Kenna. I've decided to join them on their patrol of the isle of Fain. I trust you will be safe in your uncle's hands while I'm gone."

I nodded, biting the inside of my lip to hide my excitement. If the king was leaving, I would get the chance to ask Isaiah my questions. Perhaps I would even be able to escape and find the Grisons. I resolved to search for them in spirit that night and try to let them know I was alive, though it was hard to communicate with mortals while in spirit form.

It seemed an eternity before the king finished eating. The rest of us stood as he left the room. Our eyes met once more, and his seemed to be searching mine. I searched his as well, trying to figure out this mystery of a man.

How could someone that appeared so kind be the one waging war against my people? How could this be the face of the bloodthirsty king I'd been imagining for years?

The captains dispersed to prepare for their voyage, but Isaiah did not follow them. Instead, he put a strong, gentle hand on my shoulder and led me back to my room, telling my maids he would escort me and they could attend to their other duties. None of them questioned him. We walked the halls in silence, and only when my door was securely closed behind us did he speak.

"Which question should I answer first?"

If I tried to sort through them and decide which to ask when, this conversation would never end, so I blurted out the first one that came to my mind.

"Are you really my uncle?"

Isaiah ran his hand through his hair. "No, Kenna. I'm not your uncle."

"Then who are you?" I breathed.

He took my hand. I stared into his gray eyes, a familiar ring of blue on the outer edges of the pupils. I searched my memory for where I'd seen those eyes before. With a shock I realized the memory was of my own reflection. My eyes widened in recognition before he spoke the words aloud.

"I'm your father."

CHAPTER TWELVE

ECHOES OF THE PAST

"**M**y father?"

I felt like my legs were going to give out and stumbled to sit down on the edge of the bed.

He smiled, his eyes misty. "You look so much like your mother. That was how I recognized—"

I wasn't listening, my fingers curling into fists against the bedsheets. "Why did you abandon me? All this time—if you were alive—" My voice cracked. I felt a void in my life I'd never really noticed before.

His smile faltered and he placed both hands firmly on my shoulders. "I love you, Kenna. I wouldn't have given you up for the world if I'd had a choice."

"Then why did you?" I whispered.

He sighed. "Because you would have been killed if you stayed with me."

The knot in my throat only tightened at this. He released my shoulders and joined me on the edge of my bed, his face somber.

"Your mother was a white witch," he began. "I met her before the majority of the Ungifted knew magic existed. In fact, I didn't know she was a witch at first."

"How did you meet?" I asked.

"I was working in a blacksmith's shop, as an apprentice," he said with a wry smile. "She came in to pick up an order for her uncle. They had a farm just outside of town..."

His voice trailed off, and he rubbed his right arm with a heavy breath. "I'd heard of the Gifted, but only that they were dangerous. If I hadn't gotten to know your mother before she told me about her Gift, I'm not sure how I would have reacted. But she showed me the truth about her powers, and it just made me love her more that she trusted me enough to share that part of herself with me."

"What happened to her?" I asked.

Isaiah gazed at the window. His expression was difficult to read, but the hardness of it made my stomach turn with dread.

"Soon after we were married, King Rafael—Kiernan's father—discovered a clan of witches while hunting. He claimed they attacked him and his men, killing four of his most trusted advisors."

My jaw dropped. "Why would they do that?"

He shook his head. "I agree that it doesn't really make sense," he muttered.

It felt like he was holding something back, but before I could ask about it, he continued. "When the king returned to the city, he demanded that anyone bearing a mark be imprisoned. You were only a baby, and your mother, being the brave woman she was, decided to try to reason with him. I tried to talk her out of it, to tell her it was too dangerous, but—she was insistent."

He began to shake. I felt the urge to take his hand, and he squeezed it in response.

"He wouldn't listen to her," he said, his grief evident in the heaviness of his tone and his watery eyes. "Instead, he executed her in front of his prisoners as an example. He found out she had a child and ordered his men to find and kill you as well."

My eyes widened. "Me? Why? You said I was just a baby!"

"I don't know, Kenna," he said, his hand tightening its hold on mine. "I never knew why King Rafael did what he did."

His jaw clenched and he let out a sharp breath. "Whatever his reasons were, I had to find somewhere you could be safe. My friends helped me steal a boat, and I began searching the coasts for a clan. Eventually, I met a woman who agreed to care for you. It killed me to leave you with a stranger, but for some reason, I trusted her."

He paused, asking his questions without words. I squeezed his hand again. "Elizabeth. She treated me like her own daughter."

He managed a pained smile before he continued. "I was right to give you up. The king was enraged that you disappeared. He found our home and destroyed everything. I changed my name for protection, but I still had to hide."

"Why didn't you stay with me?" I asked.

Isaiah released my hand with a sigh and crossed the room to look out the window at the city below. "I thought you would be safer without me," he muttered. "And I wanted to help here. There were so many people imprisoned and scared. And the king's mania only worsened. It wasn't long before he decreed that anyone with magical abilities be put to death. I stayed to help the Gifted escape the city."

I pressed my palm into the mattress, my eyes watering. I wanted to tell him that was a brave and noble thing to do, but I didn't feel like words could really do his selfless actions justice.

His expression remained pained and he crossed his arms. "After seven years, hostility toward magic holders died down, but things didn't stay peaceful for long. Unfortunately, there were some Gifted who were not content living in hiding. Five years ago, a sorcerer broke into the castle and tried to force King Rafael to surrender the kingdom to him. When he refused, the sorcerer—Pious, his name was—broke into the castle, seized the queen, and brought her into the throne room where he melted her with his gift."

"*Melted* her?" I breathed, a chill running down my spine as I gripped the edge of the bed.

Isaiah nodded grimly. "Yes. He melted King Rafael as well."

The horror of the scene played out in my mind, and I shut my eyes as if that would erase the images. "What about the king—Kiernan, I mean. How did he escape?"

"One of the servants smuggled him out through a secret passage," he explained. "Pious took control of the kingdom. Everyone, Gifted and Ungifted alike, was afraid of him. He had so many people imprisoned on nonexistent charges that the dungeons were overflowing. It was a year before the knights managed to overpower and kill him, and Kiernan became the new king. He was only nineteen. That was when, at Captain Lewin's counsel, he officially declared war, and the Slaughters began."

"But why did you join the knights?" I interrupted.

"I didn't," he said. "I did everything I could to avoid being recruited—moving often, hiding out with friends—but eventually I realized that hiding wasn't doing anyone any good. But," he smirked, "if I was a scout, I would be able to find clans and give them time to relocate before the rest of the knights caught up."

"Then why didn't you warn us?" I asked softly, trying to hide the hurt from my voice. If we'd known ahead of time that the knights were approaching, we could have hidden ourselves, or at least had enough time to gather our supplies. I wouldn't have had to stay behind—I could still be with Gideon and Neal, even if it meant establishing a new shelter once again. My heart ached at the thought.

"Lewin suspects me," Isaiah said with a grimace. "He transferred me to the supply division at the back of the march two months ago, and there's no contesting an order from the captain of the guard. I've done my best to put up resistance—throwing away food, hiding weapons—but it's not easy."

He shut his eyes tightly and rubbed his arm again. "When your spirits attacked, I abandoned my post and hurried forward, hoping I could help the clan. I can't describe how I felt when I saw you, Kenna—I knew from one glance you were my daughter. I felt I would die if you died."

His eyebrows creased with emotion. I stared at him, speechless. All these years I'd wondered why my family hadn't loved me enough to keep me, but he'd loved me so much he gave me up to save my life. And he hadn't stopped with just saving me. My heart swelled with pride at the knowledge that this brave man was my father.

Unable to find words to express myself, I stood, crossed the room, and threw my arms around him in a tight hug. I felt him take in a deep breath, wrapping his strong arms around me in return.

"I'm sorry you haven't known any of this until now," he said into my shoulder, something catching in his throat.

We sat like that for a while. I wasn't really sure how to describe my emotions, and he seemed to be just as much at a loss for words now that his story was through. Eventually, I shifted and pulled away from the hug to look more directly at him.

"What was my mother like?" I asked.

He smiled softly. "She was the most beautiful woman I've ever seen—you look just like her. She was curious about everything and succeeded in anything she put her mind to. And she loved you so much. She made me promise that no matter what happened to her, I would keep you safe. It was her last wish."

"What was her name?"

"Arabella," he said, a fond reverence in his voice.

I smiled to myself before another question surfaced. "You said you had to change your name?"

"Yes."

"What was it before?"

"That's not important," he said, brushing a strand of hair out of my face. "And it's better that you don't know. What's important is that I found you again. And that you're safe."

He pulled me into another tight hug. I returned the embrace, my mind spinning as I registered all of this newfound information. It exhilarated me with its answers and overwhelmed me with knowledge I never would have guessed. But most of all, it made me feel...complete. I'd found a part of my story—my identity—that I didn't know I had been missing.

As much as I wanted to just stay there asking him question after question, he insisted on giving me some time to rest and left. But, though I tried to rest in one of the soft chairs by the window, I was too preoccupied to close my eyes.

Maybe this king wasn't the monster I thought he was. I actually felt sorry for him—a sorcerer invaded his home and murdered both his parents, with the intention of murdering him as well. I had to admit that as horrific and destructive as his actions were, I now understood them. It was only natural that he would want to hunt down people like the man who destroyed his family.

I thought back to all the hurt and anger I'd harbored in the months since losing Elizabeth and the rest of my clan. Like him, I'd wanted revenge. It had never once occurred to me to put myself in his shoes and try to understand his actions, just as it had never occurred to him to ask questions about the Gifted community.

But wanting revenge on his parents' murderer was one thing. Going after an entire population was another. Even if he had been misled by his father and Lewin, it seemed so obvious to me that killing all these people wouldn't feel right to him if he had a conscience.

As I lay there, there was a soft knock on my door. I didn't immediately respond, not entirely registering it. After a few minutes, a maid entered slowly. It was the same girl who'd been helping me since I arrived.

"Excuse me, M'Lady," she said as she curtsied, "but the king has requested that you attend lessons."

I stared at her, pulled out of my thoughts. "Lessons?"

"To learn to be a lady of the court. You are to attend today and every day at this time until dinner, until His Majesty is satisfied with your learning. If you will follow me, M'Lady, I will take you to Miss Grayson. She is to be your teacher."

For a moment, I considered refusing, but since I still hadn't figured out what my plan was, I nodded and followed her. We again entered the maze of halls. She walked a ways in front of me, partly because she didn't take the time to stare at all of the artwork around her. She'd undoubtedly passed it hundreds of times. Once or twice she took a turn that I didn't notice and I scrambled to find her. Each time this happened, a small smile crossed her lips, but she hid it expertly. It was almost as if she wasn't allowed to be amused by anything, and it seemed my continual astonishment was making that very hard for her.

When we finally stopped, a pair of large, ornate double doors stood at the end of the hall, towering over me. It almost felt like standing in front of the golden gates, but far less comforting and much more intimidating. I stared, wondering what lay behind them, feeling suddenly nervous. The maid cleared her throat and brought my attention to a smaller set of doors directly in front of me, and I relaxed.

"Miss Grayson is inside. I will be around for lunch, and to escort you to dinner and then to your room."

She curtsied and turned. Just as she was about to leave, I took a few steps toward her.

"Excuse me!" I called, bringing her to a sudden stop. "What's your name?"

She blinked, as if surprised I would ask. "Abigail Cobb," she said, her face brightening. Almost as soon as I saw her expression, it was gone, and she disappeared around the corner.

Puzzled by her reaction, I turned back to face the door, only to stumble back in surprise. A tall, very elegant woman stood in the doorway, with graying black hair pulled into a very tight bun. She wore a gloomy black dress with subtle silver accents and a gloomy expression.

"You must be Miss Grayson?" I inquired when she didn't say anything.

She pursed her lips. "First rule," she squeaked, her voice sounding like the creaking of a door that hasn't been opened for decades. "A lady never yells, especially not after a servant."

I opened my mouth to respond, but thought better of it and just nodded.

"I can see we have a ways to go," she observed, her lips permanently pursed.

Reluctantly, I stepped through the door she held open. Once I was inside, she shut it with a loud thud. I jumped.

"A lady is always composed," she snapped.

"But you just slammed—"

"And a lady never interrupts or talks back to her elders," she said, her eyes flaming. "Are we clear on those three rules at least?"

I was speechless.

***

Me being speechless turned out to be exactly what Miss Grayson wanted. According to her definition of 'lady,' I was supposed to be completely silent until told otherwise by a member of the opposite sex. No wonder she never married.

I thought when Abigail brought lunch that I would get a break, but I was sadly mistaken. Instead, Miss Grayson took the opportunity to criticize everything about how I ate—the way I was holding my fork, my posture as I sat at the table, and even the way I chewed my food. No matter how hard I tried to follow her instructions, I inevitably fell short of her expectations.

"We have a long way to go," she creaked dismally.

By the time the day's lessons were done, I was eager to return to the privacy of my room. The exquisite hallways didn't hold nearly as much wonder in them as they had earlier in the day, or at least that wasn't where my thoughts were focused. Now that I had had some time to recover from the harrowing journey here, I was eager to see if I could find where the Grison clan had gone. It was ironic that I had spent so much time thinking about how to get *here*, but now all I could think about was getting back to them. Neal's parting actions certainly had something to do with it, but it was so much more than that. They had become my family—especially Gideon—and the thought of not seeing them again was painful.

Abigail offered to help me undress for the evening, but I declined. I shouldn't have. My fingers fumbled unsuccessfully with the complicated laces on the back of my dress for so long that I almost gave up. Eventually, I found one spot that was just loose enough to pull and break myself free from bondage. With a sigh of relief, I let the fabric fall to a pool at my feet, not bothering to change out of the looser underclothing before laying on the bed.

I closed my eyes. My spirit floated from my body and out the window to soar over the top of the castle. I had to admit, seeing the castle and its city from above was breathtaking. I had never imagined so many people together in one place, nor had I ever seen so many buildings of various sizes and makes. There were even buildings made of wood, which wasn't common on the rocky islands of Orkeia due to the lack of trees. They must have shipped it over from the mainland to have enough to build, and I could only imagine how much that cost.

Tearing my eyes from the slanted wooden roofs of the city, I began to explore the perimeter of the island I was currently on. Of course, they could be on any number of islands, and wherever they were, it would be hard to spot them if they were being careful, but I had to start somewhere.

I focused on any suspicious-looking or isolated mounds but didn't find anything that resembled the first shelter I'd shared with them. There were some lone structures in the middle of the hills or scattered on the edge of the beach, but those all seemed to be abandoned. I supposed I shouldn't have been surprised. If any clans had been living this close to the castle, they were likely the first to be targeted by King Kiernan's armies.

When my search of the main island didn't yield any results, I traveled southward over the ocean. I had never really considered the expanse of the kingdom of Orkeia before. There were islands in all directions, some of them closer together than others. Most had the same rocky cliffs as where we'd been living before, and before long I even spotted our second shelter, the wedding decorations abandoned and trampled. I couldn't help but pause and stare at Gideon's pond, remembering with an ache the joy on his face when he created it.

I explored two more islands before the strain of the magic I was using began to take its toll. The spirit and the body are not meant to be separated for long and I had been searching for what was likely hours. I did my best to commit to memory the path I had taken and which islands I had already searched, hoping that I hadn't missed a telltale sign of their new location. Then, reluctantly, I traveled back towards the castle.

As I approached my body, the room seemed darker than before. At first I thought it was just because the sun had gone down, but the darkness felt heavy somehow, especially in spirit form. I stopped at the window. I had never felt the effects of cold while in spirit form before, but somehow, I was *freezing*. It felt like there was a wall of ice between me and my body on the bed, stopping me from going any further.

That's when I saw it. At first, it looked like just a dark mist floating over my body, but as I stared it began to take shape. The form of a man appeared leaning over the bed, the same form I'd sensed the previous night. I'd only been able to make out the silhouette before, but now that I was in the spirit realm, I could see it more clearly. It was pitch black, the darkness emanating from it in a way that seemed to steal what little light there was in the room. The edges of the figure were wispy like smoke rather than solid. When it raised its head to look at where I floated, it had bright, red eyes burned into a featureless face.

Slowly, it lowered its head once more to look at where my body lay. I watched in terror as it reached out a hand, its fingers stretching out as if they were long tendrils and reaching for my closed eyes.

In a panic, I forced my spirit to move through the invisible wall of ice, rushing towards the creature. Just as those tendrils were about to make contact with my body, I rushed back into it, immediately opening my eyes. I could still see it, though not as clearly as before, and I threw out my hands on instinct, willing with all my might to push it back.

There was a sudden flash of light, one that began at my fingertips and quickly filled the room. I heard a shrill scream, but not with my ears. It was screaming in my mind.

As quickly as it had appeared, the flash was gone. The flickering of the candle on my bedside was the only light that remained. I scrambled backwards on the bed, sitting up and desperately searching the room for any remaining sign of the creature.

It was gone.

CHAPTER THIRTEEN

PLAYING THE PART

As much as I wanted to find the Grisons, I didn't dare try to explore the islands in spirit after that. I'd never seen one before, but I felt certain that the creature in my room two nights in a row was a demon. How it escaped the Land of the Lost and why it was interested in me remained mysteries, but there wasn't any other explanation. And while I knew little about demons and the workings of the Lost One, I knew enough to know that leaving my body unprotected when there was one around was extremely unwise.

This meant that, at least for now, I didn't really have anywhere else to go. I was sure no one would stop me from leaving the castle, but then what? Finding my way out of the city would be hard enough, and I had no idea where to go from there. And for all I knew, this demon would just follow me wherever I went. There was no way to tell if it was attached to the castle or to me. I knew there were certain types of stones that could be used as a magical focus to protect an area from evil, but I obviously didn't have anything with me and I couldn't think of a natural way to ask for them.

Luckily, when Abigail brought my breakfast in the morning, I noticed a small bowl of salt on the tray next to the food. It wasn't nearly as effective as other things, but it at least would provide some sort of protection. While she picked out my dress for the day, I took it from the tray and slipped it into the top drawer of my nightstand so I could line my room with it later that evening.

To my relief, the visitations stopped. I still didn't feel confident enough in my defenses to attempt to leave my body again, but at least I was able to sleep through the night. As the days went on, I made it a habit to regularly refresh my supply of salt from my breakfast trays, not wanting to take any chances that the demon would come back and catch me off guard.

I fell into a reluctant routine at the castle. My lessons with Miss Grayson were by no means horrible—they were complete and utter torture. Everything I was required to do was either dim-wittingly simple or absolutely absurd, and I had to prove I could do it over and over again. I wasn't given any freedom. Even when I wasn't in that dreadful room, the maids and butlers monitored my actions and reported to Miss Grayson.

The one positive thing about the lessons was walking to and from them with Abigail. She was charming, lighthearted, and my same age. I learned about two weeks after I arrived that her surprise at my outburst that first day came from the fact that no one aside from other servants had asked her name before.

"How long have you been a maid, Abigail?" I asked.

"About three years."

I raised my eyebrows. "And no one's asked your name before?"

"As long as the job gets done, it doesn't matter who does it, M'Lady. If someone knows your name, it's usually because you've made a mistake."

My nose wrinkled in disgust. "Why do you work here?"

Her face fell. "My mum died when I was young, and my dad was killed by a sorcerer when the Great War first started. I have three younger brothers, M'Lady. We had no way to support ourselves, so I came here so they wouldn't have to live on the streets. People aren't always friendly, but it's good work and pays well. I send all my earnings to my brothers."

I stared down at the expensive carpet beneath my feet. I'd always lived in a society where, instead of money, we shared our talents and provisions with others in return for theirs. I couldn't imagine having to sacrifice as Abigail had.

We arrived at Miss Grayson's door, and Abigail left in polite silence. Sighing, I lightly tapped on the door. Ladies didn't *knock*, but they didn't just open doors either. When Miss Grayson first said that, I almost asked if I was supposed to wait at the door and hope someone inside sensed my presence. I thought better of it.

She opened the door, her lips pursed as always, and curtsied in greeting. I did the same, making sure my eyes didn't leave hers. The only person whose eyes you avoid is the king, since everyone else should feel you are either superior or equal to them.

"Your curtsy is too low," she criticized as I straightened. "And you rose too quickly."

I attempted the feat once more and, though she was still unsatisfied, I apparently improved enough to be let into the room. The door slammed behind me, something I thought very unladylike, but which Miss Grayson persisted to do each and every morning. I felt that way about a lot of things she said and did, but what would be the point of contesting them? Even if the customs didn't make sense to me, this wasn't my society, and whether I liked it or not, she was the one the king had chosen to teach me the ways of the court.

So I was subject to Miss Grayson's lessons about dining etiquette, how to walk around different people, how to speak when in the presence of royalty versus knights, how to give orders to servants—all things that were completely useless. I thought that at least learning about history might be interesting, but all she wanted me to do was memorize the names of the kings. If I asked questions about events in the kingdom's history, they were dismissed.

The only lessons I didn't seem to be utterly failing were reading and writing. Miss Grayson seemed surprised that I knew how to read and write at all and kept trying to catch me copying something she'd written rather than coming up with the words on my own. It was one of the skills Elizabeth had taught me when I was young, and I realized now that I had been taking it for granted. Apparently, in Ungifted society it wasn't common at all for women to learn to read and write unless they were from wealthy or noble families. Still, if Mrs. Grayson was impressed, she didn't let it show, instead focusing on criticizing my handwriting and insisting I practice calligraphy for an hour or more each day.

Miss Grayson's harshness wasn't the only reason I didn't enjoy being locked up in the castle. From the king's perspective, I had more freedom than half the kingdom. From mine, I had little more than a prisoner. Every second of my day was scheduled for me, and I was obliged to follow that schedule if I wanted to avoid suspicion.

It was a huge relief when Abigail informed me one morning that Miss Grayson was feeling ill and I didn't have any lessons to attend. Instead, Isaiah and I took the opportunity to spend some time together in the gardens. We obviously had to be careful about what we talked about in public, but given the fact that everyone believed he was my uncle, it wasn't hard for him to find ways to tell me stories about him and my mother. He didn't mention her magic, of course, but instead talked about how she helped her uncle around their farm, how she laughed at the smallest things, and how she was always looking for ways to help those in need. It was clear how much he loved and missed her, and I resolved that if I ever had access to summoning candles again, I would find a way for them to see each other once more, however briefly.

A thought occurred to me as we left the gardens just before dinner, and I slowed my pace and lowered my voice.

"What if we left?" I asked. "We could search for my clan, or another..."

Isaiah sighed, his lips tightening into a frown. "I don't think that's a good idea, Kenna."

"Why not? Why would you want to stay?"

"You're safe here," he said, stopping and putting a hand on my shoulder. "Out there, you'd just be running again until your people were inevitably found."

"But what if someone finds out the truth here?" I whispered. "Isn't that even more dangerous?"

"As long as you're not careless, no one will find out," he insisted.

I opened my mouth to respond, but held my thoughts as hurried steps approached from the front entrance of the castle. A young man ran around the corner, stopping when he saw us.

"Sir Balton," he panted, bowing sloppily. "Excuse me, Sir, but your presence is requested in the council room."

My father raised his eyebrows. "By whom?"

"His Majesty the king, Sir."

My father and I exchanged glances. He hurried after the servant as I heard running from the other direction. Abigail ran straight for me. She stopped and curtsied deeply, looking at the floor and not my eyes, before speaking.

"I am to prepare you for dinner with the king, M'Lady," she said.

I nodded, and we rushed up the stairs. I couldn't imagine why the king summoned Isaiah to the council room, but my being prepared to meet him wasn't a surprise. There had been much talk over the past few days of the king's returning and that a banquet would be held in his honor. Since I lived in the castle as a member of the court, I knew I would be attending whether I wanted to or not.

Abigail opened the door to my wardrobe and stepped to the side. "Which one would you like to wear, M'Lady?"

I finally cracked. "Would you please stop calling me that?"

She blinked. "What do you mean?"

"My name is Kenna," I said. "I understand you're being respectful, but it's ridiculous. I'm not a noble. I'm just a girl the king took pity on. I don't want you to avert your eyes when you curtsy to me, and I don't want you to call me by any silly titles. We're equals, Abigail."

She blinked again, and a smile slowly formed on the edges of her lips. "If Miss Grayson heard you say that, she would refuse to teach you."

I smirked. "Then maybe I should say it again tomorrow."

My smirk turned into a grin when she started laughing. There had been many times when I could tell she was about to laugh, but she always suppressed the impulse. To see her let down her guard was comforting, and I felt the first real sense of happiness I had since I learned Isaiah was my father.

"All right then, Kenna," she said when she gained control of her laughter. "Which dress would you like to wear to the banquet?"

I shrugged. "Why don't you pick, Abi?"

Her eyes lit up at the nickname, and she spun to face the dresses, biting her lip. Eyes shining, she snatched a deep red gown with beautiful floral designs on the bodice and held it up to me. "You'll look wonderful in this color."

I couldn't help but smile. Usually getting dressed in the uncomfortable clothing I was expected to wear was a chore, but for once, I actually enjoyed the process. There was plenty of laughter involved, and Abi even asked for my opinion on my hair. For the first time since I'd arrived at the castle, I was able to wear it down, even though according to Miss Grayson this was a sign of someone who was uneducated and simple. Personally, I thought my hair looked better when it was left to fall mostly at its own will, with maybe a few curls pinned up to make it look more refined. Abi agreed.

Besides, I was tired of doing everything Miss Grayson told me to do. I didn't belong to her society, so why should I follow her rules? Most of them were ridiculous anyway. And if the king thought I was unable to master being a lady, he might dismiss me from the castle, leaving me free to go wherever I wished without any suspicion. It had become more and more clear as I'd spent time here in the castle that my initial plan of trying to take things down from the inside wasn't one I was actually capable of carrying out, but I also knew I couldn't exactly just leave now that the king had extended his welcome to me. But by rebelling in small ways, such as leaving my hair down and showing up late to gatherings, I could make him less inclined to keep me here as part of his household.

As Abi finished fussing with my hair, the golden idea struck me. If I disrespected him directly, I would no doubt be dismissed from the castle. All it would take was some eye contact as I curtsied—a simple statement that I didn't consider myself inferior to him. It would be so easy, and within the week I would be free.

I followed Abi to the dining room. The doors were wide open when we arrived. She bid me goodnight, leaving me to the care of my guardian and the king. The dining table had been temporarily moved for dancing prior to the meal, and a small group of musicians sat at the end of the hall playing lively music. Isaiah was already present, as were all the king's captains. I recognized Captain Stole, but his countenance appeared quite a bit older than at breakfast a month ago. On the other side of the hall, Lewin stood in a corner, but he didn't seem as dreary as usual. In fact, I thought I saw some twisted happiness in his eyes, and I shivered.

The room was also full of people I had not seen at my initial breakfast in the castle. Clearly, local nobility had been invited to join the captains and king in celebrating their return. There were a number of young women mingling among the knights, all of them dressed in fine fabric with corset bodices so tight that I was surprised they could breathe. There were a variety of hairstyles represented, some of them looking ridiculous to me with the way their hair was piled on top of their heads, but notably none of them were left down as mine was. They also seemed to be wearing heavy makeup, some of them with skin so powdered that they almost looked like statues.

Suddenly, a loud voice interrupted my thoughts.

"Lady Kenna Balton!"

I jumped as the servant announced my arrival. All eyes turned in my direction, and many of them filled with surprise. Even my father couldn't help but stare at my hair, knowing how out of place the style was.

The king approached from where he'd been mingling with some of the nobles. Like when I'd first met him, I was surprised by his kind and welcoming countenance. The story of how he lost his parents returned to my mind, and once again I felt a kinship and understanding as I thought of my own experiences.

I found myself studying his face, searching for any sign of the monster that still lived in my mind. Instead, I was struck by how young he was, and how handsome. For this banquet, he wore his dark blonde hair down instead of pulled back, the slight waves perfectly framing his clean-shaven face and strong square jaw. His dark blue eyes held a softness within them that didn't match what one would expect from the regal and imposing presence of the king. As I stared into those eyes, I didn't feel like I was in the presence of royalty or a threat. In fact, they reminded me of Gideon's eyes.

When he reached me, I forced those thoughts aside. Remembering my earlier decision, I lowered myself into a deep curtsy, but I kept my eyes locked on his. I saw a flash of shock in his blue eyes, but his face remained impassive. A strange sensation went through my body as I straightened, but I didn't break eye contact.

Whispers echoed across the room—the act of defiance had certainly been noted. And yet, he didn't seem angry or frustrated. In fact, I thought I saw a smile on his lips. My mind filled with confusion as I tried to discern what he was thinking, and for some reason I felt like it was a little harder to breathe.

The musicians ended their song and moved on to the next. The captains, noblemen, and ladies resumed their conversations. A few couples moved toward the center of the room, and I realized they were about to start one of the kingdom's most popular dances, one that Miss Grayson had taught me just the day before. As the dancers formed their position, King Kiernan held out his hand.

"May I have this dance?"

I felt a tightening in my chest. Nervousness?

"I would be honored," I breathed.

He smiled. The tightening in my chest intensified. His fingers intertwined with mine and he led me onto the dance floor. Already, I felt like I was tripping over my feet. A slight shiver ran down my spine as he placed his other hand on the small of my back. My eyes remained locked on his. As we danced, we hardly broke eye contact for more than a few seconds.

When the music ended, he bowed and I curtsied. Again, I did not avert my eyes. He took my left hand and kissed it before escorting me to Isaiah's side. The next dance began, and he returned to the dance floor with a new dance partner, a very thin blonde woman who had a long face. Her small, narrow eyes glanced towards me briefly before they began to dance

"You made quite an entrance," my father muttered, making sure no one else could overhear us.

I noticed with alarm that I was still staring in the king's direction and tore my eyes away.

"What do you mean?"

"You know exactly what I mean," he said, an edge to his voice. "That was very dangerous, Kenna."

Not as dangerous as it should have been. My eyes wandered back to the king. Why had he not been more offended by my actions? Everyone else in the room obviously did not approve, but he had immediately asked me to dance. It didn't feel like a challenge as we maintained eye contact—I almost felt he agreed that I was no less than him. I shook my head at myself. He was the king, and had been taught his entire life he was superior to all those around him.

So why hadn't he reacted?

After two more dances (neither of which I was asked to participate in) the king clapped his hands. Servants entered the hall, quickly setting up the banquet. I took a seat next to Isaiah on the left side of the table, tensing when Lewin sat directly across from me. The socializing continued as wine was brought to each guest. When everyone's glasses were full, King Kiernan stood, causing immediate silence.

"Today is a day to be celebrated," he said, raising his glass. "For today marks our return from a very successful mission."

There was a rounding "Huzzah!" from the captains, but he motioned for silence with his free hand. "As you are all aware, for the past month I have been traveling with the best of my knights through Fain and Hairan. I am delighted to tell you all that we were successful in finding and destroying four encampments of witches, from which no one escaped."

There was applause from the women at the table and the men again sounded a cheer. My heart sank to the bottom of my stomach. Isaiah squeezed my hand under the table, but it didn't calm my nerves.

Just moments ago I'd been unable to take my eyes off of him, almost admiring him. How could I have lost sight of what he really was? How could I have forgotten what this man was doing to my people?

What if they found the Grisons? Were Neal and Gideon dead? My mind flashed back to the dream I had my first night in the castle. I fought back tears.

The captains shared their stories from the conquest, as did the king himself. I closed my eyes tightly and willed my body not to shake with agony and anger as they made toast after toast, their laughter filling the air. After what felt like hours of torture, the king stood, jerking me from my thoughts. The rest of the table also stood out of respect. I was the slowest to my feet, but I don't think anyone noticed my hesitation.

"Thank you all for coming!" he said, laughter in his voice and joy in his eyes. "I hope we have many similar celebrations in the future. Good night!"

The men bowed and the women curtsied before dispersing. Isaiah and I were two of the last people to leave aside from the king and his captain of the guard. Both sets of eyes followed me as I left. A deep sigh of relief escaped my lips when the doors closed behind me.

We walked in silence to my room. I was about to enter without a word, but I felt Isaiah's strong hand on my shoulder and turned to face him instead.

"Be careful, Kenna," he said after a moment, a troubled frown on his face. "With how you behave around the king and with your emotions."

"So I'm supposed to pretend I didn't just hear that four clans were murdered?" I whispered, my voice cracking.

"Yes," he said grimly. "I know it's difficult, and likely even feels impossible, but you must play the part to remain safe." His hand tightened on my shoulder. "I can't bear the thought of losing you again."

Then we should leave, I thought to myself, but the knot in my throat was so tight that I couldn't form the words. Isaiah's frown deepened as I turned away from him and shut my door between us.

I tried unsuccessfully to distract myself by going through my nightly routine of replenishing the salt protecting the room, but soon I was sobbing. My body shook as I collapsed on the bed, not bothering to undress, burying my face in the pillow. It felt like hours before I managed to drift off to sleep.

CHAPTER FOURTEEN

A PRIVATE AUDIENCE

I squinted as light flooded into my room, trying to remember the dream I'd been having. I could just hold on to the memory of Neal smiling at me, and the sound of children's laughter in the background. Everything felt so peaceful...

"Rise and shine, Kenna!"

I grumbled at Abi's voice and forced myself to sit up, blinking furiously. "What time of day is it?" I yawned.

"Almost noon," she said, placing my breakfast tray on the bed and sitting next to it. I smiled a bit. It was nice to see her more relaxed around me and less formal.

"Shouldn't I be in lessons then?" I asked, starting to eat.

"The king canceled them for the day. He would like to have lunch with you."

I almost choked on my eggs. "Even after last night?"

"Even after last night."

I stared at her. Something in the way that she repeated my words told me that she knew about my subtle act of defiance at the banquet. I supposed I shouldn't have been too surprised that the servants would spread gossip. Part of me expected her to be angry or disappointed in me, but instead, I thought I saw an amused glint in her eyes.

Abi urged me to stand and prepare for the day before I'd even finished my food. At random, I picked out a deep blue dress with gold accents, which Abi liked well enough, but instead of letting me leave my hair down, she braided it loosely in the back. "At least it's considered done up that way," she said when I complained, a teasing edge to her tone.

When she finished, I followed her out of the room reluctantly. I quickly realized we were walking through the same halls we took to Miss Grayson's lessons.

"Why aren't we going to the dining hall, Abi?" I asked

"You're dining with the king alone. In his quarters."

I almost stopped dead in my tracks. "What did you say?"

"You heard me the first time," she said, winking.

My mind raced. Maybe my plan had worked after all—maybe he just wanted to tell me in person that I was being dismissed from the castle. What else could it be? He couldn't have discovered the truth about my magic.

Could he?

We turned a familiar corner into the hallway where I had my lessons each day. I opened my mouth to tell Abi she must have taken a wrong turn, but I closed it just as quickly. We were headed directly for the ornate, imposing doors I'd stared at so often, wondering what lay behind them. I should've known an entrance of that magnitude could only be reserved for royalty. I'd been walking past the king's rooms every day for the past month and hadn't realized it.

Abi knocked on the impressive doors. I stood back, surprised at my nervousness. What did I have been nervous about? Plenty if he did know my secret, of course, but this felt—different. It almost reminded me of when Neal would put his arm around me, which didn't make any sense. I felt suddenly sick, and I was grateful Abi pulled my hair back.

The doors opened, revealing one of the king's personal servants. He nodded to Abi. She turned and curtsied to me, purposely averting her eyes from mine. When our eyes did meet, I could tell she was, again, teasing. Her friendly behavior did little to ease the growing panic I felt as she turned the corner and disappeared from view.

The servant bowed deeply. "If you will follow me, Lady Kenna."

Cautiously, I stepped through the doorway. My heart dropped as the doors closed behind me. If I thought I felt out of place in the rest of the castle, it was nothing compared to the king's rooms. We stood in an open sitting room, obviously seldom used, furnished with real wood from the mainland kingdoms and rich, bright fabrics the likes of which I'd never seen. There was a feminine touch to the decor that made me think his mother must have spent a lot of time here before she died. It reminded me of what he'd been through, and I again pitied him, whether or not I should.

The servant turned to the left. I followed him, dazed. Another pair of doors loomed in front of us, though hardly as foreboding as the main entrance. He opened it to reveal a small dining area. A beautiful chandelier hung from the high ceiling, and light poured in from the large windows on one side of the room, framed by blue floor length curtains.

The king sat at the far end of a small circular table, taking a long sip from his wine glass. He stood as we entered. The servant opened his mouth to introduce me, but King Kiernan held up his hand, and the servant bowed respectfully before backing out the door, closing it behind him.

We were alone.

The king crossed to my side, taking my right hand in his and kissing it. He very deliberately did not break eye contact with me, and a shiver ran down my spine. His gaze was not harsh or judgmental—it was almost inquisitive.

"Thank you for joining me," he said as he straightened. "I hope you're hungry."

I thought of the eggs I'd eaten before Abi told me I was coming here. "Starved," I said. My eyes slipped from his for just a second. His lips curved upwards as he caught my lie, but he didn't say anything.

He guided me to my seat. As he did, he kept hold of the hand he'd kissed, only releasing it to pull back my chair. When I was seated—however awkwardly—he sat as well, clapping his hands once. A second servant entered from a side door, carrying two plates of salad and setting them in front of us.

We sat in silence. On the opposite side of the table, my host ate very little, staring at me with curious eyes, as if he was searching for something. Even though I told myself over and over again that I didn't care what he thought, I followed everything Miss Grayson had taught me. I even attempted holding the fork 'properly,' but gave up when my fingers fumbled and it fell for the third time. My eyes flickered upwards to meet his, and my cheeks burned when I read his amusement. I probably ate quicker than I should have, but with my mouth full at least I didn't have to make conversation. I'm sure a shaky voice would have betrayed my nerves. King Kiernan seemed content in the silence, anyway.

When I finished, he summoned a servant, his own salad hardly touched. My plate was cleared and a platter of seafood was placed in front of me. My eyes recognized the clam, oyster, and octopus, but my taste buds didn't. Though I'd had several meals in the castle, this food was on a different level. I'd never tasted spices quite like these, and I raised my eyebrows in surprise. It was delicious. I did not attempt the 'proper' fork placement again—he certainly would have laughed at me if I did.

Once my plate was empty, he clapped his hands again and a servant instantly cleared the table. I remained seated, shifting my gaze to the table-cloth and studying the lace pattern intently as I felt his eyes remain on me. He leaned back in his chair for a moment before speaking.

"Would you like a tour of the castle?"

I don't know what I expected, but it hadn't been that.

"I would love it, Your Majesty," I stammered.

"There's no need to use that formality with me, Kenna," he said, standing and circling the table to stand at my side. "Just Kiernan is fine."

Our eyes locked once more. My mouth felt suddenly dry.

"Very well...Kiernan," I said.

His blue eyes shone. "Shall we, then?"

I stood, and he led me out of his quarters into the hallway. "I expect you're already familiar with the kitchens and the dining halls," he said. "Have you been in either of the courts yet?"

"No, I haven't."

"Then we must make a stop there. You've been in the library by now, haven't you?"

I shook my head. "Any books I need for my lessons Miss Grayson brings to me."

He raised his eyebrows. "Have you not done any exploring on your own?"

My cheeks burned. "Honestly, I didn't feel it was my place to go wandering around your home."

"Consider it yours as well," he said quickly. "I didn't bring you here to imprison you, Kenna."

He seemed to think what he'd said was amusing, and I did my best to smile in response. Strangely, I felt he was being completely sincere.

"Thank you, Kiernan," I said, surprised to hear the sincerity in my own voice.

"We'll start at the library, then. Do you enjoy reading?"

"I haven't had much opportunity to read for pleasure," I admitted. "I didn't have access to many books in my youth, and Miss Grayson doesn't really seem to value it in our lessons. But I've always enjoyed listening to stories."

"Well, I'll be certain to tell Miss Grayson to give you time to explore our collection. There is much literature I'm certain you would enjoy," he said enthusiastically. "I spent all my time as a boy in the library. My mother was too busy to entertain me herself, and my father—well, he was ruling the kingdom. But I rather enjoyed my time with those books."

As he mentioned his parents, his hand clenched by his side, and I felt the strange urge to comfort him. After a few minutes of searching for something to say, I finally sighed, deciding just to tell the truth.

"I never knew my parents," I said. "Isaiah's told me some stories, but ... obviously, it's not the same. I don't entirely know how to fill that empty space."

He slowed his pace and turned to face me. As his eyes traced my face, he gently took one of my hands in his.

"Maybe we can figure it out together," he said.

My cheeks burned a bit more, a sudden knot in my throat keeping me from giving a clear response. He released my hand almost as soon as he'd taken it, silently resuming our journey to the library.

As we entered, my mouth fell open in awe. There were more books shelved in that room than I could count, and books were hard to come by. Kiernan stood back, a smile on his face, as I wandered, gingerly touching their leather spines with my fingertips. Even not knowing what they contained, I felt the urge to pick one at random and start reading until I'd finished the entire collection.

Kiernan showed me his favorite sections, pointing out where the history and legends of the kingdom were kept. I had to admit I was curious about what the Ungifted believed about the origins of their kingdom, so I made a mental note of where it was. To my surprise, he also showed me the children's section, picking up one of the books fondly as he did to straighten it on the shelf. "It's a great place to get lost and wander," he said, his voice more wistful than I would have expected from a king.

We tore ourselves away from the bookcases and Kiernan led me down the stairs toward the main entryway. I'd walked past here a few times since arriving at the castle, but my eyes were always drawn upwards to the doors into the upper court. I'd never taken the time to notice the doors to the lower court on the ground level.

We didn't spend much time there—a simple throne sat at the end of the room and posts stood along the wall where guards were stationed. There were no seats or benches, but those who wished to attend the trials of lower-level criminals could stand behind the ropes separating Kiernan from the people. "Unfortunately the guards are necessary," he said with a wry laugh. "People often grow impatient."

From there, we climbed the magnificent front steps to the throne room. This room doubled as the upper court, for holding trials for nobles or those guilty of higher crimes such as murder or treason. This was probably where my mother was sentenced to death. I quickly pushed the thought out of my mind.

"What do you think?" Kiernan asked.

"It's breathtaking," I said, staring at the stained glass behind the throne. "It's a pity its purpose is so dismal."

He shrugged. "It's not always dismal. Occasionally I hold balls in here—I haven't for quite some time, but I'm hoping to again soon."

He paused for a moment, looking like he might be about to say more, but seemed to think better of it and simply smiled instead.

"Now I'd like to show you my favorite place in the entire castle," he said, a youthful glimmer in his eyes. He held out his arm invitingly. I draped mine through it, feeling the same tightness in my chest as the night before.

We left the throne room by a hidden side door, leading into a dark hallway. Kiernan took a torch off the wall and held it in front of us. The walls around us were hardly worn, as if this secret passage had been created recently. It occurred to me that it likely had been because of how Kiernan's parents met their end. If that was the case, I was shocked he would reveal it to me.

When we reached the end of the passage, a plain looking door opened to reveal the same sitting room we'd passed through in Kiernan's quarters. He again led me out of his rooms and we headed in the direction of mine. Instead of continuing on the familiar hallway, however, Kiernan veered to the left, going through a door that led outside.

We stood on a pathway to one of the watchtowers, the beautiful castle gardens below us to the right and the majestic cliffs to the left. I slowly spun to take in the whole sight. I'd spent some time in the gardens, and they were admittedly very beautiful, but seeing them from above was breathtaking. There were so many different colors blooming even in the cold air, and every bush was meticulously pruned.

The cliffs were equally as distracting. I could hear the sound of the water crashing against the rocks and smell the salt in the cold sea breeze. The magnificent cliff range seemed endless. Directly in front of us, though I couldn't see the actual cliffs, I could still see the sea beyond, extending into the horizon. Since I was safely on land, I didn't feel the same panic I'd felt seeing that endless expanse on the knight's ship, and instead was able to appreciate the beauty of it. As the wind blew through my hair, I closed my eyes.

"What do you think?" he whispered.

"It's amazing up here," I sighed. "It's so peaceful."

"It's a wonderful place to come and think." His right hand took a hold of my left, awakening my skin. "No one bothers you, and everywhere you look there's something beautiful."

I opened my eyes to find that he was once again studying my face. The uncomfortable tightness in my chest intensified in that instant. I took a small step back, releasing his hand. My cheeks burned, and I turned to face the gardens. As I stared down at them, my mind wandered to Neal again for some reason, and a stabbing pain struck my heart.

Kiernan placed a hand on my shoulder. I was torn between feeling comforted and running away. In the end I simply turned to look at him. His smile faltered at the melancholy expression on my face. He opened his mouth to speak, but I forced the best smile I could, trying to act like everything was fine. Thankfully he didn't press the subject.

"I have something for you," he said after a moment.

He pulled out a small box from one of his inside pockets and extended it to me. I accepted it, eyeing him curiously as I took off the lid. When I saw what was inside, my eyes widened.

"Do you like it?"

"It's gorgeous," I muttered. Inside, a beautiful ruby necklace glimmered in the midday sun. The chain was made out of pure gold, and the casing was simple yet elegant, wrapping across the gem in a curled design.

Kiernan took the box from my hands. "Turn around."

I did as he asked. He fastened the beautiful jewel around my neck, his fingers brushing against my skin. My hand automatically reached up to feel the gem, to make sure I wasn't dreaming. I slowly turned to face him, dropping my hand to my side so he could see what he'd given me.

His smile widened. "I knew it would look beautiful on you."

"Where did you get this?" I breathed, barely able to form the words.

"When we were traveling to the other islands," he said, pleased that I liked it so much. "I picked it up in one of the camps we found."

All the happiness on my face disappeared. I felt as if I were going to vomit. Kiernan's smile faded.

"Did I say something wrong?"

"No."

My voice shook unconvincingly. He would just as readily take this necklace off of my dead body and give it to someone else if he knew what I was. How could I have been so *stupid*?

"Are you all right?" he pressed.

"I'm actually quite tired," I lied, avoiding his gaze. "I didn't sleep very well last night."

He opened his mouth to say something else, but seemed to think better of it and nodded. "I'll take you to your room then."

We re-entered the castle, the darkness a stark contrast to the sunlight we'd been enjoying. The walk to my room was completely silent. I tried to act natural, but it was impossible with the feeling of the cold metal of the necklace against my skin.

"Is there anything I can do for you?" he asked when we reached my door.

"No," I murmured. His face seemed to fall and, despite my horror and hatred, I managed to say politely, "Thank you for the gift."

"You're welcome."

Before he could say or do anything else, I curtsied half-heartedly, entering my room and shutting the door between us. He was still for a few moments, and only when I was certain the sound of his footsteps had reached the end of the hall did I move away from the door. Shakily, I reached behind my neck and I attempted to unclasp the necklace, silent tears fighting to escape my eyes. When I finally unfastened it, I laid the piece of jewelry carefully on my desk. I couldn't give it back to the sister who lost it, but in honor of her, I would never wear it again.

What hurt most wasn't that I'd been given something that once belonged to a sister—it was the fact that I'd found myself befriending and caring for her murderer. I still had trouble believing he could cause all of this, but the evidence couldn't be denied any longer. He readily admitted to the crimes he committed against my people, and he even seemed proud of them.

Surprisingly, my tears were not just for those he'd slain, but him as well. I didn't understand how I could feel like I had so much in common with him—this man who killed simply because he didn't understand. I wanted so badly to embrace the good in him that I had seen, but ultimately, his objective was to destroy all magic and any who held it in the kingdom.

And that included me.

CHAPTER FIFTEEN

OPEN EYES

I sat on the edge of my bed for what must have been hours, staring out the window. My thoughts wandered far away, searching the surrounding islands for Gideon and Neal, and I almost broke the rule I'd made for myself not to risk separating from my body again. Once more I contemplated simply leaving, but the image of Kiernan's smile and the sparkle in his eyes when he looked at me replaced the thought no matter how hard I tried to push it away. It was hard to remind myself I couldn't trust him.

As the sun set, Abi knocked softly on my door and entered. I sent her a weak smile, but she wasn't fooled.

"What happened?" she said as she closed the door. "What did he want?"

"Nothing. He just gave me a tour of the castle."

She blinked. "Did you talk about anything?"

I sighed. "Nothing in particular. He just wanted to make me feel at home."

"Are you sure he *just* wanted to make you feel at home?" Her eyes widened as she picked up the ruby necklace from my desk.

I averted my eyes. "It's just a necklace."

Seeing the expression on my face, Abi slowly set down the beautiful object, her eyebrows pressed together. She bit her lip when I remained silent, probably trying to think of a way to cheer me up.

"Well, you haven't seen the best part of the castle yet," she said after a moment, her voice turning mischievous as she took my hands in hers.

I raised an eyebrow. "You know the castle better than the king?"

"I know this castle better than anyone alive." She winked, pulling me to my feet. "When you're a lady in waiting without a lady to serve, you have a lot of free time on your hands. I've used mine to explore every nook and cranny I could."

She could tell I was skeptical, but her smile only widened. "Come on," she said, lowering her voice. "Everyone else is at dinner, so we won't be missed. The king thinks you retired for the night."

Curious, I let her lead me from the room. She checked that the hallway was deserted before motioning for me to follow. We turned left down the hall, away from the dining area and toward the castle entrance, checking around corners. Just as I was about to ask where we were going, she stopped and leaned her shoulder against the stone wall. A secret door opened quietly, and she smiled at my surprise.

"Get in," she urged excitedly. I could tell she'd never shared her knowledge of this door with anyone, and she enjoyed seeing my reaction. I stepped forward, but hesitated.

"How will we see?" I said, ashamed to hear the fear in my voice. It was silly to be afraid of the dark, but there was—or at least had been—a demon somewhere in the castle, after all. While they weren't forced to stay in darkness, it certainly seemed like the darkness gave them some amount of power. Otherwise, why would it only have appeared at night?

Her face softened even though she didn't know the real source of my fear, and she touched my shoulder. "There's a torch just a little ways down. I try to keep them lit."

"Them?" I asked, stepping through the doorway cautiously. There was indeed a light a ways down the hall, but I still felt uneasy. My uneasiness grew when she closed the door behind us, and I briefly closed my eyes and reached out with my magic in an attempt to sense anything else in here with us. I was relieved when I didn't and tried to force my tight shoulders to relax.

"These passageways are all over the castle," Abi explained, taking my hand and leading me forward. "They haven't been used for years, but when

I found them I went ahead and lit them. The torches burn for a while, and since I use them almost every day—"

"Every day?" I asked, surprised.

"It makes it much easier and quicker to get around," she said, then winked at me. "There are also a few places where you can look out into the hallways and rooms...to watch a dramatic entrance at a banquet, for instance."

I raised an eyebrow and laughed unexpectedly. "You were *spying* on me?"

"Not spying! Just—observing," she said with a smirk.

I shook my head, still chuckling. "So they go to the dining hall...where else do they lead?"

"All over. Where would you like to go?"

I thought about it as she took the first torch off the wall. "How about the library?"

"Right this way, M'Lady," she said, curtsying to me. We both chuckled, though we did our best to keep our voices down in case someone heard us through the walls.

Since I grew up separate from other children, I didn't know what it was like to be a curious young girl, but I imagine I felt like a young girl that night. Abi and I never even made it to the library—I kept changing direction on her, determined to get lost somehow, but she knew her way around too well. When we were too tired to continue, we carefully left the tunnels and stepped out into the main hallways, still giggling. When we reached my room, Abi suddenly pulled me into a tight hug.

"I had fun with you tonight, Kenna," she said into my shoulder.

"I had fun with you too," I replied.

In her friendly embrace, I realized how much she felt like a sister to me. If I stayed here, there would inevitably come a time when I would have to tell her what I really was. The thought made my stomach turn over with nerves, but I suppressed it for the moment.

When she backed away, we both curtsied to each other, suppressing giggles. But once I was alone in my room, I let out a heavy sigh before changing, reapplying my salt, and climbing into bed. Even as I lay there with my eyes closed, I couldn't rest. At first I worried again that the demonic presence had returned, but every time I sat up to look there was no sign of it, and I couldn't sense it when I reached out with my gift.

After a couple sleepless hours, I finally stood, frustrated, and lit my candle, drawing an overcoat over myself. I didn't know where I was going to go, but I knew I had to walk around if I ever hoped to get to sleep.

The halls were empty, as expected in the middle of the night. I wandered for a few minutes before deciding to go to the library. With all those books, there would certainly be something to distract me. Part of me wished I'd let Abi actually show me the way in the secret passages earlier that evening, but as much fun as I'd had with her, the thought of trying to navigate them alone was alarming. It was much easier to take the route Kiernan had shown me.

It still took me some time to find it, since I'd only been there once. When I entered, my eyes roamed the shelves in the dim candlelight, searching for a place to start.

I eventually made my way towards the history section. Kneeling close to the ground, I noticed a book sticking out, the pages tattered. It looked like it would fall apart in my hands, but I gingerly removed it from the shelf anyway. Though its pages were covered in dust, the faded writing was still legible. I sat down in one of the chairs and placed the candle on the table to my right, settling in to read.

As soon as I started, I almost stood up again. *I can't have read that right.* My heart pounding, I reread the first sentence over and over again until I couldn't dispute what it said:

'A record of Hanson the sorcerer, written by his wife, Kindra.'

There was no denying what it said. But this couldn't *possibly* be Kindra's lost record! How could I be holding her original writings in my hands, and in the castle no less? Even if it had been held here by kings long ago, why and how wouldn't it have been destroyed with every other magical item the knights got their hands on when the Slaughters started?

Before I had time to read anymore, the main door to the library opened with an echoing creak. Quickly, I tucked the book into my robe under my arm. The door closed, and a shadow turned the corners of the bookcases. Even though I knew they didn't need doors, my imagination immediately jumped to the demon that was haunting me. My hand shook as I snatched the candle from the table and spun towards the approaching shadow, lifting my other hand as I had towards the creature in my room weeks ago.

"Kenna?"

It was Kiernan's voice. He stepped into the light, and I set my candle down with a heavy breath, relief washing over me.

"Are you alright? What are you doing here by yourself?"

"I could ask you the same question."

He sighed. "I couldn't sleep. Reading always helps."

"I had the same idea," I admitted.

"But you don't have a book with you," he observed, looking at the table.

"I haven't picked one yet," I lied. "I didn't know where to start."

He smiled. "Then let me pick for you. Do you mind?"

I shook my head. He approached one of the nearby bookshelves, one of the ones in the children's section he'd shown me earlier. While his back was turned, I quickly tucked Kindra's book a bit more securely under my arm. Kiernan found the book he was looking for effortlessly in the darkness and returned to my side, flipping through the pages until he found what he wanted. With another smile, he handed it to me, pointing to the start.

"It's the story of the Mother of the Sea," he said. "A children's tale, really, but one of my favorites. It tells of her constant struggle against the Father of Storms, and how she would avenge the sailors' lives that he took. When I was younger I always wished I could control the sea or sky—until I saw what power like that actually does."

His face fell, and he was serious once again. "But you can read this in your room, can't you? I don't want you wandering around yourself when it's so late."

I stared at him, his words echoing in my mind. Maybe he didn't want the death of magic after all. Maybe he was just scared of the damage bad people could cause with incredible power. If I could open his eyes, if I could show him that not all Gifted used their powers for evil ...

He took a step closer to see me better in the dim light. "Kenna, what's troubling you?"

"Nothing," I said quietly, my eyes locked on his. For a moment we just stared at each other. And despite my racing thoughts, I felt surprisingly calm.

I can show him there is good in magic.

"Let me walk you to your room," he said.

I hesitated, feeling Kindra's book slip a bit under my arm. "I'm fine. I'd like to sit here and read a while, if you don't mind."

He hesitated, but nodded. "Of course. As I said earlier, I want you to consider my home your home."

There was another pause between us. He looked as if he was going to say more, but when he spoke he simply said, "Good night, Kenna."

"Good night, Kiernan," I replied. With a warm smile, he picked up a book for himself and left. I didn't move until the library doors had shut, leaving me alone in my thoughts with Kindra's book pressed against my side.

After some indecision, I returned to my room, bringing my find with me. It wouldn't be missed from the collection, and I didn't want anyone else to discover it. I couldn't bear the thought of this record being destroyed, and I vowed to prevent such a tragedy from happening.

Of course, I didn't just want to protect it—I wanted to study it.

But now was not the time to start. By the time I had reached my quarters, the hour of night had caught up to me. I sighed as I hid the treasure under my bed and laid down, quickly drifting off into a dreamless sleep.

***

I awoke to a knock on my door, as I always did when I had lessons. I turned away from the window, expecting Abi to come in and open it as she usually did, letting in the sun. After a few moments, however, another knock sounded. Slowly, I got out of bed and pulled a robe over my nightgown. Abi never waited for me to actually get out of bed and open the door.

In the hallway stood a maid with cat-like eyes, a little shorter than Abi, dressed in a higher-ranking uniform. She curtsied low to the ground, ignoring the surprise on my face.

"Good morning, Lady Kenna. My name is Marinda. I am your new maid."

I blinked. "My what?"

"Your new maid," she repeated, waiting patiently for me to let her in.

"What's happened to Abigail?" I frowned.

"She has been reassigned," Marinda said matter-of-factly. "The king requested I take her place as your attendant."

My heart dropped. "Where has she been assigned? Has she been demoted?"

"No, My Lady," said Marinda, seeming confused as to why I would be asking all these questions. "She's been moved to a different part of the castle."

I stared at her, searching my mind for a reason to turn her away, but I couldn't find one. Servants were not supposed to grow attached to those they served, and I would probably get Abi into more trouble pressing the subject than if I let it alone.

Reluctantly, I stepped back. Marinda curtsied once again, striding past me and directly to my wardrobe. She didn't open the window, but worked in the darkness, only lighting a couple candles to see her way around. She didn't speak either—the most she said was "turn around" or "sit down" to give me direction. She also didn't ask for my opinions, forcing a dress on me before I'd really even seen it and fastening the ruby necklace around my throat without a word. She pulled my hair up so tightly that it rivaled Miss Grayson's stern style when I knocked on her door in low spirits a few minutes later.

"Thank you, Marinda," Miss Grayson said, nodding to her. Marinda curtsied to the both of us, very low to the ground, her eyes clearly averted. I stared after her as she walked away, desperately hoping I wouldn't be stuck with her for long.

Miss Grayson cleared her throat. "Now then, Kenna. We have a lot of work to do today."

She didn't seem nearly as harsh as before, and even *shut* the door, not slammed it. I wondered if taking a break had improved her mood, but I doubted two days off would be enough to change her that much.

"Have a seat," she said, gesturing to the chair by the table. As I complied, she opened the drawer to a desk in the corner, removing a few pieces of paper and a couple of parcels. She set them on top of the desk and thought for a moment. At length she nodded and took one from the bottom, bringing it to the table and setting it down before sitting opposite me.

It was a map of Orkeia. I recognized some of the Southern layout from when I had searched for the Grison clan my second night in the castle, but it was strange to see it drawn out on paper. It was also strange to see the names for the different islands. Remembering some of my former lessons, I realized that they were all named after the noble families that lived there or previous kings. I was sure that the Gifted used to have different names for them, but it wasn't something I had ever really considered before.

"What's this for?" I ventured to ask, since it didn't seem she was going to snap at me whenever I spoke today.

"To start learning and memorizing the land," Miss Grayson explained, not even a twinge of annoyance on her brow. "Who lives on which isles and what they export to the mainland kingdoms."

I raised an eyebrow. "I thought you said I wouldn't need to learn any trade."

"It's valuable knowledge," she said dismissively. "Now, let's begin with Caldsen and Terran."

The next three hours were spent learning how each island received its name, who lived there in the past, which noble families lived there now, how they made their money, and the succession of kings were Kiernan to die without an heir. My head spun, but I tried to soak it all in. It would be useful when I left this place to be more aware of my location, instead of just wandering. I would be able to help the clans I came across as well.

She'd just finished testing me on the names of all of the lords when Marinda entered with our lunch. We ate in silence as always, but with one major difference: Miss Grayson wasn't glaring at me. When we finished, she returned to the desk, gathering a different stack of papers. They proved to be miniature portraits of the lords and their families. We spent the next hour and a half matching the names to the faces. Soon, I was exhausted.

"Very good," she said when I'd finished telling her everything I could about Lord Everett and his family. "Now the nobles living inside the city."

"Excuse me, Miss Grayson," I said as she stood to gather even more portraits. "But why am I learning all of this?"

"It's useful to know who the leaders of the kingdom are."

"I don't really see how," I said as respectfully as I could. "I've been here a few months and this is the first time you've tried to teach me about the nobles."

"If you're going to be a member of this society, Kenna," she began, rejoining me at the table, "you're going to need to mingle with the upper levels. They will all know who you are, and it will be expected that you know who they are."

"Why would they know who I am?" I said, unable to hold back a laugh.

"Well I should hope they would take the time to learn about someone who could be their future queen."

The silence in the room was deafening. I couldn't have said a word even if I wanted to. All I could do was stare at her. A smile twitched on the corners of her lips as she watched my struggling expressions.

"Certainly this can't come as a surprise to you," she said, failing to hide the mocking edge to her tone. "You are a beautiful woman, Kenna. His Majesty hasn't been able to take his eyes off you since he returned, and you've only encouraged his interest by not taking your eyes off of him."

I opened my mouth, but no sound came out. Miss Grayson obviously found the situation amusing, but she wasn't about to show it. It wouldn't be ladylike.

"Now, let's continue," she said, placing the portraits in front of me. "There will be a banquet four months from now in celebration of Orkeia's founding, and all of the nobles will be here. You will be expected to know each of their names, so let's start now."

Somehow I repeated names as she said them, but I wasn't retaining any information. My stomach was in knots.

Could that *really* be his intention?

He'd talked about us helping each other in the future, that he hoped to hold a ball sometime soon—he'd dropped so many hints, and I'd remained oblivious. He was courting me, and there was no logical reason for me to reject him.

Except that if he knew about my mark, he would kill me.

I didn't master these names as I had the previous ones, but Miss Grayson released me for the day anyway. "We have time to get you ready," she said. "We'll continue tomorrow."

When I opened the door to leave, Marinda was waiting to help me prepare for dinner. She altered my hairstyle, though I didn't notice any difference, and added a hairpiece to match my necklace and dress. The necklace felt even heavier than before as I considered the intentions behind the gift, and I almost felt like it was strangling me.

When Marinda thought I looked presentable, we went down the stairs to the dining room. She opened the doors for me, curtsying to guests at the table. The men all stood, and I curtsied sloppily at the last minute, distracted by my racing thoughts. Kiernan smiled in my direction, but this time I did not meet his eyes. There was an empty seat next to Isaiah, and I took it, grateful when the guests returned their attention to individual conversations. Kiernan didn't speak to anyone, however—his eyes were fixed on my face, and try as I might to ignore him, I could feel his gaze searching me.

"What's wrong, Kenna?" Isaiah asked as I picked at my food.

I forced myself to look at him, smiling as best as I could. "Nothing," I said, not sounding as convincing as I would have liked. Isaiah frowned, unconvinced, but with a slight shake of my head I silently communicated 'not now,' and he began to eat.

It was only then that I realized that not all of Kiernan's captains were present—Lewin was missing. I obviously wasn't bothered by this, but I was surprised. Isaiah noticed the direction of my gaze and nodded to where Lewin usually sat before speaking.

"Men are deserting the knights," he explained in a whisper. "They aren't happy with the Slaughters, whether it be because they're laying their own lives on the line or they're just tired of fighting an enemy that's not actively attacking them. Lewin's hard at work rounding up deserters and punishing them."

I shivered. It was bad enough being held in that horrible dungeon for only a couple days. I didn't want to imagine what the captain did to deserters.

These thoughts were overshadowed, however, by a strange sense of happiness. Maybe not everyone had fallen for this lie after all—maybe there were those out there who knew in their hearts there was no real reason to be killing all these innocent people. It might be possible to win them over, especially if they already had some doubt in their hearts.

But would it be possible to convince their king?

I looked up and our eyes locked. He'd hardly eaten anything on his plate. He smiled warmly. I could feel my heart pounding uncomfortably against my chest. I knew everything he'd done, that he planned to destroy my people completely, but was it really *his* plan or was he just carrying out his father's wishes? Was he really so bloodthirsty that he wouldn't listen to reason?

I thought back to our interaction in the library the night before and the childlike wonder he'd shown when recounting the story of the Mother of the Sea and the Father of Storms. The thought that I could show him there was good in magic returned stronger than before.

As we continued to stare at each other, another thought crossed my mind. I tried to push it away, but it kept finding its way back, no matter what I did.

Do I have feelings for him?

The idea was absurd, but it wouldn't leave. The more I looked into his eyes, the more lost in them I became. I found myself fantasizing about a life with him where he accepted my Gift and ended the Slaughters.

Desperately, I looked away. The more I tried to make sense of my thoughts, the more my head hurt.

When the meal ended, I'd eaten hardly any of my dinner, but I wasn't hungry. We all stood when Kiernan did. I suppose I shouldn't have been surprised when instead of simply leaving the room, he moved to my side and offered his arm.

"Would you care to take a walk with me, Lady Kenna?" he asked.

His closeness only intensified the bundle of confusing emotions in my chest. "Of course," I said, trying to ignore the prying eyes of everyone else in the room as I took his arm.

He led me into the gardens. It was a cool night, but not so cold that it was uncomfortable. My thoughts were too jumbled for me to figure out a way to start a conversation, so I remained silent as we strolled through the paths. Kiernan was also quiet for a long time, occasionally gazing at the sky with a distant expression.

"Are you enjoying life in the castle, Kenna?" he finally asked.

I bit my lip. "It's...been an adjustment."

"What can I do to make you more comfortable?"

There was an eagerness in his tone that couldn't be missed. I slowly looked up at him to see an expression of genuine concern on his face.

"I'm not sure," I admitted quietly.

He sighed, stopping in the middle of the path and releasing my arm so he could face me more directly. "I feel I've done something to offend you," he said gently. "I assure you, whatever it was, I had no intention of doing so."

"No, you haven't—" I started to say, but I realized that it would be a lie. The ruby around my neck still felt like it was choking me, and I resisted the urge to yank it off. There was another silence between us as I tried to determine what to say, really not sure where to even begin.

"My life, as you observed when we first met, has been ... complicated," I started, fumbling with my words. "I've lost a lot of people close to me, and never even had the chance to get to know others. I—it's hard for me to adjust to something as new and different as life in your court."

He frowned. "Has Miss Grayson not been helpful with those adjustments?" he asked.

"Miss Grayson doesn't seem to have much patience with me," I admitted, my lips twitching with some amusement. "She's not exactly the warmest tutor. But...I don't think she's the reason I'm struggling."

Gently, he took my hands in his. "Then what is?" he said. "What can I do to help? I can only imagine what you've been through..."

I shifted uncomfortably where I stood. Those words were so familiar, almost the exact same words that Gideon had said to me when I first joined the Grison clan. And what's more, they were said with just as much sincerity. My heart twisted in my chest, but I brought my eyes up to meet his once more. In those deep blue eyes, I saw a true and genuine desire to help. I saw a man who wanted to right the wrongs he'd seen and protect his people at all costs.

He's a good man.

Slowly, I drew my hands back from his and reached up to unclasp the necklace. His frown deepened as I removed it and placed it in one of his hands, letting out a heavy breath.

"I cannot accept this," I admitted quietly. "It's beautiful, but...I can't bear the thought that someone had to die so I could have it. Death...death should never be celebrated, no matter who it is."

He stared at me for a long moment. Part of me expected him to say that there was no reason for me to feel uncomfortable if the person who had to die was a witch. But to my relief, he didn't. With a slow, small nod, he placed the ruby in his pocket.

"I apologize," he said, genuinely sounding remorseful. "Perhaps I have been too cavalier when it comes to this war. You are right of course. I hope you can forgive my oversight."

I nodded, trying to swallow the knot in my throat. He gingerly took my hand and kissed it before offering me his arm once more to lead me back into the castle. We didn't speak on the way to my room, but it wasn't really an uncomfortable silence like before. It was a silence of understanding.

As we reached my door, another thought occurred to me and I let out a breath.

"Kiernan, I wonder if I might ask for one more thing."

"Of course," he said without hesitation. "What is it?"

"I'd like my old maid back—Abigail Cobb."

He raised his eyebrows. "I thought you would appreciate having a higher-ranked maid."

"I do appreciate the thought," I said sincerely, "but it would mean so much to me if Abigail was reassigned as my attendant. She's—well, she's become a close friend. I don't want to lose her."

His expression softened. If he was bothered by the idea of me being friends with a maid, he did a good job of not letting it show. "Of course. You can expect to see her in the morning,"

I beamed at him. "Thank you," I breathed out with relief. My heart feeling considerably lighter than it had for the rest of the day, I curtsied once more. Again, I did not break eye contact. He responded with a bow, watching me turn to enter my room. Out of the corner of my eye, I saw him put his hand in the pocket that held the ruby, a thoughtful expression on his face.

Closing my eyes, I leaned against the door as I shut it. I noticed with some alarm that my breathing was heavier than normal and I took a few minutes to try to steady it. My fingers curled against the wood of the door as my thoughts wandered.

Giving him back the necklace had been a risk. I wouldn't have been surprised if he'd reacted with deep offense. Instead, he was humbled and willing to admit that, at least to some degree, he'd been wrong in his attitude towards this war. It was a small start, but a start nonetheless.

If he was that receptive to a gentle correction, perhaps given time I really would be able to persuade him that what he believed about magic wasn't the truth. And if I could do *that*, I might actually be able to put an end to this war.

My palms pressed against the door and I opened my eyes as I pushed away from it. A sense of determination and resolve gradually replaced my confusion and uncertainty.

I would allow this relationship to continue, and if he did propose, I would accept. Yes, it meant never returning to my clan and committing to a life within these stone walls, but that was a small price to pay if I could save my people.

CHAPTER SIXTEEN

LIGHT IN THE SHADOWS

The days following were unbearably monotonous: I woke up, Abi prepared me for the day and served breakfast, I attended my lessons with Miss Grayson, Abi brought lunch, we continued my lessons, and I ate dinner with the king and whomever else happened to be present. Some days I took a walk in the gardens with Kiernan on his request, and others I returned to my room directly after dinner. When I did walk with Kiernan, Abi was always in my room the moment he was down the hall, pressing me for details. When I didn't, Isaiah escorted me to my room, 'subtly' trying to discover my feelings toward the king.

I didn't tell him about my resolution. I was sure he would be against it. But as the days had passed, I had just become more committed to my decision. If Kiernan proposed, I would accept and face whatever consequences came. If he accepted me, we would work together to stop this war. If he didn't, I would die for my people.

But as almost a month passed, my decision became less and less about ending the war. Surprisingly and almost against my will, I found myself falling for him. He was even more charming than Neal and never let a moment pass without doting on me with gifts or compliments. He even stole me away from my lessons on occasion, for which I was eternally grateful. More and more I caught myself blushing in his presence, and soon enough I had convinced myself that he was courting me for more than my looks. In my heart, I had come to believe that he would accept me as a witch.

We spent many hours together in the library, pouring over books together. He told me about his ancestors and folklore his mother had relayed to him when he was young. One of them was a legend about the Mother of the Sea raising Orkeia's islands from beneath the surface to provide protection from the Father of Storms. In the story, there was even a large sea serpent that the Father of Storms created to sink the ships of local fishermen. As I listened, my eyes widened.

"That sounds like the story of Hanson," I said before I could stop myself.

He paused, looking up from the book he was holding. "Hanson?"

Realizing my mistake, I shifted in my seat, nervously tucking a loose curl behind my ear. His curiosity was apparent, and I knew that there wasn't a way out of explaining myself.

"A legendary sorcerer," I muttered.

Kiernan cocked an eyebrow. "A sorcerer?"

"Yes, I—I heard the story while I was with the clan," I said, clasping my hands in my lap and attempting to remain casual. "It's very similar. This sorcerer used his Gift to darken the moon in order to weaken a sea serpent terrorizing the region, then lifted an island from the ocean floor to bury it forever and keep the people safe."

I watched his reaction carefully. His eyebrow remained raised, but I wasn't sure if it was in an incredulous expression or one of interest.

"His Gift?"

"That's what they call their powers," I said, just managing to catch myself before saying 'we' by accident.

"Fascinating," he muttered. His expression softened, and he briefly stared at the window in thought. I unclasped my hands, the tension in my shoulders slowly starting to relax.

"What else did you learn about their legends and customs?" he asked, bringing his gaze back to mine. He then added, "Of course, if it's painful to remember, please don't feel any obligation to talk about it."

"No, I—no, I don't mind at all," I blurted out, perhaps a little too quickly. My heart was suddenly beating harder against my chest, but I tried to hide my excitement. This was a golden opportunity to begin to change his perspective on who the Gifted really were.

I was careful about how I told the stories. Some of the details I left vague on purpose, not wanting to try to give him too much to process all at once. It was clear that he knew almost nothing about how magic worked, which shouldn't have really surprised me. After all, all he'd known was the destruction the evil sorcerer, Pious, had caused when he overthrew the kingdom. To him, there hadn't been much reason to study more about the nature of Gifts—it was more important to eliminate the perceived threat of magic from the land. But even with his comparative ignorance, he expressed that some of the stories were very similar to ones his mother had told him, even pulling out books from the library's collection to show them to me.

That night, we were both deep in thought as he accompanied me back to my quarters. Making connections between our two cultures was illuminating. We had each grown up in a world where they were kept starkly separate, but clearly that hadn't always been the case. If so many of our respective legends shared similar themes and characters, they had to have come from a common source.

Desperately, I wished I had my summoning candles so I could ask Hanson personally about what society had been like when he was alive. But while that was currently impossible, I had the next best thing.

Once Kiernan bid me goodnight, I shut my door and rushed to retrieve the fragile book from under my bed. I had been kept busy enough in the past month that I hadn't had the energy or time to begin to delve into Kindra's record, but even more than before I felt eager to learn as much as I could about her and Hanson.

Sitting on the floor, I opened it on my lap. Reading the first sentence again, I shivered and turned the page in anticipation.

'I met my husband when I was thirteen years old. He had been the Father of his clan for a year but still hadn't chosen a counselor. For some reason, just months after my family joined the clan he approached me and asked if I would fill the position. I initially refused, feeling he should have a counselor who

was older and wiser, but eventually accepted the offer. To my surprise, my parents and the rest of the clan supported his decision, and we began working together.'

I reread the paragraph once, surprised. I hadn't realized how young Hanson was when he became Father of his clan, and thirteen was extremely young for Kindra to be called as a counselor. A counselor is not only someone who supports and advises the Father or Mother of the clan, but they are also the one who's in charge if the Father or Mother is unavailable for any reason. The way Kindra described the role sounded more like a marriage, the wife supporting and advising her husband, even before the two of them were actually married.

She described the workings and some of the history of her people. After a year, the Mother white witch of the clan died of natural causes, and the talisman chose Kindra in her place. Reading her reflections on how unprepared she felt was very familiar, and I had to pause for a moment and close my eyes as I remembered Sybil, her sacrifice, the confrontation with Ethel, and so much more that had happened while I was living with the Grison clan.

For a brief moment, I questioned my resolve to stay here, my heart aching to find them again. But I knew that ultimately, the best thing I could do for them—and the rest of the Gifted people living in Orkeia—was continue to develop my relationship with Kiernan and help him see the true nature of magic.

I was a bit surprised when Kindra mentioned some of the Ungifted members of their clan. I almost didn't catch the reference, since it was treated casually and normal. It confirmed the suspicions I'd had as Kiernan and I exchanged stories in the library, and I frowned to myself, wondering how and when things changed and the people separated.

If we'd lived together in harmony once, was it possible for us to do that again?

I read until my eyelids drooped so much that I could no longer continue. Carefully, I hid the book under my bed once more, eager to resume reading it the following day. Almost as soon as I climbed into bed, I was fast asleep, dreaming of a day when Gideon, Neal, Shae, and Jo could live in the city with me, free to practice magic among the Ungifted. It seemed so real, and I did everything I could to remain asleep when the sunlight shone through my windows.

"No lessons today," Abi was saying. "Miss Grayson said she's not feeling well, but I expect she's just tired of you. I told her you wouldn't mind."

"Then what in the world are you waking me up for," I grumbled, only partially sarcastic.

"I've already let you sleep in much too late," she grinned, setting what was clearly lunch and not breakfast in front of me. "I was starting to worry you were never going to wake up."

"Maybe I didn't want to," I grumbled, taking a bite of the delicious salmon on my plate. The image of Gideon's smile and Neal's wicked grin were still fresh in my mind, and I stared longingly out the window.

If Abi noticed my wistfulness, she didn't say anything as she opened my wardrobe.

"The king's having a private dinner with his captains tonight," she informed me. "So what do you say we pick out something for you to explore in?"

In the occasional moments when I wasn't occupied with lessons or spending time with Kiernan, Abi had taken it upon herself to show me more of the secret passageways in the castle. The more time I spent in them, the more comfortable I was, and it was exciting sneaking around the castle unnoticed. Besides, Abi always made good company, and I had to admit that it was entertaining to listen in on the conversations of the servants and knights.

I smiled at her idea and stood, moving to her side at the wardrobe. "I'll wear the yellow one," I suggested. "I would love an excuse to dirty it up."

She laughed and pulled it out. "It's beautiful!"

"It makes me look like a ghost." *And I should know.*

"Well, I don't know how dirty you'll get," she said, laying it on my bed and unlacing the back. "I've spent most of your lesson time in the last couple weeks cleaning out the passageways."

"Oh, well, I'll just have to deal with the clean," I joked as I took off my nightgown and stepped into the dress. As always, I was careful to make sure that my underclothes stayed secure so Abi wouldn't catch a glimpse of my mark.

She spent minimal time on my hair, pulling it back with a ribbon matching the dress and letting some curls hang in the front. "Have you been to the watchtower passageways yet?"

I raised my eyebrows. "You didn't show me those."

"They're a little tight," she shrugged. "But you'll fit. The greatest thing about them is that there are small holes in the walls. It's fascinating to see what the guards do when they think no one's watching."

She winked, and I couldn't help but giggle. "Then what are we waiting for?"

We walked into the hall, trying to appear casual. I followed Abi down the stairs and toward the dining hall, nodding politely to those we passed. When there was no one around, Abi opened up a small concealed doorway near the watchtowers. I entered first, and she closed the door lightly behind us just as footsteps were heard coming down the hall.

"That was close," she chuckled, keeping her voice low. "All right, shall we stay on this level or go up the stairs?"

I was still listening to the footsteps. There were at least two people walking together, and I could vaguely hear their conversation. Though I couldn't make out the words, I thought I recognized Kiernan's voice, and I bit my lip. I knew I should allow him his privacy, but I couldn't help the pull of curiosity I felt as I strained to hear what he was saying.

"Are there any places to look out close by?" I whispered.

Abi nodded and squeezed past me, leading me to the hole. As we drew closer, it was easier to hear the conversation. The voice was definitely Kiernan's. When we reached the opening, I knelt and looked through, waiting for the men to appear.

"—quite the coincidence, don't you think?" he was saying.

"Lies and deceit," came Lewin's rough voice. He sounded particularly sour this morning, and when he moved into view, there was a clear, angry grimace on his face. "You don't really think we have anything in common with those heathens, do you?"

"I don't know," Kiernan sighed as he came into view. "Kenna seems to think so."

"And why should you consider that? She was their prisoner. No doubt they fed her those lies and warped her mind to have pity for them. For all we know, they deliberately left her behind to send her here with lies in her head as a plot to sow seeds of doubt in our cause."

Kiernan's lips tightened into a frown and he stopped walking, luckily still within view of the hole. "I trust her, Lewin. She is of sound mind."

"Can you really be sure of that?" said Lewin, turning to face him. The speech sounded rehearsed. "We know nothing about her past. The only source we have for her lineage is her uncle, if he even is who he claims to be, and he hasn't told us anything other than claiming she was abducted as a child when her parents were killed. He has given no details to us about who they were or how they died."

"And why should those details matter? Isn't her character more important?"

There was a long pause before Lewin spoke again. "Kiernan," he said in a warning tone, almost sounding like a father ready to scorn his child. "Don't tell me that the rumors are true."

"What rumors?" Kiernan said.

"Rumors of your intentions to court and marry this woman," he said, his voice dripping with disdain.

My breath caught in my throat. I knew I should leave at this point, but even if I'd been capable of pulling myself away from the conversation, Abi was directly behind me, and she didn't seem at all inclined to move.

Kiernan stiffened, standing up a little straighter. "That's not really any of your business," he said firmly.

Despite the king's tone, Lewin was undeterred. He straightened as well, clearly trying to exert control over the situation. I remembered vaguely what Isaiah had said about Lewin heavily influencing Kiernan to declare war against magic, and my stomach turned in my chest. This man was trying to control the kingdom from the shadows and take advantage of Kiernan's youth. My fear and hatred of him only increased as I thought of how much damage he'd caused, not just to the kingdom, but to Kiernan and his perceptions.

"Forgive me, Kiernan," Lewin said, not sounding sorry for what he was about to say in the slightest, "but the queen should be someone with noble ancestry, not an orphan of no particular background."

"In case you've forgotten, Captain, I'm an orphan as well."

"Her blood is not noble, Your Majesty."

"And there was one time in history when the blood of my ancestors was not noble," Kiernan retorted matter-of-factly.

"There are plenty of suitable young women with noble heritage across the kingdom eager to catch your eye. Lady Ina, for instance—"

"Yes, too eager," Kiernan said bitterly. "They're interested in the throne. Kenna's different. She's interested in me."

The fondness in the way he said my name made my chest tighten and blood rush to my cheeks.

"You don't know that for certain," Lewin warned.

Kiernan straightened once more. "You haven't spent time with her, Captain. I have. I know her character. She is kind and considerate. She cares about even those who have hurt her. And while she may not be as *refined* as Lady Ina, she is certainly more noble of heart. She is exactly the type of person I want at my side leading the kingdom."

There was a very long moment of silence at this, Lewin's eyes narrowing. "You are decided, then," he said grimly.

"Yes. I love her."

The firmness with which he said it seemed to surprise even Kiernan. We could have heard a pin drop in the silence. Lewin seemed too taken aback to respond. I couldn't have made a sound had I wanted to, because I could barely breathe.

"Love is a strong word, don't you think?" the captain said carefully.

"It's the truth," Kiernan said. His thoughts were moving away from the tension of the beginning of their conversation, and I saw his eyes begin to shine as he looked past Lewin down the hall. "I love her," he repeated, a note of excitement in his voice.

"Consider this, Kiernan," Lewin said, changing his tactic. "How do you know she returns your feelings? You are the king after all, and it would be easy for any woman to receive you, however she felt."

"There's only one way to find out, then, isn't there?"

Without another word, Kiernan walked past the captain with purposeful steps, moving out of the watchtowers and in the direction of my room. Lewin stood stunned, his expression hardening in the silence. Then, with determination written on his face, he hurried after his king. Abi and I were rooted to the spot, staring breathless at where they had been.

"Let's go," Abi whispered excitedly. "We can get there just after he does—"

"No," I managed to breathe, sliding down the wall and sitting on the ground. "I can't."

Her mouth hung open. "Why? He's going to tell you he loves you!"

"But he'll expect me to say it back."

Abi shut her mouth tightly and joined me on the floor. "And you don't love him?"

My fingers shook, and I grasped them together in my lap to try to stop the tremors. "I don't know."

Hearing him say those words had sent my thoughts into a spiral. On the one hand, my heart had started to race with excitement. This was what I had wanted, wasn't it? To win him over so he would see me for what I really was? And I couldn't deny that the more time I spent with him, the more I'd come to care for him, regardless of his status as king.

But even when I was with Kiernan, sometimes his eyes would remind me of Gideon, or the touch of his hand would bring back memories of Neal and the last moments we shared. Hearing Kiernan say those words brought so much doubt into my mind about my own feelings and if they could match what I had felt for Neal in that moment.

I'd never been so confused.

I could tell Abi wanted to say more and prod about what I was thinking and feeling, but I was grateful that she didn't. Eventually, I stood, my legs sore from the awkward position I'd been sitting in, and exited the tunnels into the main halls. Abi followed, and I was extremely relieved when we didn't cross paths with Kiernan, or anyone else for that matter.

"Do you want me to stay?" she asked, breaking the silence as we entered my room.

I hugged myself tightly, sitting on the edge of my bed and staring out the window. "I think I need to be alone for a while," I muttered.

She hesitated but gave a slow nod. "I'll bring up your dinner in a few hours. Anything else I can do for you?"

I shook my head. She opened her mouth to speak again, but bit her lip instead. Hiding her concern, she left the room, leaving me alone in my thoughts. Desperate to quiet them, I tried to sleep, but seeing as it was the middle of the day, that was impossible. Not knowing what else to do and not wanting to grapple with my conflicting emotions, I took Kindra's book out once more and opened it to where I had left off.

'While he was already a talented sorcerer and very talented at manipulating the elements, Hanson eventually admitted to me that he wasn't sure what his Gift actually was. He said that using his magic didn't feel as innate and natural as others made it sound like it should and it took a great deal of practice and focus for him to use it.

'I suggested he might have Varan's gift, power over the universe. Hanson was understandably incredulous, but I searched the other worlds anyway and was not disappointed. Varan was waiting for me when I arrived in the Land of the Saved. He told me I was correct, that Hanson was his descendant and had the same power he held. I was tasked with helping Varan mentor him by relaying messages back and forth, teaching Hanson how to control his gift and telling Varan what he was struggling with.'

Once again, I was struck by the similarities between her story and my own. My grip on the book tightened as I thought of Gideon and the hours I'd spent with him on his lessons. But as I sat there, my thoughts quickly wandered away from his lessons to other moments we had shared, simple moments when we were walking along the beach or enjoying a meal together. I felt tears begin to form in my eyes and carefully shut Kindra's book, not wanting to wet any of the pages and not sure I could emotionally continue to read—at least not now. It was too painful to remember everything I had lost and everything I was giving up.

Picking up the book had been the exact wrong thing to do to try to distract myself. More than ever, my thoughts were split between life here in the castle and life with my former clan. Neal, Gideon, and Kiernan's faces all swam in my mind at once, and I felt the tears roll down my cheek as I shut my eyes tightly.

Why did this have to hurt so much?

As my emotions began to overwhelm me, the air seemed to turn cold. At first I hardly noticed it, since my body shook regardless of any change in temperature. But when I opened my eyes, I couldn't deny that there had been a sudden shift in the amount of light in the room. I could still see the sun high in the sky out of the window, but the room was filling with darkness.

I realized what was happening just as an icy cold hand with impossibly long fingers clutched my throat from behind. A strangled gasp left my lips as I tried to stand and pull myself away from the presence, but I couldn't move. My vision began to darken as a black, suffocating mist surrounded me. I tried desperately to summon my strength and thrash against the evil power that held me in place, opening my mouth to scream but unable to make a sound. The icy grip enveloped me and, in addition to being cold, became sharp. I felt deep gashes form on my arms and chest, the pain intensified by the cold.

My lungs begged for air, and it took every ounce of what I had left to lift my arms from my sides and extend my fingers. In what I was sure would be my last moments of life, I silently cried out to the Giftgiver, pulling the magic inside me from deep within and willing with all my might for it to banish this presence.

The room exploded in light, and a terrible, rattling scream filled my mind, more terrible than I had heard it before. For an instant, I saw in my mind the horrible forest in the Land of the Lost and felt myself being dragged down into a deep, endless pit within it. As suddenly as it had appeared, the vision was gone, and I collapsed, unconscious.

***

"Kenna! Kenna, what happened?"

Abi's frantic voice was the first thing to hit my senses. The second was her shaking fingers fumbling at my wrist for a pulse. When I managed to open my eyes, she let out a choked sob of relief.

I looked down at my body. Blood dripped from beneath my sleeves and stained the yellow bodice. The cuts had penetrated beneath my clothing but hadn't disturbed the fabric. They stung horribly, and I gasped as I attempted to sit up, wincing in pain.

Clearly panicking, Abi reached for the rope next to my bed. I felt a sinking sensation in my stomach and instinctively reached out to stay her hand, wrapping my fingers around her wrist.

"Abi—don't—"

"We need to get a nurse," she insisted shakily.

"Please! I'll—I'll be fine."

I was sure I was unconvincing, but I had to try regardless. It would be clear to anyone who saw me that this attack had been magical in nature, and I couldn't afford to let Kiernan get word of it and double down on his previously conceived notions about the Gifted. He would attribute this to some witch or sorcerer targeting me, perhaps in an effort to hurt him, and I didn't know how I could possibly explain to him that it had been something entirely different without revealing my abilities—something I didn't think he was ready for just yet.

"Kenna, you're bleeding all over," Abi breathed, clearly thinking I was just in shock. Once again she reached for the rope, but I summoned my energy and took both of her hands in mine as I sat the rest of the way up.

"I know," I stammered. "Just—help me get out of this dress."

Her eyes kept darting to the rope, but at least for the moment she relented. I winced as I stood, shaking more from the turmoil of the experience than the pain. The yellow dress was definitely ruined from the amount of blood soaking the inside, and I heard Abi take in a sharp breath when the cuts that were the source of it were revealed.

"We need to clean these cuts," she said, her voice insistent and determined. "You *need* a nurse."

"Wait," I pleaded.

I shut my eyes tightly, focusing on my breathing to keep it steady. In the pit of my stomach and on the edge of my fingers, something tingled. The feeling began to spread up my arms, then down my chest and torso towards my legs. A warm, soothing sensation accompanied it, and Abi gasped as she released me. I heard her stumble backwards, something falling off of my nightstand as she bumped against it.

When I opened my eyes, the stinging from the cuts on my body had subsided. I furrowed my eyebrows in confusion, looking down at my arms. The cuts that had been there before had disappeared. The only evidence I had been injured was the blood smeared on my now undamaged skin.

"What just happened?" Abi breathed.

I looked at her and saw that now *she* was shaking. Her eyes were wide with shock, fear, and wonder. I opened my mouth to try to think of a way to respond, but the truth was, I didn't exactly understand what had happened myself.

"You—you started to glow," she said, her voice barely above a whisper. "And then the cuts just—they just faded. It—it was—"

"It was magic," I finished, trying to stop myself from shaking.

The fear in her eyes at those words was unmistakable. My lips quivered as I gently took a hold of her hands.

"I'm fine, Abi," I said as calmly as I could. "I promise."

She didn't look at all convinced, and I could tell she was resisting the urge to run for help. There was no choice but to tell her the truth, and she deserved to know.

I sighed. "You may want to sit down."

Chapter Seventeen

UNDER THE RAIN

Abigail sat stunned on the end of my bed.

"You're a witch?" she whispered for the fifth time.

"Yes," I said. But even as I said it, I wasn't entirely sure. I had never heard of a white witch being able to heal physical injuries before. That was something that was usually associated with green healing magic. My mind spun with confusion as I tried to rationalize what had happened with everything I knew. But for now, at least, the primary concern was keeping Abi calm.

Her voice shook. "And...the thing that attacked you was...a demon?"

"Yes."

"Will it come back?" she asked, trembling.

"I don't think it can anymore," I said with a heavy breath of my own, slowly sitting on the edge of the bed next to her. "I—I think I managed to banish it back to the Land of the Lost...somehow."

"Using...using your magic?" she said, still sounding afraid to say the word out loud.

I nodded, a knot forming in my throat. "Yes. Abi, magic—magic itself isn't good or bad. It's—sometimes people *use* it for evil, but most—the majority of us—we see our powers as Gifts. And I—I mean, could I really have banished a demon if my own powers were evil?"

She stared at the blood-stained dress on the floor, her hands still trembling in her lap. I covered them with my own, even though I was definitely still shaken myself.

"What about the mark?" she asked after a long silence. "You don't have one."

"Yes, I do," I admitted quietly.

She slowly raised her eyes to look at me with a confused frown. I lifted my underdress just high enough to reveal the clearly defined heart on my skin, and a gasp escaped her lips.

"What does it mean?" she breathed.

"It means—" I hesitated. "Well, most people think it means I'm a white witch."

She raised her eyebrows. "There are different types of witches?"

I did my best to explain the different branches of magic. The more I talked, the more Abi's shoulders slowly—very slowly—began to relax. She started to ask questions, and as the conversation continued her eagerness to understand grew.

"So the magic holders—sorry, the Gifted—that you were with were good people?"

"The best," I responded with a pained smile.

She clearly had more questions, but now that both of us were no longer shaking uncontrollably, she set them aside as she looked with concern at the blood still covering my skin.

"Let me draw you a bath," she said, standing.

I frowned a bit, standing with her. Usually, two or three maids would work together to set up a bath for me, and the last thing I wanted was for someone else to walk in on the scene of my room covered in blood. I was about to express my concerns, but then Abi continued to speak.

"I'll get rid of the sheets and dress," she said, gathering up any fabric that was stained with blood. "While I get help to prepare the bath, you can hide in the wardrobe so no one sees you and asks any questions."

I watched her for a moment. My eyes started to sting, and I realized it was because they were filling with tears. Abi didn't notice, focused on stripping the bed. The tears continued to build up with my emotions until I couldn't hold it in any longer. I threw my arms around her and pulled her into a tight hug, letting out a shaky breath. She dropped the sheets as I did, and after just a moment of surprise she returned the embrace, holding on to me just as tightly. It was the warmest hug I'd ever felt.

"Thank you," I said into her shoulder through a choked voice.

She somehow squeezed me even tighter. "I'm so sorry," she breathed out.

Slowly, I pulled back from her, my eyebrows furrowed. "For what?"

Her eyes were on the ground. "All this time, I thought magic was just evil. I mean, my father was killed by a sorcerer, and so were the king and queen, so I just assumed—"

"It's all right," I said quickly. "I don't blame you. I'm just glad you trust me enough to see the truth. Hopefully Kiernan will as well."

Her eyes shot up to meet mine and her jaw dropped. "You're going to *tell him*?"

The silence was deafening. You would have thought the king had just told her *he* was actually a sorcerer.

"I won't have much choice if I marry him, will I?" I said a little awkwardly.

"*What?*"

Just hours before, she had been eager to encourage my relationship with the king, and disappointed when I expressed that I had reservations. Now, she looked absolutely appalled at the thought.

"How could you even *consider* marrying him?" she blurted out. "The king will never understand, Kenna, he'll kill you as soon as he knows!"

I frowned. "I don't think so. I think he would listen—"

She began to pace the room, ignoring me. "You need to run, before anyone suspects anything. There are a few passageways out of the castle. I could get you out, my brothers could meet you in the city and help you leave—"

"Abi, stop!" I half-yelled, putting my hands on her shoulders to stop her pacing and force her to look at me. "Please, I just—I have to do this. If there's *any* chance he'll listen, if there's a chance I can help the rest of the Gifted and stop all this bloodshed—"

A knot caught in my throat. "These people are my family, and they're dying," I finished in a whisper. Abi's lips tightened into a concerned frown, but after a few minutes her expression softened with understanding.

"All right...if you're sure," she muttered.

I pulled her into another hug. She once again held me tightly, and I felt her sigh as she did. When we parted this time, there was a gentle, concerned smile on her lips.

"Now...I really should get you a bath at least," she said, attempting a bit of a teasing tone. "Try not to get blood on any of the other dresses, I don't want to have to come up with an excuse to the tailor for replacing your entire wardrobe."

I chuckled, the laughter cathartic after the ordeal we'd both just been through. Abi chuckled as well and gathered up the sheets once more, placing the dress inside of them and carefully folding it to hide the stains. As I watched her leave the room, I felt lighter than I had in months. Whatever happened with Kiernan, I had changed the mind of at least one person.

***

I hid in the wardrobe like Abi had suggested when I heard her approaching with two other maids. When the bath was in place and the others had left, she stayed to help me scrub the blood from my skin. Since she knew about my Gift now, I didn't insist on the privacy that I normally had to in order to hide my mark. Both of us kept examining my healed skin with wonder.

"Can you heal others, too?" Abi asked, her voice filled with wonder.

"I actually didn't even know I could do that until today," I admitted. "It's not something white witches can usually do. I've never heard of it before, at least."

She stopped scrubbing my arm and leaned over the edge of the tub a little to see my face better. "You didn't *know*?"

"No," I said with a sigh. "I mean, Gid seemed to think I might be a sorcerer after all, but I had just never had any evidence for that."

"Who's Gid?" she asked immediately. "And what's the difference between sorcerers and witches?"

This led into another endless set of questions. I did my best to answer all of them, and despite the macabre image of the pink bath water from the blood, the atmosphere in the room felt much lighter than before. She was very curious about what life was like with the Grison clan, and though I avoided talking too much about Neal, the twinkle in her eyes told me she could tell there was a history there. When she tried to prod for more details, I quickly changed the subject. It was too hard to think about him with everything I'd overheard Kiernan say to Lewin echoing in my mind. For the most part, I tried to move the conversation away from the people I missed so much and instead explain how magic worked the best I could.

"And you're sure this demon isn't coming back?" she asked with a frown as I dried off.

"I...can't be *sure*," I admitted a little hesitantly. "But for a moment, I thought—well, it almost felt like I was experiencing what it was experiencing, being dragged down into the Lost One's pit."

"How did it get here?"

I shook my head, wrapping the towel tighter around me. "I don't know. I've never really studied the dark side of spirit magic, but I always thought they had to be summoned by a white witch or sorcerer in order to escape the Land of the Lost. But I don't know who, when, or how it would have been brought here, or why it targeted me specifically."

"Could it have been summoned by Pious?"

"Maybe," I muttered. "But if it's been in the castle since he had power, wouldn't it have attacked someone else in all that time?"

We both were quiet as we considered the possibilities, but ultimately, Abi knew even less than I did. There was a sinking feeling in my stomach as I considered the three attacks, and especially the fact that the third and worst of them had taken place in the middle of the afternoon. I found it hard to believe that they were random, but if they weren't, that meant there was someone else at the castle secretly practicing magic—someone who wanted me out of the way.

Since speculating wouldn't get us anywhere, we let the subject drop, and Abi returned to questioning me about my clan and magic in general. It was such a relief to have someone to talk to so freely, and for the first time in months I felt like I could truly be myself. Soon enough, the sun had completely set, but our conversation likely would have continued well into the night if it hadn't been for a sudden knock on my door.

We both jumped and exchanged a surprised glance. As I quickly pulled on a robe over my nightgown, Abi crossed the room to open the door. I thought of the conversation we overheard between Kiernan and Lewin, and I felt my breath catch in my throat remembering how eager Kiernan had seemed to speak to me. If this was him, I was even more unprepared for that conversation now than I had been earlier that afternoon.

Abi opened the door, and from where I stood I couldn't immediately see past her into the hall. She curtsied, lowering her gaze.

"Good evening, Sir Balton," she said. "May I help you?"

I closed my eyes and let out a relieved breath.

"I need to speak to Lady Kenna in private, please," he said from the other side of the doorway. I couldn't see his face at the moment, but his tone was almost monotonous, something that I had learned was a clear sign that he was troubled.

"Of course, Sir," Abi said with another curtsy. She shot me a glance as she straightened, her eyebrows slightly raised, but didn't say anything else as she left the room, the door hanging open behind her. My father quickly stepped through it, and the conclusion I'd come to while listening to his voice was mirrored in his expression. His lips were pressed tightly together, his jaw set and his brow furrowed with concern.

"What's wrong?" I asked as he closed the door behind him. For a brief moment I thought he somehow knew about the demon attack, or that I'd revealed my mark to Abi, but he couldn't possibly have knowledge of the events of the afternoon without Abi or myself having told him directly.

"There's something you need to know, Kenna," he said, the concern in his eyes deepening as he spoke. "The king approached me this evening. He asked for your hand in marriage."

I bit the inside of my lip, pulling the robe tighter around myself. "What did you say?"

"I said yes, of course," he said, but his tone was still the troubled monotonous tone.

"So you approve?" I asked quietly.

The concern in his expression shifted to a flash of surprise, and even possibly anger. "Of course not."

"Then why did you—?"

"Refusing such a request from the king would arouse suspicion," he said firmly. "Which is why you need to dissuade him from the idea. Stop spending time with him. Come up with excuses. Make yourself absent for meals. Do whatever you need to do to lessen his affections for you short of making an intentional offense."

My fingers curled against the fabric of the robe, and I straightened slightly, attempting to look more confident than I felt.

"No."

He raised his eyebrows. "No?"

"I won't dissuade him," I said, my voice softer than I meant it to be.

"Please don't tell me you return his affections," he said, his jaw tightening.

My cheeks warmed. "He's a good man—"

"In case you've forgotten, you're a *witch*, Kenna!" my father whispered harshly, looking around as if someone would hear. "Once the king learns the truth, there will be no more compliments, no more presents. You'll be hanged in front of the entire kingdom."

I sighed, and my lips quivered. Before I could find the words to explain myself to him, he let out a grunt of frustration and rubbed his eyes with his thumb and forefinger.

"You were right," he muttered. "We should never have stayed here."

"I was wrong," I said, taking a step towards him. "You yourself told me that *Lewin* was the one who convinced him to start the Slaughters. He's not bloodthirsty and out for revenge. He just wants to protect the people, and he doesn't understand—"

"You can't be sure of any of that, Kenna," he said, struggling not to raise his voice. "I know he's a charming man, but don't let that overrule your better judgment."

"My judgment is just fine," I said, setting my own jaw as frustration began to take hold.

His eyes narrowed. "We're leaving in the morning," he said with finality.

I crossed my arms defiantly. "You can leave if you want—I'm staying."

"*Kenna*—"

"If there is even the *slightest* chance that I can convince him to stop this war, I have to take it!" I snapped. "Isn't that what my mother would do?"

His eyes softened, those words clearly striking a cord. Slowly, he stepped towards me, sighing as he pulled me into a strong hug, one of his hands resting on the back of my head. I forced my shoulders to relax, sighing as I leaned my head against his shoulder.

"You're just like her," he muttered in my ear, his voice cracking. His hold on me tightened slightly and his chest shook against me with his heavy breath. "Kenna...I can't bear the thought of losing you, too."

I shook my head, his beard scratching my cheek. "You won't lose me."

He pulled back from the embrace to place his hands on my shoulders. His eyes were watery as he gave me a very stern look. "Listen to what you're saying. This is the man who killed your clan, who ordered your death. His father executed your mother."

"He's not his father," I said firmly. "Kiernan's different. He will accept me, I know it."

"He's lived his whole life believing the Gifted are evil," he said, desperately trying to convince me to reconsider. "How do you think you're going to change that?"

"Didn't you say that once you'd gotten to know Arabella you couldn't believe magic was evil?" I asked in place of a direct answer.

At that, he pressed his lips tighter together and slowly let his hands fall to his sides, his gaze dropping to the ground as he became lost in thought. I uncrossed my arms and reached for one of his hands, giving it a gentle squeeze.

"Trust me," I pleaded.

He shut his eyes tightly, gripping my hand. After what felt like an eternity of silence, he gave a very reluctant nod.

"Promise me that at the first sign that he's not going to accept you, you run as fast and as far as you can," he said firmly, opening his eyes to meet mine in earnest. "With or without me. Go to Northtown, find the Dreys. They're good friends, they'll get you out of the city and to safety."

"I'll be fine," I reassured him.

"Just promise me," he said, and I saw a few of the tears that had been welling up escape his eyes.

"All right...I promise."

He kissed my forehead lovingly, his hands returning to my shoulders. He lingered in that position for a very long moment, clearly reluctant to leave. But eventually, he did make his way to the door and bid me goodnight.

When I was finally alone, the muscles in my body began to buckle. I was overcome with exhaustion, both emotional and physical. Letting the robe fall from my shoulders, I moved to the bed. Briefly, I considered reaching for Kindra's book, but the moment I sat on the mattress I knew that any further efforts to remain awake would be in vain. It had been a long, trying day, and in my last moments of consciousness as my head hit the pillow, I couldn't shake the feeling that the next day would be just as eventful in its own way.

***

The routine of the day was the same, but it felt vastly different. I was more comfortable with Abi than I had ever been, but the thought of seeing Kiernan at dinner made me increasingly nervous. He had sent a request that I dine privately with him that evening, and I had no doubt that he intended to confess his love to me. The problem was, however determined I was to go through with this, and however much I did care about him, I still wasn't entirely sure how I would respond. I wanted to say it back, truly, but I wanted to be sure that I *meant* it when I did.

I was barely able to focus during my lessons, a fact which Miss Grayson was quick to point out. Right around lunch time, she pushed a stack of papers under my nose, slamming the table as she did. "You're supposed to be reading the history of the kings," she said as I jerked my head up from where I'd been staring at my hands in my lap. "Honestly, what has gotten into you today, Kenna?"

I sighed. "I've just been thinking."

"Which is not part of your lessons," she said, only somewhat sarcastically. "Now, repeat to me the Frewin family genealogy, starting with Kiernan."

Our lessons ended early that afternoon to give Abi more time to prepare me for dinner with the king. With much persuasion, she let me wear my hair down. All she did was braid two strands and bring them together in the back, letting everything else fall naturally. As we both stared at my reflection in the mirror, she let out a breath, a small frown forming on her lips.

"Are you sure about going through with this, Kenna?" she whispered. "He could propose to you tonight. You need to be ready with a response."

My stomach filled with butterflies, but I nodded. "I'm sure."

But despite my words, deep down, I hoped I didn't have to give that answer tonight. I was mentally ready for his declaration of love, but not an official proposal. Not yet.

The walk to the king's rooms felt even longer than usual, the echo of my footsteps in the halls almost deafening. Abi accompanied me to the door, curtsying as was expected when she turned to leave. She flashed me an encouraging smile when her back was to the other servants, and I returned, albeit a bit shakily.

"Right this way, Lady Kenna," said the servant who'd opened the door, bowing deeply.

I still paused when I entered the beautiful sitting room, but not in awe this time. If what Kiernan said was true, if he really loved me, this room would be mine. All of these rooms would be mine. I would live here by his side, aiding him as he ruled the kingdom that I'd been hiding from for my whole life. I had to catch my breath before I could enter the dining area.

Kiernan stood, not waiting for his servant to announce me. "Kenna! I hope you're well?"

"Very well, thank you," I said, allowing him to kiss my hand like always. The feeling of his lips on the back of my hand sent a shiver up through my arm, prompting my cheeks to flush. His eyes met mine as he straightened, their deep blue color shining. He pulled out a chair from the table for me to sit, which was good timing as I felt my knees about to buckle. I closed my eyes as he took his seat and discreetly let out a breath, desperately trying to control my nerves.

The dinner was excellent, as always. We ate much slower than usual. Kiernan was awfully talkative and, despite my nerves, the conversation felt natural and unburdened. He asked how my lessons with 'the old crab' were going, and I couldn't help but chuckle, even with the rich pudding in my mouth. The more we talked, the more my shoulders relaxed. I found myself tracing his jawline with my eyes, reflecting once again on how handsome he was.

When the table had been cleared, we strolled outside onto the towers, enjoying the view on both sides. My heart started to beat a bit faster as I stared out towards the sea, watching the waves rise higher as clouds began to roll in. It looked like it was going to rain, but neither of us seemed intent to move back inside, at least not immediately. After a moment, Kiernan cleared his throat, and I turned to face him.

"I wanted to give you something," he said, shifting his feet with an uncharacteristic show of nerves. From his pocket, he withdrew a small pouch and gently placed it in my hand.

"The last time I brought you here to give you a gift, I was misguided," he said slowly, as if he had thought about and rehearsed what to say many, many times. "I can't change that, but I wanted to make it up to you somehow."

His eyes were locked on my face as I pulled the string to open the pouch. Inside was an emerald pendant. I caught my breath as I carefully lifted it, looking at the thin silver casing around the gem. So much of what I had been adorned with at the castle was elaborate and complicated in its design. By contrast, this was elegant and simple, and much more akin to something I would choose for myself than what I seemed expected to wear as a member of the court.

"I had it commissioned a few weeks ago and have been waiting for the right time to give it to you," he said, almost as if to fill the silence and calm his own nerves. "I hope it's to your liking."

"It's perfect," I said breathlessly, looking back up at him.

Kiernan beamed, taking the pendant from me and clasping it around my neck. As his fingers brushed against my skin, thunder sounded overhead, and rain began to fall, but neither of us moved.

Tenderly, he reached up to tuck a stray lock of hair behind my ear, his hand lingering on my cheek. I closed my eyes, my lips parting with a shaky breath. I felt his other hand on the small of my back, and my heart skipped a beat as he gently pulled me against his chest.

"I love you, Kenna," he breathed against my ear.

Before I had time to even think, his lips were on mine. Instinctively, I returned the kiss, my heart pounding against my chest as I lifted my arms to wrap them around his shoulders. His hand on my cheek moved to the back of my head, his fingers slowly entangling in my hair as he deepened the kiss. I held him tighter, shivering both inwardly and outwardly as the rain began to fall in earnest. Still, neither of us moved.

Eventually, he pulled back just enough to take a breath, pressing his forehead against mine. Our grips loosened around each other, but neither of us completely let go. I was breathing heavily as we stood there, water running down my arms. Both of us were completely soaked.

I didn't care. With that kiss, all doubt and uncertainty had melted away. "I love you too, Kiernan."

CHAPTER EIGHTEEN

A COURTLY DANCE

I shouldn't have been surprised when Abi burst into my room unannounced. In retrospect, she obviously had been spying on us, and she even brought a handful of towels without even being asked. I had to shush her multiple times to keep her squeals of excitement and delight from escaping into the hallway and attracting the attention of anyone who might happen to be nearby. To be fair, I had to suppress plenty of my own as well. For the moment, the fact that he didn't know about my Gift didn't seem to matter, and Abi's fears that he would reject me when I told him were replaced with enthusiastic confidence that the opposite would be true.

If I thought Kiernan had paid me attention before, it was nothing compared to after we kissed. He took me out of my lessons early more frequently, much to Miss Grayson's chagrin, and it became customary for us to have breakfast together. With the celebration of Orkeia's founding approaching, dinner was held in the dining hall with any visiting lords and ladies, but that didn't stop us from spending time together in the evenings. He almost always stole me away immediately after the meal, no matter who wanted to speak with him. According to Abi, this caused whispers of his intentions to quickly spread through the castle. I saw Lewin scowl every time we left together, but I pretended not to notice. If Kiernan wasn't going to pay him any mind, neither would I.

Of course, the days were still busy, for both of us. Miss Grayson tested me daily about each of the nobles, where they were from, and their genealogies. Economics was a high topic of study as well, since she assumed there would be people discussing it with me at the celebration. She also pointed out who might be most likely to start these conversations, a rare kind gesture from her. All of the lords of the various isles and many of the nobles would be attending, along with the higher ranked knights, and I was expected to know all of them.

On top of all this, she brought in one of the king's servants, Franklin, and had me practice the dances with him. They were all far too difficult to be enjoyable. I kept tripping over the train of my dress (which Miss Grayson insisted could not be shortened) and falling off beat. Her pursed lips each time we had to start over told me she expected me to fail miserably.

As the day approached, I grew more and more nervous. I knew everyone would be watching me closely to determine if I was worthy to become queen, and Miss Grayson's apparent doubts that I would be able to impress them made me feel less and less confident. Ironically, the only person I wasn't worried about assessing my performance was the king himself.

It didn't help that I hadn't had an actual conversation with any of the lords and ladies yet, despite having dinner with them as they arrived. In the beginning, they just hadn't paid me any mind. After they began to notice my relationship with Kiernan, I received considerably more curious glances (and sometimes jealous ones from the young ladies), but Kiernan was still the one the lords were eager to ingratiate themselves to and engage in conversation. The night before the ball, I mentioned this to him in passing as we strolled through the garden, and he stopped dead in his tracks.

"Goodness, Kenna, why didn't you say anything?" he said with a frown. "I can't believe I haven't formally introduced you to anyone!"

"It's nothing, Kiernan," I insisted. "I'll meet them at the celebration tomorrow."

He shook his head, a smile creeping up his lips. "All the same, you'd probably prefer to only be forced to socialize with them for one night."

I couldn't help but laugh. "They can't all be that horrible."

"They're rich, power-hungry members of society," he grumbled. "Whatever I feel for you, I'm sorry you'll have to deal with them."

My cheeks burned and I looked toward the paved pathway under my feet. It was the first time he'd hinted at my future as queen in any of our conversations. Gently, he lifted my face with his right hand, coaxing me to look into his eyes.

"I love you," he said quietly. "But if this isn't what you want—if the pressure of life here feels like it's too much—I would never force you into something you don't want to do. I want you to know that."

I placed my hand on his cheek and kissed him lightly, reassuring him. In response, he wrapped his arms around me, bringing me into a more passionate kiss.

***

Miss Grayson had ordered a new dress for me to wear at the celebration. I'd expected it to be as austere and stiff as she was, but when I finally saw it, I was pleasantly surprised. The gown was a deep green color, its silky fabric flowing in waves down to the floor. Delicate embroidery swirled in intricate patterns along the hem, cuffs, and bodice like golden vines. A train trailed gracefully on the ground, adorned with the same golden motifs.

It was truly a gown fit for a queen.

I tried to calm myself as I ran my hand along the fitted bodice, taking in my reflection in the mirror. Looking the part was just the beginning. For the first time, everyone was going to see me in a formal, high social situation. There was no reason I should be nervous about what Kiernan thought of me, but I still was.

Abi put my hair up in a very traditional style, pulling back part of the hair in braids before pinning the rest into a loose bun. Though I preferred to have my hair free to lie where it may, I had to admit that a more casual style would have been woefully out of place with the elegant dress. As a final added touch, I put on the emerald he'd given me the night we kissed.

Hopefully I would be able to fit in.

My father knocked on the door, and Abi let him in. He was dressed in full knight regalia, complete with a new blue and gold tunic portraying a seahawk. I knew he was still uncomfortable with my decision to stay and encourage this relationship, but he smiled when he saw me all the same, placing a hand on my shoulder.

"You look beautiful, Kenna," he said warmly.

"Have a good evening, M'Lady," Abi said, curtsying. I nodded to her as she left, barely catching a glimpse of her winking at me. My father still didn't know how close Abi and I were, and I wasn't sure if I wanted him to know. If he found out that I'd told her my secret, I would never hear the end of it.

"Shall we go?" he asked, offering his arm to me. I smiled and took it, allowing him to lead me to the dining area.

We would be dining in the hall that exited into the gardens for the celebration. After the meal the tables would be cleared and the ball would begin. I was surprised Kiernan wasn't using the larger and more decorative throne room for the actual ball, but he seemed to prefer to have the option to escape to the gardens.

We were announced as "Sir Balton and his niece, Lady Kenna." Hardly anyone reacted to my father's name, but everyone's heads turned at mine. I took in a deep breath through my nose and straightened a bit more as I walked, attempting to appear confident and composed. Kiernan smiled as I approached, kissing my hand when I curtsied to him. I heard a few whispers when the two of us maintained eye contact, but it didn't faze either of us. In fact, I think at this point Kiernan would have been uncomfortable if I looked away from him.

Isaiah gave a deep bow and stepped off slightly to the side, but he still hovered protectively nearby. Kiernan remained at my side as guests continued to be announced. Taking comfort from his presence, I surveyed the crowd. Many of the ladies glanced at me before quickly whispering to one another, and I squirmed a bit where I stood. One woman in particular couldn't seem to keep her eyes off me, and her gaze was less than friendly.

I recognized her at once from the portraits, thanks to Miss Grayson's endless tutoring. She was Lady Ina, daughter of Lord Everett and Lady Nerissa, who ruled over Orkeia's most northern island, Roldsay. I remembered that Lewin had mentioned her as an alternative prospect to me when speaking with Kiernan, and with a start I remembered that she had also been the woman who glared at me during the first banquet I attended in the castle—when I danced with Kiernan for the first time.

She was a generally attractive woman, about my age, but living so far north brought a coldness to her appearance that wasn't tempered by her demeanor. Because of the lack of sun and warmth, her skin was paler than candle wax, and her white blonde hair, pulled back in a tighter style than mine, looked as if it would lay completely flat against her head were it let down. She had a long neck and seemed to be trying to make it longer as she stared at me through the crowd.

Kiernan noticed my gaze and turned. When he saw Ina, his smile faltered. But I didn't get the chance to ask him about her before a tall, brunette man strode up to us.

"Your Majesty!" he said loudly, bowing deeply to Kiernan, almost to the point of mocking the action. "And Lady Kenna!" He straightened only to bow deeply once more, taking my hand in his and kissing it slightly longer than I was comfortable with.

"Kenna," Kiernan said, composing himself. "May I introduce you to—"

"Lord Hamon," he interrupted, smiling widely. "Very pleased to make your acquaintance."

My lips curved into an amused smile. "Pleased to meet you as well, *Sir* Hamon," I said.

He raised his eyebrows. "I think you mean 'Lord.'"

"Oh, my apologies," I said innocently. "Did something happen to your brother? I was under the impression Lord Kaden still held the title. Have you and Sophronia moved to Fain? You were living in the city before, correct?"

I suppressed a chuckle at Kiernan's smirk, still feigning innocence. Hamon opened his mouth to respond, but closed it quickly. A sly smile formed on his face and he nodded to Kiernan before returning to his wife's side on the other end of the room. Kiernan chuckled.

"You passed his test," he whispered. "Hamon's one of my oldest friends, and he's taken it upon himself to make sure you've been studying well."

"They're not *all* that bad, then."

Kiernan shook his head. "Hamon still wants power—he'd love to rule his brother's island—but he's a good man at heart. At least, I can tolerate him more than once a year."

I smiled wryly, quickly returning my attention to the guests. Now that Hamon had spoken to me, everyone else felt comfortable enough to introduce themselves. Lord Kaden did come up, warning me not to believe a word his brother spoke. I hid my laughter.

After a few minutes, the men surrounded Kiernan and the women pulled me away. All of them had very similar gowns, mostly in the kingdom's colors of blue and gold, and I couldn't help but feel a little out of place wearing green. I wondered why Miss Grayson had chosen it.

The only woman not joining the group was Ina, and it wasn't hard to guess why. Her eyes darted from me to Kiernan, always lingering on Kiernan with longing and me with contempt.

"So, Kenna," one of the ladies said suddenly, interrupting my thoughts. It was Lady Eloise of the southern island, Caldsen. "Which house do you descend from?"

"I'm an orphan, Lady Eloise," I said calmly. "I never knew my parents."

She raised her eyebrows. "But surely your uncle has told you your lineage."

"He doesn't know it," I said, receiving a few odd glances. "If there is nobility in me, it's in my mother's line."

"Then why on earth are you living in the castle?" Lady Ariadne blurted out disdainfully. She was Eloise's sister, and Lady of Terran to the south.

"His Majesty took pity on me," I said, meeting her eyes as I smiled sweetly. "He invited me to stay here under his protection."

"Why would you need protection?" asked Lady Rosalyn, surprise in her voice.

I had assumed the story would have already gotten out, so I didn't know exactly how to respond. They all stared at me as I thought, trying to find wording that would satisfy them and keep me from condemning the Gifted.

"I was kidnapped five years ago," I finally said. "His Majesty worried the kidnappers would pursue me."

The women exchanged curious looks, surprisingly disdainful. Except Lady Rosalyn. "That's dreadful!" she gasped. "I can't imagine what a struggle you've been through!"

"Never mind that, Rosalyn," Lady Nerissa, Ina's mother, said coldly. "Tell me, Lady Kenna, how do you think we could speed up the war against magic holders? They're not being destroyed fast enough."

The dinner bell relieved me from having to respond. Everyone had finally arrived, and we each found our designated seats at the table. Kiernan sat at the head, of course, and had designated that I would sit directly to his left. Lewin sat to his right, which unfortunately meant every time I looked up I saw his small, dark eyes watching me. If I looked to my right, I met Kiernan's gaze, and if I looked down the table to the left I met Ina's. I spent the majority of the meal staring at my food.

When the meal ended, Kiernan clapped loudly, and everyone stood. A servant immediately took the chair I'd been sitting on to the edge of the room. Within minutes, the floor was clear, and the musicians began to play.

No one made any move to dance, however. People were paired off, either with their spouses or acquaintances, but no one moved. I didn't realize why until Kiernan led me onto the dance floor. He stopped in the center of the room and his strong arm spun me into dancing position.

My feet and legs suddenly felt numb. I'd never completed any of the dances Miss Grayson taught me without either falling down or tripping over myself or my partner. I was dreadfully paranoid of stepping on Kiernan's feet, but I tried to smile and not let my fear show.

When we actually started dancing, my worries disappeared. From the very first step, Kiernan effortlessly took the lead. I didn't even have to think about the steps I'd studied for so many hours before performing them—the feeling returned to my legs as he guided me into each move, our two bodies flowing together as one. The room seemed to fall away, and for a moment, it was just the two of us.

When the music ended, he released me, and I curtsied. He led me back to the edge of the room, kissing my hand before finding a new partner for the next dance. I was so entranced as I stared after him that it took me far too long to notice Sir Hamon asking me to be his dancing partner. By the time I was aware of his presence, the dancing had started. He grinned and kindly told me he'd be back later.

It was the only dance I did not participate in. If Kiernan didn't make his way back to me in time, one of the lords or knights would undoubtedly lead me onto the floor. After the sixth dance, however, Kiernan strode toward me before any of the other men could, smiling as he firmly took my hand in his.

"Don't get any ideas," he teased. "I'll just have anyone you choose killed."

When I'd first met him I would have taken that statement seriously, but now I couldn't help but laugh. "Then I shouldn't tell you that Sir Brenden seemed very keen to steal me away?"

"Sir Brenden would steal any woman away that he could," he said, not bothering to lower his voice.

"I noticed as much," I said, chuckling at the disapproving look on Kiernan's face.

When he heard my laugh, he forgot about his irritation with Brenden and was once more absorbed in the music. For the next four dances, he didn't even lead me back to the edge of the room, but kept his hand in mine at all times. He was making a statement, not only to Brenden but to everyone else present: he had made his choice, and his mind wouldn't be changed.

I didn't realize just how tired I was until we stopped dancing. Even though the music hadn't stopped, neither Kiernan nor I had had a break, and we both were about to collapse. We passed through the crowd together into the gardens, lit by nothing but dim candles and the moon, bracing ourselves against the cool summer breeze. My hair started to come undone, but I ignored it. As the night progressed, I'd realized that none of the opinions of the nobles mattered to me. All that mattered was him.

"I hope you're enjoying the celebrations?" Kiernan said as we moved further from the sound of the music behind us.

"Very much," I responded, a little surprised by how sincere I was. I had expected to be much more nervous around the nobility, but while I could certainly sense judgment from some of the women, the majority of the people I'd interacted with had been pleasant. Part of me wished Miss Grayson was here to see just how successfully I was navigating the social side of things.

"I'm glad," Kiernan said, moving his arm around my waist as we walked. My smile warmed at the sensation and I leaned slightly into his side.

The happiness I felt was tempered somewhat as my thoughts wandered in the silence. Lady Nerissa's words about destroying magic holders rang in my mind. In all the time we had been spending together, I still hadn't told him about my Gift. There had been a few times I'd intended to broach the subject, but I always lost my nerve. I knew he loved me, and I knew he trusted me, but I also knew that he would undoubtedly feel betrayed to learn that, from the very first day I met him, I had been lying to him about something so consequential. The moment to bring it up had to be just right, and I simply hadn't found it yet.

I tried to push away the intrusive thoughts as we continued our stroll. When we reached the other end of the gardens, he steered me towards one of the benches.

"Would you like to sit down?"

I expected him to sit next to me, but instead he knelt on the ground, taking my hands in his. My heart jumped into my throat and I drew in a deep breath, mentally preparing myself for the words to come next, for how I would respond—

"You must be thirsty. Can I get you anything from the ballroom?"

It took me a full minute to respond. His smile grew wider and his eyes twinkled. "Yes, thank you," I said weakly, still in shock when he stood and walked back toward the castle.

You must be thirsty?

Where had that come from? Had he lost his nerve at the last second? Did he doubt my answer? Could he sense that there was something I was still holding back?

Then I remembered the glint in his eyes, the smile on his face as the confusion on mine increased. When I finally realized what had just happened, I was torn between laughing out loud and yelling after him. I shook my head, chuckling as I plotted how to repay him for his moment of fun.

It occurred to me that he might propose for real at some point in the evening, and my chest tightened. For the most part, I was eager for the proposal. I really did love him, and I was confident in saying yes, even if I hadn't yet revealed my secret.

But as much as I tried to ignore it, there was still a lingering fear that his love for me wouldn't be enough to overcome years of hatred towards an entire population of people. Yes, I had seen him soften as time went on, but it would still be a major change to his world view, and one that would have significant political and social consequences. Even if he accepted *me*, it would just be the first of many, many steps we had to take together to change the perceptions of an entire kingdom.

My thoughts wandered to the fantasy of Gifted and Ungifted living together peacefully in the kingdom, which naturally meant that they made their way towards Neal and Gideon. I felt a pang of guilt as I thought of them, shifting where I sat on the bench. If things had been different—if there had never been a war in the first place and I had met the three of them under the same circumstances—would I still have chosen Kiernan?

Shutting my eyes in an attempt to banish these thoughts, I pulled my shawl tighter around me. It was taking a bit longer for him to return than I had initially expected, but I supposed I shouldn't have been surprised. No doubt someone had pulled him aside at the first opportunity, and he was too polite not to engage in conversation for at least a moment.

Eventually, his voice floated through the silence from the entrance to the ballroom. A woman spoke as well, but I couldn't make out anything being said. I stood to see over the hedges.

It was Lady Ina. It didn't surprise me to see her confront him, but I was taken aback by the way she spoke to him. Though I couldn't understand her words, her tone was harsh and inappropriate for a lady, especially in the presence of the king. Kiernan seemed to be trying to be polite, but he grew impatient as the conversation went on.

Finally he turned away from her, headed toward me. As I watched, she grabbed his arm and pulled him back, kissing him forcefully. He dropped the glass he'd been bringing to me and it shattered as he pushed her away. She stepped toward him, but he held out his hand and shouted at her, his voice angry and powerful. Ina stumbled back.

I turned away and sat back on the bench, doing my best not to listen to his words. If I'd been listening hard enough, I would have been able to hear everything he said, but it didn't matter to me. What mattered was that he hadn't welcomed her advances—even when he didn't know I was watching he had remained faithful to me.

It was then that I resolved that my doubts weren't going to stand in the way any longer. I had chosen Kiernan, we loved each other, and nothing else mattered. I just had to believe he would still feel the same when he knew the truth.

He returned a while later, a new glass in hand. He smiled as he handed over the refreshment and sat down next to me. If I hadn't watched the interaction with Ina, I wouldn't know anything had happened. I decided it would probably be better if I didn't bring it up.

The rest of the night passed quickly. We did eventually have to return to the ballroom, though I think both of us would have preferred to remain hidden in the gardens. I met more of the nobles and danced with Kiernan until I thought I was going to drop. Overall, I enjoyed myself, but I was grateful when the celebrations died down. I was exhausted, but lingered in the ballroom as it began to empty. Even as Kiernan wished goodnight to the guests, his eyes kept darting to me, and I had the sense he didn't want me to leave just yet.

My father offered to accompany me back to my room, but I declined, deciding to wait until Kiernan was available to do so. I saw Isaiah's shoulders tense when I did, and the fatherly concern in his eyes was unmistakable. I couldn't blame him. As confident as I was that Kiernan would accept my Gift, there was no guarantee I was right. But I had faith that his love for me was strong enough to overcome the shock.

When the last person finally left, Kiernan sighed heavily, turning to me with a tired smile and offering his arm. I mirrored his expression as I took it, shutting my eyes briefly when he kissed my forehead before we made our way into the halls.

He didn't take the path to my room that I would have expected, apparently wanting to extend the night a little further. I could feel my feet throbbing with each step, but I pushed the sensation aside. I didn't mind bearing a little more discomfort to spend a few extra minutes with him.

As often was the case, he led me to the towers once more. My lips tingled as they curved into a smile at the memory of our first kiss. Kiernan slid his arm out of mine and around my waist as we paused about halfway across the overlook, facing the garden side of the view. Beyond the castle grounds, flickering lights illuminated various parts of the city below. Though distant, I could hear the sounds of music and laughter in the brightest area, signs of the more local celebration of the kingdom's founding.

"The people seem to be enjoying themselves," I remarked, somewhat surprised that the party was still noticeable from this distance at this hour of the night.

"A good celebration does a lot to lift peoples' spirits," Kiernan said. "We should hold another one soon."

I bit the inside of my lip and reached to tuck a loose curl back into my bun. "What did you have in mind?" I asked, feigning ignorance.

"Your uncle tells me your birthday is coming up. That would certainly be a reason to celebrate."

"Yes, but how many of the people are really going to care about one person's birthday?" I said. "It should be something more exciting than that."

He hummed a bit in response, as if deep in thought. "I suppose you're right. Perhaps I could organize a special festival. Or a tournament. We haven't had one in some time, since the majority of the knights have been away from the city."

"Perhaps," I muttered.

Slowly, he slipped his arm from my waist and took a small step to the side. "Oh perhaps …"

His voice trailed off. My heart jumped into my throat as his silence prompted me to look away from the view and turn to face him. He was no longer standing.

He was kneeling.

His eyes shone. "I think a wedding would be a grand celebration, if you'll have me," he said softly. He took my hands in his, rubbing his thumb across my skin. I felt my eyes begin to well up, but I willed myself to keep my composure, squeezing his hands lightly. There was a shaky edge to his voice as he spoke again.

"Kenna Balton, will you do me the honor of becoming my wife?"

My lips quivered but I shrugged. "I'm not sure I'm very fond of weddings."

Kiernan blinked, his smile faltering as he stared at me. After an agonizing moment, he caught the glint in my eyes, the same glint that had been in his earlier that evening in the gardens. A laugh of relief escaped his lips and he stood to wrap me in an embrace, lifting me off the ground and spinning me around above the city. The instant my feet were again on the ground, our lips met, and I melted into his arms.

"Yes," I whispered against his lips as we began to part, to which he responded by immediately resuming the kiss. I'd never imagined I would be this happy when the moment came, but I felt as if my heart was going to burst out of my chest.

It was hard to say goodnight after that, but we both had to admit that we needed rest after such an eventful day. He escorted me to my room, randomly stopping in the hall to pull me against him and kiss me three more times before we reluctantly parted.

I collapsed on my bed with a wave of elation and exhaustion, and I wasn't surprised at all when Abi ran into the room just moments later. She squealed and jumped onto my bed, throwing her arms around me. I returned her embrace, laughing with the purest joy.

CHAPTER NINETEEN

THE WEIGHT OF THE CROWN

Preparations for the wedding started immediately. Over breakfast, Kiernan and I discussed when to have the wedding and decided on two weeks later. When he told Miss Grayson the date, I thought she was going to pass out. She was determined to make sure everything I did on the wedding day was perfect, from what I said to how I said it to who I said it to. I had to practice walking to the altar, practice my curtsy even more, and learn an entire new dance for the reception. Again Franklin helped me, and again he left with bruised feet. Clearly she did not think I was ready to be queen, but her opinion didn't much matter.

When I wasn't sequestered in Miss Grayson's chambers, I made an effort to spend more time with the lords and ladies who remained at the castle. At the announcement of the wedding, most of them had opted to extend their stay rather than travel back to their respective islands only to return two weeks later. Lady Ina and her family were an exception, leaving immediately the morning after the celebration, I presumed at Kiernan's insistence.

Of all the ladies in the kingdom, Lady Rosalyn was the most agreeable. The other women seemed to think she was too talkative, but I didn't mind. She was still fairly shallow but in more of a childlike way than the others. Her husband, Logan, was also pleasant to be around. He was by far the least power hungry of all the lords, and he and Kiernan were as close to being friends as Kiernan was with anyone.

That fact bothered me. Kiernan had no real friends—not among his servants, the knights, or the lords. I couldn't help but wonder if his feelings for me were brought about more because he hadn't had many social interactions that weren't guarded. I didn't think they weren't genuine—I couldn't possibly think that—but I made it a personal goal to help him develop other genuine relationships in the future.

Two days after the proposal, a tailor came to take my measurements. She asked me what felt like a million questions about what I wanted, intending to completely personalize the garment for the woman who was going to be queen. I felt overwhelmed and for most of them had no idea how to respond. When she returned a week later with the finished dress, it was worth it. I gazed in awe at the mirror. The dress was covered in the most beautiful lace and beading, and it fit me perfectly, better than any of my other dresses ever had.

My belongings were transferred from my room to the queen's room in Kiernan's chambers. For the moment, I had Abi take Kindra's book for safe keeping, not wanting to risk it being discovered and destroyed. My stomach flipped upside down during this process. I couldn't doubt his love for me, but the thought of revealing to him who I truly was still made my head feel like it was about to explode. I knew I had to tell him before we were married, or both of us would regret the consequences.

The problem was, we never had a moment alone. We always dined in public, and afterwards were pulled in separate directions. Kiernan worked on planning the banquet and ball while I mingled with the ladies or went back to more lessons with Miss Grayson. We were only together when eating meals and working on the decorations, and servants buzzed around us during both.

But aside from my growing nervousness, it was a happy two weeks. Apparently I had made a good impression with the nobility at the ball and in the following days, or at least if I hadn't, they were gracious enough to accept Kiernan's decision. Even Lady Ariadne and Lady Eloise, who had been clearly shocked to learn that I wasn't of noble blood myself, went out of their way to congratulate me, paying me frequent compliments and expressing that they were certain I would be a wonderful queen. I felt a bit more nervous as I started to truly consider what 'being queen' meant, but I decided that was something I could focus on after everything else was taken care of.

The only person clearly unhappy with the match, aside from my father, was Lewin. His scowl deepened every time he saw me and more than once I caught him whispering to Kiernan at meals or in the halls. Kiernan always ignored him, but he seemed to be growing increasingly frustrated at his persistent objections. I didn't understand why he tolerated the behavior at all. From everything I had seen, Lewin was a manipulative and bloodthirsty man who wanted nothing more than to control the kingdom from the shadows, something I was eager to convince Kiernan to put a stop to.

A few days before the wedding, I desperately needed a break. Abi and I escaped into the passageways during my lessons, laughing as Miss Grayson and my other attendants scrambled around the building to find me. We headed to the library on a whim, snickering as we climbed out of the bookcase that hid the secret door. Abi was about to say something when we heard voices coming from the entrance. Quickly, we scrambled back into the passageway, but instead of running, pressed our ears against the wall.

"It's Kiernan," she whispered.

I frowned. "He's supposed to be meeting with the captains."

"Your Majesty, I really do need to speak to you," another man's voice said.

"And you may, Captain Stole," Kiernan said. "I just have a couple books I need to find for reference."

Stole cleared his throat. "You love your betrothed, yes?"

"Of course."

"Then you would want her to be as safe as possible, wouldn't you?"

I could hear the frown in his voice. "I don't see why she would be in any danger."

The captain took a deep breath. "I believe one of your knights may be plotting her death."

Kiernan's footsteps stopped. So did my heart. I heard Abi gasp and she grasped my hand.

"Who might that be?"

I knew the answer before Stole spoke.

"Captain Lewin."

Kiernan sighed, sounding relieved. "You're mistaken. Captain Lewin is loyal to me and the crown. He would do nothing to harm Kenna."

"With all due respect, Your Majesty, I'm not so certain that's true. He's openly against this union."

"As he's made known to me, many times. But I've made it clear to him that his opinions on the matter are irrelevant."

"But Your Majesty—"

"I've heard enough of this, Captain Stole," Kiernan said, his voice growing more stern. "Captain Lewin's concerns are based on me being hasty, and since I have made my thoughts clear on the matter he has nothing more to fear. Concern yourself with the security during the wedding service rather than accusing one of your fellow officers of such a thing."

Stole didn't say anything else, and soon we heard their footsteps leaving the library. I leaned against the wall, letting out a deep breath. Abi didn't let go of my hand.

"Do you think Kiernan's right?" Abi said, her eyes full of concern.

I bit my lip. "I certainly hope so."

"Lady Kenna!" a voice called from the entrance to the library. "Are you in here?"

Abi and I chuckled, shaking off our feelings of uneasiness, and hurried back down the passageway.

***

The day before the wedding was the most hectic. I spent almost all day in Miss Grayson's room, being tested and retested over everything she'd taught me during my entire time at the castle. I was shocked when, just before I left for the evening, she smiled and let her always crossed arms fall to her sides.

"You will make a fine queen, Lady Kenna," she said, curtsying deeply, avoiding eye contact. "I look forward to serving you."

A knot caught in my throat. I could feel her sincerity, and all the stress from those lessons melted away in that moment.

"Thank you," I stammered, not knowing what else to say. She curtsied again as Abi knocked on the door.

I wasn't supposed to see Kiernan the day before the wedding. It was some silly tradition I had no intention of following. I needed to speak with him before the ceremony in the morning—he couldn't marry me without knowing the truth. I had tried desperately to catch him after dinner the last few nights, but inevitably one of us had been pulled in another direction before I could actually approach the subject privately. It was now or never.

"He's dining with the lords right now," Abi whispered as Miss Grayson's door closed. "When the meal is finished, he'll most likely go for a walk along the towers as usual. You wait there, and I'll watch for him."

I hugged her tightly and hurried to the tower. As I waited, I played out the conversation in my mind, preparing myself for two different scenarios. I believed and desperately hoped he would understand, however hard it was for him, but the fear grew ever stronger that he wouldn't be able to overcome years of building hatred and fear.

Hurried steps came down the hall and Abi poked her head through the doorway and winked. Kiernan was on his way. The butterflies in my stomach multiplied to an immeasurable number. I took a hold of the tower edge, steadying myself. As always, the waves of the ocean beat against the cliffs in an almost hypnotic fashion. I closed my eyes, the sound bringing me back to years and years of living on a beach, first with Elizabeth and then with the Grisons. Everything about my life and expectations had changed. If my worldview could alter so drastically, surely Kiernan's could as well.

My eyes were still closed when he came outside, and I heard his footsteps stop.

"Kenna," he said, torn between surprise and delight. "What are you doing here? You're supposed to be in bed."

I smiled softly as I turned and opened my eyes to meet his eyes, trying to take comfort in the thought I had just had and remain calm. "I needed to see you."

He smirked. "We're not supposed to see each other tonight."

"Too late," I said. He laughed, and my nerves subsided. He closed the distance between us and wrapped me in his arms.

"Is everything all right? Are you satisfied with the flower arrangements? I know you spent a lot of time planning the decoration for the ballroom—"

"Everything's wonderful," I said sincerely. "There's just ... something I need to tell you."

He raised an eyebrow. "What is it, Love?"

I took a deep breath, trying to remember how I'd decided to start the conversation. He waited patiently. I focused on how strong he felt holding me there, feeling another dose of comfort as his hand gently rubbed my back.

"There's something you don't know about me," I started. "When the Knights found me six months ago, I—"

"*What in the world are you doing out here?*"

Both of us whirled around to see Miss Grayson storming over to us, her eyes furious. Kiernan released me instantly, stepping backward out of surprise and a small amount of fear.

"You're supposed to be in bed!" she exclaimed. "Your Majesty, you should know better than this! It's bad luck to see the bride the night before the wedding!"

"Miss Grayson—"

"You're coming with me right now," she said, interrupting her king without a second thought and taking a hold of my arm. "I can't believe you would disregard something as simple as not seeing him for one night."

Kiernan stood back in surprise as we left. I had no choice but to let Miss Grayson lead me back to my room, scolding me the entire way. I couldn't speak to Kiernan in the presence of anyone else, not about this.

It was the most sleepless night of my life. Despite Abi's comforting words, I tossed and turned, haunted with nightmares of him drawing his sword as soon as I revealed my secret and killing me in front of all the guests. I was drenched in sweat when I awoke.

I lay awake in my bed for hours before hearing a knock. I hurried to make myself presentable, but as soon as I opened the door, I regretted it. A throng of maids and attendants stormed into my room, pinching and prodding every part of me, hurriedly feeding me breakfast, forcing me into my wedding gown, and confirming decoration choices. It was unbearable. People pulled at the hair on my head at the exact same time that others pinched my cheeks. My attendants put accessories on my wrists, neck, and anywhere else they could. I took deep breaths and tried to relax, but nothing helped. By the time I was completely dressed and ready, I felt too dizzy to stand, let alone walk to the altar.

The dizziness left at the sight of my reflection. The dress was just as beautiful as I remembered, with gold, swirling details against the white of the fabric. The intricate circlet braided into my hair fit perfectly, and for once I didn't mind having my hair pulled up. I wore a beautiful pearl necklace and earrings, and my shoes were surprisingly comfortable for their elegance.

As I stared in disbelief at my reflection, hardly recognizing myself, Abi answered a knock on my door. My father entered, dressed in a light blue tunic with gold embellishments. Through my nerves, I smiled at him. To my surprise, he smiled as well.

He approached and took my hands in his. "My, you look like your mother. Of course, she was dressed simpler than you, but I had never seen anyone so beautiful—until now."

A knot formed in my throat and I squeezed his hands. Lovingly, he kissed my cheek and took my arm, leading me to the entryway. The wedding was being held on the front steps of the castle so all the citizens of the city—carefully controlled by Kiernan's personal guard—could watch through the gates if they so wished. The lords, ladies, and knights filled the courtyard itself. Music already played outside as I approached. I gripped my father's arm tighter, not entirely sure if I was nervous or excited.

When the front doors opened, deafening cheers filled the air. I could barely hear the fanfare over all the noise. The gates were so crowded I couldn't see where the crowd ended. The nobles in the courtyard stared upwards, extending their necks. My ears rang uncomfortably as I stepped into the bright sunlight.

All the noise turned to silence when I met Kiernan's eyes. If I hadn't been certain of his love before, that look was enough to convince me. His eyes were shining.

It seemed to take ages to reach him, when in fact it was only a few steps. My father released my arm somewhat reluctantly. Kiernan was too focused on me to notice. He took my hands in his and gave them a squeeze.

Hierarch Gordon raised his arms for silence. He was the most revered hierarch in the kingdom and had traveled down from Fain to perform the ceremony. He married Kiernan's parents as well, so he seemed a natural choice. Though he was growing older, the happiness of the event had caught hold of him as well, and there was a youthful glow around him.

"My lords and ladies," he began as the crowd died down, "misters and misses, we thank you for coming to witness the union of Lady Kenna Balton and our beloved King Kiernan Frewin."

Another cheer arose, and he continued the service when they quieted, but my legs kept shaking. Soon Kiernan repeated the words Hierarch Gordon spoke.

"I, Kiernan Frewin, King of Orkeia—vow to take you, Kenna Balton, as my wife and queen—to cherish you with a love as deep as the sea—as powerful as the storms—as constant as the sun and the moon—"

His already bright eyes brightened as he said the last phrase, holding onto my hands slightly tighter. "May the Mother and Father forever bless our union."

The crowd cheered for a moment, but the ceremony wasn't over yet. Hierarch Gordon turned to me, the same smile on his face.

"I, Kenna Balton, Lady of the kingdom—" he said loudly so the crowd could hear.

I took a deep breath, doing my best not to speak too softly. "I, Kenna Balton, Lady of the kingdom—"

"Vow to take you, Kiernan Frewin, as my husband and king."

"Vow to take you, Kiernan Frewin—" Something caught in my throat. "—as my husband and king."

I continued to repeat each of the lines: "To cherish you with a love as deep as the sea—as powerful as the storms—as constant as the sun and the moon—"

Hierarch Gordon smiled at the last line. "May the Mother and Father forever bless our union."

The enormity of this moment took all the air from my lungs, and I had to take a moment to remind myself how to breathe before I could manage to speak the final words.

"May the Mother and Father forever bless our union."

The cheers were deafening. Without waiting for the hierarch's permission, Kiernan pulled me into an embrace and kissed me passionately. My entire body trembled against his, and I threw my arms around his neck.

"I present King Kiernan and Queen Kenna Frewin, holy sovereigns of Orkeia!" Hierarch Gordon announced, though the words were impossible for most people to hear over the crowd. Kiernan reluctantly broke the kiss to face the people, taking my hand in his and raising our interlocked fingers in a celebratory gesture. As he did, my legs began to shake once again.

I'm the queen.

It's fortunate Kiernan carried me into the castle, because I don't think I would have been able to walk. Since I didn't hold any actual political power, a coronation ceremony was unnecessary—being Kiernan's wife automatically made me queen of Orkeia. I, a white witch, was the wife of the king, the man waging a war against my people. The queen of Orkeia was one of the very people he and his knights had sought to destroy, and he didn't even know it.

The thought dug a deep pit of guilt and regret in my stomach. I had to tell him before tonight, and I didn't know when the opportunity would present itself.

We held a late, celebratory lunch. There was no opportunity for privacy. Kiernan and I sat together at the head of the table, naturally the focus of all conversation. I didn't eat much—I felt like I was going to be sick.

I'd hoped we'd have a moment alone after the banquet, but I wasn't so lucky. We immediately climbed the stairs to the throne room, now decorated with flowers of all kinds and colors. I'd been nervous about people approving of the decorations, but it didn't seem to matter now.

A second, smaller throne had been placed next to Kiernan's, and he led me to it. Sitting there at the head of the room, I could almost feel the weight of the entire kingdom falling upon my shoulders. Kiernan's smile was wider than I'd ever seen it as the nobles and knights entered, each in turn approaching the throne and bowing or curtsying to the two of us. With each greeting, I felt more and more like a fraud. Somehow, I still managed to smile and thank them.

When the musicians took their places, Kiernan escorted me into the middle of the floor. All the guests watched us dance together, clapping as the music faded into the next dance. The sensation of dancing with him thrilled me just as before, and at least momentarily quieted my thoughts and fears about the secret he still didn't know I held.

The ball went on for hours. Every once and a while Kiernan and I returned to the dais to catch our breath, but we were soon on the floor again. He loved to dance, and even though I lacked the talent, I loved dancing with him. But I kept looking for an opportunity to step out, to have a private word with him, to confess what was eating me up inside. The more time that passed, the harder it was to keep myself from hyperventilating.

"Kiernan," I breathed once when we sat down for a break. "I need to speak with you."

"What is it, my love?" he asked, leaning on the arm of his throne. His face was flushed red from all the dancing, but his smile was as wide as ever.

I glanced nervously around the room. "Could we step out for some air?"

Hearing the shakiness in my voice, he furrowed his eyebrows. "Is everything all right?"

"I just want some air. Do you think we could leave the party for a few minutes?"

He opened his mouth to respond, but I never heard his answer. The doors opened loudly and trumpets sounded. A large man with a jet black beard entered followed by a swarm of attendants. He wore a deep purple robe with brilliant gold trim over a shining golden tunic, a large crown filled with jewels of all kinds adorning his head. I recognized him at once as King Simeon, the ruler of the neighboring kingdom of Cogfaire.

Kiernan immediately stood, and I joined him. It was rare for Simeon to leave his kingdom, and even rarer for him to attend celebrations. He'd been invited to the wedding, but no one had actually expected him to come.

"My friend!" Kiernan said, stepping down from the dais. I knew very well that he and Simeon were far from friends, but that was the language of politics. "So glad you could make it! I thought you would be too busy fighting off the invaders from the south."

"How could I miss your wedding?" said Simeon, patting Kiernan on the back. He was much older than Kiernan, and obviously more experienced, but Kiernan didn't let that intimidate him. He laughed loudly and returned the gesture.

"Another throne for His Majesty," he called.

Servants quickly moved to do as ordered, but Simeon waved his hand dismissively. "Not on your wedding day, Kiernan. I'm here as simply another guest."

Somehow I highly doubted that a king—particularly one who chose to dress so exuberantly and make such a grand entrance—would truly see himself as 'simply another guest,' and I was sure Kiernan didn't think so either. But it wouldn't do to insist when Simeon had already 'humbly' refused.

"Very well then," Kiernan said, dismissing the servants with a nod. "Everyone, carry on!"

The music resumed, and the couples on the floor returned to their places. Simeon's attendants joined the dance, but Simeon remained where he was, his eyes flickering to me.

"My, I do envy you," he said, a disturbing glint in his eyes. "Queen Kenna, you are the fairest jewel I have ever seen."

"That she is," Kiernan said, motioning for me to step down and join him. I did so somewhat reluctantly. King Simeon was notoriously a warlord, and not in the same way that my husband had been waging a war. As wrong as the Slaughters were, they were motivated by a desire to protect the people of Orkeia. Simeon's only desire in the battles he waged seemed to be conquering as much territory in the mainland to the south as possible.

Despite my discomfort, I smiled and curtsied deeply, averting my eyes. "Honored to make your acquaintance, King Simeon."

"The honor is all mine," he said, his lips resting on my hand too long.

Kiernan's eyes flashed, and he pulled me closer to him. "How long will you be staying, Simeon?"

"Just the night," he said. "I'm on my way to the next set of islands, just North, across the Barren Ocean. I decided I might as well stop and join in the celebrations."

"You are most welcome," Kiernan said, but his voice wasn't as strong as before. "Anything you wish, you need only ask for it."

It was clear from his tone of voice that the term *anything* was very subjective. Simeon grinned, making me extremely uneasy.

"Well, I won't keep you any longer," he said, stepping aside. "Congratulations, Your Majesties."

Kiernan nodded civilly and escorted me back onto the floor. I stared straight ahead. These were the people I was going to be socializing with for the rest of my life, constantly feigning politeness and friendship. The only relief I found was in Kiernan's comforting smile, relaying without words that everything would be all right. He obviously didn't enjoy socializing with Simeon any more than I did.

We didn't get the chance to talk anymore during the dance. Even when we were sitting and resting, someone was always there to give us their congratulations. Sir Hamon insisted on dancing with me, no matter how many times I said I was too tired. Eventually, the hall cleared, until only a couple of the lords and captains remained.

Among them was Lewin. He grimaced even more than usual, and I shivered when he caught my eye as I remembered Captain Stole's concerns. To my relief, he kept his distance, and eventually left with a number of King Simeon's attendants. Kiernan remained oblivious to Lewin's displeasure and continued to entertain, a huge smile on his face, until the very last person left the ballroom.

Finally, we were alone.

Kiernan breathed a sigh of relief and faced me. His eyes sparkled in a way I hadn't seen before. As he held out his arm, my stomach turned. I knew what was on his mind. My whole mind had been on revealing my identity. How could I have forgotten about this next part? Numbly, I took his arm and let him lead me to my new quarters, my mind spinning.

"I'm so happy, Kenna!" he said lovingly as we traveled through the secret passage from the throne room to his—*our*—sitting room. "You are the best thing that's happened to me."

"You really don't have to say that," I muttered, my heart beating uncomfortably. What if my father was right? What if he did reject me, claim that I used sorcery to seduce him? How could I convince him that I was telling the truth, that magic in and of itself wasn't evil? That *I* wasn't evil?

I ran out of time to think as we reached the end of the passageway and passed into the sitting room. The servants had retired to their own quarters for the night, granting us privacy. I opened my mouth to speak, still unsure what to say, but my thoughts left me as Kiernan opened a pair of double doors.

Slowly, I entered the extravagant, scarlet room, furnished with eclectic and beautiful furniture from all parts of the world. My eyes widened at the sight of the silk tapestries and rich rugs. I stood quite still, taking it all in, hardly daring to believe I could ever feel at home in this place—if I even had the chance to try.

Kiernan closed the doors behind us. I felt him place a hand on my shoulder, and his lips brushed my neck. I closed my eyes at the sensation, shivering as his hand traveled down the laces on my back.

"Kiernan," I breathed, stumbling forward. My cheeks burned hotter than a fire. I turned to face him, but couldn't meet his eyes.

"There's something I need to tell you."

"I'm sure it can wait," he said, pulling me into his arms. Our lips met, and he backed me up against the wall, pressing his body against mine. I felt the urge to simply melt into the kiss, but instead broke it, pushing gently against his chest to prompt him to stop.

"No, it can't," I gasped.

He only backed up enough to give me space to breathe. After recovering from his surprise, he smiled playfully at me. "What great secret have you been keeping from me, Dearest?"

I couldn't smile in response. My heart was racing uncontrollably, the air in the room suddenly suffocating. "When your men found me, I wasn't being held captive."

His expression questioned why in the world I would bring it up *now* of all times, but he took a small step back, finally sensing I was serious. His arms remained loosely wrapped around me. "You had escaped, then?"

"I didn't escape. I was never their prisoner." My voice cracked. "I was living there."

He frowned. "Kenna, I don't understand."

My vision blurred as my eyes began to water. I could tell he was concerned with the appearance of the tears, but I imagined that would change in a moment. The crushing guilt of springing such a huge revelation on him made me swallow a sob. Just as he opened his mouth to speak again, I finally worked up the courage to say it.

"I'm a witch, Kiernan."

Time seemed to stand still, my heavy breathing the only sound in the room. His confusion quickly changed to shock, which then morphed into anger. Just as I thought he was about to demand my death, his anger changed to something else. His eyes filled with pain and distress, and his arms fell to his sides. He stumbled away from me, sitting down on the bed.

"A what?" he croaked.

My hands trembled as they pressed against the wall behind me. "They were my family. I was protecting them. I should have died, but Isaiah lied to save me."

"Why?"

"Because he's my father."

Kiernan showed no additional surprise at this newfound knowledge. I held my breath, waiting for him to say something, anything, that would tell me how to act. There were so many things I wanted to say to him, to explain and apologize for, but none of them came out. He struggled to find his voice as well. He kept opening and closing his mouth, his eyes staring in my direction without actually seeing me.

Desperately, I knelt at his feet, the tears beginning to escape my eyes and roll down my cheeks. "I am so sorry," I stammered. "I tried to tell you last night, and so many times before that, I—I didn't want it to be like this. At first I was keeping it from you for my own protection, but that doesn't matter anymore. Don't punish Isaiah for this, it's not his fault—I should be blamed. I never meant to hurt you—"

I stopped myself, knowing that if I continued I would just keep stumbling through words in a verbal circle. He kept his head down, refusing to meet my eyes. My heart broke more with every moment of silence. I wanted so much to tell him that I loved him, but I knew those words would only deepen his pain.

I swallowed another sob and bowed my head. "I am your wife now," I whispered, "and you may do as you will with me. According to the law, I should be put to death. I only ask that if it is your wish to kill me, I die by your hand."

He seemed surprised by this statement and opened his mouth, but still didn't make a sound. I sat on the ground in front of him in silence, knowing that there was nothing more to say.

"Your room is through that door," he finally muttered, nodding to his right.

I felt tears come to my eyes, but held them back. "Kiernan, I—"

"Good night," he said, his voice stronger as we made eye contact once more. I'd expected to see anger or sadness in his expression, but instead I saw nothing. His eyes were as cold and emotionless as when we first met.

Slowly, I stood and crossed the room to the door he indicated, leaving him sitting alone on the bed. I paused as I turned the knob, taking one last look at him. He stared at the floor again, gripping the edge of the bed with white knuckles. I barely made it through the door before the sobs I'd been holding in began to escape my throat of their own accord.

I fell onto my bed in my wedding dress, shaking, the lace, trimmings, and jewelry all pressing into my skin like accusing daggers. How could I ever have believed he would accept me? After everything he'd been through and how long he'd been working to eliminate magic, how could I think he'd still love me knowing how much I had lied?

That night, I dreamt of Kiernan coming in the night and stabbing me in the heart before going out in search of more magic holders. I watched in spirit as he traveled straight to the Grison's home, as if he'd already known where they were. They tried to fight him, but one by one every member of my family fell. He sliced open Gideon's throat with his sword, and I awoke with a stifled scream. I could have sworn the door between our rooms was open when I first opened my eyes. When I looked again it was closed, no light coming through the cracks.

Chapter Twenty

BREAKING THE SILENCE

I caught my breath as my back hit the wall. Kiernan advanced, his eyes colder than I'd ever seen them. He drew his sword and placed the blade against my throat. Warm blood trickled down my neck, and my eyes clouded with tears.

"Please," I whispered. "I love you."

"How could I ever love such a vile creature?" he hissed.

A sob escaped me as he drew back his sword, aiming for my heart. I couldn't move. His expression hardened. He thrust forward, and my chest exploded with pain—

For the third night in a row, I awoke screaming. I stifled the sound as quickly as I could. Kiernan appeared to be asleep in the next room, but then again, I wouldn't know. I hadn't seen him since the wedding three days ago.

He hadn't left his room. The first morning, Franklin seemed surprised when Kiernan didn't join me in the dining area for breakfast, but he didn't ask any questions. I ate in silence, staring at the doors to my husband's bedroom and waiting for him to come out and tell me my fate. He never did.

Franklin was the only person allowed in the quarters for those three days. It was supposed to be a time for us to be alone, away from Kiernan's duties as king, free from obligations. Instead, it was three days of torture, dreaming of my death each night and waiting for it to come during the day.

The one time I knocked on his door, there was no response, and I didn't have the courage to enter uninvited.

The second morning, I tried to write letters to Abi and Isaiah, to let them know I was all right and put their minds at ease. But after several attempts, I threw the parchments in the fire, my eyes filling with tears as I watched it be engulfed in flames. How could I reassure them when, for all I knew, their worst fears might still be realized?

Now, on the third morning, I stared at his door, the nightmare fresh in my mind. All my tears were spent. There was part of me that just wanted my heart to stop beating. At least then I wouldn't have to deal with the agony of dreaming of my death every night.

Slowly, I climbed out of bed, pulling on a robe over my nightgown. The sun had barely begun to rise. I stepped out onto my balcony, shivering in the cold, and looked down at the courtyard below, covered in frost.

Eventually, the sounds of stirring from his room caused me to turn. A glow of candlelight leaked under his door into my room. It seemed we were both always up at this hour, but we never spoke. I closed my eyes, listening to his footsteps, familiar with the sound of his pacing by now. I remained where I was, wishing he would open the door but knowing he never would.

I would have to end the silence.

Whether he accepted or killed me, it would be today. I wasn't going to endure one more night of those nightmares. If he chose to kill me, I wanted it to be over with. I wanted to live in the Other Worlds in peace.

Determined, yet terrified, I approached the door, pausing with my hand on the handle. His footsteps had stopped. Breathing deeply, I turned the knob and opened the door.

He sat on the edge of his bed, still in his nightclothes. His hair was more unkempt than I'd ever seen it, and the wrinkles in his clothing told me he hadn't changed for at least a day. The sight only heightened the guilt I felt for what I'd put him through, and it took all my will to stop myself from retreating back into the other room.

I was sure he'd heard me enter, but his gaze remained fixed on the ground. Leaving the door open, I stepped toward him, trying desperately to stop my hands from shaking. Silently, I sat on the ground at his feet, and just—waited.

I thought I would go mad in the silence. Unable to look at him, I stared at the rug. I had the intricate pattern memorized before either of us spoke. There were a few times he breathed deeply and my heart jumped in fear and anticipation, but no sound escaped his lips. By now the sun was bright in the sky. It felt like we were going to sit there forever.

Finally, he shifted, pressing his hands against his legs.

"Why don't you have a mark?"

It wasn't exactly what I'd expected, but I answered quietly. "I do."

"Where is it?"

I hesitated a moment before shifting my weight to my left side. He was my husband now, after all, and he had the right to see it. Slowly, I pulled up my nightgown to reveal the heart on my thigh, feeling some heat come to my cheeks. From the position of his head, I could tell he was looking at it, but I was still unable to see his eyes.

Slowly, he slid off the bed onto the floor next to me. He leaned down, sweetly kissing the middle of the heart. Tears that I thought were well spent began to fall as he straightened, his face inches from mine.

"I love you," he said, his voice cracking. Tears formed in his own eyes—the same warm eyes I'd fallen in love with, full of life and emotion.

"Oh, how I love you!" he exclaimed breathlessly, wrapping me in his arms. Our tears intermingled as the kiss deepened. As he stood and lifted me from the ground, my heavy heart lifted as well, and for the first time in a long time, I could finally breathe.

***

I could have stayed there wrapped in his arms forever, but since Kiernan hadn't been out of his room for days, we dressed for breakfast. My heart bursting with happiness, I was finally able to sit down and write letters to

Abi and my father, assuring them I was safe. Once I'd finished and sealed both letters, Kiernan and I walked hand in hand out of his room.

When we entered the dining area, Franklin stood a little straighter. He still didn't ask questions, but he seemed to linger more than was necessary or usual even after the meal was served. Kiernan politely dismissed him, saying he would ring for him when we finished. As he left, I handed him the letters, telling him to ask both Abi and Isaiah to visit the next day. I wanted at least one day to enjoy my time with Kiernan.

"I'm sorry," my husband said for the millionth time once Franklin closed the door behind him. "It just took me so much by surprise—"

"How many times do I need to tell you I've forgiven you?" I interrupted, shaking my head. "I'm the one who needs to be forgiven. I should have found a way to tell you sooner."

He reached across the table and squeezed my hand. "There's nothing to forgive," he whispered, kissing my hand before returning to his food.

We ate in comfortable silence. We hadn't yet discussed the Slaughters, but if the king of Orkeia could fall in love with a witch, anything was possible.

As if hearing my thoughts, Kiernan sighed and set down his fork. "I've been too convincing, Kenna—the entire kingdom believes witches are evil."

"It's not going to happen overnight," I acknowledged. "I mean, it took you three days to decide not to kill me."

He shook his head. "I decided not to kill you that first night."

"But you hadn't decided whether or not I was evil," I said as I took his hand and gave it a squeeze. "If we stop spreading the idea that the Gifted need to be destroyed and start subtly introducing the things that connect us, people's attitudes will begin to change. No one *wants* to be living in a kingdom at war."

His smile warmed as he gazed at me. "You are going to be a magnificent queen," he said.

I laughed, surprised at the sudden shift in conversation. "Oh? And what makes you so sure?"

"You once told me that death is never something to be celebrated," he recalled. "It was a bold statement to make to the king, but more than that, it was a wise observation, and one filled with charity towards all people. I don't know if I would have said it myself were I in your shoes—in fact, I wouldn't blame you for having wanted *me* dead."

"I did," I admitted with a wry smile. "For a long time. But then I met you."

He squeezed my hand in response, his dark blue eyes admiring me for another moment before he spoke once more. "Tell me more about your people. About magic."

As I began to describe the differences between sorcerers and the different types of witches, he listened intently. As joyful as it had been to share this with Abi, it paled in comparison to the joy I felt sharing it with him—with my husband.

"I'm sorry you've had to hide this for so long," he sighed after what must have been an hour of conversation, leaning back in his chair and shaking his head.

"It's all right," I insisted, then added in a bit of a teasing, flirtatious tone, "I'm sure you'll make it up to me."

He lifted his head to look at me again and smirked a little, his gaze lingering on my lips. "I certainly intend to."

Standing, I moved the small distance between us to sit on his lap. He slowly wrapped his arms around me as I did, rubbing my back. I reached out and ran a hand through his hair, then resting it on his cheek as I gazed at him for a moment before gently bringing my lips to his in a sweet kiss.

"I love you," I said.

"And I love you," he said softly, pulling me slightly closer against his chest. "Every part of you."

On that beautiful day, all of my worries seemed irrelevant, and the world was completely peaceful. Nothing existed but the two of us. Things would soon be different as we attempted to change the way an entire kingdom of people thought, but it didn't matter just then. I felt as if we'd already succeeded, and there was no doubt in my mind that one day I would entertain the Grisons and Patersons in the castle.

That night, my dreams were far from nightmares.

***

I awoke to feel Kiernan tracing patterns on my back. My lips curved upwards as he kissed my neck. Seeing my body shift, he realized I was awake and sat up to light a candle on the bedside table.

"Good morning," I mumbled, rolling over to see him. He kissed me sweetly, but I could tell his thoughts were elsewhere.

"I have to conduct a few trials today," he explained when he saw the curiosity in my eyes. "We're supposed to start in an hour."

"Trials for what?"

He climbed out of the bed and began dressing. "I'm not sure. Lewin organizes them. I don't know who's being tried or what their crime is until the trial is presented."

"That sounds...stressful," I said. I wanted to say more about my misgivings about Lewin specifically being in charge of arranging trials given his treatment of me and the other prisoners he'd held in that horrible dungeon, but for the moment, I kept those thoughts to myself.

Sighing, he nodded in agreement. "I'll have Franklin bring you breakfast."

"Actually...do you think I could come?" I asked.

"You want to observe the trials?" he said, raising his eyebrows.

"I mean...I am the queen now," I said with a shrug. "I should probably educate myself more on this side of things. Besides, if I come I can spend more time with you."

He smirked a little, climbing back onto the bed and kissing me again. "I don't think you would like spending time with me there," he whispered, pressing his forehead to mine.

"I want to come," I replied earnestly. "Is there any reason I wouldn't be allowed to?"

Kiernan thought for a moment before shaking his head and heading back to his wardrobe. "If you're that determined, I won't stop you. I'll have Franklin call for your maid."

He gave me another tender kiss and briefly left the room. I went into my own room and pulled on a dress, realizing how much I'd missed Abi these past few days. It occurred to me that he may have arranged for a higher-ranked maid for me, since I was now the queen, but I didn't want anyone but her.

When I heard him return, I stuck my head through the open door between our rooms. "Kiernan, about my maid..."

He pulled his tunic over his head. "I thought you liked your old one, so I've been having some of the higher maids train her over the past few days."

My face lit up, and I rushed into his room and threw my arms around him, making him drop his tunic belt. He chuckled, kissing the top of my head.

"Thank you," I said with a sigh of relief as I stepped back so we could both resume dressing.

"Does she know your secret?" he asked, retrieving the belt from the floor.

"Yes. She found out a couple months ago."

"How did she find out?" he asked curiously. "Did she notice your mark?"

I paused, slowly lowering my hands from trying to tame my hair. I stared in the mirror with a frown. In all the preparations for the founding banquet and then the wedding, and all the emotional ups and downs I experienced during that time, I had pushed aside memories of the demon. There hadn't been a sign of the creature returning, and I felt confident now that the vision I'd had of it being banished to the Lost One's pit was, in fact, what had happened. I hadn't really had the time or mental energy to ponder more about *how* I did that, or how I had healed my cuts for that matter. So many other things had occupied my time and mind.

Kiernan finished dressing and stepped into my room, an eyebrow raised slightly with some concern at my silence in response to his question. "Is everything all right?" he asked.

"Yes," I muttered quickly, then sighed as I sat at the vanity, placing my hands in my lap and still staring at my reflection. "Now, anyway. But she found out...well, she found out because I was attacked."

A flash of shock on his face very quickly turned concern, then anger. Swiftly, he closed the distance between us and put his hands on my shoulders, standing behind me.

"What do you mean attacked? By whom?"

"By what," I corrected, shakily placing a hand on top of his. "There was a demon in the castle. I sensed it my very first night here, and I tried to ward myself against it, but eventually, my protections weren't enough."

His eyes widened as he met my gaze in the reflection. The anger was still there, but shock had returned a bit more to his face—shock, fear, and deep concern.

"You were attacked by a *demon?*" he breathed, his hands squeezing my shoulders.

I nodded slowly. "I don't know how it got here, or why it was targeting me. Demons—usually they can only leave the Land of the Lost if they're summoned."

His eyes flashed with rage, and his grip on my shoulders tightened even more as he shook slightly. "Someone summoned a demon to attack you?" he almost growled.

"I don't think so," I said quickly, turning on the vanity bench so I could look directly at him instead of just through the reflection. "I'm pretty sure it was already here when I arrived months ago. It—it definitely decided to target me for some reason, maybe just because I'm Gifted. I really don't know. It's gone now, I—managed to banish it."

"Even if it wasn't meant to attack you, someone summoned it regardless," he said through clenched teeth. "That means they could do it again."

Those words brought a shiver through my spine, and my lips quivered as I looked up at him. I wrapped my fingers around his. I was trying to keep myself calm and hold on to the safety I'd felt with him in the last twenty-four hours, but I knew he was right. Just because the threat had been momentarily dealt with didn't mean there wasn't still someone or something at work in the castle with evil intentions.

Before either of us could gather our thoughts and emotions enough to continue the conversation, there was a knock on my door. Kiernan was still shaking as he very reluctantly released my shoulders and moved to answer it.

He had barely turned the knob when the door crashed open, and Franklin entered as if pushed into the room.

"Miss Abiga—"

Abi pushed past him before he could finish, practically running. I stood just in time for her to squeeze the breath out of my lungs with her hug.

"I was *so* worried! I didn't know if you were alive or dead! I hadn't heard from you, no one had seen you in three days, and even when I got your letter yesterday—"

She suddenly became aware of Kiernan's presence and released me, straightening her skirt. "Your Majesty," she said, curtsying. "My apologies, I was just concerned..."

Her cheeks turned red and she stared at the ground. Franklin looked between the two of us with a raised eyebrow, no doubt surprised at her audacity to hug the queen and confused by her words about life and death.

"Franklin, you are dismissed," Kiernan said, smiling at Abi with laughter in his voice. "Inform the captain I will arrive at court shortly."

Franklin nodded, glancing between me and Abi once more before leaving the room. Abi remained still, unsure how to act around the king, no matter her relationship with me.

"You may call me Kiernan," he said, and her head snapped up. "Any friend of my wife's is a friend of mine."

Abi let out a deep breath. Without warning, she ran forward and practically jumped on Kiernan, wrapping him in another tight embrace. I laughed at the surprise on his face. He patted her back awkwardly. I didn't tell him it was something he should get used to.

"So what's the plan?" she asked enthusiastically when she'd released him. "What do we do first?"

"The plan?" Kiernan asked.

"To end the Great War," she clarified, as if it should have been obvious, sitting down on my bed. Kiernan raised his eyebrows at her familiarity, glancing at me briefly before looking back at her with some amusement. Despite my distracted thoughts, I couldn't help but chuckle.

"Right now, the plan is for you to fix my hair so I can join Kiernan in court," I said, holding up a brush and waving it.

***

Abi's lighthearted, bubbly presence was a sharp contrast to the heaviness of the conversation Kiernan and I had been having just before she arrived. As wonderful as it was to see her again, my thoughts remained on the demon while she tamed my hair. I tried to push them aside and focus on my happiness, but when Franklin returned to inform Kiernan that Lewin was waiting in the hall, my breath caught in my throat.

Was it Lewin?

Of all the people I'd met in the castle, he was the only one that I was sure was truly evil. Sure, my initial experiences in the dungeon had a lot to do with how I saw him, but I didn't think that was all that it was. After all, he'd been keeping the dungeons a secret from Kiernan until I arrived, and I'd seen him resist Kiernan's authority and attempt to exert his own on more than one occasion. And he seemed particularly bothered by my presence in the castle.

But he also clearly hated the Gifted. Unless he was Gifted himself and pulling off an elaborate, twisted ruse, I couldn't imagine him working with a white witch or sorcerer to summon a demon, no matter how much power that would give him. Was that really a line he was willing to cross?

My mind spun with that terrible possibility as I shakily stood. In the mirror I saw Abi frown.

"What's wrong?" she whispered.

I took her hand and squeezed it, managing a smile. "Later," I promised, then, in a rush of emotion, pulled her into a tight hug. I buried my face in her shoulder taking in a deep breath. We held each other tight, releasing all of the stress and tension we'd both felt in the last few days.

When I released her, I looked to where Kiernan stood in the doorway. The corners of his lips were curved downward.

"Are you sure you want to come, Kenna?" he said. "It's not expected."

I stepped towards him and took his hand. "I think the people should get used to the unexpected from their new queen," I said with a bit of a wry smile.

Kiernan chuckled despite his concern. He kissed my hand before draping it over his arm. "That they should," he said fondly.

As we left the room, I caught Abi's eye once more. "Will you tell my father to meet me here after the trials?" I asked.

She assured me that she would, and Kiernan and I followed Franklin into the hall. Lewin waited there, his expression stoic. I tried to keep my composure, not wanting to be obvious about my suspicions and the increased fear I was feeling around him. It was easiest not to look directly at him, so instead, I looked past him at the decorations in the hallways, focusing my thoughts on the feeling of my hand on Kiernan's arm as a grounding point.

"I've come to escort you to the trials," he said to Kiernan in a very business-like tone, giving a slight bow. The bow was certainly not deep enough for the respect he should have been showing his king, but then again, Lewin had never shown the proper respect and deference to Kiernan.

"Thank you, Captain," Kiernan said with a nod.

Lewin looked at me, his lips still pressed together as he seemed to be attempting a professional address. "Would you like me to escort you to the dining hall or the library on our way, My Queen?" he asked, those last two words subtly laced with disapproval.

"Queen Kenna will be joining us," Kiernan said when I didn't immediately find my own voice to respond. "She will preside with me over the trials."

Lewin's gaze snapped to him, then back to me. "The High Court is no place for a woman, Your Majesty."

"She is coming with us," Kiernan repeated in a commanding tone. "She has requested it."

Lewin bowed in response. To my surprise, I thought I saw a sly smirk come to the corner of his lips just before he turned his back to us. He didn't speak again as we walked down the halls. I frowned, staring at the back of his head. I had expected a much colder reaction from him.

I forced myself to shelve the thoughts as we reached our destination. Members of the royal guard lined the staircase to the throne room, now being used for the High Court. It was jarring to be entering the same room where we had celebrated our marriage just days ago under such a different atmosphere and purpose. The nobles and others seated within stood as the doors opened.

"King Kiernan and Queen Kenna," a servant announced, his booming voice echoing across the walls.

Those present exchanged curious and confused glances when they saw me enter with my husband. Miss Grayson had never specifically said anything about me *not* appearing in court, but it also was not something she had ever mentioned as part of my expected duties. But whatever the regular customs were, and however inappropriate it may seem to people like Lewin, it was important for me to be here. I needed to become familiar with the justice system so I could help Kiernan change the current laws and practices against my people.

More guards lined the walls of the court, armed and prepared to defend us should the need arise. It was comforting. We were about to be in the presence of multiple criminals, and it was in this same room that Kiernan's parents had fallen victim to Pious's attack. My eyes darted to the secret passageway, reminding myself where it was and how to open it just in case the escape was necessary.

The crowd didn't take their seats until Kiernan and I did. We sat in an eerie silence as Lewin left the room through a door to the right—evidently one of the rooms that held criminals before trial—and returned with a young man in his grasp.

The boy had sandy blonde hair and was rather tall and lanky for his age. His hands were bound. His nose looked as if it had been broken several times, and he avoided looking anyone in the eye. From the dirt under his fingernails and on his face, I assumed he lived on the streets. His countenance was scarred and hardened, likely from years of struggling to survive, and he seemed not even to care that he was being tried for a crime.

"Colin Randal," Lewin read from a sheet of paper. "Guilty of theft and murder."

"I didn't murder no one," the boy piped up, receiving a dark look from the captain.

"You are not allowed to speak in this court," he said harshly.

"What?" I said under my breath, so only Kiernan could hear. He turned to me, his face full of concern.

"You don't have to stay—"

"Why is he not allowed to speak?" I whispered, leaning in closer to him. Lewin read a list of witnesses, and the rest of the room was silent as three men approached the dais.

Kiernan leaned in close to me as well, keeping his voice low. "He's not allowed to speak unless I ask him to," he clarified. "Apparently my father didn't consider it important to hear people defend themselves. Don't worry, I'll hear his story."

I frowned, straightening to face the accused once more. The more I learned about Kiernan's father, the more convinced I was that he had not been the benevolent ruler the majority of the people claimed him to be. He not only made judgments without hearing both sides of the story, but he had built a secret prison to hide people away in regardless of their guilt. I thought of my mother standing before him in this room and gripped the armrests of my throne.

When Lewin finished reading, the trial officially began. The first witness to the event stepped forward now and bowed deeply before speaking. His voice oozed like oil. "Your Majesties, I witnessed young Randal bludgeon the baker on my street not a week ago before stealing two loaves of bread."

The boy stared at the man with clear surprise, opening his mouth to protest. But he reluctantly closed it when he saw Lewin's warning look. The second witness greeted us the same, telling a similar story about a butcher on his street. The third man seemed convinced that Randal murdered one of his fellow fishermen. None of them could tell us what reason the boy had to commit these crimes other than thievery.

"Mister Randal," Kiernan said when the third man had finished. "Did you or did you not steal food from these men?"

Randal's head snapped up, looking both surprised and relieved that he was being allowed to speak. Lewin pressed his lips together in apparent disapproval, but he said nothing.

The boy blinked. "Yes, Yer Majesty," he confessed, though he didn't sound scared or ashamed. "Fer me and me brother."

"The three victims lived in various parts of the city, far from one another. Not very convenient for a thief," Kiernan observed, leaning forward in his chair. "Why did you travel such distances?"

"I didn't," he said matter-of-factly. "I stole from all o' them on Market Day, when they was in the same place."

"Have you ever been to the shore?"

"No."

"Did you know these men?"

"Not at all, Sire. I stole from them is all."

Kiernan leaned forward even more, his eyes fixed intently on the young man. "And did you attack any of these men?"

"No need, Sire," he said, a small smile on his lips. "They didn't even see me."

Kiernan was quiet for a moment, surveying the boy and the three men who spoke against him. All three witnesses had become very nervous as soon as the boy started speaking. My husband motioned to one of his guards to come up to the dais and whispered instructions so quietly not even I could hear. The knight nodded in understanding. As he motioned to two more of his men, Kiernan sat up straight, his eyes narrowing when he looked out at the four men. I realized that throughout the entire trial, my nails had been digging deeper into the fabric on the armrests of my throne, and I let out a slow breath and willed them to relax, watching my husband intently.

"Murder is a serious crime," he said, his voice powerful in a way I'd never heard before, "and the only punishment available for such an action is death in return. Therefore, you, Brent Jacobs, Liam Barter, and Charles Newnan are sentenced to death by beheading."

There were gasps of surprise as the knights seized the three shocked men, but their guilt and devastation of having been caught in their lies clearly showed on their faces. None of them fought the guards holding them. I let out the breath I hadn't realized I'd been holding and forced my hands to relax, moving them from the armrests to my lap.

"Take them to the dungeons," Kiernan commanded.

As the men were taken from the room, Randal stared straight ahead at Kiernan, mouth hanging open. He seemed too amazed to celebrate that he was going to live.

"As for you, Mister Randal," Kiernan continued, his tone still serious. "Thievery is not tolerated here. You are to spend two months in jail, followed by three months of service."

The crowd murmured as the boy was led away. I saw the surprised expression on his face shift to a relieved smile as he left, hardly believing his luck. I looked at Kiernan sideways, seeing his hard expression. My lips curved into a frown of my own and I reached over to place one of my hands on top of his. He turned his palm upward and gave my hand a squeeze, his countenance softening for a brief moment as he did before the next person accused was brought into the room.

There were four more trials that day. The second was a case of treason—the man had been passing information about the inner workings of the army to King Simeon. Though Simeon wasn't yet attacking us, we all suspected he would sometime in the future. Our islands would eventually not be excluded from his goal to conquer as much land as possible. The man was sentenced to life in prison, a punishment that many people watching didn't seem to think severe enough, but none would argue with the king.

The third and fourth were two men who worked together to plan the death of their main competitors in the farming market. They not only killed the farmers, but their wives and children as well. Both of them were sentenced to death just as the first three men, and their executions were scheduled for that evening. Kiernan took my hand once more as they were dragged away, seeing how pale I'd become.

I was relieved there was only one more trial, and had just decided to avoid coming in the future when the fifth man entered the room. Immediately, my heart stopped.

It was Gideon.

CHAPTER TWENTY-ONE

A HEALING TOUCH

My nails dug into Kiernan's palm so much that he winced and turned to look at me. I wasn't looking at him to see his expression, however—my eyes were locked on Gideon.

He was staring at the marble floor, his jaw clenched. His golden blonde hair was disheveled and much longer than I remembered it. The clothes he wore were filthy and too loose, as if he had lost a significant amount of weight. My throat tightened as if I was being strangled to see that both of his arms, all the way up to the shoulder and the base of his neck, were horrifically burned, the skin red and scarred, completely masking any sign of his mark.

Lewin's voice sounded dull to my ears, almost as if I was hearing it from underwater.

"This man will not give his name. He is suspected of witchcraft."

My mind spun, and my chest rose up and down dramatically as I struggled to keep myself from hyperventilating. I could feel my eyes welling up with tears, but I knew that if I let them fall, I would make the situation infinitely worse. Somehow, I needed to keep my composure, to pretend I wasn't absolutely terrified to see Gid standing there, scarred and malnourished, wrists bound tightly in front of him. He still hadn't lifted his eyes from the ground, and as a result had not seen me. I had to bite the inside of my lip to keep myself from calling out to him, and in an effort to control what little I could of my expression.

The room felt cold, and not just to me. Everyone present had stiffened at the mention of witchcraft and was eerily silent. Kiernan, too, was silent for a long time. I could feel him squeezing my hand, clearly able to discern that I was distressed. Each moment felt like an eternity.

"Who issued the arrest?" Kiernan asked. There was a cold, menacing edge to his tone that alarmed me enough that I jerked my head away from Gid to study my husband's expression. With relief, I could tell that his eyes were still soft, and even as he scowled down at Gideon, I felt his thumb rub the back of my hand in an attempt of comfort. For the moment, he had to keep up pretenses, or the people would become alarmed and we would be suspected.

"Captain Stole, Your Majesty," Lewin said in response to his question, nodding in the other captain's direction as he approached the dais. Stole gave a deep, respectful bow when he reached the front.

"Captain—describe the arrest and why witchcraft is suspected," Kiernan ordered.

"Your Majesties," Stole began, giving a smaller, second bow and nodding at both of us in turn. "I accompanied my command on a routine patrol of the Southern shore two days ago. As we approached the village of Braen, one of my men reported movement in a small forest just west of the village. We decided to investigate. The moment we entered the trees, the forest caught fire from an unknown source, and I heard someone cry out. As my men retreated and searched for a way to stop the spread of the flames, I searched for the source of the voice and discovered this man. He was badly burned and unconscious. I removed him from the danger."

"Why is witchcraft suspected?" Kiernan interrupted before Stole could continue. "It sounds like this man was a victim."

"That was my initial assumption as well, Your Majesty. But he had this with him."

Stole motioned to another guard who approached with a canvas bag—*my* canvas bag. I was barely able to hold in a gasp by instead biting my lip harder, hard enough that I tasted blood. Apparently my nails also dug deeper into Kiernan's palm, because I heard him clear his throat subtly as he tapped my hand with his thumb. I willed my grip to loosen, not wanting to hurt him, but if I had tried to remove my hand from his I was certain it would shake uncontrollably.

The guard opened my pack and Stole reached inside of it, producing two of my summoning candles. There was a low murmur through the crowd in response, and I saw several people towards the front take significant steps back, as if being near the candles would somehow harm them. Gid still had not looked up, but I saw him shift in place in response to the sound.

"When he awoke, we questioned him about why he was traveling with magical objects," Stole said as he placed the candles back into my pack. "He refused to say a word to us. I became suspicious that he may have been the source of the fire, which he neither confirmed nor denied under penalty of arrest. Since he refused to explain himself, I determined the best course of action was to bring him to you for judgment rather than come to a conclusion on my own. He has not said a word for the past two days since he awoke."

"Did you see any sign of a mark on his skin?" Kiernan asked, his tone difficult to read.

"No, Your Majesty. But given his burns, it is possible the mark could be obscured."

The murmurs in the crowd resumed at that, but Kiernan quickly raised a hand to indicate a demand for silence. At this point, I had no choice but to close my eyes for a moment. If I didn't, I was sure the tears would begin to fall profusely. Part of me desperately wanted Gideon to look up, to see his bright blue eyes again. But another part of me—the wiser part—hoped he would keep his gaze down, not sure he would be able to disguise his reaction at seeing me sitting before him on the throne of Orkeia.

It felt like hours before the silence was broken. Kiernan continued to rub the back of my hand with his thumb. I was barely stopping myself from calling out an order to release Gid, knowing how incredibly foolish and inappropriate that outburst would be. It would start rumors and doubts among the people around me that we couldn't afford to be spreading until we'd actually come up with a plan for ending the Slaughters.

Finally, Kiernan spoke. "Take him to the castle dungeons. I will question him privately at another time."

My eyes shot open as the room erupted in an uproar. A number of people stood in protest, Gideon's possession of my pack and summoning candles more than enough to condemn him in their eyes even though he had done nothing to threaten the knights. I heard shouts of "Kill him now!" and "The king's been charmed!" Lewin drew his sword and stepped forward, ready to defy Kiernan's order.

"Stop!" Kiernan shouted in a booming voice, releasing my hand and standing. Everyone quieted down almost instantly, and Lewin reluctantly sheathed his sword. All eyes were on Kiernan, his presence captivating and commanding. Even Gideon looked up, his brows slightly furrowed in confusion.

Our eyes met. I gripped the armrest of my throne, desperately willing my body not to tremble. Gideon's mouth fell open in shock. He looked as if he was about to say my name, but thankfully he thought better of it an instant later and forced his mouth closed. Immediately, tears began to roll down his cheeks, and his lips quivered, his eyes locked on mine.

It took every ounce of will I had to shut my own eyes and break the connection. I couldn't risk breaking down myself in front of this irate crowd. Even if everyone's focus was on Kiernan's standing presence, there was no way the people wouldn't notice my emotions if I continued to look at Gideon. My breathing felt staggered and shallow, like my body was going into shock.

"I have given an order and I expect it to be obeyed," Kiernan said authoritatively in the uneasy silence. "Take him to the dungeons, and do not harm him."

There was a murmur of discontent and confusion among the crowd, but no one else shouted out a protest. I heard footsteps as Gideon was escorted from the room, and did not open my eyes until I heard the crowd beginning to empty out as well. When I did, the first thing that I saw was Kiernan standing directly next to my throne, holding out a hand to me. His eyes were questioning, but also filled with deep concern.

My entire body shook as I took his offered hand and very slowly stood. Immediately, Kiernan wrapped his arm around my waist to support me, an action which turned out to be necessary to keep my legs from dropping out from under me when we began to walk. Since the room had emptied almost completely other than the royal guard, Kiernan guided me towards the secret passageway rather than the main hall.

Feeling a prickling on the back of my neck, I made the mistake of looking over my shoulder as we left. Immediately, my gaze locked with Captain Lewin's. There was a wicked smirk on his face, one that only grew when our eyes met. My stomach felt like stone as we disappeared into the passageway and the secret door closed behind us.

"Let's get you sitting down. Then we can talk," Kiernan whispered once we were alone in the passageway. His voice was filled with worry, and I was a bit surprised to hear a shaky edge to it. It was such a contrast to the commanding, confident tone he had used in the courtroom.

Even if I had been ready to talk at that moment, I didn't think I could have made a coherent sound right away. So we walked in silence through the passage. By the time we reached the sitting room, my fingers were numb from gripping his arm so tightly.

Franklin and Abi had already prepared lunch and were in the process of setting the table. When she saw my obvious distress, Abi immediately abandoned the task and rushed to help me into a seat.

"What's wrong? What happened?" she said with a frown.

The tears I'd been holding back for the entire trial began to fall. Abi's frown deepened and she pulled me into a tight hug. Across the table, Franklin paused, watching us curiously. Kiernan cleared his throat.

"Things are set up enough, Franklin. Will you give us some privacy, please?"

Franklin set down the platter he was holding and bowed. "Of course, Your Majesties," he said. His eyes lingered a moment on Abi, who made no movement to join him, before he left the room.

Kiernan pulled a chair next to mine and sat. Abi released me as he did, taking a step back and allowing my husband to take one of my hands in his own. With his free hand, he tenderly rubbed my arm.

"Who is he?" he asked softly.

It was still another minute before I gathered enough breath to speak. "His name is Gideon," I croaked out.

Abi gasped. "Gideon? As in *Grison*?"

I nodded and she covered her mouth with her hands, her eyes wide.

Kiernan's glance flickered to her briefly before returning to me. "You were close to him," he observed.

I swallowed. "Very close," I admitted.

"I won't let anything happen to him," Kiernan assured me, wiping some of my tears. "I'll go to the dungeons this evening and release him myself. There are passages leading to the cliffs that not even my captains know about. My mother showed them to me when I was young."

I shook my head. "I—I need to speak with him," I breathed through a sob.

Kiernan took in a sharp breath, but nodded, taking my shaking hands in his. "If you'd like, I can have him brought to one of the studies where we can meet with him away from prying eyes."

"Thank you," I breathed, giving his hands a squeeze.

***

Abi wanted to come with us, but I told her I needed her to wait there in case Isaiah came while we were gone. Even though I'd sent him messages, I knew my father must be worried sick. I wondered why he hadn't come to see me already, but that thought was very much in the back of my mind.

Kiernan took my arm in his as we walked towards the study where Gideon would be waiting. It was exceedingly hard for me not to break into a run, and I focused on the feeling of his fingers lightly brushing against my arm to keep me grounded. With each step, my heart beat just a little faster.

There was a guard stationed at the door, and he bowed to us as he opened it. Gideon was already inside, flanked by two additional guards. He stood in the middle of the room, staring at the rug on the floor, but the moment the door opened his head snapped up. Our eyes met again, and he let out a shaky breath, his eyes immediately watering again.

"Thank you, gentlemen. You may wait outside," Kiernan nodded to the guards.

The two of them exchanged a glance. For a moment, they remained where they were, clearly uncomfortable with the idea of leaving the king and queen alone in the room with an accused witch. But with another look at Kiernan's determined expression, they bowed and reluctantly left the room.

The moment the door closed, I crossed the room, sobbing as I threw my arms around Gideon. He let out a sob of his own, unable to wrap his arms around me due to the ropes that still bound his wrists. I pulled back just long enough to fumble with those ropes and remove them, throwing them to the side before embracing him again, burying my head against his shoulder. I felt him wince and suddenly realized that his burns were probably still fairly painful if they were so recent. Quickly, I stepped back.

"I'm sorry, I'm sorry!" I gasped through another sob. I reached up and brushed his hair out of his face as he trembled, his blue eyes misty staring down at me.

"I knew you were alive," he choked out. "I always knew, but what—how—what are you—?"

His eyes darted momentarily past me to Kiernan, but were quickly locked on mine once more. "Are you safe?" he whispered, practically just mouthing the words, clearly concerned about the king's presence.

"Yes," I said quickly. "Yes, I—Gid, this is—King Kiernan is my husband. And he knows."

It was hard for me to fully interpret his reaction. There was definitely surprise in his eyes, but undoubtedly he had put some things together after seeing me on the throne. But his eyebrows furrowed with confusion, and his lips quivered with—something else. In the end, he let out a deep, shaky breath of relief, closing his eyes as a few more tears fell and pressing his forehead against mine. I closed my eyes as well.

Kiernan cleared his throat and stepped forward. "Mr. Grison. I sincerely apologize for any mistreatment you may have received. Please, do sit down."

Carefully, I led Gideon to the settee, taking a seat next to him. Kiernan hovered next to me for a moment before sitting across from us in an armchair. He leaned forward, looking between the two of us with a concerned and empathetic frown. I thought I saw a hint of guilt in his eyes and flashed him a weak but supportive smile. I reached across the distance between us to hold his hand and give it a squeeze. When I looked back at Gideon, he was staring at our hands, but quickly brought his gaze back to my eyes.

"How did you get here?" I asked, my own surprise and confusion evident in my shaky voice. "We heard what Captain Stole said, of course, but what were you doing in that forest? Where is the rest of the clan?"

Gid sighed, leaning back against the fabric of the seat and closing his eyes again. I could tell that he was experiencing a similar sensation to the one I had my first time laying in a bed in the castle, and for a moment he just breathed before attempting to answer my questions. Neither Kiernan nor I rushed him.

"I don't know where the clan is," he admitted quietly when he finally opened his eyes again. "I never left with them."

I stared at him. "But—the shelter was clear when the knights searched it. How did you—?"

"I jumped out of the circle right before my father completed the spell and went to the shelter to grab your pack. When I heard the knights coming, I opened up a pit in the floor, jumped down, and closed the opening just before they arrived. After I waited long enough for them to leave, I tried to follow the army's tracks, but I wasn't able to keep up."

Across from us, Kiernan shifted in his seat, and I met his gaze. I could tell he wanted to ask questions about the magic Gid was referring to, but I also knew it would be difficult to explain succinctly. After thinking for a moment I landed on, "Gideon can manipulate earth and the elements."

Kiernan nodded, keeping his face steady, but his eyes widened slightly. "Were you responsible for the fire, then?"

Gideon looked up at him, and I saw his shoulders stiffen. Much like me when I first arrived, he clearly didn't trust the man sitting across from him. But the fact that I had chosen to marry him logically won over his instincts to remain silent, and he nodded, letting out another breath as he looked down at his arms.

"I was trying to start a campfire," he said, shaking his head. "But—Kenna, you know I hadn't practiced much with fire. It got away from me and sort of...exploded. That's how this happened." He lifted both arms slightly. "I suppose I was lucky, all things considered."

I released Kiernan's hand and gently took a hold of one of Gid's. He winced again, looking down as I tenderly placed one palm underneath his and the other on top of the back of his hand. The skin was rough and raw, and my eyes watered once more as I thought about how much it must hurt.

As I examined his injuries, an insane thought occurred to me, and I let out a breath. For a long moment, I continued to just stare, thinking through the night of the demon attack once more and trying to remember the sensation I'd felt as I'd somehow healed the cuts on my skin. Closing my eyes, I tried to draw upon wherever that power had come from and direct it into my hands, my fingers tingling with warmth.

Something awakened within me, and when I opened my eyes, I saw that my hands were glowing, just as Abi had described months before. The glow spread from my hands and up Gideon's arm slowly.

"Kenna," he gasped. "How are you—?"

I didn't respond, keeping my focus on the raw, unfamiliar magic I was performing. Eventually, the glow covered his entire arm, and when I slowly withdrew my hands, it dissipated.

His arm was completely healed. There was no sign that a burn had ever been present, and the clear circle on his shoulder was once again visible.

Both of the men in the room stared at me. Their expressions were similar, but while my husband's was filled with awe and wonder, Gideon's was pure shock.

"How did you do that?" he breathed almost reverently. "That's not—white witches don't heal."

"I know," I breathed. I could hear that my voice was shaking and realized that I felt drained. But without hesitation, I reached for his other hand and closed my eyes to heal the other arm. The room was silent as I did so, and when I was finished Gideon lifted up both of his arms and examined them with wide eyes. Performing the second attempt had been a bit more draining than the first, and I closed my eyes and leaned back against the settee with a breath.

It occurred to me as we sat in silence that healing his burns had probably been a bit unwise. There wasn't a logical way to explain their sudden disappearance to the guards waiting outside the room other than a magical source. This must have occurred to my husband as well because after recovering from his surprise, he stood and crossed to the door, opening it just enough to speak to the guards on the other side, but not enough to allow them to look in.

"Bring this man a change of clothes and some gloves so he can protect his hands and arms. Also bring me the bag he had with him, including its contents."

I imagined that the guards bowed in response, even if they were confused by the orders. As Kiernan shut the door, Gideon reached over and took my hand. His was trembling slightly, and when I looked up to meet his gaze, his eyes were still misty with tears, but he was smiling, the expression somewhat pained.

"I told you you were a sorcerer," he muttered, a teasing edge to his tone.

I rolled my eyes. "We still don't know that."

"Really? Then how do you explain what just happened?"

"I don't know. I haven't had much time to think about it," I said with a quiet sigh, closing my eyes once more as I gave his hand a squeeze.

I felt Kiernan touch my shoulder and released Gideon's hand, looking up at my husband. The awe in his expression from earlier had been replaced with a concerned frown as his eyes flickered from me to Gideon and back again. There was a tightness in the frown, but as I took his hand, it softened.

"I'm all right," I assured him.

While we waited for the guard to return, Gideon explained more about his journey. He was able to work out that the army had taken me to the village, but following the ships was a different challenge. He waited until nightfall before going to the beach and stealing some supplies and a small fisher's boat. Using his Gift, he steered the boat towards the next island.

Of course, he didn't know which island I had been taken to or even the layout of the various islands in the area. For months, he traveled from island to island, searching for any information he could. He guessed he was looking for the main city, assuming that I would be taken to be tried.

At length he came across another clan where one of the members happened to have the Gift of scrying. She used her Gift and confirmed that I was still alive and was, in fact, in the castle, but she wasn't able to glean much more information. By asking for help from a white witch in the clan, he was able to orient himself towards the castle and finally reach the main island, landing his stolen ship just west of the village of Braen.

The entire time he was telling the story, I fought back tears. He had done all of this just to find me and make sure I was safe. A knot caught in my throat as I thought about everything he'd been through—all the cold nights, days without food, and loneliness.

Kiernan listened intently to the story, asking questions periodically to help clarify his understanding of the magic involved or simply to understand more about Gideon himself. Though I could tell that Gid was still guarded with him in the room, he trusted me enough to be truthful and honest. As I looked between the two of them, I was reminded of the dream I had had not long ago of entertaining the Grisons in the castle. I had certainly imagined them meeting under different circumstances, but it was still thrilling to see the two of them conversing.

At length, there was a knock on the door, and Kiernan stood to open it, thanking the guard and quickly closing it once again behind him. He returned carrying the requested clothing, my pack slung over his shoulder. I felt another surge of emotion and sat up straighter. Seeing me stare at the bag, Kiernan set down the clothes and shrugged it off, offering it to me.

He remained close by, watching with interest as I opened it with trembling hands.

Inside were my candles, a few items of clothing, and at the bottom a few flowers—now very dead and dried out—that I vaguely remembered Neal giving me a day or two before the attack occurred. There was also a small amount of food that Gideon must have gathered or been given by the clan he met on his journey. I swallowed as I pulled out one of the candles, holding it against my chest and letting out a deep breath.

"Elizabeth helped me make these," I muttered. "I never thought I'd see them again."

"Elizabeth?" Kiernan asked gently.

"The woman who raised me. She was killed by the knights about a year ago, just before I met Gideon and his clan."

My husband frowned and placed a hand on my cheek. "I'm so sorry, My Love," he said, the words catching a bit in his throat with guilt. While my lips trembled with sadness as I remembered coming upon the scene of my murdered clan, I reached up with my free hand and cupped his cheek, giving him a tender kiss in comfort. Out of the corner of my eye, I saw Gideon shift where he sat, turning his head away from us awkwardly.

With a sigh, I placed the candle back in the pack. Kiernan coaxed me to my feet once I did.

"You both need some rest," he said, looking from me to Gideon. "You will need to change here, Mr. Grison, so no one sees your arms. I will have a room prepared for you and accompany you there. We can discuss what you would like to do next in the morning."

For some reason, Gid wore a small frown, but he nodded. "Thank you," he said.

"What are you going to say to the guards?" I asked my husband, glancing at the door.

"I will explain that he was simply in the wrong place at the wrong time," he said confidently. "He ran to try to escape the sudden fire and tripped over this bag, which must have been left behind by someone else. He was still in shock from the pain and fright when he awoke to the interrogation and simply shut down, but with some reassurance you and I were able to discover the true story and determine that he was innocent of any crime."

"And you think they'll accept that story?" Gideon asked skeptically.

"Whether or not they immediately accept it, there are some benefits to being king," Kiernan said with a bit of a smirk. "Very few people are bold enough to question my word once it has been given."

My thoughts immediately went to Captain Lewin, and I felt a pit in my stomach. I thought about mentioning the look he'd given me as we were leaving the trials, but before I said anything, Kiernan turned back to me and tucked a piece of hair behind my ear.

"I know there's much more you want to discuss, likely with both of us. But for now, you need to rest," he said firmly. "I will meet you in our quarters shortly."

With some reluctance, I sighed and nodded. Gideon stood, and I gave him another hug. This time, I didn't shy from holding him as tightly as I could, since there were no longer injuries to worry about. He held me just as tightly, breathing in heavily against my shoulder and placing a trembling hand on the back of my head.

"I can't believe I found you," he breathed into my ear. "I'm so glad you're safe."

"I can't believe you're here," I breathed back, and he squeezed me just a bit tighter for a moment before slowly lowering his arms and taking a step back.

My husband put an arm around my waist and walked me to the door. "I'll stay here to make sure Mr. Grison makes it safely to his guest quarters," he said.

Kiernan kissed my cheek. As he ushered me into the hallway, I glanced back at Gid once more. He had sat back down on the settee and closed his eyes. Clearly, he was exhausted, but he was safe. Peace washed over me, and despite my own exhaustion, each step back to my quarters felt lighter than the last.

Chapter Twenty-Two

BONDS AND BURDENS

Kiernan's intention had been for me to rest when I got back to our quarters, but I didn't immediately get the chance. When I opened the doors to the sitting room, my father paused where he was pacing by the windows, eagerly turning to face me.

His eyes met mine, and I smiled. A weight visually lifted off his shoulders. He crossed the room in just a few swift steps, wrapped me in his arms, and kissed the top of my head, shaking.

"I told you I'd be all right," I said into his shoulder, to which he took in a sharp breath and held me even tighter. For a long time we just stood there until he eventually released me and stood back to gaze at me, his hands on my shoulders.

"You are one of the bravest women I've ever known," he said.

My cheeks burned a little, but I smiled softly. It wasn't until then that I noticed Abi behind him. When our eyes met, she took a step forward.

"How did things go with Gideon?" she asked quietly.

My father looked between the two of us with a slight frown. "Who's Gideon?"

As I recounted our conversation, the three of us sat. Abi and my father each took an armchair, while I rested on the longer settee, trying to hide just how tired I was. They both asked a lot of questions about Gideon and his Gift, fascinated by how rare it was and the amount of power that he held.

Suddenly, Abi jumped up, gasping.

"The book!" she said. "The one you asked me to look after—let me get it for you, I think there's something in it you need to read."

I raised an eyebrow as she ran from the room, returning not too much later with Kindra's record in hand. Frantically, she flipped through the pages, rambling as she did.

"I was so restless the past few days—when I wasn't in the middle of training, I couldn't think of anything to do other than read," she explained. "I mean, I'm a pretty slow reader and a lot of it went over my head since I didn't really know anything about magic until you, but this seemed familiar and I wondered if you'd seen it yet—"

She cut off her speech suddenly and pointed to a passage, handing the book to me.

"Remember how you glowed? That night with the demon?" she breathed.

"What demon?" Isaiah interjected, his body suddenly tense.

I didn't immediately answer him, looking down at the page she'd opened to and quickly beginning to read. As I did, my eyes widened.

'The talons left long gash marks in Hanson's arm. He insisted he would be fine, and I knew that once we returned to camp our green witches would be able to help him, but by now I also knew that I loved him. It broke my heart to see the amount of pain he was in. I ripped off a piece of my skirt and began to bind the wounds, gently pressing my hands around the bindings when I was finished.

'That's when something very strange happened. As I thought about how much I wished I could heal him, my hands started to glow, and within moments, the gashes were, in fact, healed. When we returned to camp, I journeyed to the Land of the Saved to speak with Varan once more and mentioned the strange occurrence. It was then that he explained that I wasn't a white witch after all, but in fact a sorceress, and another one of his descendents. Through his male line, the Gift of power over the planets had been passed down. But through the female line, another Gift had been inherited, a very special and sacred Gift, and I was the Bearer.'

I stared at the page, scanning the next few paragraphs and turning the pages wildly in an attempt to read what the Gift actually was. She never said. All she would say was that it gave her the ability to heal physical injuries on the body (like the cuts and burns I had healed) in addition to communicating with spirits. According to her, it was exceptionally unique and sacred, and another Gift that only manifested itself every fourteen generations.

A sorcerer?

"That has to be the same thing, right?" Abi said excitedly. "And just like you, she thought she was a white witch at first, didn't she?"

"What demon?" my father asked again before I could find my voice to respond. His firm tone demanded an answer, and concern and fear filled his eyes.

I sighed, rubbing my temples with my thumbs. "I was attacked by a demon in my room a couple of months ago."

As I recounted the story, Isaiah's fists clenched tighter and tighter. "Why didn't you say something before?" he demanded in a scolding tone.

"Because I banished it!" I said defensively. "It was no longer a threat."

"Kenna, if there was a demon in the castle attacking you, there is very much still a threat," he said matter-of-factly, pressing his lips together. "You can't be so naive as to think that whoever sent it after you has just given up."

"We don't *know* if someone sent it after me."

My father opened his mouth to argue with me further, but he was interrupted by the sound of voices and footsteps coming from the hall. The voices were immediately recognizable as Kiernan and Lewin, and Lewin in particular was not attempting to hide his anger and frustration. I stood as the doors to our quarters opened.

"—ridiculous notion, Kiernan," Lewin was saying. I could just see him past my husband through the open door, and his eyes were blazing.

"I made myself clear, Captain," Kiernan said as he walked briskly through the door, a tired look of frustration on his face. He had my pack over his shoulder, and I saw Lewin glare at it from behind him.

"It's a sign of weakness," Lewin growled. "Think logically, Kiernan. People will think you've been enchanted. Especially with you pardoning the prisoner from this morning—"

I felt a stab of panic, thinking Lewin somehow knew the truth about Gideon. Kiernan spun around in anger. "Last time I checked, Captain, *I* was the king. You are to follow my orders with no further questions."

Before Lewin could open his mouth, Kiernan slammed the door in his face. In the brief moment before it closed, I made eye contact with the captain, and I felt a cold chill run down my spine as his eyes narrowed with what could only be described as hatred.

The anger emanating off of my husband subsided only slightly when the sound of Lewin's footsteps could no longer be heard. He didn't move, breathing heavily and facing the doors. Abi and my father both remained silent, staring at him as well. Cautiously, I stepped around the furniture and placed a hand on his shoulder. He let out a deep breath and put his hand on top of mine before facing me, exhaustion written on his face.

"What was that about?" I asked, trying to keep my fear in check.

Catching the edge to my voice, Kiernan squeezed my hand. "Your friend is safe," he said reassuringly. "Captain Lewin's just angry."

Despite his reassurance, my shoulders tensed. "About what?"

"He found me while I was on my way here," he explained. "He was still upset about the trial and suggested increasing searches on the island. I said no and told him to begin disbanding the witch patrols instead."

"*What?*" I breathed. "Kiernan, why would you—?"

"Gideon was lucky, Kenna," he said, lifting my hand from his shoulder and clutching it tightly. "*You* were lucky. I can't bear the thought that if things had been even the slightest bit different, you would have been killed before—before I even had the chance to know you."

His voice caught in his throat and he cupped my cheek with his free hand, his thumb caressing my chin. "I can't let the patrols continue."

"Kiernan, Captain Lewin's right," I stammered, the words sour in my mouth. "It's—this isn't going to happen overnight. We're trying to change the way an entire kingdom of people has felt for years. People *are* going to think you've been enchanted—"

He shook his head. "People are ready for this war to be over, Kenna. The men actually fighting it—they've been away from their families for far too long with nothing to show for it other than innocent bodies piling on the shore."

"But they don't *know* those bodies are innocent," I retorted. "Not yet. We need to make changes more gradually—"

"I only told him to start disbanding the patrols," he said, his tone firm and calm as he took both of my hands in his and held them tightly. "I didn't tell him to declare the war over or stop attacking magic holders. But the active searching for the Gifted—*that* I needed to stop. I love you, Kenna, and seeing you in so much distress when Gideon walked into the courtroom...I had to do something."

As I stared into his eyes, the love I saw in them made my heart feel as if it was going to burst. My eyes watered. As concerned as I was about how others would view this decision, I also felt a rush of gratitude, and I leaned forward to press my lips against his. He placed a hand on the back of my head as he returned the kiss, and when it broke he pressed his forehead against mine.

"Thank you," I breathed after a moment, slowly pulling back to meet his gaze again. "But...I don't think you should make any more changes. Not this fast. You may be the king, but you still have to be careful."

He sighed and squeezed my hand. He was about to say more when he looked over my shoulder and suddenly straightened, clearing his throat and releasing my hand.

"Good afternoon, Sir Balton," he said with a bow. I felt a rush of heat to my cheeks as I turned to look at my father, honestly having forgotten he and Abi were in the room.

Isaiah was standing, observing the two of us with an expression that was difficult to read. I could tell that he was still upset about the demon, but at least for the moment he was letting the subject drop. He bowed in return to Kiernan, keeping his gaze low. But when he straightened, I was relieved to see a hint of a smile on his lips.

"I am glad to see that you, unlike your father, have enough sense to listen to reason, Your Majesty," he said.

"My father didn't have someone as persuasive as Kenna to help him see the truth," Kiernan replied.

Isaiah's smile faltered, though I wasn't entirely sure if it was because he was thinking about my mother or because of what he said next. "She is wise, as well. Forgive my candor, but you should not have been so hasty in your orders to Lewin."

There was a biting edge to the way he said the captain's name. Kiernan pressed his lips tightly together, and for a moment I thought he was angry with Isaiah for speaking out of turn.

"Perhaps you are right. I would be grateful for your strategic advice moving forward, Captain Balton," Kiernan said.

Isaiah raised an eyebrow. "Captain?"

"Yes. Effective immediately. I need someone I know I can trust at the highest ranks."

My father bowed deeply. "Thank you, Your Majesty."

Kiernan cleared his throat. "Now," he said, turning to face me again and brushing a hair out of my face, "I believe I told *you* to get some rest."

I was about to argue with him, but a yawn betrayed me. My husband was right. I was exhausted both emotionally and physically, and I really did need some rest.

Abi quickly moved to my side, linking an arm with mine. "I'll get her in bed," she said, gently pulling me with her. My husband invited Isaiah to speak with him privately in his study and the two of them left the room as well.

Once alone in my room, Abi asked me questions about the last four days as I undressed, like what Kiernan's initial reaction was when I told him the truth. But once I was sitting on my bed, she could see how tired I truly was and ended the conversation, giving me one last hug before leaving the room. I laid down and closed my eyes, almost instantly asleep.

***

I slept through not only the rest of the afternoon, but the entire night as well. Kiernan was waiting for me in our dining quarters when I emerged for breakfast. With some surprise, I saw that Gideon was there as well. He looked up as I entered and stood, pulling a chair out for me. He was wearing long sleeves and gloves to keep up the pretense that his arms were still burned.

"How are you?" I asked with some concern, keeping my eyes on his face as I sat. Despite the fact that he had been given a proper bed and room to rest in for the night, there were bags under his eyes.

"I'm fine—still a little overwhelmed to be a guest in the castle," he said, sitting down next to me. He managed a somewhat amused smile and added. "I never thought I'd be able to say I was best friends with the queen."

I chuckled and reached for my fork. Gid didn't immediately begin to eat, looking a little uncomfortable to be sitting at the table with me and Kiernan, but as the meal went on he slowly started to relax.

Kiernan asked both of us many questions throughout the meal about how to earn the trust of the Gifted society, but ultimately, it was Kiernan himself who came up with the best start to a plan.

"What if you were to return to your people?" he suggested to Gideon as the meal finished. "You could begin spreading word among them. Perhaps I could even designate one of the islands as a sanctuary for the Gifted. The active witch patrols are being disbanded, but we could choose an island to keep the army away from entirely while we work to change the minds and hearts of the people."

I set down my glass, raising my eyebrows slightly and feeling my face brighten as I looked at my husband. "A sanctuary is a brilliant idea."

Excitedly, I turned to look at Gideon. But to my surprise, a tight frown was on his lips.

"What's wrong?" I asked.

He searched my face for a long time before letting out a heavy sigh. "I just found you," he said quietly. "Yes, I know you're safe, and you don't need rescuing, but leaving feels...wrong."

My lips quivered a little as I took his hand and gave it a tight squeeze. "I don't want you to leave, either," I admitted. "But if we're going to really make this work—if we're going to be free to practice our magic together again—we need someone working among the Gifted as well as the Ungifted."

As he looked down at our hands, I thought I saw some color come to his cheeks, and he slowly drew his hand back. My smile faltered.

At length, he nodded, still not meeting my gaze. "You're right, of course. You always are."

There was an attempt at some light-heartedness with his second statement, and I saw his lips twitch, but he didn't quite manage a smile, and he still didn't look up. My concern deepened.

"Kiernan," I muttered quietly, looking up at my husband, "do you mind if I speak privately with Gideon for a moment?"

Kiernan's gaze moved between the two of us, and I saw a flash of emotion in his eyes. I wasn't really sure what it was, but it reminded me of a look Neal had given Gideon more than once. I parted my lips to ask about it, feeling an odd tension in the room, but then, Kiernan nodded.

"Certainly," he said, clearing his throat. "I'm sure there's much you have to talk about."

There was some hesitance in his tone, but when he met my gaze again he put on a smile. Standing, he moved to my side and kissed my forehead, lingering there for a moment, before stepping back and looking down at Gideon.

"I have a meeting with the captains this morning," he said. "Afterwards, I'd like to discuss options for the sanctuary with you and Captain Balton, Mr. Grison."

Gideon nodded, finally managing to look up. "Of course. Thank you."

Kiernan nodded at him as well. He kissed the top of my head again and rubbed my shoulder briefly before leaving the room. Gideon looked away again, his expression somber.

"What's really going on?" I asked with a bit of an exasperated sigh. "I know the last months have been hard..."

My voice trailed off as I stared at him in concern. Gideon stared at the tablecloth for a while before closing his eyes. Were they watering just before he did? It was hard for me to tell.

"It just feels like losing you again," he admitted, his voice cracking slightly.

I sighed and reached for his hand again, but he pulled it away when he felt my touch. The action felt like a stinging stab to my heart, and while I wasn't sure if his eyes were watering, I could feel mine begin to do so.

"You're not losing me," I said quietly. "Before you know it, I'll be helping you train with Hanson again. But this time, we won't need to hide it."

This thought didn't seem to comfort him, but he reluctantly nodded nonetheless. We continued to sit there for a while, until Franklin entered the room to begin to clean up breakfast. When he did, the spell of silence seemed to break around us, and both Gid and I stood. As I turned to leave the room, Gideon gently touched my arm.

"It's a good idea—the sanctuary, I mean," he said. "I'm sorry for letting my emotions get the best of me."

I gave him a supportive smile. "It's all right. It's...we're all emotional right now."

"Once we've decided where to place it, I'll start traveling," he said. "Even if I don't find my own family right away, I can start spreading the word."

I shifted where I stood, tucking a curl that had come loose behind my ear. "You shouldn't travel alone," I mused, unable to hide my concern.

"Well, I don't think it would go over well for the queen to disappear from the castle with a strange man who showed up being accused of witchcraft," he said, managing an amused smile.

A chuckle escaped my throat and I shook my head. "No, it wouldn't. But...maybe my father..."

He raised an eyebrow. "Your father?"

It was then that I realized that while he had relayed much of his story to me, I'd hardly told him anything about the months I'd spent here in the castle since we were separated. It was also then that I remembered we weren't alone in the room. Over his shoulder I saw Franklin watching us curiously. I cleared my throat and linked my arm with Gideon's.

"Let's go for a walk," I said.

I brought Gideon to the towers, where Kiernan and I often retreated for our own conversations. Not many servants or knights were around, but I was still careful about how I spoke. I told him everything I'd learned about my parents, about Pious, and about Kindra and Hanson from reading her book. He was eager to see the book himself, but when I offered—somewhat reluctantly—to let him take it with him on his journeys, he quickly refused. "I'll study it whenever I get back here," he said, clearly trying to be more optimistic and positive than he had been during breakfast.

Like my father, he was particularly concerned about the demon I had battled months ago. But rather than focus on any looming threat, I tried to keep the focus of the conversation on my newfound power to heal. He was obviously intrigued by it, especially when I told him about the passage Abi had found in Kindra's record.

"Well, you have your candles again," he said. "Maybe you could find Kindra in the Other Worlds and get some more information from her."

I nodded. "I intend to," I said. "Hopefully Hanson will still be close enough to the gates that I can get a message to her soon."

We both fell silent for a while as we watched the waves of the sea beat upon the cliff's edge. It was so reminiscent of all those afternoons we'd spent on the hills near our shelter, and I closed my eyes and sighed. I almost leaned into him, but realizing how inappropriate that would be, I stopped myself.

Abi found us just before it was time for lunch and said that Miss Grayson wanted to speak with me. I was surprised, given the fact that I had explicitly told Kiernan that I didn't want to attend lessons anymore, but I followed her nonetheless. Gideon gave me a tight hug and said he would see me at dinner before returning to his guest room.

When I entered Miss Grayson's room, she gave a very deep curtsy, practicing the same technique she had taught me so rigorously. It was a strange exchange of roles, and I quickly motioned for her to stand up, having to remind myself that I was no longer required to curtsy to her in return.

"You wanted to see me?" I asked.

"Yes, Your Majesty," she said, her voice as creaky as ever but filled with respect that I wasn't quite sure I had earned. "We need to review the duties and schedules of the staff."

I furrowed my eyebrows slightly, but then remembered that this was just one of the many queenly duties she'd taught me that I would be expected to perform. I held in a sigh and nodded, sitting as she placed a mountain of papers and charts in front of me on the table.

***

Miss Grayson kept me occupied for the remainder of the day, and I didn't leave her chambers until it was time for dinner. Even though all we'd been doing was going over schedules and staffing responsibilities, for some reason, the task was exhausting in its own way. Part of me wanted to just go straight to bed, but knowing Gideon would likely be leaving soon, I didn't want to miss the chance to spend a little more time with him.

Gideon, my father, and Kiernan were already seated when I arrived. There was a rolled up map on the table next to my husband. I opened my mouth to ask about it, but Kiernan nodded subtly to where Franklin stood in the corner of the room, pouring drinks, and I closed it. When he was finished serving us, Kiernan dismissed him, and only then were we able to speak freely.

"We've been discussing possible locations for the sanctuary," Kiernan explained, unrolling the map and spreading it across the table. "We've talked about Hairan and Roldsay as options, but I think it's best to do some canvassing of the isles first. See what the general attitudes are more locally towards the Gifted before designating a gathering place."

I nodded, glancing at Gideon. "I'm assuming that will be where you start, then," I said.

He nodded. "We'll leave first thing in the morning."

"We?" I asked, looking at the other two. For a brief moment, I felt a rush of panic, and blurted out, "You're not going, are you, Kiernan?"

"No," he said with a laugh and a shake of his head. "I wouldn't leave you to run the castle on your own less than a week after our wedding."

"I will be accompanying Gideon," my father clarified. "Kiernan has assigned me to manage the affairs of local garrisons. With my new position, I'll have the excuse to travel, and some pull over the local lord and lady once we decide on a location. I'll be able to reorganize their military forces to keep the Gifted safe. Besides," his lips curved into a wry smile, "I have my own connections, and a knack for finding clans in hiding."

I nodded. While it had been my idea for my father to go with him, it was definitely bittersweet to think of both of them leaving. Kiernan reached under the table to take my hand as I became lost in thought, and I met his gaze.

"Why don't we drop the subject for the moment and just enjoy our dinner?" he suggested.

"That would be nice," I said, squeezing his hand.

Kiernan had asked plenty of questions over the past few days, but this time, Gideon showed the most curiosity throughout the conversation. He asked Kiernan about growing up in the castle and his favorite activities. To my relief, he didn't ask any questions damning Kiernan's former actions against the Gifted—he could tell that Kiernan's guilt was already eating at him enough.

When the meal was over, I felt my eyelids drooping. My work with Miss Grayson had apparently left me more tired than I realized. Gideon noticed almost immediately and frowned.

"Are you feeling alright, Kenna?" he asked.

I nodded and yawned. "Yes, I'm just...tired."

"Do you want me to have Abi summoned?" Kiernan asked, standing.

"No, I'm all right," I insisted as I, too, stood. "I can prepare for bed on my own."

Kiernan nodded and kissed my forehead, leading me to the door. My father and Gideon both stood, and I paused before exiting, my heart heavy as I gazed at them.

"I'll see you in the morning," I muttered.

"See you in the morning," Gideon repeated softly.

With that, I left the dining area, the door closing behind me. Entering my room, I let out a heavy sigh as I changed into a nightgown and took out the pins in my hair. But when I went to place them on my vanity, I paused.

Sitting in the middle of the vanity was a sealed envelope. I picked it up, turning it over to see if it was addressed in any manner. It was not. The seal was also not one that I recognized, looking almost like whoever had sealed it did so with a coin rather than an official symbol.

Curiously, I opened it. It contained just five words, but I stumbled backwards when I read them, almost dropping the parchment.

'I know your secret, Witch.'

CHAPTER TWENTY-THREE

THE TETHERED SOUL

Franklin didn't know where the letter had come from—he had just returned from meeting with the kitchen staff to arrange meals for the following day when I burst into the sitting room. The truth was, the note could have been left at any point in the day while both Kiernan and I were occupied. And even if Franklin hadn't seen anyone, there was no doubt in my mind who the note came from.

Shaking, I instructed Franklin to have guards posted at the door to our quarters as well as the entrance to the tunnel in the throne room. As he left to relay the message, Kiernan, Gideon, and my father exited the dining room together.

Immediately upon seeing me, Kiernan frowned and moved to my side. "What's wrong, My Heart?"

His use of my old nickname made my breath catch in my throat, but now was not the time to get sentimental. Glancing at my father and Gideon, I saw concern in both of their expressions, but Gideon in particular was averting his eyes. With a rush of heat to my cheeks, I realized I was in nothing but a nightdress, and had been the entire time I was speaking with Franklin.

"Let's—speak privately," I muttered. Kiernan nodded and wrapped an arm around my waist, leading me into his room.

"I thought I told you to rest," he chided as the door closed.

I let out a breath. "I intended to. But when I got back to my room, I found this."

My hand shook as I offered the note to him. Kiernan released me with a frown and took it. As he read the words, his grip on the parchment tightened, crumpling it in his hands. His expression hardened.

"Did Franklin deliver it?" he asked.

I shook my head. "He didn't see anyone come in, either. But...I'm certain I know who it was."

"Who?"

"Captain Lewin."

Kiernan looked up from the note and stared, his hard expression shifting to one of surprise. After a long moment of silence he sighed, shaking his head.

"I understand how you feel about him, Kenna," he said, choosing his words carefully. "I really do. But Captain Lewin has always been loyal to the crown—"

"Kiernan, he's constantly questioning you," I interrupted, my chest tightening with frustration. "*Especially* when it comes to me. How can you not see that he's been suspicious of me from the start? He's never let go of those suspicions."

"He's just used to tradition," Kiernan said, reaching to take my hands. "It's not necessarily about *you*, it's about any young woman I choose to be with that breaks from that tradition—"

"He locked me in a dungeon for two days!" I yelled, my frustration turning into anger. I snatched my hands from his and stood, crossing the room and spinning around to face him. "A dungeon that he was keeping hidden from you and secret to carry out his own justice. I was in complete darkness, without food and water. He would have left me there forever if my father hadn't come to you! And since then, he's done everything he can to separate us. Even Captain Stole had suspicions about his intentions, and if he had access to this demon—"

"You can't seriously think that Lewin is a magic holder," Kiernan said with a sudden, surprised laugh.

"I don't know if he is or if he isn't, or if he may be in league with someone, or what's going on!" I snapped. "All I know is that he was *pleased*

I was going to be in court this morning, because he knew Gideon would be one of the prisoners being tried and he wanted to see my reaction to confirm his suspicions once and for all."

"And how do you know that?" Kiernan asked, his sigh sounding exasperated.

I felt like my heart was caught in my chest. My eyes began to well up with tears and my fingers shook as I gripped my hands into fists.

"Why do you have more faith in him than in me?" I breathed out, my whisper harsh.

At that, Kiernan frowned, his own frustration replaced by hurt. "How can you say that, Kenna?"

"Because you're not listening to reason. You're ignoring what's right before your eyes."

He slowly stood, venturing to take a step towards me. I took a step back in response and he sighed, stopping in place and observing me sadly.

"Kenna, I've known Captain Lewin all my life," he tried to explain gingerly. "He is a harsh man and set in his ways. But he is also a man fully devoted to protecting the kingdom. When Pious took the throne, Lewin was the one who managed to smuggle me out of the castle so I would remain safe. He taught me how to defend myself and worked secretly with the remaining captains in the castle, putting his life and safety on the line hundreds of times, in order to plan an attack that would rid us of Pious's tyranny. He is a cunning strategist—"

"And that's exactly what I worry about," I breathed out, the tears beginning to roll down my cheeks. "He *is* cunning. He's had a lot of influence over you in the past, and I don't think he wants to give that influence up."

Kiernan's eyebrows furrowed at that and he pressed his lips tighter together. For a long moment there was silence between us as we stared each other down, neither of us seeming willing to change our minds about the man. Finally, after what felt like an eternity, Kiernan let out a breath and closed his eyes, shaking his head and reaching up to rub his forehead.

"What do you want me to do, Kenna?" he asked, sounding defeated. "Have him tried?"

"I don't think there's enough proof for that," I admitted. "But investigating and trying to gather evidence would be a good start. I'm sure Captain Stole would be up to the task. He already has his own misgivings about him."

"Very well," Kiernan muttered, still sounding unconvinced. "But I am confident he won't find anything. Captain Lewin is a hard man, but one that I trust with my life—and yours."

There was no point in escalating the argument. So instead, I just muttered, "Thank you," before moving towards the windows that overlooked the cliffside. My arms were still shaking as I folded them across my chest, watching the way the waves crashed against the rocks and the clouds floated on the horizon. The sun was setting over the horizon, and I closed my eyes just trying to breathe enough to keep myself calm.

As I thought about the sun, my mind wandered to Gideon, then Hanson and what I'd read in Kindra's book. If she was a descendent of the world-builder before Hanson, did that mean that I was a descendant of Hanson just as Gideon was? She had called herself a 'Bearer' of this inherited Gift, a Gift that was given only once every fourteen generations...

I need to talk to her.

I felt Kiernan's hands on my shoulders and sighed, my eyes remaining closed. I hadn't heard him approaching over the storm that was my own thoughts.

"I'm sorry, My Heart," he said gently, slowly wrapping his arms around me from behind and kissing my neck. "I want you to feel safe, and I will do everything in my power to ensure that you are. I'll talk to Stole, and I'll check on the guards you summoned. For now...for now will you please rest? You've had an eventful few days..."

Slowly, I placed my hands over his, focusing on my breathing. He kissed my neck again, and I felt a bit of a shiver on my skin where his lips pressed against it. The bliss of our time alone felt so distant, but at least for a moment I was reminded of the love we held for each other. It was real, and it was strong. Whatever challenges remained before us, we would face them together.

"I'm sorry, too," I whispered.

He released me with one more kiss to my neck, coaxing me into my room. But I still couldn't rest—not just yet.

My heart beat a bit faster as I closed the door behind me. My pack sat on my bedside table, and I approached it almost reverently, pulling the candles out one by one. The knot in my throat was extraordinarily tight. It had been so long...

Very carefully, I set up the circle. I must have checked and rechecked the runes a dozen times before finally stepping inside of it. The magical energy from the circle tingled in the air, almost feeling like a gentle breeze against my skin. I closed my eyes and let out a shaky breath, chanting the Sacred Words of Passage once more.

Nothing happened. I did not hear a voice asking me where I wanted to travel, despite the clear magical energy in the room. Instead, I felt a pit in my stomach, as if there was a weight grounding me to the earth.

Furrowing my brows, I tried again. Still nothing. There seemed to be something preventing my spirit from separating from my body, something that was keeping me in place. It couldn't be possible that just discovering that I was a sorcerer and not a white witch would be enough to do this—sorcerers could learn to wield the same magic that witches held, after all. There must be some other reason.

Beginning to feel desperate, I stepped out of the circle, the tingle dissipating as I did, and moved to lay on my bed. Closing my eyes once more, I willed my spirit to leave my body as I had done many times before. Again, I felt a pit in my stomach, my spirit completely tethered to my body. They would not separate.

Was I just that out of practice? Or was there something else—some sort of curse or spell that had been placed upon me or the castle to block my Gift? I had just used it to heal Gideon, so that also did not make sense to me.

Why can't I separate?

Keeping my eyes closed, I opened myself up to sense any spirits in the room, initially worried that I would sense another demon sent to attack me, as my father had feared. At first, I didn't sense anything, my surroundings feeling devoid of any other spiritual presence. But after a few minutes of focusing, I noticed the faintest trace of a soul somewhere nearby, young and innocent, more pure than anything I'd felt before.

And it was inside me.

With a gasp, I sat up. My eyes were wide as I stared at my reflection in the mirror, and a hand shot to my stomach.

I'm pregnant.

***

I don't know how I ever fell asleep that night. I paced my room, stopping in front of the door to Kiernan's at least half a dozen times. When I did finally lay down, I tossed and turned until Abi arrived to help prepare me for breakfast. I almost blurted out the news to her, but I wasn't ready to admit it yet—not to her, not to Kiernan, and not even really to myself. But now that I had identified it, every time I closed my eyes, I could sense the small, developing spirit.

I had never thought about how pregnancy could affect the ability to travel between the other worlds, in large part because I hadn't really considered marriage as I was growing up. Elizabeth was unmarried, after all, and until I met Gideon and Neal, I hadn't spent time around people my own age. It was a question I'd never thought to ask, but apparently the presence of a second spirit sharing the same body made it impossible to complete that separation.

To my relief, Kiernan didn't say anything at breakfast about the note. I was sure that if Gideon and my father knew about it, they would refuse to leave. As much as I would miss both of them, I didn't want to delay their journey. Saying goodbye was hard enough as it was.

When we all stood up from the meal, Isaiah gave my forehead a tender kiss before pulling me into a parting hug.

"Remember what I told you to do if you needed to run?" he whispered in my ear.

I frowned against his shoulder. "Yes…"

"Tell me."

I hesitated, confused. He'd given me these instructions in case Kiernan chose not to accept me, and I had more or less discarded them now. But as he pulled back from the embrace and placed his hands on my shoulders, I saw the lingering fear and concern in his eyes. Even though no one had mentioned the threatening note, he knew just as well as I did that other threats still existed.

"Tell me, Kenna," he urged.

"Find the Allreds in Northtown," I repeated.

He nodded, the tension in his shoulders subsiding. "Good. Remember that."

With a breath, he kissed my forehead once more before stepping aside. Gideon stood behind him. The black long-sleeved tunic and gloves covering his arms were so different from anything he'd ever worn when we were with the clan. On anyone else, the look would have been austere at best and intimidating at worst. But regardless of what he wore, his blue eyes were still the same warm, kind eyes that had brought me comfort when I'd lost everything. Only now, they were misty with emotion.

My vision blurred as mine, too, began to fill with tears. I stepped past my father and threw my arms around Gideon, suppressing a sob as I buried my face into his shoulder. He took in a sharp breath through his nose, one of his hands resting on the back of my head and the other wrapped around my waist. I felt him trembling, but then he let out the breath he was holding and his body relaxed. He slowly released me, meeting my gaze with a heartfelt smile, and wiped away a tear as he had so long ago on the beach.

"It means everything to me to know that you're safe," he whispered.

My breath caught in my throat. "Promise me you'll make sure *you* stay safe," I stammered.

"I promise," he said. The hand wiping away my tears lingered for the briefest moment on my cheek before he drew it back and stepped away, tearing his eyes from mine to look at Kiernan.

"Take care of her," he said. I was surprised to hear a commanding edge to his tone.

Kiernan stepped up beside me and wrapped an arm around my waist, holding Gideon's gaze. He didn't look angry at how he'd been spoken to—in fact, they looked at each other as if there was a shared understanding.

"Always," Kiernan said.

His arm remained around me as we watched Gideon and Isaiah leave the room. Though my heart was heavy at the separation, the feeling of Kiernan's steady support next to me brought with it all the comfort I needed.

I leaned into him, and he wrapped both arms around me, kissing my cheek. I felt the way his hand brushed against my stomach as he did, and my thoughts spiraled back to my revelation from the night before. Just as I was about to speak, however, Franklin entered the room with a bow.

"Your Majesty—they are waiting for you in the High Court," he said. "And My Queen, Miss Grayson has requested an audience."

We both sighed as Kiernan pulled away from me. "The duties don't stop," he muttered, brushing a hair out of my face with a wry smile.

My smile was definitely more forced, but I managed one nonetheless. Tenderly, I placed a kiss on his lips. "I'll see you at lunch," I said, trying to keep my voice steady.

***

We actually didn't see each other again until dinner that evening—the trials went longer than expected, and afterwards Kiernan left for a scheduled tour of the military quarter with Captain Stole. I was desperate for a distraction, and, no matter how un-queenly it was, enjoyed a few hours with Abi exploring the castle's passageways. More than once, I had to stop myself from telling her about the pregnancy. I wanted Kiernan to be the first to know.

Dinner was held in the main hall that evening with the majority of the captains and some of the local nobles, including Sir Hamon and Lady Sophronia. As Sophronia went on about how gorgeous my wedding gown was, I studied the room. Lewin was conspicuously absent, and after a second look, I realized that Stole was as well. Meeting my husband's eyes, I realized he must have spoken to Stole while they were in the military quarter about keeping an eye on his fellow captain. I reached under the table for his hand and gave it a gentle squeeze, which he returned.

It felt like something was bubbling in my stomach for the entirety of the meal. I didn't let go of Kiernan's hand, not even to eat, which resulted in me using entirely the wrong fork technique. Kiernan made no effort to pull his hand away, seeming just as eager for the connection as I was, even if he didn't yet know what was on the forefront of my mind.

When we finally returned to our quarters, Kiernan sighed heavily with exhaustion, but smiled when I sat on the edge of his bed. Joining me, he placed one hand on my cheek and wrapped his other arm around me, pulling me close and giving me a tender kiss. I returned it, trembling a bit against him, gently resting my hands on his arms as I took in a sharp breath.

When he pulled back, he pressed his forehead against mine, tracing figures along my back as we both just breathed for a moment. "It's been a long day," he whispered.

I nodded. Though I was trying to find the words to speak, something seemed to be blocking my throat. Kiernan didn't immediately notice, kissing me tenderly once more, the kiss growing in emotion as he held me tighter.

It was a relief to let myself get lost in his embrace. For at least a short time, I didn't have to think about Lewin, the demon, the army, my Gift, or even the pregnancy. I allowed myself to focus on nothing but him and the connection we shared, a connection that was growing deeper by the day.

A while later, I rested my head on his chest, slowly running my fingers through his hair. His eyes were closed and his breathing even and relaxed. The more we laid there, however, the more I felt my heart beginning to race with nervousness.

I was a little relieved when he was the first to speak. "What's on your mind?" he asked in a whisper, rubbing my arm. He could probably feel the way my body was stiffening against his the more I thought about my news.

Taking in a deep breath, I slowly sat up. He did as well, looking at me with a curious expression.

I swallowed. "What if we were to have children, Kiernan?"

He sat up straighter, taken aback. I waited as he eyed me, anxious to hear his response.

"Of course we'll have children, Kenna," he finally said, his tone suggesting he hadn't really thought about it before, "but it's a little early to be planning on it, don't you think?"

"Maybe not," I said, feeling more and more nervous as I took his hand in mine. "Maybe—*now* would be a good time to start thinking about it. Because I'm...I'm pregnant."

It came out so much clumsier than I had hoped. My heart was pounding. Kiernan's eyes widened.

"You're pregnant?" he repeated. "Are you sure?"

"I'm sure."

"But how—how could you possibly know this soon?"

I gestured to my mark, and he seemed to understand. For a long moment, he just stared at me, clearly struggling to find a way to respond. I took his hand in mine, and he squeezed it tightly. I leaned forward and kissed him, trying to ease both of our nerves.

"Now what's on *your* mind?" I asked, keeping my voice as even as I could.

He let out a shaky breath. "My own father...our relationship was complicated. I can't say he showed me how to be a father, only how to be a ruler. I don't want this child to have the same lonely childhood I had, but I don't know how to give them a better one."

I ran my fingers through his hair again, gazing into his deep blue eyes. "I know how you feel. I don't know how to be a mother any more than you know how to be a father. So...we'll just have to figure it out together."

To my relief, he leaned forward and kissed me sweetly, lingering longer than I'd expected. When he placed his hand on my stomach, I saw a hint of excitement glinting in his eyes. That was enough to let me open myself up to the emotion as well, and I breathed a sigh of relief and happiness as we retired for the night, dreaming of a baby in my arms.

CHAPTER TWENTY-FOUR

BURIED SECRETS

The next morning, anyone walking past my door would have sworn something exploded inside my room. Abi bounced around in excitement.

"I can't believe it! An heir already! Oh, Kenna, this is wonderful!"

I caught the pillow she threw in excitement and laughed. While the thought was still overwhelming, the tender night spent with my husband and seeing Abi's enthusiastic reaction had done quite a bit to help ease the tension I'd felt about it the day before.

When she finally calmed down enough to start getting me ready for the day, I sat up a little straighter on the vanity bench, eyeing her seriously in the mirror. "I would like you to be my midwife, Abi."

Her eyes widened and she stopped in the middle of braiding my hair. "I don't know anything about that sort of thing," she stammered. "I wouldn't trust myself—"

"It has to be you," I said. "The midwife will see my mark and any mark the child might have. We can't plan on the war being over by then, and you're the only one I can trust."

She shook her head. "I couldn't—I don't know how."

"You have a while to learn," I urged, reaching up to take one of her hands.

She sighed in surrender, releasing the braid and putting up her hands to accompany the sound even as she smiled. "Whatever you say, Your Majesty."

I slapped her hand rather hard for her false modesty and we both laughed. She spent the rest of the time preparing me for the day talking about possible names for the baby and speculating on if it would be a boy or a girl. I had to make her swear not to say anything to anyone else, knowing it would be difficult for her to contain her excitement, but she promised she would keep it to herself until it was time to officially make the announcement.

***

The following days and weeks were by no means peaceful, but the stress and busyness of life in the castle soon became the norm. As time wore on, I saw less and less of Kiernan—I refused to attend the trials again, and I wasn't welcome in his meetings with the captains (though I was told everything afterwards anyway). Kiernan spent more time in the Military Quarter than before, making sure his orders were carried out and reforming the training program. He often came back to the castle exhausted but did his best not to burden me with the stress he felt, particularly concerned about putting too much pressure on me during my pregnancy.

Not that I was idle. I was kept busy managing the household, which was a more complicated responsibility than I'd thought it would be when Miss Grayson first explained it to me. Thankfully, she was experienced in the task herself, since Kiernan hadn't had a queen to assist him up until then, and provided a lot of support. And despite how tense our relationship had begun, I was soon very grateful for her diligence and assistance.

When I did have free time, I spent it in the library, reading the oldest books I could find. The more I looked, the more books I found on the Gifted. People I'd believed to be legends had records in their own hand here in the castle's library, the writings preserved carefully with magic. The biggest surprise came when I found a book containing drawings of ancient magical symbols and discovered that many of them were incorporated in my circlet and Kiernan's crown. I was initially shocked, but was quickly reminded of Hanson's legends, and how Kindra had mentioned so casually the Gifted and Ungifted living together. Obviously the Gifted had been part of Orkeia's founding. What was difficult to figure out was when and how that changed.

Another thing that remained a mystery was the true nature of my Gift. Frustratingly, Kindra never revealed it explicitly in her writings. She talked about some of the things she did, but most of them still seemed to be related to white witch magic, only on a larger, more powerful scale. It was difficult not to take my candles out of their storage space in my cabinet and try again to communicate with her, but if it hadn't worked when I was only a few days pregnant, it certainly wasn't going to work now.

The nausea started after a little over a month. I wasn't sure how mild it was compared to other women's experiences, since I didn't really have anyone to talk to about being pregnant other than my husband and Abi. Though Abi began training with a midwife in town immediately, we decided to wait to make any official announcement until a couple months had passed. After all, there was no reason we should have known sooner under normal circumstances.

When the formal declaration was sent out after about three months, we were soon receiving letters of congratulations from all over Orkeia as well as the surrounding kingdoms. We even received a letter of congratulations from Gideon and my father, in which they also gave us an update on their progress. The island of Hairan had been designated as the sanctuary, and they were encouraging clans to relocate. Many of them were understandably hesitant, but slowly, my people were beginning to gather in one.

While we were making steady progress, Kiernan was still having a hard time making his captains trust his judgment. The fact that he was king gave him great control, but the fact that he was only twenty-five made most of them feel they knew better than he did. Captain Stole was an exception to this and seemed fully supportive of all the decisions his king was making. But the louder voices—such as Lewin's—were difficult to discount.

Two months after we had officially announced the pregnancy, Kiernan returned from the Military Quarter late at night. He'd been trying hard not to worry me about what was going on with the knights, but I knew it was taking its toll on him. I was in his room reading a letter of congratulations from King Simeon when he entered.

He stared at me with bloodshot eyes. "Why are you not in bed?"

"I wanted to see you," I said, setting down the letter. "I'm worried about you."

"Don't," he sighed, removing his cloak and letting it fall onto the bed. "We both knew what we were getting into."

I stood, ignoring the slight stretching pain in my abdomen when I did. "You don't have to do everything on your own, you know, and you don't have to do it all now."

He closed his eyes as I placed a hand on his cheek. "What if the child is Gifted?" he said, stress in his voice. "Everything's happening so fast—"

"Then we'll hide the mark. That's why Abi's training to be the midwife, remember?"

"I know," he breathed. "I just don't want our child to have to live a lie."

"Everything will work out," I said for the millionth time. "We've made it this far, haven't we?"

He shook his head and stepped past me to reach his bedside dresser. "I just wish I knew why my father started the Slaughters in the first place," he said as he took off and folded his tunic. "He never spoke to me about it, and no one else seems to know."

"Fear?" I suggested.

"Maybe. But my father never did seem afraid of anything."

He leaned against the wall. Suddenly, the stone he was touching sank into the wall, making a startlingly loud noise. Kiernan whirled around, and I jumped out of the bed in shock. We stared, listening to the sound of stone grinding against stone, as a hidden door opened directly behind my husband.

"Kiernan," I said quietly when the door had stopped moving. "What is this?"

"I have no idea," he said, his mouth hanging open. He grabbed the candle from his nightstand and stepped cautiously through the opening.

"There are steps leading down. Why didn't I know about this?"

"I wonder where it leads," I said, making my way to his side. The passageway was wide enough to accommodate the two of us side by side, and we both stared down into the darkness.

"I'm going to find out." He descended the first couple of steps. "I'll tell you what I find."

I put a hand on his shoulder. "I'm coming with you."

"No, you're not," he said, almost laughing at me.

I put my hands on my hips. "Yes, I am."

"Kenna, you're five months pregnant."

"So I can't climb down some stairs?" I said, raising my eyebrows.

He shook his head as he took my hand in his. "Fine," he said reluctantly, holding the light high above his head. From where we were, there was no foreseeable end to the staircase. I was reminded of the stairs leading into the cell Lewin kept me in, and I shivered. I kept a tight hold on his hand as we descended deeper and deeper into the darkness.

After a few minutes, we reached level ground, and a large, oak door stood at the end of a dark hallway. We approached carefully. Kiernan pushed it open, and it creaked eerily as we stepped inside, the dim light of our candle illuminating the room.

My eyes widened. Hundreds of bottled potions sat on dusty shelves. Many of them were labeled, most of them with names and ingredients that I was unfamiliar with. There was a summoning circle in the middle of the room, the runes set in an order that I recognized but had never used, and for good reason. Within the circle was a chalk drawing of an upside-down pentagram. The child inside of me jumped violently and I gasped, leaning against the doorway.

"Is everything all right?" Kiernan asked.

"We need to get out of here," I breathed, my voice shaking as I stumbled backward.

He didn't ask for an explanation. Quickly, he followed me out of the room, shutting the door firmly behind us. As we made the long journey upwards and away from the energy of the room below, I felt the child inside of me start to calm down. When we were safely back in Kiernan's bedroom, he guided me to the bed, and I sat down in a daze.

"What was all that?" he said, concern written on his face. He searched for the same stone he accidentally pushed before, and the door closed.

I stared straight ahead, unable to answer him. Now that we were out of the room and I could think clearly, I remembered many of the symbols inscribed on the walls and their meanings from the books I'd been reading. Elizabeth had taught me long ago about some of the ingredients for the potions as well, and my breath came staggered.

"Darling," he said, trying to hide his fear as he sat on the bed next to me. "What is it?"

"Dark magic," I stammered. "Everything we saw—all of the potions, the order of the candles—it's all forbidden."

He furrowed his eyebrows. "I don't understand."

My hand grasped his tightly. "I've already told you that the candles are used to visit the other worlds. A witch using his or her powers correctly can also summon spirits into the circle to speak with them. When you summon spirits with the candles, however, they have a choice of whether or not they come, and they can't come at all unless you knew them personally in life."

I started shaking again. "Not when the runes are placed in that order. The spell you saw down there—the symbol of the pentagram upside down, the candles—summons demons."

"*What?*"

Immediately, he jumped to his feet, dragging his desk across the floor to slam it against where the secret opening was, as if to stop any demons from getting out. I knew that even if there were demons in that passage, a physical barrier would do nothing to stop them, but I didn't bother saying anything, in large part because my panic was building as I remembered more details from the books I'd read.

"How—and *why*—is there a passageway to a room full of dark magic in my quarters?" Kiernan said, sounding equally horrified and furious.

"That's not all," I breathed. "The spell that white witch was casting—whoever it was—is a spell used to bind a demon to their soul."

His eyes widened. "Why would someone want to do that?"

"To get power—they would have complete control over the demon. But the summoner loses their identity in the process."

"That must be how the demon that attacked you got here in the first place," Kiernan said, tensing even more as he looked back at the wall.

With some trepidation, I gave a small nod, hugging myself tightly. "But who summoned it?" I breathed. "And was it still being controlled?"

He stared at me, processing everything I'd said. When he finally spoke, it was definitely not what I'd expected.

"You said you can visit the Land of the Lost—could you find my father?"

I frowned. "What makes you so sure he's Lost?"

"If he was involved in this—binding demons to his soul—he would most definitely not be Saved."

"We don't know it was him," I said with a tight frown. "It could have been Pious."

"I don't think Pious would have hidden this," Kiernan said with a shake of his head. "He was very public with everything he did. This—this was meant to stay a secret. My father must have been working with witches to take advantage of their magic, regardless of what he told the people."

"You're jumping to conclusions," I said, though I couldn't deny the logic behind his words.

"All the same—I've waited for answers from my father long enough," he said definitively, taking my hands in his. "I know you can't use this magic until the baby's born, and I don't want to ask you to put yourself in any more danger, but...will you try to find him?"

My lips tightened. Traveling to the Land of the Lost is very different from traveling to the Land of the Saved. Although the spell for getting there is the same, the process of finding people and returning are both different, and dangerous. I'd only been there once, and it was with Elizabeth as my guide and protector. If I wasn't careful, I could easily become one of the Lost myself in that forest.

Kiernan tucked my hair behind my ear. I took a deep breath, staring at the secret door. Whether I liked it or not, we needed answers, and there was only one way we were going to get them. Slowly, I nodded.

He kissed my cheek in gratitude, wrapping me safely in his arms. I closed my eyes, doing my best to calm myself and the child, trying to forget the horrible sense of evil in that room. The force with which I'd felt my child jump told me they had felt it as well, and there was only one explanation.

The child was a white witch.

Chapter Twenty-Five
A New Light

For the next week, Kiernan spent nights with me in my chambers, even moving my vanity in front of the door that connected our rooms. While I knew that the physical barriers he was attempting to place between us and the chamber wouldn't do anything, I did make sure Abi brought a large supply of salt from the kitchens to place a magical barrier that would, in fact, be effective. But despite the evil I'd felt emanating from that room, I doubted there was an actual presence. Whatever had started there had already been released, and was now banished back to the Land of the Lost.

At least, the one that had attacked me was banished. As terrifying as it was to admit, for all we knew, there were more demons roaming the city. When I reviewed the next castle supply order with Miss Grayson, I requested a large order of quartz from the kingdom of Cogfaire to have something more powerful than salt to protect not only our quarters but the castle in general. She was confused by the order but didn't question it, accepting the explanation that I was just fond of the gem and wanted to use it to add my own decorative touch to the castle.

The order arrived about a month later, and I immediately arranged for skilled craftsmen from the city to integrate it into every doorknob in the castle. Luckily enough, one of the runic symbols for warding off demons happened to be woven into my circlet, so no one asked too many questions about the design I had them use. But my anxieties were still ever present, especially with the eerie silence from the note left in my room months before.

I was still convinced Lewin was responsible. It was true that he hadn't tried anything—in fact, he seemed to be avoiding me at all costs—but his dangerous eyes still met mine with malice at every opportunity. When Kiernan followed up with Stole about the investigation, the captain admitted that he hadn't been able to uncover any evidence to support his theory of Lewin's ill intentions. If Lewin was planning on trying something, he was biding his time.

Whenever the subject came up in conversation, it inevitably turned into an argument. For reasons I couldn't fathom, Kiernan continued to defend Lewin's actions, even when he actively spoke out against his king in front of other captains and knights.

"Why haven't you at least demoted him?" I demanded after one such occurrence.

Kiernan raised his eyebrows. "Demoted Lewin?"

"You're right," I said, crossing my arms. "You should dismiss him."

He frowned. "Kenna, I know how you feel about him, but he's only doing what he thinks is best. He's spent his life training for war, and when he feels there's a threat he wants to be prepared for it."

"And kill it," I mumbled.

"He's a brilliant strategist. If King Simeon were to attack—"

"Simeon's too busy with the southern invaders to attack us."

Kiernan groaned, moving to sit on the edge of the bed. "You're not going to let this go, are you?"

"No," I said matter-of-factly. Kiernan sighed and pinched the bridge of his nose. Taking a few calming breaths, I moved to sit next to him on the bed.

"I know you have history with him, and it's hard for you to see what I see," I said, placing a hand on his knee. "But Kiernan—he doesn't respect you. I'm worried—I'm worried that if he feels like he can't control you anymore, he'll..."

I choked on my words and Kiernan slowly looked up at me with a raised eyebrow. Upon seeing the degree of fear on my face, his expression softened, and he pulled me into a tender embrace. The child in my stomach kicked gently, and I held Kiernan tightly in response.

"I just want our family to be safe," I breathed against his neck. "All of us."

He gave me a gentle squeeze, and I felt him let out a long, slow breath. When he pulled back, he ran his fingers through my hair, his eyes tracing my features tenderly.

"I may have a solution," he said a little hesitantly. "At least, a temporary one to help ease your fears."

I raised an eyebrow, and he continued. "King Simeon has proposed we send a military envoy to him for a few months. He would like to send an envoy here as well. The intent is to form an alliance in case the invaders start moving further north."

"An alliance with Simeon?" I said, holding back a scoff. "He would never honor it."

"Probably not," Kiernan acknowledged. "But ignoring him isn't wise. Simeon is a proud man, and once he is no longer focused on this imminent threat, he will turn his attention to anyone he feels has wronged him and seek to take revenge. It is better to play along for the moment, and perhaps we can even gain some valuable information ourselves from the man that we send."

I frowned but nodded, knowing he was right. Though despite my misgivings about forming any sort of connection with Simeon, the plan Kiernan was implying did help my shoulders slightly relax.

"And you'd be willing to send Lewin?" I said, trying not to sound too hopeful.

"I'd already been considering him for the job," he said, brushing my hair back again before lowering his hand to rub my shoulder. "As much as I still believe his work is invaluable here, as I said, he is a brilliant strategist. He will know what to look for and what knowledge would be useful should Simeon choose to turn on us and attack. And he will be able to gather this information much more subtly and efficiently than others might."

I nodded, feeling more calmed by the moment. "How long is the contract?"

"Four months," Kiernan said, giving my shoulder a squeeze. "He would return after the baby was born, just in time for the founding celebration."

Closing my eyes, I couldn't help the small, relieved smile that came to my face. I felt Kiernan's thumb on my chin as he cupped my cheek with his free hand. Keeping my eyes closed, I let my hands travel up his arms to gently wrap them around his neck and press my lips against his.

"Thank you," I muttered.

He reached for my hand and squeezed it soothingly. "I'll give the order in the morning," he said.

I returned the squeeze and kissed him again, wrapping my arms tightly around him.

***

According to Kiernan, Captain Lewin was less than pleased to receive the order, but for once he did not argue. The more Kiernan had been asserting himself as a military, the more Lewin had realized he was no longer able to dictate the king's mind. Only three days later, I stood on the tower wall as the ship he was on sailed south, feeling like the entire world was a bit brighter than it had been before.

With Lewin gone, I no longer felt a looming threat anywhere I went on castle grounds. And though he didn't directly admit it, Kiernan felt some of that relief as well. He was much less anxious after meeting with his captains and grew more confident with each day that they would support ending the Slaughters.

Captain Stole became Kiernan's chief military advisor. A little over a month after Lewin left, I returned from a trip to the library to find the two of them in the sitting room.

"The people will be thrilled, Your Majesty," Stole was saying as I entered.

I looked between them. "About what?"

Upon noticing me, both men stood. Captain Stole bowed. Kiernan crossed the room and put an arm around my waist, giving me a short but meaningful kiss. He rested his other hand on my stomach for a moment, his blue eyes shining, as he answered.

"I am repealing the current drafting laws," Kiernan explained. "Young men are no longer required to serve two years in the military when they come of age. Enrollment in the knights will be strictly voluntary from now on."

I beamed at him, placing my hand over his and giving it a squeeze. "That's wonderful."

"I will leave you, Your Majesties," Stole said with another bow, taking a few steps towards the door. But Kiernan put up a hand.

"Please sit, Captain. Queen Kenna is welcome to join our conversation if she would like. I value her insights."

For many captains, this would have been a shocking statement. But to my surprise, beneath his neatly trimmed beard, Captain Stole smiled. His eyes met mine with a profound respect that made me stand just a little straighter.

"I am sure I will value them as well," he said.

"Thank you, Captain Stole," I said, my breath catching in my throat.

Kiernan released me, briefly and lovingly rubbing my stomach before he did, and returned to his seat. There were papers and maps scattered across the small table between the two armchairs. He sat in one and Stole took the other. I considered going into my room to lay down, but sat across from them on the settee instead.

"I will give the command for messengers to immediately be sent to the isles announcing the change," Stole said, picking up a piece of parchment and writing down a note for himself. "But there is still the matter of those currently serving their compulsory terms."

"We will allow them to choose whether or not they wish to continue to serve," Kiernan said matter-of-factly. "Anyone who wishes to end their service and return to their families will be allowed to do so."

Stole nodded, but his brows creased slightly. "I suspect that will significantly decrease our current numbers."

"And what is the problem with that?" I blurted out. "The active witch patrols have already been disbanded, and our local garrisons are overflowing. Are our current numbers really necessary?"

The captain considered me for a moment and, again, I thought I saw him smile. "No, Your Majesty," he said with a nod. "Though some would argue it would be unwise to let down our guard."

"Against?"

"Against any possible magical attacks."

I bit the inside of my lip, struggling to find a way to respond. Kiernan watched me for a moment before clearing his throat.

"Captain...when was the last time we experienced a magical attack that wasn't provoked?"

Stole's gaze rested on my husband, his expression difficult to read. "Not for some time, Your Majesty."

Kiernan and I made eye contact. Silently, we seemed to come to the same conclusion, and I let out a deep breath.

"If the magic holders aren't attacking us, should we really be attacking them?" I asked, choosing my words carefully.

There was a brief silence as the captain set down the parchment in his hands. He shifted in his seat to face me a bit more directly.

"I've had that question myself, My Queen," he admitted, a softness in his voice.

My heart thumped a bit harder in my chest and I pressed my hands against the settee. I had to choose my words carefully to avoid revealing the whole truth.

"We have not seen any increase in attacks since ending the witch patrols," I said. "If anything, there has been a decrease in violence because our men are not initiating it. It appears that, if we leave the clans alone, they are content to simply live their lives independent of the crown."

Stole nodded, his expression thoughtful. Kiernan leaned forward, and though the three of us were the only ones in the room, he lowered his voice.

"Captain—it is my intent to end this war entirely," he said. "It has been for some time now. Can I count on you to support that decision when the time comes?"

I clutched the edge of the settee so hard that I was sure my nails would leave marks in the fabric. Kiernan appeared much more calm than I felt, confidence and determination written on his face.

Captain Stole looked between the two of us. He sat up a little straighter, and as his expression brightened, I felt like the entire room did with it.

"Absolutely."

***

Kiernan didn't make his intention known to the rest of his council, but having Captain Stole's support made everything that much easier. There were still plenty of people—captains and nobles especially—who harbored a deep hatred of magic holders, but Stole helped us strategize how to start conversations that would have them questioning things for themselves. He also helped Kiernan better plan when and how to make military changes with the least amount of resistance.

Fears still persisted, of course, especially among the castle staff. Many of them had been personally subject to Pious's tyrannical rule, and Abi told me they still shook whenever his name came up, or any mention of magic, really. She had tried to talk to a few of her fellow servants about the possibility that not all magic holders were evil and malicious like Pious was, but most of them simply wanted to avoid the topic. Franklin actually told her it was treasonous to question the Great War. Thankfully, she was level-headed enough to hold her tongue in the moment, but when she told me about it, she couldn't hide her anger.

"*He's* the one being treasonous!" she blurted out, throwing her hands up in frustration as she worked on my hair. "His *queen* is a wi—"

"Keep your voice down, Abi," I said with a frown, shifting on the vanity bench and glancing at the door to the sitting room warily.

She let out a puff of air and dropped her arms to her sides. "If he knew—"

"We don't know how he'd react," I interrupted. "Not everyone is going to be as open-minded as you."

I sent her a sideways smile at that, and she sighed. She put down the brush in her hand and wrapped her arms around me from behind. I reached up to touch her arm. Resting her head on my shoulder, she met my eyes in the mirror.

"No one who knows you could keep believing those lies about magic," she said, giving me a gentle squeeze.

I closed my eyes and sighed. "I hope you're right," I muttered.

After that, I was much more careful how I spoke around him. When I told Kiernan about the conversation, he revealed that Franklin had worked for his father before him, and then for Pious himself. Franklin's attitude was understandable, and as loyal as he was to Kiernan, I didn't want to tempt fate by making him suspicious of my secret. I could only hope that when the truth did finally come out, Abi would be right.

***

The castle remained as busy as ever, and my duties started to take more of a toll on me as time went on. The last two months of my pregnancy somehow felt like both the longest and the shortest stretch of the experience. Things that were normally mundane and simple, like dressing for the day, became increasingly difficult and taxing. Miss Grayson took complete control of the household, partially at my request and partially at her own insistence. A woman 'in my state' shouldn't be making important decisions, she said.

Occasionally, however, she came to visit me in my quarters, saying she needed my approval for one thing or another. About a month before I was due to give birth, she asked me to approve the week's meals, and I sat up a little straighter on the settee and raised my eyebrows.

"Miss Grayson," I said, "surely you are more than capable of approving the cook's menu."

Her persistently pursed lips tightened even more. "Of course, Your Majesty. I just thought—"

My lips curved into a smirk. "You're worried about me?"

She blinked. "I beg your pardon, Your Majesty?"

"You don't need my help with anything at all," I laughed. "You're just making up excuses to come check on me."

I was certain she would deny it. But to my surprise, this was one of those rare occasions where her expression softened.

"I...have become rather fond of you, My Queen," she admitted, sounding almost like she was trying to swallow the words.

My smirk shifted into a smile. "I've become rather fond of you as well, Miss Grayson."

She tensed her shoulders, clearly uncomfortable with the informality of the conversation. But I thought I saw her lips twitch upwards.

She cleared her throat. "I will let you rest now, Your Majesty," she said, curtsying and turning to go.

"Call me Kenna," I called after her.

From the way she stumbled through the door, I thought she was going to pass out.

***

When the time finally came for the baby to be born, it was a long ordeal. Through it all, I could hear Kiernan pacing back and forth outside my door. If Abi hadn't blocked both entrances into my room, I'm sure he would have burst in at hearing my first scream, but it wasn't considered proper for the man to be present during birth, as ridiculous as I thought that was.

Abi kept telling me to focus, but my thoughts were running in all different directions. I didn't know the first thing about being a mother, and now that the moment was actually here, I was more terrified than ever. Was I ready? How would I know what they needed? Would they be a good ruler when they grew up? How could I teach them everything they needed to know? Would they know I loved them?

And then there was the biggest question: could I protect them? The world was still at war against us. How long would it be before Orkeia was safe for its own heir? How could I keep them safe until then?

The pain eventually chased out all other thoughts, and when I finally heard cries other than my own, my heart soared. Through my tears, I gazed at the beautiful baby girl Abi handed me, taking her in my arms in awe and wonder. She stopped crying at my touch, and I closed my eyes in pure joy as I held her against my chest. The warmth of her steady breaths against my skin made all the pain and worries disappear.

When I opened my eyes again, I met Abi's gaze. Her cheeks were streaked with happy tears of her own. She beamed while cleaning the baby girl in my arms. After a moment, she paused.

"Look," she said.

I tore my gaze from my baby's blue eyes to look at her arm. A small spiral swirled near her shoulder.

"She's a white witch," I confirmed. The knot in my throat tightened. Seeing the physical proof of what I already knew brought with it a mix of emotions. But for the moment, I suppressed any fearful thoughts and instead just focused on the wonderful feeling of holding my daughter.

After she made the room more presentable, Abi unbarred the door and had to practically run to get out of Kiernan's way. Once he was inside, his pace slowed to a walk, and he numbly made his way to my side. His eyes shone and his lips split into a wide smile. He sat on the edge of the bed, staring at the child in my arms. I handed her to him, and he cradled her in his arms, his eyes full of more love than I thought one person could hold.

"She's beautiful," he breathed, a sob forming in his throat as he gazed at her before looking up to meet my eyes. "Just like her mother."

Full of emotion, he leaned forward and pressed his lips lovingly against mine, the child nestled between the two of us. Whatever pain I may have been in, it didn't matter. I'd never felt such pure, unimaginable joy.

Carefully, he passed her back to me, and I again held her against my chest. "We never decided on a name if it was a girl," I said with a bit of a chuckle, reaching up to wipe my eyes with my free hand.

"What if we named her after your mother?" Kiernan suggested. "Arabella."

I felt a lump in my throat. "Arabella," I agreed quietly.

Kiernan beamed at both of us, kissing her head before kissing me once more.

Chapter Twenty-Six

WHERE THE DEAD WEEP

The next week was even more hectic than when we'd been preparing for the wedding. Word was published throughout the kingdom of Arabella's birth the very next morning. All of the lords and ladies visited in turn. We were very careful to make sure Arabella's dresses covered the mark on her arm, but I don't know if anyone would have noticed even if it was visible—they were all blinded by her charm. Lady Rosalyn was the most excited to see the baby girl, and squealed as she insisted that Arabella smiled at her.

Every time I saw Kiernan now, there was a smile on his face. He kept canceling meetings in order to spend his time with the two of us, ignoring my insistence that he needed to work as well. Nothing else seemed to matter. He even stayed up all night on occasion to look after Arabella so I could rest. Abi would have performed the task, but Kiernan didn't seem to want to let his daughter out of his sight for longer than absolutely necessary.

As much as we wanted to continue to bask in the wonder of our daughter's birth, our responsibilities couldn't be put on hold indefinitely. Kiernan continued to work towards declaring the Slaughters over, and while he didn't feel the time was right to reveal the truth about magic to the Orkeian people—and certainly not the fact that the queen and new princess were both magic holders—we grew increasingly confident that the time was coming soon. The letters we were receiving from Gideon and my father were encouraging as well.

"'Last week, a few of us went into town,'" I read out loud to Kiernan, holding Gideon's letter in one hand while I cradled Arabella with my other arm. "'Neal was with us and decided not to cover his mark. Your father wasn't very pleased with that decision, but it turned out to be enlightening. When one merchant noticed it, he was surprised, but then he lowered his voice and asked if there was anything we could do to help his crops grow more effectively. It turns out that most of the people, at least on Hairan, are more curious about magic than scared by it. In fact, the knights' armies were more intimidating to them than we ever were, and they've been relieved ever since the patrols stopped.'"

I paused, letting out a bit of a sigh and setting down the letter to readjust my hold on my daughter. Seeing that my arms were beginning to get tired, Kiernan stood from his desk and took her from me, kissing me quickly before kissing her sleeping forehead.

"That's incredible," he muttered as I sat down. "I don't know if the people here in the city will be so easily swayed, but if those in more remote villages are receptive, it's certainly a good sign."

I nodded in agreement, picking up the letter and continuing to read. It had been a relief to get word a couple months before that they had found the Grison clan, and even more of a relief to hear that everyone was still safe and accounted for. Darius had fought the idea of moving the clan to Hairan, especially hesitant to gather in larger numbers as a Gifted community, but Julius eventually convinced him. And with Julius's help, they were able to traverse the islands with more efficiency, using his Gift to find more clans and help them travel to the sanctuary instantly.

Though I didn't say it, I missed all of them dreadfully. Part of me wanted to arrange a trip to Hairan just so I could see them in person, but even though I had recovered uncommonly quickly from giving birth, Bella was too young for me to feel comfortable with the journey. For the moment, I had to resign myself to reading through Gideon's letters.

Shae often wrote her own letters and sent them with his, all of them full of questions about life in the castle, what the king was like, and if I could please describe the wedding in detail. I received occasional updates on the other members of the clan, but I noticed that Gideon didn't say much about Neal. I wished Neal would write to me himself, but I suppose I understood why he didn't—I doubted he'd taken the news of my marriage very well, let alone Arabella's birth. Still, I felt confident that when we did eventually meet again, it would be a joyous reunion.

Abi came in a few minutes later to take Bella from us and put her down in the nursery for the night. Both Kiernan and I began to change into our night clothes. Through the open door between our rooms, I noticed Kiernan pause with his nightshirt only halfway on. When I turned to get a better look at him, he was staring at the wall—the wall that held the door to the secret passage we'd discovered months before.

My shoulders tensed. I hadn't forgotten my promise to try to find his father, but I had been avoiding the topic, using the excuse of taking care of our daughter and the resulting exhaustion to justify myself. And it wasn't exactly a lie—I hadn't even tried traveling to the Land of the Saved yet to find Kindra. But the real truth was that I was just out of practice, which worried me. It had been over a year since I'd last traveled to the other worlds, and more than seven years since I'd attempted to make my way through the dark forests of the Land of the Lost.

Kiernan sighed, finishing putting on his nightshirt. As he did, he caught a glimpse of me, frowning a bit when he saw my expression.

"What is it, My Heart?"

I hesitated. Whenever I felt nervous about trying to use my Gift when I was young, Elizabeth always said that the only way to get over that fear was to take the leap. My eyes drifted past Kiernan to the wall for a moment and I let out a heavy sigh. My hands trembled slightly as I turned away from my husband and moved further into my bedroom. I opened up the cabinet where I'd stored my candles and began pulling them out.

Kiernan entered my room as I began setting up the circle, watching me intently. "Can you summon my father?" he asked after a long silence.

I shook my head. "I can only summon people I've already met," I explained, willing my hands to remain steady as I set up the last of the candles. "If I've only ever heard of someone, I need to make the trip in spirit myself."

Kiernan watched intently as I stepped into the circle. Looking up, I met his gaze.

"You're confident he'd be in the Land of the Lost?" I asked.

He nodded. "Even if he's not the one responsible for the demon, he...well, he wasn't a good man. I suppose it's possible I could be proven wrong, but somehow I doubt it."

"All right," I said quietly, closing my eyes. My nerves were threatening to take over and make me step outside of the circle, but I willed myself to stay still. It wasn't enough to keep Kiernan from noticing my shaking voice and trembling hands, however.

"Kenna, you don't have to do this," he said with concern. "I know I asked you to, but if it's this dangerous..."

"I just have to be careful," I breathed, lifting up a hand to begin to trace the pentagram over my chest.

"I wish I could come with you," Kiernan sighed.

A sudden idea occurred to me, and I opened my eyes. Lowering my hand, I stepped outside the circle once more, rearranging the candles. I had seen Elizabeth do this when training me, of course, and had read about Kindra doing the same thing with her daughter, but I hadn't ever heard of someone attempting it with an Ungifted partner. But something told me it would still work.

Kiernan stepped forward curiously. "What are you doing?"

"Take my hand," I said instead of answering, practically pulling him into the circle with me. Holding his hand tightly, I traced a pentagram over my chest with my right hand, chanting the words of passage. Kiernan jumped when the candles around us lit, but he didn't try to leave the circle.

"Do you desire to visit the Saved or the Lost?"

Kiernan looked around the room with wide eyes. "Who said that?"

"The Lost," I said in answer to the voice.

The voice spoke again. "Do you desire to bring this traveler with you?"

"Yes," I said.

Kiernan's hold on my hand tightened as a heavy gust of wind blew through the room, extinguishing the candles. My spirit left my body and traveled quickly downwards, landing on the edge of a thick, dark wood. When I opened my eyes, I was relieved to see the spirit of my husband next to me, staring around in wonder and fear.

"It worked," I breathed.

"Is this the Land of the Lost?" he croaked.

I looked into the dark forest. "Yes. This is the only entrance and exit for our spirits."

"So if we get lost in there...?"

"Our spirits will be lost," I confirmed. "Do you want to go back?"

After a moment, he shook his head. "I want to be with you every step of the way," he said. He reached out to take my hand, and was surprised when his went through mine.

"We're mortal spirits now," I explained. "When a spirit is still mortal, it can't interact with other spiritual things, only physical and mortal things."

He smiled wryly. "So I won't be able to punch my father?"

I grinned. "I'm afraid not."

He sighed, losing his humor as he stared into the never-ending expanse of trees. "So how do we find him?"

I took a deep breath. "We walk into the forest."

We both shivered, but the decision had been made. Kiernan had the urge to take my hand again, but drew back at the last second. Now that we weren't speaking, we could hear horrible and heart-wrenching screams and sobs coming from every direction. Slowly, we made our way into the trees, leaving the light behind us.

We searched for hours, walking straight in one direction, then moving to the right and walking straight the other way in hopes of preventing ourselves from getting lost. Most spirits, when they felt our mortal spirits approaching, coiled away from us. Some, however, drew closer, trying to pull us into the darkness with them. They knew that if we lost our way, we would have no way to return to our bodies and be trapped down here. Kiernan began to understand more why I'd been hesitant to search for his father in the first place, and seemed to regret asking me to try, let alone bring him along.

I was careful not to go too far into the forest. Though his father might be deeper within, it wasn't worth the risk. If we ventured too far, we would fall off the edge of a sudden cliff into a dark abyss. The only thing past that cliff is the Lost One's castle, standing on a high, steep hill miles from the edge. Many spirits see the castle and head toward it, inadvertently finding themselves trapped in complete darkness instead of just the darkness of night. Even in the front of the forest it was difficult to see, and I didn't want to imagine what it was like at the bottom of that cliff.

When we turned around for the seventh time, Kiernan stopped. "Maybe we should just give up," he said. "I don't know how much help he would be anyway."

"Kiernan," I said, coming to his side. "If we—"

"Kiernan, did you say?"

We both turned sharply to see a horrid looking creature approaching us. He clearly used to be a man, but boils and cuts covered him head to toe and his overgrown, gray, knotted hair disguised his youth. I shrank back as he neared us, repulsed by the image. Kiernan, on the other hand, stepped closer, staring at the man intently.

"Father?"

King Rafael gave us a toothy grin, showing rotten teeth. "Hard to recognize me, isn't it?" he said, partly in humor and partly in sadness. "I was always so put together in life. But this is what happens when you bind your soul to a demon. I wouldn't suggest it, Son."

Now that he stood so close, I could see the resemblance, however eerie the setting. He'd clearly been very handsome once, but his actions turned him into a vile and disgusting creature of the Lost One. Kiernan's mouth hung open, and his father laughed at his expression.

"I never thought I'd see you here, let alone while still alive. When I was alive, it was hard to find white witches willing to travel into the Land of the Lost, and near impossible to find ones willing to bring me along. Looks like you're following in your father's footsteps."

Kiernan stood up straighter and closed his mouth, his expression hard.

"I'm nothing like you."

His father raised his eyebrows. "Then what are you doing here?"

Kiernan got straight to the point, ignoring the continuing screams in the forest around us. "Why would you have started the Slaughters when you were using dark magic yourself?"

"I thought you would have figured that out by now," he said, his eyebrows still raised. "I left a record of the prophecy in the chamber."

"What prophecy?" I said.

Rafael smiled wickedly at me. "She's a fine one. Where'd you find her?"

"What prophecy?" I repeated as Kiernan stepped forward protectively, eyes narrow.

"You'll find it all in my record," he said, bored of the conversation. "Life would have been grand if I'd just ignored it."

Before we could ask anything else, he turned away from us, disappearing in the darkness. His cackling echoed through the trees, and Kiernan's face hardened even more. He stepped forward, ready to follow him.

"Kiernan, *no!*" I reached out to stop him, even though I knew it would do no good. Thankfully, he paused before disappearing in the dark, dense forest, facing me with fury in his eyes.

"He hasn't told us anything we needed to know!"

"But he told us where to find it." I took a careful step toward him, making a note of which direction we'd come from. "Let's go."

"He's not going to get away with not talking to me," he yelled. "He never spoke to me in life, but I'm going to make him when he's dead."

"He's tricking you!" I cried as he turned away from me again. "He wants you to follow him and get lost!"

Kiernan wasn't listening, hurrying after his father's laughter. I searched in my mind for a way to stop him, to bring him back—

"Think of Arabella!" I cried out, my voice cracking. "Think of your daughter!"

He stopped, staring ahead of him into the darkness. His father's laughter could still be heard, but he slowly turned and made his way back through the darkness toward me.

"I'm sorry," he muttered when he reached me. "I couldn't control myself."

"It's all right," I said, my voice shaking.

Carefully, we turned back to make our way back. I felt a huge wave of relief when we reached the edge of the wood, a small ball of light visible a little ways from us. We ran toward it, eager to get away from that horrible forest.

When we reached the light, my heart sank in realization and I bit my lip. "I'm not going to be able to just bring you with me this time."

"Why not?"

"Because we can't touch," I explained. "You're going to have to return yourself.

"How?"

Though he seemed confident I wouldn't lead him astray, I was terrified of him never being able to return to his body. I hadn't thought this far in advance. I took a deep breath, trying to recall how Elizabeth had explained things to me so many years before.

"Think of your body—how you were last standing, where you were, what you were feeling. Close your eyes, and imagine your spirit returning. But think about what you're going to do *after* you return to your body, not simply returning."

My instructions were definitely confusing, but he closed his eyes to focus. I let out a deep breath when his spirit slowly rose, disappearing from my view. Only then did I close my own eyes, relieved when I opened them to see that his were open as well.

Without speaking, he hurried to the wall, pushing aside his desk and searching for the stone to open the secret door. He was out of sight before I could say a word, taking the one lit candle in the room with him. Anxiously, I waited in the little moonlight coming through the windows. I didn't even think about joining him—I wasn't going to go back to that evil space if I could help it, especially not immediately after returning from that horrible forest.

He returned quickly, a small brown book in his hands. Out of breath, he closed the door and sat next to me on the bed, holding the dust covered record between us.

"He'd better have been telling the truth," he breathed.

I placed a hand on his shoulder. "Maybe we should wait until tomorrow."

Kiernan shook his head. "He's kept secrets from me long enough."

He opened up to the first page, and we both began to read. It was a log of the experiments King Rafael performed down in that room with a trusted group of sorcerers and witches. At the time, very few of the Orkeian people even knew that magic was real. He had learned of its existence through reading in the library and sought out Gifted members of the community, using their power to increase his. Many of the names Kiernan recognized as captains or nobles from his childhood. The first thirty or so pages went on like this, detailing ceremonies performed and who had performed them. I shivered uncomfortably, knowing full well how the magic they were performing could twist someone into barely a human being at all.

After about an hour, we came to the last entry. My eyes widened. It was dated almost nineteen years ago, on the day I was born.

Everything's changed today. Wendell had another one of his visions. Luckily he and I were alone. He spoke these words:

> *In the midst of Slaughter, the King will be conquered—*
> *Magic will reign and Witches be royalty—*
> *Until Life leaves the Kingdom—*
> *Souls will wander the new World—*
> *Carefully watching the Heir—*
> *And the fate of the Gifted will be decided.*

Needless to say, I killed him the moment he finished. Orkeia will not be ruled by magic, and I will not be deposed. On our next hunting trip, I will kill the rest of them myself and blame it on their own kind. Then the people will join me in destroying every last one of them, preventing this prophecy from coming true. They need not ever know.

Kiernan and I stared at each other. Suddenly, everything made sense. Prophecies were ambiguous, but from his interpretation of what it meant, King Rafael had decided to kill all magic holders, including his own captains, to protect his throne. Battling the witches had been a complete lie—he led his captains to a secluded place and killed them himself, and all because of these six lines.

"'Until Life leaves the Kingdom,'" Kiernan muttered, frowning. "What does that mean?"

I looked at the line he was referring to, but my eyes flickered to the one above it. *Magic will reign and Witches be royalty...*

I sat up straighter.

"It's me."

Kiernan's frown deepened. "What did you say?"

"It's me—the prophecy's talking about *me*, Kiernan."

My husband shook his head. "It can't be—"

My mind raced, putting the pieces together. "It was given on the day I was born. Prophecies aren't random, they're triggered by events."

"It could just be a coincidence—"

"'In the midst of Slaughter,'" I read, pointing to the page. "I was captured because of the *Slaughters*. 'The King will be conquered,' 'Magic will reign,' 'Witches be royalty'—"

"But I haven't been conquered."

"Maybe not in a political or military sense, but one could say I conquered your heart." I flashed him a teasing smile before continuing. "Prophecies are often figurative in their speech and descriptions."

Kiernan's eyes widened. "So my father *caused* the prophecy to come true," he said quietly. "If it hadn't been for this war, we would never have met."

We sat in silence for a few minutes. I'd never heard of a prophecy not coming true, no matter what anyone did to try and prevent it. The Slaughters were part of the prophecy, and King Rafael had inadvertently put all the events in motion that would bring us to this day.

He closed the book with a sigh. "It still doesn't tell us much."

I put my hand on top of his. "Prophecies can be hard to understand," I acknowledged. "But now we know that we were fated to end this war and unite our people. It must be possible."

He turned his palm upwards to interlock his fingers with mine. His grip was tight.

"We know something else, too," he said, a quiet anger in his tone. "We know where the demon came from."

I frowned slightly at that, not as sure myself. Usually, if a demon was bound to someone's soul, they would return to the Land of the Lost when that person died. For one that King Rafael had summoned to remain at the castle was abnormal. I thought back through everything we'd read over the past hour, but the king's journal wasn't always detailed with who was involved in the ceremonies and what exactly the goals of them were. Perhaps there had been someone else who had bound themselves, someone close to him...

Kiernan stood, determination on his face. "It's time the people knew the truth," he said firmly, tossing the book aside with enough force that it slammed against the wall with a thud.

My breath caught in my throat. "Kiernan—"

"Things are never going to change if I keep acting like I'm content with how they've been," he said firmly, pacing the room. "I am the king, and I owe it to my people—Gifted and Ungifted alike—to bring this treachery to light."

"Do you really think they'll be ready?" I asked in a whisper, slowly standing as well, wringing my hands.

He stopped pacing and faced me, taking my hands in his and holding them tightly. "I'll make a speech at the founding celebration," he said, his mind clearly made up. "I'll tell them everything we've learned, about my father, about the true founding of Orkeia, all of it. Yes, it will be a shock, but who is going to question the king?"

My frown remained, but I was reminded once again about Elizabeth's advice—that when you were scared, you just needed to take the leap. Swallowing hard, I nodded gently.

He cupped my cheek and kissed me deeply. "We're going to end this once and for all," he said, already sounding triumphant. He then rushed to his desk and pulled out a parchment and quill, writing furiously as he began to plan his speech.

Chapter Twenty-Seven

TRUTH UNVEILED

Isaiah returned about a week before the founding celebration, leaving Gideon behind with his clan and the rest of the Gifted he had gathered on Hairan. My father was overjoyed to meet his granddaughter, spending every spare moment he could with her. It raised my spirits to see the two of them together, particularly given how nervous I was about the upcoming celebrations.

Kiernan continued to be convinced that the founding was the perfect time to reveal the truth to all of Orkeia. Reading over his speech, I had to admit that it was well crafted. He highlighted the legends of the Mother of the Sea and the Father of Storms, pointing out the clear magical influence those stories contained, and went on to reveal that forgotten and lost records from the founding of Orkeia had been discovered within the castle's library. While he didn't mention Hanson by name, he emphatically stated that a sorcerer lifted these islands from the sea, and he and his people collaborated with those who held no magic to establish a kingdom upon the land. While it wasn't the most accurate or descriptive history, it was certainly effective at getting the point across.

But the eloquence of his planned speech wasn't enough to completely ease my concerns. After all, as part of this speech, my identity as a magic holder—and that of my daughter—was about to be revealed to the people. It was a reveal that I'd prayed and hoped would happen eventually, but now that it was approaching, I didn't feel ready for it.

How would the people react? Would they revolt? Would the lords and ladies who had come to trust me distance themselves out of fear?

As much as I didn't want to admit it, there was only one way to find out.

***

"Kenna, get in here!"

"Just a minute, Abi," I called, smiling at my two-month-old daughter. Bella smiled back, cooing as I made a funny face.

"We only have an hour to get you ready for the banquet!"

I sighed, kissing Bella's forehead before straightening in front of her crib. I didn't want to leave my daughter's side, not tonight. Kiernan had grown more and more confident as the days went on that his speech would be received favorably, but I couldn't help the gurgling feeling in my stomach.

Abi barged into the room, her hands on her hips. "This might just be the biggest moment of your life, and I am *not* going to let you experience it with your hair looking like that!"

Despite my nerves, I laughed, turning around and smiling warmly at her. Reluctantly, I left my daughter in the care of another maid, a young girl named Diana. My father had recommended her, explaining that he was close friends with her father and trusted her to keep the secret about Bella's gift until it was officially revealed. Diana hadn't seemed fazed at all to discover that the queen was, in fact, a magic holder, and that at least brought some hope that others would react positively as well.

Abi had already decided what I was to wear, and in record time I was dressed and having my hair done. She smiled at me in the mirror.

"You're going to do great," she whispered excitedly, giving me a tight hug from behind.

"What matters is that everything goes smoothly." I sighed.

"It will," she reassured. "As long as you're there on time."

I chuckled before relapsing into silence. Once my hair was finished, circlet included, she removed the emerald necklace Kiernan gave me so long ago from my drawer and latched it around my neck.

"There," she said. "Now you look like a queen."

I laughed at her, standing and giving her a tight hug. As always, Abi's excitement was infectious. And beneath all the nerves and uncertainty, I started to allow myself to feel some excitement as well.

We're actually going to do it. We're going to officially end the Slaughters.

When I stepped out of the door, Kiernan was waiting in the sitting room. He grinned when he saw me, sweeping me into his arms and kissing me swiftly. "You look beautiful as always, My Heart."

"And you look handsome," I said, fixing a loose strand of hair that was in his face. Kissing his cheek, I leaned in close and whispered, "Why don't we skip the party altogether?"

He smirked, but ignored my comment, leading me into the hall. I tried to hold on to Abi's infectious excitement, but with each step I held on to Kiernan's hand a little bit tighter. He rubbed his thumb along the back of my hand encouragingly.

"It's going to go well," he whispered, kissing my cheek. "You'll see."

My smile was shaky, but I still managed it. When we arrived, the dining room was already crowded with guests. They all bowed or curtsied as we entered. I saw many friendly faces that I had come to know over the past year—Sir Hamon and Sophronia, Lady Rosalyn, and Captain Stole were all particularly warm and welcoming presences. As I met each of their gazes in turn, I told myself that they, at least, would accept the truth, and by extension, accept me. Like my husband, they knew my character, after all.

There was one face that was the opposite of friendly, however. Lewin stood towards the head of the table, not directly next to our seats but closer than I would have liked. He had returned just a few days previously from his assignment with King Simeon and seemed even more hardened and angry than he had been before. I tore my eyes from him, pushing aside my fears. After tonight, even if he was the one who had left the note almost a year ago, it wouldn't matter. Everyone would know the truth.

Kiernan and I took our seats next to each other at the head of the table. Instead of staring at my plate as I had two years before, I met the lords' and ladies' gazes, nodding and smiling at each of them in turn. Somehow, I'd become the queen, not just a girl the king dragged out of a cell. It was strange how natural certain actions had become, but none of that really mattered. What mattered was the man sitting to my right and the child in the rooms above.

Once everyone had been served, Kiernan stood. He beamed at me before speaking, placing his free hand on my shoulder.

"I would like to begin with a toast," he said, and I looked up at him with a raised eyebrow. This was not the opening line that he had been rehearsing, but he just winked at me upon seeing my surprise and continued.

"You all first met my wife two years ago on this very day, the celebration of our kingdom's founding. You didn't know what to think of her then, and rightly. She was kind, beautiful, and refined, but she didn't necessarily follow all the customs of our society."

Chuckles were heard around the table as everyone recalled the shock they'd felt when I refused to avoid Kiernan's eyes. I smiled to myself, remembering that the entire reason I'd done that in the first place was to disrespect him. Now it was a sign of mutual respect between us.

"But now you see her before you," he continued. "Loving wife, devoted queen of her people, and mother of our perfect Princess Arabella. Her companionship and wisdom has been invaluable to me as I have worked over the past year to bring peace and prosperity to our people. Tonight, in addition to celebrating Orkeia's founding, I would like to celebrate her beauty, bravery, and leadership."

He raised his glass of wine to me. "So here's to you, My Heart. I will love you forever."

As he drank, the rest of the guests took up their glasses and toasted to me as well. My cheeks were burning profusely, but I beamed at him. As he lowered his glass, I let out a slow breath, keeping my eyes fixed on him as he officially began his rehearsed speech.

"You are all familiar with the history and tales of our people," he said, taking a moment to clear his throat. "When I was young, my mother told me stories—stories of—"

He coughed, a hand going to the edge of the table to steady himself. At first I assumed he had just taken in too much wine at once, but as his coughing continued, my amused smile faded. Suddenly, he dropped his glass and it shattered on the floor as he fell to the ground.

"Kiernan!" I cried out, falling to my knees beside him.

His hands grasped desperately at his throat, and foam started coming out of his mouth. In a panic, I pulled him into my arms. Before I could even cry out for help, the life and love in his eyes vanished. He lay still in my embrace, no sound coming out of his open mouth.

"*No*," I whispered, my mind spinning. I pulled him tighter to me. Tears clouded my vision as I realized he wasn't going to meet my gaze, that his eyes were going to remain empty forever. I shut my eyes tightly, the sounds of shock and fear from everyone else in the room barely reaching my ears. My entire body shook and I buried my head against his chest.

"NO!"

The magic within me erupted. Through my tightly shut eyelids, I perceived a bright flash of light—light that I knew was coming from me. With all of my might, I directed the magical energy into my husband, desperate to keep him with me, to bring his spirit back to his lifeless body.

I collapsed on top of him sobbing as the light disappeared. Desperately, I waited for his chest to rise, to feel his arm wrap around me.

It didn't.

My sobs turned into wails and I clutched his body even tighter. There was no sound in the room other than that of my grief echoing off the walls. If I had been able to focus on anything else, I'm sure I would have been able to feel the shock and fear present in our guests. As I gasped for air, I heard the first terrified whisper.

"*She's a witch!*"

The whisper began a murmur, one that I was hardly coherent enough to combat, still sobbing and holding on to my husband's lifeless form. I thought I heard my father trying to speak up in my defense, but anything he was about to say was quickly drowned out by Lewin's booming voice.

"She murdered the king!" he growled. "It was all an act! She's been planning on taking Orkeia as her own since the beginning! GUARDS!"

There was an uproar of sound, some people screaming and rushing away from the table towards the door, others protesting to Lewin that he was jumping to conclusions. Two guards stepped in from their stations and hoisted me to my feet, wrenching me from my husband.

Lewin drew his sword. "Take her to the dungeons. You two! Get the child!"

The world turned upside down. "*LEAVE HER ALONE!*" I screamed, struggling violently against the men who were holding me. "*DON'T YOU TOUCH HER!*"

All of a sudden, I fell to the ground. Spinning on the spot, I saw my father dueling both of the men who'd been holding me at once. "Run, Kenna!" he exclaimed as I staggered to my feet.

I ran, but not nearly fast enough. Two more guards seized me on Lewin's orders, dragging me toward the dungeons. I screamed, fighting to break free. Isaiah let out a yell of frustration, besting both of the guards he was fighting and trying to make his way towards me. I continued to struggle against my captors, my sleeve ripping in the process, and succeeded in releasing myself from one of them by elbowing him in the stomach. Only Lewin had come to the celebration with his armor on.

As I fought to free myself from the second man, Lewin approached my father from behind. He raised his sword, and a scream escaped my lips. Lewin's sword protruded from Isaiah's stomach, spilling blood on the spotless ground. The light left my father's eyes.

"Bring the child to me," he said once again. "These abominations must be destroyed."

"*MONSTER!*" I screamed as four more men took a hold of me, dragging me away from the bodies of my father and husband. Lewin's face split into a disturbing, uncharacteristic grin as he pulled his sword from my father's body, letting the blood drip onto the floor. He met my eyes with fire and malice in his just as I was pulled around a corner and into darkness.

I continued to scream and sob until I couldn't make any more noise. Even though my vocal chords refused to cooperate, the tears didn't stop, and neither did the fighting. I'm sure the guards were relieved when they threw me in the dungeon, locking the bars behind them. All my energy spent, I fell in a heap on the floor, weeping.

Until Life leaves the Kingdom...

Why would I have been fated to become queen if this was how it was going to end? Why was I blessed with a caring father, a wonderful husband, and a beautiful daughter just to see them murdered?

The door at the top of the stairs slammed, and I heard heavy footfalls on the steps. I knew it was Lewin. He paused outside my cell before unlocking the door and entering, closing it behind him.

"Good evening, *Your Majesty*," he said, mocking laughter in his voice.

I screamed and threw myself at him, clawing at his face. He punched me in the jaw—*hard*—and I flew into the wall. I crumbled to the floor, and he cackled under his breath.

"You're not an easy person to get rid of, Kenna Gale," he spat. While the surname clearly meant something to him, it was foreign to me. But that was far from important right now.

"Where is my daughter?" I demanded, ignoring the pain in my jaw as I grit my teeth.

His lips curled into a grin. "Dead. I killed her myself."

A horrible choking sound escaped my throat. He drew his blood-stained sword and stroked the blade, his squinty eyes dancing with pleasure as he advanced. Leaning over me, he grabbed a fistful of my hair to force me to look into his eyes.

"I thought I'd take the most pleasure in killing your father," he hissed. "I've been hunting him for years. Did he ever tell you the truth? About who he really was? About why he changed his name? Or even how he met your foolish mother?"

"What do you know about my mother?" I spat through a sob.

His evil grin spread. "More than you'll ever know. I'm sure she can tell you all about it herself when you join her in the Other Worlds."

My eyes widened and he laughed horribly. "Oh, yes, I know of them. Intimately, in fact."

The way his eyes glinted made my blood run cold. "It *was* you controlling the demon," I breathed shakily.

"An old present from King Rafael," he said mockingly, but his grin turned into a sneer. "And you had to go and *banish* it."

I screamed and tried to throw his arm off of me, kicking wildly on the ground. His hold on my hair only tightened and banging my head against the stone wall. The room spun, and when it came back into focus again, his murderous face was inches from mine.

"Clever, clever girl," he growled, pushing the hair out of my face with the tip of his sword. "You wouldn't believe how many times I've imagined killing you, imagined what it would feel like. King Rafael gave me the order seventeen years ago. Your father saved you then, and he saved you on that beach. But he isn't here to save you now."

He forced my head back, placing his sword at my throat. I whimpered from a sting of pain as the sharp edge drew blood. His eyes were full of fire. I stared straight into them, unable to look away. My breath came in short spurts as I waited for him to end it.

Cackling, he withdrew his sword and threw me to the ground. He exited my cell and sheathed his sword. The lock clicked behind him.

"You will be executed at sunrise," he said before disappearing back up the stairs into the darkness.

I sobbed on the cold, stone floor. My entire body was numb with grief. Of all the horrible things I'd imagined might happen, this—this was so much worse than any of my nightmares. I felt broken beyond repair, too overcome with despair to move from where Lewin had thrown me on the ground.

It couldn't have been more than an hour when I heard the door to the dungeon creak open again. The sound was so quiet that I almost thought

I imagined it. But then, hurried footsteps echoed through the stone walls, and I lifted my head just as Abi rounded the corner. I scrambled to my feet.

"Abi," I croaked, finding what little of my voice remained. "Lewin—he killed them—Bella, Kiernan, Isaiah—"

"Bella's safe," she said, fumbling with a ring of keys. I didn't know how she had gotten a hold of them or how she even knew where to find me, but I wasn't going to question any of that at the moment. With a sob, I rushed to the bars, holding on to them desperately as she placed key after key in the lock.

"How?" I breathed.

I thought I saw a flash of anger in her eyes, but before she spoke, another voice interrupted.

"Later," a man said.

Looking over Abi's shoulder, I saw a tall, cloaked figure coming down the stairs after her. He moved quickly, but almost silently. In the cracks of moonlight coming from the barred windows, I caught a glimpse of a dagger in his right hand. It was dripping with blood.

I squirmed and almost took a step away from the bars, but Abi reached through briefly to take my hand and squeeze it. "It's alright, Kenna—this is Alex. You can trust him."

My lips quivered, but I met her gaze and nodded.

"Hurry," Alex said.

Abi tried the last key and finally, the cell door opened. I pushed it out of the way and threw my arms around her, holding her with all the strength I had left. She returned the hug with her own shaky breath, and I realized that she, too, had been crying. But at least for the moment, she was holding herself together enough to keep a level head.

"Come on," she whispered urgently as a glow of light appeared in the stairway. Seizing my hand, she pulled me around a corner and into the shadows. Alex followed, moving almost as if he were invisible.

Panicked voices came from my cell as she pressed on a stone in the wall, opening up a small doorway. She pushed me in first, sliding in herself as light began to fill the hall. Alex joined us and the door closed just as the knights were about to turn the corner. Abi held on to me, panting.

Alex moved past us and motioned for us to follow and keep quiet. Abi kept hold of my hand, which I was thankful for in the darkness. Eventually, the passageway opened wider and sloped downward until it was large enough for five people to fit across at once. After we'd been running for about ten minutes, I saw a light and dark figures in the distance, and I tried to pull back.

"Don't worry," Abi said, continuing to pull me after Alex. "They're with us."

For the moment, I didn't ask any questions. Finally there was enough light to recognize the figure of my little Arabella in Diana's arms, and I ran ahead of my friend and our mysterious protector as fast as my feet could carry me. I scooped her up and held her tightly, letting tears that should have already been shed fall. She cried as well, confused and frightened by the panicked energy around her.

"We have to hurry," said another man to my right. "Before they discover the boats."

Through my tears, I saw with some shock and gratitude that it was Captain Stole. But there wasn't enough time to slow down and thank him. I held my daughter tightly as the group moved forward. Eventually, the passageway opened like a cave, and we filed one by one onto a cliff ledge. I didn't count how many people there were or even wonder where they came from—all that mattered was that my daughter was alive.

The ledges weren't extremely thin, but I was still nervous with each step I took of falling to my death and bringing little Bella with me. Four small boats waited for us on the beach, and we filed in without any words. As we pushed off into the ocean, a war horn sounded above. I shut my eyes tightly, focusing instead on the sound of the waves crashing against the wood of the boat, clutching Bella to my chest. I did my best to shush her and calm her cries, whispering to her that everything was going to be alright, even though I couldn't see how.

Until Life leaves the Kingdom...

ACKNOWLEDGEMENTS

To properly acknowledge everyone who has been a part of this process would be an entire book in and of itself. So here is my paltry attempt at saying thank you.

First, to my family: Mom, Dad, Kenn, Allison, and Derick. This book is fifteen years in the making. Your constant support is what made it finally happen.

Second, to my husband, Michael. Thank you for always supporting your wife's crazy dreams and for being truly the best husband and father anyone could ask for.

Third, to my alpha readers, Amber and Alicia. I couldn't have done it without the ping pong balls.

Fourth, to my beta readers for helping me hammer out all the little dents and dings: Ruthie Cobb, Sophia Garner, Carlee Hemmelgarn, Shannen Ingram, Beth Lloyd Lowe, Sarah Lund, L.C. Meyer, Amberly Plourde, Tanya Roundy, Tori Saccoccio, Kylie Shake, Allyson Wilkins

Fifth, to my incredible editor, Dana Boyer. You truly helped me take Kenna's story to the next level!

And last, but far from least, to YOU, my amazing readers! Thank you for stepping into my world and going on this journey with me!

A QUICK FAVOR

If you enjoyed THE GIFTED HEART and want more of Kenna's story, please leave a review! Even just a sentence or two saying what you liked about the book really helps indie authors like me keep writing! You can review on:

Amazon

Goodreads

Anywhere else you review your books!

Thank you so much for reading, and I hope to welcome you back into the Marks of Inheritance books soon!

ABOUT THE AUTHOR

Tiffany Davis was born in Utah, but spent her childhood moving all across the United States. Growing up, she had a passion for theatre and story-telling that led her to begin writing Marks of Inheritance series as a senior in high school. Now, it is finally time to share her rich fantasy world with this one. When she isn't writing, you can find her teaching in the junior high classroom, participating in community theatre, singing, and taking care of her two beautiful daughters.

Join the magic!

Instagram: @tiffanydavisauthor
Website: www.tiffanydavisauthor.com

Join the newsletter and get access to the FREE short story, "The Fall of Orakys"